Louise James is a Sc[illegible] Paisley. She has previously worked as a poultry-woman and local journalist, but is now a full-time writer of short stories, novels and plays. She is married with two grown-up sons.

Also by Louise James

Gold Round the Edges
The Promise Box

Penny for a Song

Louise James

HEADLINE

First published in 1989
by Century Hutchinson Ltd

First published in paperback in 1990
by HEADLINE BOOK PUBLISHING PLC

10 9 8 7 6 5 4 3 2 1

All characters in this publication are fictitious and any resemblance to real persons, living or dead, is purely coincidental.

ISBN 0 7472 3415 9

Printed and bound in Great Britain by
Collins, Glasgow

HEADLINE BOOK PUBLISHING PLC
Headline House
79 Great Titchfield Street
London W1P 7FN

This book is dedicated to PS *Waverley*,
the last of the Clyde paddle-steamers,
and to her owners, the Paddle-Steamer
Preservation Society, and her crew.

1

Night in South Africa was a blue-black velvet cloak, sprinkled lavishly with huge stars. Dawn always arrived as swiftly and skilfully as a practised thief, slipping the cloak from the land's shoulders so carefully that its going wasn't really noticed until the glow from the lamps burning in the corrugated iron ward turned pale and sickly and the orderly began to put them out, one by one.

That was Rose's favourite time – more than adequate recompense for being on night duty. As light filtered in through the windows, touching the bare, dreary ward with fingers of palest dove grey, then shell pink shading to gold as the sun began to near the horizon, she put the finishing touches to the bandage and straightened, smiling down at the man who had lain submissively beneath her capable hands. 'There – you'll soon be well enough to be discharged.'

Piet van den Burgh's lithe body and bearded young face had been tense in anticipation of the pain he had become used to. But this time it hadn't bored through his wound as expected. He moved his right shoulder tentatively then relaxed and nodded, a grin beginning to spread over his features.

'You're right. It's much better. You're not a nurse, Rose, you're a magician.'

Although he had been using her first name, strictly against regulations, for the past week, it still sounded foreign to her when spoken in his strange Dutch-English accent.

'No, I'm just one of Princess Christian's Army Nurses,' she said briskly, and set herself to tidying his bedcovers, reluctant to move on to the next patient. She enjoyed talking to Piet.

The day's noises began to intrude from outside. The chink of metal on metal, a horse blowing through its nostrils, the bark of an order. Then all at once the sun hoisted itself into the sky, the ward was washed with gold and the new day had begun.

The orderly roused the last of the patients who had managed to sleep, the armed guard on duty inside the hut at all times yawned and stretched, the walking cases began gathering basins and lining up at the door, waiting for it to be opened so that they could go out into the small wired-off compound round the ward to fetch washing water.

'Have you finished the book yet?'

Piet glanced at the volume on the table by his bed. 'Almost. You live in a romantic country.'

'Och, books always exaggerate. Though I suppose that some parts of Scotland are romantic.'

'But not the place where you live?'

'Oh no. It's a very ordinary town – though the River Clyde's lovely, with all the islands. On summer mornings at home,' Rose said, remembering, 'the water's usually like a millpond, with a mist on it, and the islands – Bute, and the Cumbraes, and Arran – floating above the mist like islands in the sky instead of in the water.'

'And yet you don't think it's romantic?'

'Not as romantic as Africa. You must go and see it for yourself some time.'

Piet's smoky grey eyes surveyed her sardonically. 'You think your people will ever set me free again, to do as I want, and go wherever I wish?'

'Of course,' she said in genuine surprise. 'One day, when this war's over.'

A tenacious fighter, the young Boer Kommando was something of a hero-figure among his own people. When the British troops had finally captured him and brought him in to Naauwpoort Hospital seriously wounded and close to death it was Rose who had brought him from the brink, refusing to let him die, watching over him until he was out of danger and on the mend.

'My little Rose –' he said now, mockingly affectionate. 'So efficient, and yet so innocent in the ways of governments.'

'What do you mean?'

He folded one arm behind his head, and asked a question instead of giving an answer. 'Why did you come here, Rose? Why travel from your country to mine? Wasn't it because you believed in your people and their cause here as I believe in mine? Did you tell yourself that we impertinent Boers should be crushed?'

'I'm a nurse. I wanted to help the wounded. I wanted to see Africa. And I wanted,' she added honestly, 'to get away from everybody at home for a wee while.'

'So there was nobody to keep you there? No sweetheart?'

'No.' But memories of Daniel had rushed to the fore at the word 'sweetheart', and the young man was quick to read her face.

'Not now, perhaps. But there was. Tell me.'

'There's nothing to tell. I was walking out with someone – a schoolmaster. He wasn't a sweetheart, only a friend. Then he met my sister. And now,' she said with difficulty, 'they're going to be married.' Then she amended it to: 'They will be, by this time.'

'He chose your sister instead of you?'

'She's very pretty.'

'And he,' said Piet with calm conviction, 'is a fool.'

'I told you – we were only friends!'

He raised a sardonic eyebrow. 'Can young men and women who walk out together only be friends?'

'They can in my country,' Rose retorted tartly. As far as Daniel was concerned, they were friends. But for her own part –

'Sister –' The medical orderly beckoned from the other end of the ward and she hurried towards him, leaving Piet. There was always plenty to be done in the prisoners' wards.

Naauwpoort Hospital was a stationary hospital, almost on the border of the Orange Free State and close to the front lines. The patients consisted of a mixture of Boer prisoners, kept in their own wards under guard, and British soldiers waiting to be shipped to the big base hospital once they were strong enough to be moved.

Unlike the British, the Boers weren't moved on to another hospital as they began to improve, but kept there until they were completely recovered.

Many of the nurses detailed to the hospital refused to look after the Boers, insisting that they were in South Africa to care for the British soldiers, not for enemy wounded. As a result there were always too many patients and too few nursing sisters in the wards within the wire compound.

By the time her relief arrived, rested and fresh, pretty as a butterfly in the white and scarlet and grey uniform that was supposed to de-feminize the nursing sisters, Rose was keenly aware of her aching back and her exhaustion, and more than ready to leave the ward without lingering.

The morning air, although heavy with the promise of the day's heat, was fresh compared to the atmosphere inside the hut. She drew it into her lungs, brushed away the flies that immediately swarmed about her face, and stopped to have a brief word with the sentries stationed permanently outside the ward door.

As she made her way through the gap in the barbed-wire fence and walked to her own part of the compound the notes of a bugle drifted across the flat area between herself and the mushroom of tents. The platoon camping on the low hills near the hospital had begun to march out towards the distant thump-thump of the guns only miles from the hospital.

A long winding line of infantry, broken here and there by the figure of an officer on horseback, was already moving into the distance, their uniforms blending with the surrounding dun-coloured foothills.

Another company, thought Rose, would be marching in within hours to occupy the conical tents that now lay empty. No doubt it would bring with it more sick soldiers, victims of one fever or another.

Most of the British patients were suffering – and dying – from enteric fever. Thirsty during a march and ignoring warnings about stagnant water, they had filled their empty water-bottles from some convenient pool.

The army, one of the doctors had told Rose bitterly, was losing as many men to disease in this godforsaken place as to the Boer guns.

She didn't think of Africa as a godforsaken place. She loved it – the great open stretches of the veldt and the hills that echoed to gunfire; the vivid blue sky, the incredibly raw, beautiful colours of the land, the velvety black skin and huge eyes of the Kaffirs.

The golden expanse of the place beneath its mercilessly blazing sun couldn't be more unlike the crags and soft mists and damp air of Scotland, but unlike the other nursing sisters, Rose hadn't suffered badly from homesickness. In South Africa she felt free for the first time in her life.

The bugle sounded again, so faint and far away now that she only just heard it.

The tempting aroma of new-baked bread flared her nostrils. Indian orderlies just a hundred yards away from the wards had begun their work round the brick ovens. For the moment it was pleasant, but soon the sun's heat would turn the pale fawn earth and rocks to searing, wantonly beautiful, red gold.

The last of the line of men disappeared into the

distance, on their way to fight. Although nobody in Britain had initially thought that the Boer dispute would ever come to war, it was still going on, the killing and the wounding and the fevers. The nurses were told little, but letters received from home indicated that there was little doubt that the British would win.

If that was the case, Rose thought wryly as another volley of distant gunfire echoed round the hills, the tenacious Boers hadn't yet realized it.

After breakfast she went to the hut that she shared with two other nursing sisters. They were both on day duty, so she had the place to herself. It was blessedly quiet, although the heat was often a deterrent to sleep.

Rose unfastened her cuffs and collar, took off her apron, then removed her cap and unpinned her long dark hair, letting it fall free. In the spotted mirror's reflection her face, pale with fatigue beneath its tan, looked eerily greenish.

She envied her half-sister Leila her small slender frame and fair skin and neat little kitten-like face, and had often thought with dislike that with her own oval-shaped face, serious in repose, she herself looked like nothing more than a boiled egg with features drawn on it.

Bella Gibb, her mother, had never made a secret of the fact that Rose was the illegitimate result of a swift coupling in the house where Bella had worked as a pretty kitchenmaid, lucky enough to have her own cupboard-like room beneath the roof slates. A room that was altogether too private and out of the way, as it turned out. Especially when there was a house-party, and young virile guests in the place.

Rose had her mother's smooth ivory complexion, now touched with warm gold under the African sun, her mother's black hair and wide brown eyes. She was taller and sturdier than Leila, whose father had been a small, neatly made man.

On the one occasion when Rose had dared to ask what her own father had looked like Bella had studied her for a moment then said, 'How should I know, in the dark? But from the look of you, he was a handsome bugger.'

Two letters had arrived in the morning mail delivery. One was from her stepbrother Chauncy, who wrote with faithful regularity. The other was from Leila.

Rose hesitated, biting her lip, then took the cowardly way out and opened Chauncy's first. As she ran her eyes down the close-written sheets, Africa's rich golden beauty seemed to fade away, to be replaced by the small coastal town where she had been raised.

Chauncy wrote a good letter. She sometimes thought that if he had been born into a more affluent family he might have become a writer, instead of taking up a humble clerk's pen.

'The wedding was a very pleasant occasion. Leila looked beautiful, and Daniel every inch the proud and happy bridegroom,' Chauncy wrote, little realizing how much pain his words would cause. 'Mother sniffed a great deal during the service. Fortunately the congregation thought that it was from emotion.'

Chauncy always called Mam by her proper title. Bella preferred it; to her it was a way of underlining the fact that her husband's son by a previous marriage wasn't of her own flesh and blood.

Rose smiled, knowing full well why Mam had sniffed her way through the marriage ceremony. Bella had been raised a devout Catholic, and when she found that she was pregnant and lost her job, she had gone home to Ireland, turning to her own people for help in her time of need.

Her parents had railed at her for bringing shame on them, and the priest had called her a fallen woman.

'If that's the way of it, Father, I'm for fallin' out with the likes o' you!' seventeen-year-old Bella had retorted with spirit, then spent all the money she had left on a ticket back to Scotland, and turned her back on her homeland and Catholicism for ever.

Even so, she must have hated to see one of her daughters married in a Protestant church. Since Daniel belonged to the Church of Scotland and Leila had set her heart on a 'proper' wedding Bella had had no option but to let the marriage ceremony take place in what she called a 'heathen place of worship'.

'We've had a wet spring and her rheumatism is worse,' Chauncy went on. 'She's had to give up work and at times she can scarcely manage to see to the house. Now that Leila's in her own home we could do with you here, Rose. I know that Mother misses you.'

Rose put down the letter and tried to ignore a twinge of conscience. Mam only missed her usefulness, and she didn't need Rose as much as the sick and wounded soldiers did.

Unable to put off the evil moment any longer she drew Leila's letter from its envelope and unfolded the single page.

Her sister's tiny feminine writing, neat as the stitches that made Leila such a successful seamstress, hurried across the paper, the inked words almost sparkling as they reflected the girl's radiant happiness.

'Just think, Rose, only three more days and I shall be Mrs Daniel Currie! Today Jinty Nelson and I went by train to Glasgow and I bought myself a smart new flowered hat to go with the coat and jacket Jinty made for me. In the evening Mrs Kemp came along to the house to admire the presents we've received. So many of them, Rose! Our own little house will be quite crowded out.'

'Our own little house –' Rose swallowed hard, thinking of Leila and Daniel together in their home, the door closed to the rest of the world. She thought of Leila's slim hand bearing Daniel's wedding ring.

'Mrs Kemp brought a very handsome crystal butter dish. While she was here my dearest Daniel came in. He was quite embarrassed to find himself the centre of attention! Mrs Kemp hadn't met him before, and she told me pertly right in front of him that I had landed myself the most handsome catch in town. Mam was pleased, but poor Daniel scowled, and I loved him even more!'

Rose could see, as though he stood right beside her, the way Daniel's thick brows would have drawn together over narrowed grey eyes. She knew just how his mouth would have twisted down at one corner in embarrassed self-derision.

'Later,' the words on the page before her chattered on, 'the two of us escaped from the house and walked down to the beach together for a breath of air before he went back to his lodgings. Oh, Rose, I do love him!'

For a few moments, while writing the letter, Leila had apparently recalled tardily that when she first met Daniel he had been her sister's acquaintance. The tone of the letter changed.

'You truly don't mind, do you, that Daniel and I fell in love with each other? I can't imagine how you could have known him before and not loved him yourself! I shall be forever grateful to you, Rose, for bringing us together! My only regret is that you won't be here to see us joined as man and wife.'

A surge of bitterness scalded Rose's soul as she laid the letter down. Although nobody, even Daniel himself, had suspected that Rose loved him, although she had stepped back into the shadows as soon as she realized that he and Leila were attracted to each other, a childish voice deep within her now screeched: It's not fair! He should have been mine! I saw him first!

Mam would have rapped back: 'And who told you that anything in this life's fair, Miss?' Nobody had. But even so – it wasn't fair! Daniel had been hers before ever he set eyes on Leila. He would have fallen in love with her in time. He would have proposed marriage.

He had been hers! And if Mam hadn't interfered, pushing Leila under his nose, he might still be hers!

As punishment for her rebellious thoughts Rose made herself sit at the hut's rickety writing desk. She drew a sheet of writing paper towards her, and dipped her pen in the inkwell.

'Dear Leila and Daniel –' She forced her hand across the page, then sat and stared at the four words for a long time before going on. 'I am so happy to hear from Chauncy that you are now married, and settled as man and wife –'

The pen splatted a large blot on to the page. Rose looked at it, then deliberately added another blot, and another. It was foolish, but it gave her some comfort.

She screwed the paper up, threw it across the room, and went to bed, wrapped in an unusual, but comforting, cloud of self-pity.

2

Once Piet van den Burgh's injuries began to respond to treatment they healed swiftly.

Within a few days he was allowed out of bed, moving slowly and stiffly about the ward and looking longingly from the doorway at the great open spaces beyond the camp.

'Don't worry, my friends,' he said in amusement to the sentries when they uneasily tightened their holds on their rifles. 'I'm not going to make a break for it – not until I'm stronger, at any rate.'

'You wouldn't try to escape, would you?' Rose asked anxiously when she overheard him.

He limped over and took a bowl from her hands, leaving her free to bandage the wound she was working on.

Now that the lines of pain and fatigue had melted from his face he looked much younger than before. He wore the rough shirt and trousers that had almost become the Boer uniform. The shirt was open at the neck to show his sinewy brown throat and a sprinkling of black hair on his deep chest.

'I should – when I'm more able.'

When he grinned at her his grey eyes reminded her of Daniel's.

'But they'd shoot you down!'

'You think they won't do that anyway – eventually? Or perhaps put me into one of those terrible camps many of our women and children are being kept in like caged animals?' he added with savage frustration.

'The camps are for their own protection.'

'So they tell you – and you believe them. You always believe them, Rose!'

'Why shouldn't I?'

'Why not?' he agreed mockingly. 'After all, they're British. And the British are honourable. The British never tell lies.'

The angry bite in his voice frightened her. So did the chill in his eyes. Looking at him anew, she could understand why he had been a thorn in the side of the army for so long before they took him.

'We do all we can to help your people! You know that we give medical treatment to the local families whenever possible.'

'Indeed you do, under the impartial flag of the Red Cross. Such irony, my little flower, to have British military medical staff living in friendly coexistence with the Boers in this area, while only a matter of miles away Boer and Briton are fighting to the death. But we have to remember that this is a civilized war. If there can ever be such a thing as civilized war!'

The man she was working on groaned, only half-conscious, and in a lightning change of mood Piet turned to speak to him reassuringly, stroking his forehead.

Rose worked on in silence, securing the bandage, easing the wounded leg into a comfortable position on the thin mattress. Piet put down the bowl and helped her, handling his sick comrade as gently as any woman could.

'At least our friendship with the Boer farmers in this area proves that both sides can live in peace,' she said when the work was done and they were moving away from the bed. 'And we will, properly, one day.'

'Not if the Boer must kneel before the Briton.' Piet spoke through set white teeth. 'Never that way again, if I and my comrades can help it!'

The senselessness and futility of it all were bitter-tasting in her mouth. 'Why do men always have to fight to prove a point? Why can't they ever respect each other's rights?'

'Ask your own Lord Roberts that question. But remember this, Sister Rose,' said Piet with quiet vehemence, 'freedom and independence are the greatest gifts that men – and women – possess. They should never, ever, be given up. Not for anybody or anything! Not even for life itself.'

The authorities seemed to find nothing strange about the coexistence of Boer and British during the war, and some of the Boer families who lived near the hospital even entertained groups of nurses to afternoon tea now and then.

The nurses gratefully responded to the opportunity to get away from the camp.

The day after her disturbing conversation with Piet, Rose sat in a Dutch farmer's parlour with four other nursing sisters, taking tea with his wife, a square-faced, stolid, calmly efficient woman who busily dispensed sweet cakes and tea and said little, seemingly content to listen to the girls' feminine chatter.

Rose, used now to wooden-planked floors and corrugated tin huts, found it odd to be in this over-furnished parlour with its papered walls and polished floor, its family portraits and its ornaments.

She looked round the room slowly, wondering if this was the sort of home that Piet had been raised in. 'More tea, Sister?' her hostess asked, lifting the teapot.

Watching her, Rose wondered what the woman truly thought of the conflict, and how much she feared its outcome. As she accepted the refilled cup she said quietly, 'I'm sorry, Madam. Your people are always so kind to us, even though this is a difficult time.'

The woman's eyes widened, then she smiled, a spontaneous, warm smile that gave a dazzling glimpse of the comely, carefree young woman she had been, perhaps not so long ago.

'We women –' she said '– all women, must hold the world together.'

Then she turned to attend to another of her guests, and the intimate moment was over. Rose sipped at her tea, feeling a trickle of perspiration run down between her shoulder blades as she sat back in her chair.

Although the Princess Christian's Army Nurses were permitted to don their own clothes when off duty, they were expected to wear as much underneath as they would have worn in Britain. Shady hats and cool dresses did little to ease the sticky discomfort of chemises, bloomers, suspender belts and stockings in the fierce heat of the African sun, although Rose, like the other nurses, had flouted authority and convention to the extent of discarding her corsets.

She mopped at her forehead, remembering with inward amusement that Mam always spoke of humidity as something the nuns dinned into her at school.

'Humidity – that's all they ever thought of!' Bella was fond of saying. ' "You've got to learn humidity, Isabella!" they said. And I did! Sweet Jesus Christ, I've had to learn that much humidity in my life that I'm surely bound for sainthood without as much as a sniff at Purgatory!'

When it was time to return to the hospital the farmer's wife and her small, solemn-eyed daughter stood on the front porch of their little farmhouse and watched the nurses tuck themselves into the little Cape cart drawn by a pair of mules, with a soldier acting as coachman.

The man clicked to the horses, the woman and child waved, and the cart jolted into motion.

Although the cart had a small canopy the sisters each carried a small parasol for added protection against the sun and the persistent flies.

A captain with a touch of the poet in his soul had once described a cartload of nursing sisters, with their colourful parasols, as a basket of flowers. The sisters had giggled, delighted with the compliment. Their superintendent, when she heard of it, frowned her disapproval.

A group of tiny, dark-eyed Kaffir children eyed them shyly as they jolted past.

'Aren't they beautiful? White babies don't look nearly as sweet as black ones.' Rose waved, ignoring the disapproving glares of one or two of the older nurses. One of the Kaffir children was bold enough to wave back.

An ostrich lying across the track rose unhurriedly at their approach, gathering its absurdly long thin legs beneath it, then bounded away with angular grace.

The mules shied a little as it ran off, and the soldier at the reins cursed them, then, red-necked, apologized to his giggling passengers.

The low hills enclosing the hospital rose before them. As the cart approached they could make out the tents and the drift of smoke from fires and hear the barking of a drill sergeant's orders.

Then the wards came into view and they were home again. Parasols were furled and the soldier jumped down and assisted each of his charges to step to the ground.

When her turn came Rose accepted the proffered hand and skipped nimbly to the ground. Then she stopped, staring in the direction of the prisoners' ward.

'What on earth's going on over there?' one of the other sisters wanted to know.

The noise that had taken their attention grew into the clamour of men shouting, topped by an authoritative voice barking out an order. Heads were turning towards the sound from all over the camp. Indian servants busy preparing the evening meal had stopped work and were staring.

Sudden panic flared in Rose's mind. She caught up her skirts and ran, leaving her discarded parasol to roll on the hot dry ground. She knew, she just knew, that whatever was happening Piet was at the core of it.

Skirting the barbed-wire barricade and rounding the side of the hut she stared, appalled.

An ambulance wagon was drawn up outside the hut and two soldiers were dragging Piet towards it. He was resisting, fighting them all the way.

The door of the ward was being held closed by the guards on duty, their faces grim. Judging by the yelling and the thump of fists against the inside of the door, most if not all of the sick prisoners were trying to get out.

Rose ran forward and found her way barred by a determined soldier.

'Let me past!'

The man knew her well. He had often been on guard duty at the ward door. Rose was one of his favourite sisters, and he had always been ready to exchange a few words and a smile with her as she passed in and out. But now his face was like granite as he advanced on her, forcing her to retreat from the path between ward door and ambulance.

'Go back to your own quarters, Sister, this has nothing to do with you.'

'That man's one of my patients!'

'Not any more. He's being sent to stand trial on charges of treason.'

'But he's injured! He's not fit to be moved yet!'

Just then one of the soldiers struggling with Piet wrenched at his arm. The Boer gave a high, involuntary cry of pain and blood suddenly flowered on his shirt.

'Let me by!' Rose lifted her booted foot and kicked the soldier as hard as she could on the shin.

Taken by surprise he gasped and jerked aside, and she flew past him towards Piet, only to be caught by two other men who stepped into her path and took hold of her arms, physically restraining her.

As she struggled with them she caught another glimpse of the young Kommando, his sleeve darkening with blood from the opened wound. The soldiers had managed to get him as far as the ambulance wagon, and they were lifting him hurriedly, clumsily, up to the doorway.

A third man standing in the wagon caught him by the shoulders to drag him in and for an anguished second Rose saw Piet's face turn grey with pain beneath his tan, and his teeth lock into his lip to hold back another cry.

'You can't – he's not well enough!' Rose was fighting like a maniac now, struggling against the men who tried to subdue her.

One of them let out a muffled curse and let her go, staring in disbelief at his bitten hand. She twisted and eeled and managed to ease out of the other man's grip, then made a dive for the ambulance wagon.

One of the guards who had pushed the prisoner into the wagon caught her shoulder and tossed her aside, deliberately using more force than was needed. Realizing just in time that she had been thrown in the direction of the barbed-wire fence, Rose threw out her arms and managed to protect her face from the worst of the tiny vicious spikes.

Before she could recover her balance the guards who had been trying to restrain her moved in, one on either side, and pinioned her arms firmly.

The man who had pushed her slammed the flat of one hand against the closed wagon doors and bellowed, 'Get out of here!'

Then, as the driver gathered up the reins and the nervous mules, only too eager to escape from the noise and confusion, strained against the traces and began to move off, he roared out more orders. A wave of uniformed men poured past Rose and through the gap in the wire fencing to encircle the hut, rifles at the ready.

'Miss Gibb!' The superintendent sister's voice snapped like a rifle shot. 'Miss Gibb – have you taken leave of your senses?'

'He's still a sick man! Miss Vernon, you must stop them!'

There was a fresh onslaught on the ward door. More soldiers ran to hold it shut as the wooden panels bulged. The armed men surrounding the building braced themselves, and with cold horror Rose heard the safety catches on their rifles click off.

'Get that female out of here!' someone bellowed.

The nurses who had been in the Cape cart with Rose stood in a numb, shocked group behind the superintendent sister. She rounded on them, and beckoned one forward. 'See to Miss Gibb, then bring her to my office.'

The soldiers holding Rose released her and took a step back. She looked down at her freed arms and saw with surprise that her forearms were scratched and bleeding where they had come in contact with the barbed wire.

The ambulance wagon taking Piet van den Burgh away was clear of the camp and rattling briskly across the veldt. There was nothing more she could do for him. It was over.

Shrugging off the timorous hand that the girl detailed to help her laid on her arm, Rose turned and walked through the group of gaping sisters, head high, to her own quarters.

3

Miss Vernon's blue-veined hands were knotted tightly together on her blotter. Her face might have been hewn from granite.

'I have never in all my years as a nursing sister seen such an outrageous lack of control!'

Rose stood straight-backed before the desk. Her eyes were hot sharp-edged rocks that didn't fit properly into their sockets. Her head seemed to have been emptied by grief and outrage. It was a large hollow place with little coherent thought in it at all.

Her torn arms had been bandaged by a young doctor she knew well. He had worked in silence, his eyes never once meeting hers. He had almost bolted from the hut as soon as his work was over.

'Well?' the older woman prompted. 'I'm waiting for an explanation.'

'Miss Vernon, the man was still in need of care. How could I – how could we allow them to take him away in such a – heartless fashion?'

'The man was a prisoner. One of the enemy.'

'He was a patient!'

Miss Vernon's nostrils flared, her voice shook with rage. 'He comes from Cape Colony, which means that he is a British subject. He raised arms against the Crown, and therefore he is a traitor.'

'But –'

'I've no intention of discussing the matter any further, Miss Gibb. I have referred it to a higher authority. A group of patients leaves tomorrow for one of the base hospitals. You will travel with them, and report to the lady superintendent in Cape Town. You are relieved of all duties until then.'

'Miss Vernon, surely –'

'That is all!'

Miss Vernon's mouth snapped shut. The interview was over, and there was no more to be said.

A great train of wagons, each carrying two patients, left on the following morning. It pulled out before dawn, so that the ox-wagons could travel in comparative coolness.

To her relief Rose had been permitted to wear her uniform and travel as one of the nurses looking after the sick men. She couldn't have borne it if she had had nothing to do but sit and dwell on what had happened.

As they drew away from Naauwpoort she busied herself caring for the men in her wagon, despite the fact that they needed little attention at this stage, being judged strong enough for the journey.

She couldn't bear to look back at the hospital. It was as though she had been torn away from her home, cast out into the wilderness.

One of the walking wounded, a man who had been shot in the shoulder and the face, hoisted himself one-handedly on to her wagon as they set off. She could feel his eyes on her as she moved between the stretcher cases, and knew that it was only a matter of time before he spoke.

When he did, some considerable time after the hospital had disappeared from sight behind them, it was in a broad Yorkshire accent.

'You're t'lass that gave them trouble over that Boer.'

'Yes.' She looked fully at him. He had a broad, square-chinned, aggressive face, scarlet and sweating now that the sun was up, and made even more threatening by an ugly raw new scar that ran from temple to jaw down the left side. This man had been very lucky to escape with his life.

His eyes were pale blue, edged by stubby fair lashes. Red hair clung with determination to a strong skull.

'You should've learned by now,' he said roughly, almost contemptuously, 'that it don't pay to interfere.'

A spurt of anger set her lips trembling, but she turned away from him and said nothing. During the rest of the journey she was aware of his eyes studying every inch of her. Once or twice he moved from his seat to help her with her work.

When he did, the two of them worked together without speaking. She was aware of the heat of his sturdy body close to hers, the smell of his sweat.

The train that waited to convey them to Cape Town was a hospital on wheels, especially shipped out from Britain, and equipped with its own kitchen and dispensary. One of the two nursing sisters on board, a cheerful Londoner, was to travel to Naauwpoort to take Rose's place.

'Not that I'm looking forward to it,' she said. 'I liked working in Cape Town. I don't fancy life at the back of beyond.'

'It's not as bad as all that.'

'I hope you're right, love,' said the girl, and stood wistfully on the small platform, watching as the train pulled out.

The base hospital their patients were bound for was a huge building, airy and well staffed and set in pleasant green gardens where convalescent patients could stroll among the flowerbeds. Rose would have liked to spend more time in the place, recovering after the train journey, but she was told that she had to travel on at once to Cape Town, eight miles further away, to face the lady superintendent at the hospital there.

It was obvious that news of her disgrace had travelled before her. The staff at the base hospital were tight-lipped and reluctant to help her any more than they had to.

She was curtly informed that her luggage would be taken to a room in the nurses' quarters.

'A soldier has been detailed to act as your escort to Cape Town,' the sister superintendent said briskly.

'I don't need a guard. I won't run away.'

'That will be quite enough of that, Miss Gibb!' said the woman, and bent her head over her work.

Rose's heart sank as she saw that the Yorkshire-born soldier was waiting outside the office.

'This way.' He set off in the right direction. Short of rebelling, and making another scene, she had no choice but to follow.

'I can find my own way perfectly well,' she informed him firmly when they were seated side by side on the tramcar.

'No doubt, lass, but I've been ordered to look after you.'

'I thought you were supposed to be wounded,' she snapped.

'I'm well enough to come and go – they know that. And not ill enough,' he said with a touch of gloom that made her sympathize with him, briefly, 'to get a spell at home.'

She didn't want to sympathize with this man. She didn't want his company, or anyone else's. So she tried to ignore him after that, and sat openly gaping at the cosmopolitan sights as the tram rolled into Cape Town.

It was as though she had just made a journey to another continent, instead of another part of Africa.

The wide streets were busy with carriages and carts and trams, and the pavements fairly seethed with people, the majority of them white-skinned. Most of the men wore uniform. The ladies tended to be dressed in the height of fashion, shading their faces from the heat of the sun with wide-brimmed hats and pretty parasols.

There were children too, well dressed and pleasantly sun-tanned, many of them escorted by black servants.

Rose had heard that a large number of civil servants and high-ranking military personnel flooding into South Africa because of the war had brought their families, but she hadn't pictured such comfort and serenity. These people looked as though they were enjoying a holiday, with not a worry or a care in the world.

'You'd not know to look at them that there was a war on,' said her companion sourly, as though reading her thoughts. 'It's like everything else – one rule for the rich and another for the rest of us.' He snorted, then stabbed a short, emphatic finger. 'Them lassies'll be from your own part of the world.'

Two Scottish soldiers, khaki-jacketed and helmeted, with tartan kilts swishing about their brown knees in place of army trousers, came towards the tram, then turned in at the ornate gates of a great park where fountains played and people strolled past brilliantly jewelled flowerbeds. In the centre of a stretch of well-tended grass a neat white wrought-iron bandstand held a military band. Several people stood listening to the music.

As the tram rattled by Rose caught the strains of 'Soldiers of the Queen'. It was all very like an exceptionally good summer's day at home – apart from black faces here and there, and the predominance of uniforms.

'We get out here,' the Yorkshireman said, and she found herself swept from her seat, escorted along the aisle, and half-lifted down the steps.

'The hospital's over –'

'I can see that for myself. Thank you – you needn't accompany me any further.'

'I've got me orders –'

She strode away from him, through the open gates, without looking back.

The hospital must once have been a grand house. It was snowy white, standing in its own grounds, with a great pillared verandah running round the four walls.

French windows were open, and convalescent soldiers were resting in wicker chairs on the verandah. Each man seemed to be attended by a cluster of fashionably dressed ladies.

With amusement, Rose recalled hearing that these 'ministering angels' had flocked from Britain, making a great nusiance of themselves as far as patients and staff were concerned. She found herself thanking Providence that Naauwpoort was too far away – and too heathenish – to attract these women.

With her next thought – that Naauwpoort was perhaps no longer her home, or her concern – depression swept over her again.

In the main hall a young soldier sitting behind a desk gave her a swift, appreciative glance, sweeping her from top to toe in the blink of a discreet eyelid, then smiled and inquired her business. When she gave her name in a clear, firm voice the smile faltered and died, and the man's eyes became sharp with interest.

'I believe that Mrs Russell is in the wards just now. You can take a seat over there and wait for her. Miss,' he added with crisp correctness.

There was no mistaking the coolness in his voice. He knew. They all must know by now, Rose thought, taking her place on a hard, upright chair by the wall. Scandal moved very quickly, particularly through a close-knit group like the army.

There was movement at the corner of her vision. She kept her eyes front as the Yorkshireman seated himself beside her.

After a while the duty soldier's relief arrived. There was a short murmured exchange, and both men glanced at Rose. She smiled at them, and to her amusement they both coloured and looked away hastily, avoiding each other's eyes in their embarrassment.

The original soldier went away. After another long wait he came back and said, 'Mrs Russell will see you now.'

'I'll wait 'ere,' said the Yorkshire soldier.

'No need.'

'I've got me orders,' he said, and settled his shoulders stolidly against the back of his chair.

The lady superintendent, waiting behind the desk of a small bare office just off the main hall, was an angular grey-haired woman with a severe face and piercing eyes of an extraordinary green colour. One look at those eyes, cold though they were, betrayed the fact that Mrs Russell had once been a beauty. A society beauty, to judge by her accent.

She surveyed Rose for a long moment without inviting her to sit on the only other chair in the room, then said, 'Well, Sister? What have you got to say for yourself?'

'Ma'am, I was trying to protect a patient who was being ill treated. His wounds weren't fully healed. It was wrong of them to take –'

The woman's voice cut through the words like a whiplash. 'Wrong? You – a military nursing sister – dare to criticize the decisions of your superiors?'

'It's as a sister that I do criticize them. Surely when a man's being nursed back to health he's entitled to better treatment!'

'One of the enemy?'

'To me he was a patient.'

'Indeed? I doubt that, Miss Gibb. It seems to me that your disgraceful display must have been the result of some other fanciful, girlish emotion.'

Rose's cheeks flamed. 'That's not true!'

'Whether it's true or not, you were sent here to cure the sick, not to impose your own irrational beliefs on the authorities. Obviously,' said the woman, 'you're unfit for military duty. You will be sent home.'

'But I'm a good nurse!'

'You think that you could stay in Naauwpoort Hospital, after what you've done?'

'There are other hospitals –'

'Not for you. I doubt if you'll find a position in Britain now, let alone South Africa. Do you have any idea – any idea whatsoever – of the setback your disgraceful behaviour will cause?' Mrs Russell asked, an angry red patch growing on each cheekbone. 'We've worked hard for years to establish our nursing sisters in military hospitals. Thanks to your impetuous foolishness we've probably lost all that ground in one short day!'

Then, as Rose said nothing, the lady superintendent added crisply, 'Passage has been booked for you on a ship leaving for Britain tomorrow. I've already notified the base hospital. They will see that you and your luggage are taken to the docks in good time. That will be all.'

Dismissed, unable to grasp that it was all over so suddenly, without a chance to put her side of the argument, Rose turned automatically to the door. As her hand touched the knob, the Irish blood she had inherited from her mother suddenly surged to the fore. She spun on Mrs Russell.

'I'll go gladly, for I'd not want to be associated any longer with such – such cruelty and such inhumanity! Just because you dress it up in the Union Jack you think it looks respectable!'

'Miss Gibb, you forget yourself!'

'On the contrary – I've just found myself. Piet was right – he was right!'

And she strode out of the room, borne along on a wave of fury that carried her past the orderly's desk, towards the outer door.

'Miss Gibb – a message has just come in for you. You have to report to the barracks immediately.'

'The barracks?' She stared at the soldier foolishly for a moment, all her anger ebbing away abruptly as she wondered if it was possible for a nursing sister to be court martialled by the army.

Dear God, was there to be no end to this humiliation and misery?

4

'I'll take you to the barracks.' Her Yorkshire shadow was at her elbow. Rose was beginning to hate the man.

The barracks lay a short walk from the main hospital. This time she didn't have to cool her heels in the foyer. A smartly turned out sergeant was waiting for her, and nodded to her escort.

'I'll take over.'

The red-headed man gave a brisk salute, and left.

Rose was led into a room where a young officer waited for her. The man's unease would have amused her if she hadn't been so tired and confused by then. No doubt he, too, was fully aware of what had happened, and was hard put to it to know whether to treat her with the gallantry he had been taught to show towards the opposite sex, or with disapproval.

'Miss Gibb, I believe you come from a town in Scotland called Sandyford.'

'Yes, I do,' she said cautiously.

He relaxed a little. 'Good. We have a man here, arrested on a charge of possible spying for the enemy. He claims to be – well, let's just say that if he's who he claims to be, you may be able to identify him. Come this way, please.'

Mystified, Rose followed him down a succession of corridors and a flight of stairs. Finally he rapped on a door which was promptly opened from within. The officer stepped aside and waved Rose ahead of him.

A guard stood to attention at the door. The stuffy windowless room's only other occupant was a dishevelled young man in crumpled, dusty civilian riding clothes.

His fair hair was untidy and darkened with dust and sweat, his eyes shadowed with weariness, his long aristocratic face scribbled over with the beginnings of a beard.

He was sitting at a bare wooden table in the centre of the room, elbows planted on its surface, chin propped in his hands. He looked up as the newcomers arrived, then scrambled to his feet, frowning his surprise, when he saw Rose. Her astonishment equalled his. For a long moment they stared at each other.

'Do you know this man, Miss?'

'Yes, of course I do.'

The prisoner's dark blue eyes surveyed her with a glance that was admiring but puzzled. His brows tucked deeper into the frown, then unknotted as he smiled faintly. 'Then you have the advantage of me, Madam, for I haven't the faintest idea who you are.'

'You wouldn't,' she said dryly. 'My stepbrother works in your office at the harbour.'

'So you do know him, Miss,' the officer said.

'Of course.' She had seen him about the town often enough, sometimes on foot, sometimes riding a handsome chestnut stallion. 'This is Mr Blair Crawford, of Crawford House in Sandyford.'

A broad grin broke over Blair Crawford's face. 'An angel in disguise!' he said triumphantly. 'Now, Lieutenant – now will you believe me and stop treating me like a criminal? Confound it, man – do I look like a spy?'

'Any man found riding through a war zone with no identification papers is suspect – Sir,' the lieutenant said stiffly. 'However, as the young lady has vouched for you –' He opened the door. 'I'll be back to sign the release papers shortly. This way, Madam.'

'Wait –' Blair Crawford said as Rose turned to go out. 'At least let me know to whom I owe my freedom.'

'My name is Rose Gibb.'

'Well, Miss Rose Gibb –' He sketched a bow that looked graceful despite his shabby, dusty clothes. 'I'm in your debt.'

'This way, Madam,' the officer repeated with the faintest hint of impatience in his voice and she followed him out of the room and back to the building's entrance hall.

'Blasted civilians –' he grumbled as they went. 'The country's full of them, all behaving as though the war was a game. That one back there was on his way if you please, to cheer on the troops at Pretoria!'

His gratitude to Rose for having solved a knotty problem for him had eased his manner towards her. 'And when he was arrested as a possible spy he seemed to think that telling us he was Crawford of Sandyford would set matters right at once. How were we to know who Crawford of Sandyford was?'

'His family are the local lairds. I heard from my brother that young Mr Crawford had made several trips to South Africa.'

'Well, if I have my way of it he'll get his marching orders back home, And with any luck the war'll be over soon, and your Mr Crawford and his like will have to find their amusements somewhere else.'

They were back in the main hall again, and the Yorkshireman was waiting, standing stiffly to attention. The lieutenant gave her a half-bow.

'Thank you, Ma'am, for your assistance.'

In silence, Rose and her escort walked down the shrubbery-lined driveway to the busy road. With the man continually at her side she felt as though she was a prisoner, and yet she had done nothing wrong. She knew how Blair Crawford must have felt before she arrived to identify him and give him his freedom.

She was so occupied with her own thoughts that she was completely unprepared for what happened next.

Just before they rounded the bend that brought the

wrought-iron gates into view the soldier's hand snatched at her arm and whisked her deftly from the driveway and into the bushes that lined its edge. She had only time for a short startled yelp before the man scooped her into his arms and his mouth found hers, his tongue slithering hungrily between her lips.

He shifted position so that one of his legs moved behind hers, to trip her and drop her neatly on to the ground.

But Rose Gibb hadn't grown up among the streets and tenements and back greens of a working-class town without learning a thing or two. Without stopping to think twice about it she took advantage of his partially spread legs and brought one knee up sharply.

It found its mark. The man gave a grunt of pain and released her. She stepped back and with flawless timing delivered a stinging slap to his jaw as he began to double forward.

Almost immediately she realized with horror that she had hit him on the wounded side of his face. Although she had been poised to run, she stopped, stooping over beside him, trying to see his face as he sagged against a convenient tree, groaning with pain.

'Oh God, I'm sorry! I didn't mean to hit your wound. Let me see –'

He raised his head, his eyes blazing blue hatred at her. She was relieved to see that the wound hadn't opened, although the area round it was a stinging scarlet.

'Get away from me, you – you bitch!' he said viciously.

It was all she could do to keep from slapping the other, uninjured side of his ungrateful face. 'Don't worry – I'm going. And the next time you try to attack a defenceless woman, make sure she's not a Scot!'

'He's dead!' He made no attempt to stop her, but his voice followed her vindictively as she fought her way through the thin screen of bushes. 'Your precious Boer's dead, did you know? They tied him on to a chair because he couldn't stand, and they shot him!'

The words slapped against her, one by one, each hurting as much as she must have hurt him. But she kept going until she was free, stumbling blindly on to the driveway, towards the road.

There was a seat by the gate. She lowered herself carefully on to it, afraid that her knees might give way if she tried to walk on.

Piet was dead. She had known it, deep within. She had known when she saw him being dragged away that his life was already over.

She locked her arms about herself, shivering despite the heat of the day. Piet had been right – this whole war was like a rotten apple. Outwardly, it looked fine and grand and colourful, but inside there was nothing but shame, with no honour.

'Freedom and independence are the greatest gifts that men – and women – possess.' She clearly remembered the words he had used, even heard them spoken in his unusual accent. 'They should never, ever, be given up. Not for anybody or anything! Not even for life itself.'

She wouldn't forget. Not ever.

She looked up into the blue sky, narrowing her eyes against its vivid colour. She loved this war-torn, sprawling, lavish country – but tomorrow, like it or not, she was going back to Scotland. Back to nursing in the local infirmary, back to Daniel, now married and out of her reach for all time. Back to Mam, who ruled the roost.

She was going to be a challenge, was Mam.

'Miss Gibb?' Someone stopped beside the seat. She blinked the dazzle from her eyes, and shaded them with one hand.

'Miss Gibb,' said Blair Crawford, 'I'm a free man again, thanks to you. Can I show my gratitude by escorting you to wherever you're going?'

Behind him, the red-headed soldier stepped through the gate, glowering.

Rose got to her feet. 'Thank you, Mr Crawford,' she said, and took his arm.

5

'Gibb –' said the heir to the Crawford wealth thoughtfully as they travelled by tramcar to the hospital where Rose was to spend her last night in South Africa. 'I know that name well, and yet I can't quite place it. It's been bothering me since we first met.'

'My stepbrother, Chauncy Gibb, runs the harbour office for your father.'

Then, as he shook his head, still puzzled, she added, 'My stepfather was your father's batman in the Sudan when they were both young men.'

His brows shot up. 'Harry Gibb – of course! I remember him. He dived into a swollen river and saved my father's life, as I recall.'

And lost his own, as an indirect result. Harry Gibb, after his army days were over, had been given tenancy of a flat in one of the better tenements down by the harbour as a reward for saving the young laird. But his lungs had been affected in the soaking he had received during the rescue, and his work in the Crawford mine hadn't helped matters. He had died of a lung complaint in his early fifties. As far as Rose knew, the Crawfords hadn't connected the life-saving, or the work in the mines, with Harry's death. They had allowed his widow and family to live on in the tenement flat, but that was as far as their generosity had gone.

'So – history is repeating itself, Miss Gibb. Now it's my turn to be indebted to a member of your family. You must let me show you round Cape Town.'

Then he added, with a grimace, 'Unfortunately, the authorities insist that I must sail for home tomorrow, but I can entertain you until then.'

'I'm going home tomorrow as well.'

Blair Crawford's infectious smile sparkled down at her. 'Excellent! In that case, we shall travel together,' he said.

After the fiery gold and bronze colours of Africa, Scotland was incredibly grey. Rose had never known it to be so devoid of colour before.

Blair Crawford's company during her last hours in Africa and on the journey home had acted as a barrier, keeping out thoughts of Piet's death and her own shameful and unfair dismissal. But once she was aboard the train from Glasgow to Sandyford the thoughts returned, weaving themselves into her mind.

Blair, no longer the dusty, woebegone creature she had been asked to identify in the army barracks, had insisted that she travel in a first-class compartment with him. He sat opposite, talking about South Africa and his determination to return there as soon as he could.

His hair was groomed, his face clean-shaven apart from a neat silky moustache, his clothes immaculate, and expensive. The elderly couple who shared their carriage were silent, and Rose could almost see their ears stretching as they eavesdropped.

She saw, as though it was imprinted in Indian ink on their faces, their approval of this gallant young adventurer who had travelled to South Africa to cheer his country's troops on.

But not so brave or gallant that he chose to become part of that army, thought Rose, recalling the sick and wounded young men who had poured into Naauwpoort's wards.

Then she scolded herself for being uncharitable enough to wish such misery on any man, particularly a man who had been such a pleasant and welcome companion.

The train swung round the side of a hill and the Clyde

lay below them, its breadth of water smooth and silvery-grey beneath the sky. Its nearside bank was fringed with shipyards and the tenement buildings where most of the ship-workers lived within sight and sound of their employment.

In the middle of the river two of the popular passenger-carrying paddle-steamers passed each other, looking from the height of the railway line like children's toys. Smoke trailed from their funnels, and the water's satin surface was torn into swathes of creamy lace as they cut through it.

The familiar sight of the plump-bellied paddle-steamers reminded Rose more than anything else could that she was almost home. Inside her gloves the palms of her hands felt hot and damp.

As though sensing her sudden nervousness the engine picked up speed, dragging the rocking carriages behind it as it careered blithely down the sheer hill towards the mouth of the Clyde, where the island-sprinkled firth opened out into the sea.

Behind lay Glasgow and other, larger shipyards. Below, strung along the mainland shore, were a series of communities. The big industrial towns, Greenock and Port Glasgow and Gourock, and the popular holiday resort of Largs were interspersed with smaller communities – Fairlie, Wemyss Bay, Portencross, Sandyford.

The elderly gentleman fussily began to collect his belongings from the overhead rack. Blair Crawford got to his feet and insisted on helping.

The driver applied his brakes and the train began to slow. As they entered the ornate station with its wealth of glass and wrought-iron, its high roof and spacious platforms, Rose felt her stomach fluttering.

A man came bustling along the platform as Blair stepped from the train, his own bag in one hand, and Rose's in the other.

'Welcome home, Mr Blair, Sir.'

'Thank you, McLean,' the young laird said cheerfully. 'Take these, will you, and put them in the carriage.'

'Yes, Sir.' The man took the luggage, eyeing Rose inquisitively as he did so, and set off along the platform.

Blair turned to help Rose out of the carriage. Dismayed, she watched her possessions being borne away in the manservant's large hand.

'I can manage fine on my own –'

Blair was busy assisting their travelling companions to the platform. When they had alighted safely and had been sent on their way in a flurry of gratitude and farewells, he said, 'I wouldn't dream of leaving you to make your own way home, after all you've done for me. I insist on escorting you.'

There was nothing she could do, short of taking to her heels and running away from him. And arriving home without her luggage.

Uncomfortably aware of the interested stares of passers-by she was escorted outside and handed up into the neat carriage waiting by the station's broad, pillared entrance.

Sandyford, like all the other Clyde coast towns, was built on a hill. The main station was situated halfway between shore and summit, and down by the shore there was a smaller goods station that coped with coal and timber to be shipped out, as well as luggage bound for the steamers that plied between the mainland and the islands.

The town was fringed on each side by a short row of respectable detached, semi-detached and terraced houses, and a few blocks of smart tenements. Between them, round the harbour, lay the working-class area, the shops and school and churches.

On the hill stood a few larger houses built over the past fifty years or so by the whisky and cotton barons who had set up fine summer homes on the banks of the

Clyde, far away from the smoke and grime of Glasgow where they had made their fortunes. The townsfolk below viewed these incomers with mixed feelings. On one hand they were beneficial to the local tradesmen when they were in residence, and they provided domestic work for the Sandyford women. On the other, the opulence of folk who themselves had working-class origins was hard to stomach.

Crawford House sat at the very top of the hill, its turrets and terraces still managing to hold sway over the younger mansions in the area. The Crawfords owned most of the land where the town stood. It was a forebear of Blair's who had first created the town of Sandyford.

Behind turreted Crawford House, on the other side of the hill, stood the small mine that Rose's stepfather had worked in. It was called, ironically, Lady's Walk, because it occupied land that had once, before its riches were discovered, been lush parkland where the ladies of the house took their daily stroll.

At the end of Station Road the coachman, following Blair's instructions, turned towards the waterline.

'You must visit my home one day,' said Blair. 'I'd like you to meet my family.'

Rose looked at him in disbelief. 'Why should I go to Crawford House?'

'Why not?'

'You surely know why not! You're the young laird, and the Gibbs are scarcely local gentry.'

'You saved my life, Miss Rose Gibb, and I've got every right to invite you to my home if I want to. Besides,' he added, 'I've never met anyone like you before. I don't intend to let you go as easily as that.'

'You've never met anyone like me before because you're not in the habit of speaking to the ordinary folk in the streets.'

'You,' said Blair Crawford, 'are not ordinary.'

The horses clipped their way down to the waterside,

then turned left. On the river side of the street lay warehouses and a yard where the wood from the Crawford timber mill waited to be shipped out by the Crawford import and export business. Chauncy worked in the shipping yard, in a small wooden office.

There was a small shipyard on the harbour too – also Crawford owned. Once the yard had built ships for the Crawford shipping business, but since then, faced with increasing competition from the flourishing yards upriver in Glasgow and downriver at Gourock and Port Glasgow it had been reduced in size. Now it built yachts for the whisky and cotton barons who had come into the area and enjoyed sailing on the river in the summers.

It was after working hours now, and the cobbled quays were silent, the crane motionless.

There was bustle and hurry, however, on the pier that the pleasure steamers used. A boat, perhaps one of the vessels they had seen from the train, had just arrived, and was disgorging its passengers. They flooded out into the street, holding back to let the glossy carriage past, eyeing its two occupants.

Some of the faces lifted to them were envious, some indifferent, some inquisitive.

Rose had never travelled in a private carriage before. She disliked the sensation of being perched high above everybody else as though she was better than they were. As though, she thought with embarrassment, she was some sort of side-show, to be stared at and wondered about.

She didn't know how rich folks could bear to travel about in such a fashion. But then, they were used to it.

A sidelong glance at Blair showed that he was quite unaware of the interest being shown in their passing. He was studying the piles of timber waiting in the yard, eyeing the lines of the smart little paddle-steamer, then turning, before Rose could look away, to catch her gaze and hold it.

The driver reined in the horses just then, and inquired, 'Is it this building, Ma'am?'

'Yes.' Rose began to get up but Blair stopped her with a hand on her wrist and waited for the coachman to dismount and open the door. Then he stepped down and offered her his hand.

Once on the pavement she held out her own hand for her bag, but Blair took it from the man and said, 'McLean, you might as well take my things to the house. I'll walk up. Tell them I'll arrive shortly.' Then to Rose: 'This entrance, is it? Which floor?'

'The first, but –'

He swung into the tiled close and went blithely up the stone stairs, the bag swinging from his hand as though there was no weight in it at all. By the time Rose caught up with him he was at the door, his hand raised to the brass knocker, a ring in the mouth of a fearsome lion.

Before he had time to lift it the door flew open and Bella Gibb burst on to the landing, resplendent in her best black silk dress, her arms wide.

'My little girl, home –' she cried, then stopped, mouth agape, and stared up at the handsome young man who stood on her doormat.

'My dear God –' she said. 'It's the young laird!'

6

'I've brought your daughter home, Mrs Gibb,' Blair said smilingly. 'Safe and sound, you'll be glad to know.'

Bella swallowed hard and managed to overcome her astonishment. 'My little girl, home from the wars –'

Her voice trembled with emotion but her eyes were dry and shrewd as she drew Rose into an embrace that smelled of eau de cologne and, surprisingly, port. Bella had always disapproved of liquor.

The embrace was short. Bella swiftly released her daughter and positively elbowed her aside. 'Come in, Mr Crawford – come in, and welcome! We're just having a wee party to celebrate Rose's safe homecoming from that heathen country.'

'Mam!'

'I'd be delighted, Mrs Gibb.' Blair swept his hat off and ushered Rose before him into the narrow dark hall.

'Well, now,' said Bella, in a flurry of pleasure, and sailed ahead of them like a small galleon to the living room at the end of the hall. She threw open the door and proclaimed, 'She's here – and she's brought a visitor!'

A hand, more determined than maternal, took Rose's elbow and thrust her into the room. It was crammed with people. Rose's first appalled glance took in a bevy of neighbours in the background; Bella's special cronies, being permitted to share in the family gathering.

Chauncy Gibb, uncomfortably awkward in his best clothes, perched on the edge of the slippery horsehair sofa. His half-sister Leila reclined elegantly on a straight-backed chair, the flared skirt of her rose-coloured gown arranged to advantage around her neat ankles.

Daniel Currie stood by the window, his hands behind his back, his face indistinct because the light was behind it.

'Here we all are, together again at last!' Bella announced archly, and there was a little appreciative buzz of agreement from the neighbours. Then the archness disappeared, to be replaced by barely concealed triumph. 'And here's Mr Blair Crawford, escorting her home!'

For a moment, as Blair followed Rose into the room and everyone saw him, there was a stunned, awkward silence. These folk were used to seeing the gentry passing through the town in their carriages or, in the young laird's case, on horseback. But never within their own territory. They gaped, as Bella had first done. Blair smiled on them all, completely at his ease.

Leila was the first to pull herself together. 'Rose!' She got to her feet, and Rose saw the soft roundness of early pregnancy pressing against her skirt just below the waistline.

She inclined a smooth violet-scented cheek to be kissed, then turned to Blair, offering her small hand.

'Mr Crawford – how gallant of you to escort my sister home.'

'It was my pleasure, I can assure you.'

Leila smiled up at him radiantly, then her long-lashed gaze swept back to Rose.

'Oh, my dear – how brown your face is! That dreadful African sun – your skin's probably gone quite leathery. Didn't you think of carrying a parasol? You must let me recommend some good creams.'

'Her skin isn't in the least bit leathery,' Chauncy said, coming forward to enfold his stepsister in a warm, welcoming hug. 'She looks beautiful.'

'I agree,' Blair said from behind Rose. 'An angel of mercy, in more ways that one. I'll be for ever in her debt.'

'Nonsense!'

'Indeed I will,' he corrected calmly. 'And I hope that one day you'll let me repay that debt.'

'What's this?' Bella asked with sharp interest.

'Your daughter saved me from a firing squad, Mrs Gibb.'

There was a gasp from the entire gathering. Rose felt her face flame. She tried to speak, but Leila and Bella were clamouring for details and Blair was only too pleased to provide them.

Everyone, even the neighbours who had been holding back shyly, crowded around him to be entertained to a dramatically embroidered version of his first meeting with Rose.

Only one person present, apart from Rose herself, wasn't hanging on Blair's every word. Daniel had left the window and come further into the room, his eyes fixed on Rose. She had no option but to tilt her chin and meet that gaze.

Piet had comforted her hurt vanity by dismissing Daniel as a fool. He was wrong, Rose thought dispassionately, but the months in South Africa had clarified her vision and put everything that had once seemed important into its proper perspective.

Even so, it was with a strong sense of shock that Rose discovered that her youthful passion for Daniel Currie had gone, burned out without her knowledge, leaving not even a few warm ashes.

Relief curved her mouth into a smile. His eyes, embarrassed and apprehensive until then, brightened, and he smiled back at her.

At that moment Leila looked up. Her glance skimmed the two of them and she laid a possessive hand on Daniel's arm and drew him closer to her side.

When Bella finally bustled into the kitchen to make tea for all her guests Rose took the opportunity to follow her.

'Mam, did you not get my letter?'

'Yes. What of it?'

'Then you knew I wanted to come home without any fuss.'

'I know nothing of the sort! You don't think I'd let you come back after risking your life among all these foreigners without giving a party for you?'

'Mam, you know that I was sent home. And you know why!'

Bella, arranging her best tea service on a tray, said, 'Escorted by Mr Blair Crawford, no less! Saving his life and all! If that's not good reason for a celebration, I don't know what is.'

'Mam!'

'Wheesht now, and bring that plate in,' said Bella, and whisked back to her guests.

It was dark outside before the party finally drew to a close. Blair was the first to go, shaking hands all round.

'I'd like to stay on, Mrs Gibb, but my father and grandmother will be waiting for me.'

'You'll come back again, now that you know your way,' Bella invited grandly.

Blair's eyes sought and found Rose. 'Indeed I will,' he said. 'And I'll not forget, Miss Gibb, that I'm in your debt. If I can ever repay you, I'll be a happy man.'

'You should have been a novelist, Mr Crawford,' she said dryly when they finally stood alone on the landing outside. 'You've got a fine way with words.'

He laughed, then took the hand she offered and raised it to his lips. His mouth was warm against her skin.

'Goodnight, Rose. I look forward to our next meeting,' he said, then left her, loping down the stairs without a backward glance.

She looked after him, smiling with mingled exasperation and amusement. The smile faded as she turned to go back into her mother's house.

Blair's going had signalled the end of the party. Bella's

friends, pink with gratification at being invited, scurried out of the door, dusting cake crumbs from their mouths and skirts, murmuring gratitude to their hostess, who received it graciously.

Then Leila rose and said decisively, 'It's getting late, Daniel. We should be on our way home. Rose, you must come and see our little house soon. We've just bought a new piano, so that Daniel can hold rehearsals for the church choir.' She offered her cheek to be kissed once again.

Marriage and the promise of motherhood suited Leila. Her brown eyes were brilliant, reminding Rose of a polished agate ring she had once seen. Her skin, always flawless, had taken on a rich, creamy texture.

Daniel, on the other hand, had become positively boring, with little to say for himself. Rose couldn't imagine what she had ever seen in him. He and Leila were a well-suited couple – better suited, she knew now, than she and Daniel would have been had they ever come to marriage.

Old Mr Kenway from the flat next door muttered something and tried without success to prise himself out of the chair where he had huddled unnoticed all evening.

'Come along, Mr Kenway –' Bella, glowing with the success of her party, eased him upright and helped him across the room.

'Good to see you home, lass.' The old man's voice was as dry and faint as the rustle of autumn leaves underfoot. His hand lay limply in Rose's for a moment, cold and brittle, then slid from her grasp.

'Goodnight, Mr Kenway.'

'Chauncy, help me to get Mr Kenway home,' Bella commanded, and her stepson hurried to obey.

'You look tired,' Rose heard her say to the old man as he tottered out of the room, Bella on one side and Chancy on the other. 'A good night's sleep's what you need. Lie in, in the morning, and I'll bring some broth across later.'

Mr Kenway, wizened and grey-skinned, a widower for so long that nobody remembered Mrs Kenway, suffered from heart trouble and stomach trouble, and had been clinging to life for many years now.

It was Rose's firm belief that he only owed his continued existence to the fact that Bella had long since taken him under her wing, and often scurried back and forth across the landing with bowls of soup and plates of food to tempt his poor appetite. Bella Gibb had more compassion for her neighbours, at times, than for her own family.

Left to herself, she began to gather up plates and cups. In the kitchen, filling a basin with hot water from the big kettle that always stood on the range, she fought back a yawn and suddenly realized that she, too, was more than ready for her bed.

But Bella returned before she had finished washing the dishes. 'Och, leave these and I'll do them later.'

She bundled her elder daughter back into the living room. 'Chauncy's helping the poor old soul to get to his bed. Now –'

The proud, loving mother had gone. In her place was a virago with flashing eyes and a hard mouth. 'I want to know all about this trouble you got yourself into.'

'It wasn't trouble, Mam.'

Bella gave a chuff of disgust. 'Don't try to pull the wool over my eyes, my girl! Your letter wasn't the only one I got, don't think that. I'd a communication from your superior, telling me all about the shameful way you tried to interfere in something that was none of your business!'

'If you'd read the letter properly, you'd know that –'

'Dear God,' Bella interrupted dramatically, appealing to a Being that she had long since denied, 'what have I done to deserve such shame and humiliation?'

'The man was ill, Mam. If you'd seen the way he was being treated –'

'I hope Mr Crawford didn't get to hear about it?'

'I've no idea. Does it matter?'

'Of course it matters! The man likes you, any fool can see that. We all heard him saying he was in your debt.'

'Mam, I've no intention of seeing Blair Crawford again.'

'But he's got every intention of seeing you, mark my words. You're a fool if you don't make the most of your chance. He could do you a lot of good, my girl.'

'Mam, you're talking about the laird's son, not a – a schoolmaster!'

'You could hold your own in any company, Rose. You were conceived in a big house,' said Bella, 'no reason why you shouldn't marry into one.'

'Marry?'

'There's our Leila well settled' – her mother swept on – 'with her first child on the way. A mother has the right to want to see both her daughters well placed before she goes to her rest.'

Rose, defeated for the moment, got to her feet. 'I'm tired, Mam. I'm going to my bed.'

As she was about to open the door of the room she and Leila had shared Bella said from the living room door, 'Not there. That's the lodger's room now.'

'The lodger?'

'You're in Chauncy's old room,' said Bella, and shut the living room door before Rose could ask where Chauncy was sleeping.

For a moment she hesitated in the semi-darkness of the hall, lit only by the gas lamp on the landing outside, shining through a small pane of glass above the door. Then she decided that she was too tired to face her mother again, and went to bed.

She meant to stay awake and have a word with Chauncy when he came back into the house, but as soon as she drew the blankets up to her neck and stretched her feet to the bottom of the bed exhaustion caught up with her, and she was swept into a dreamless sleep.

*

She wakened to darkness, with no way of knowing whether it was minutes or hours later.

The front door closed with a faint, cautious click, and Rose realized that she must have been wakened by the scrape of a key in the lock.

Someone walked softly along the linoleum in the lobby, then the door to the room that had been hers and Leila's opened and closed. Mam's lodger had arrived home.

Rose caught the light sounds of the wardrobe door opening and closing and steps moving round the adjacent room.

She wondered where Chauncy was, for there was no other bedroom. Bella slept, as she had done since her marriage, in the wall-bed in the kitchen. There was nowhere else.

With no warning, sleep took her again and she slipped without a struggle into its comforting arms.

7

The only time Bella Gibb was free of the pain and discomfort of rheumatism nowadays was when she was highly elated about something, or in a furious temper.

On those occasions, she managed to transcend the stabbing, corkscrewing discomfort that haunted her joints night and day, and could tackle any work that needed to be done.

On the morning after Rose's return from South Africa Bella was in such high spirits that she was in the middle of ironing her way through a huge pile of freshly laundered clothes, working with great sweeps of the iron, when her eldest child walked into the room.

'I didn't realize it was that time already, Mam. You should have wakened me.'

'Och, time enough to go up to the infirmary and get your old job back later. You deserved the rest,' Bella said indulgently, taking the teapot over to the steaming kettle.

'I'll do that.'

Bella relinquished the kettle without an argument and went back to ironing one of Chauncy's shirts. 'They're all talking about it this morning,' she said smugly.

Rose measured tealeaves into the pot and filled it with boiling water. 'Talking about what?'

The iron soared over the shirt. 'Mind and put in plenty tealeaves. About Blair Crawford driving you up to this very close in his own carriage – what else? About him coming in and making himself at home in this house. That's set their tongues wagging!'

'Mam, we just travelled together in the train from Glasgow, and he insisted on escorting me to my door.

And that –' she said firmly, to forestall any more of her mother's nonsense '– is all.'

'He'd not have wasted his time on you if he wasn't interested.'

Rose said nothing, setting two cups on the table and pouring her own tea, then putting the pot back on the hob. Her mother liked her tea black and well stewed.

Bella put the iron back on to the range to heat and turned her attention to slicing a loaf she took from the cupboard.

Over the rim of her cup Rose noticed that her mother's hands were badly swollen, the skin red and shiny and looking as though it might split if the tissue beneath expanded any further. Her knuckles were twisted and lumpy, and her wedding ring had sunk into the puffed flesh of her third finger.

'I'll do that, Mam. What's this about a lodger?' she added as her mother handed the knife over with suspicious readiness.

'He's a decent enough young man who pays his rent on the dot, without fail.'

'But where does Chauncy sleep?'

'In the wee room between here and the living room.'

'The wee – Mam! That's only a cupboard!'

'It's big enough for Chauncy. No doubt he'll be leaving soon enough to get married.'

'Has he a sweetheart?' Chauncy, tall and broad-shouldered, open-faced and blue-eyed, was presentable enough to please most girls. But he had never, as far as Rose knew, walked out with a girl more than once or twice. His shyness always got in the way, and the lassies went off, some with a regretful backward look, to find a man more forceful than Chauncy.

Bella spat on the iron, decided that it was hot enough, and went back to work. She took great pride in the knowledge that every piece of material in her house was perfectly laundered. Rose and Leila had been raised to believe that terrible things happened to girls who didn't iron their clothes properly.

'Not yet. But he will, one day. Then it'll be off with him and never a word of gratitude. You wait and see.'

'It's not right that he should have to sleep in a cupboard!'

'He's not complaining.'

'Oh, I know that well enough!' Chauncy was like his father, a gentle man, too courteous and easygoing for his own good. Bella had always ridden rough-shod over him.

'It's as big as the rooms in some of the tenements in Atholl Row.'

'The houses in Atholl Row should have been pulled down long since. It's a slum, and this building isn't. The cupboard's got no window and no ventilation, Mam!'

'He manages perfectly well with the door open. And how else, tell me, could I bring in money, with both you and Leila away from the house?'

'I sent home most of what I earned.'

'But not a penny do I get from your sister now that she's wed. And what with having to give up my own work because of my joints –' Bella wrenched the words out, bitter at having to admit to her own physical failings '– I had to do something to bring in enough to keep us.'

'What does this lodger do?'

'Nothing much.'

'Then how does he manage to pay for his board?'

Bella hung the immaculate shirt on a clothes horse to air, then started work on a sheet.

'He's got private means. You'll remember Harriet Darroch? Her that was married to the man that made a fortune then gambled it all away?'

'She came into my ward at the hospital once, suffering from pneumonia.' Rose recalled the name more clearly than the woman herself. She had been a nondescript creature with scarcely a word for anybody.

'God rest her poor soul,' said Bella. 'If that man of hers hadn't died of apoplexy when he did he'd have gambled away the very bedclothes she lay under, and landed her in the workhouse. But die he did, and now she's gone as well, and left what little she had to her nephew.'

The sheet joined Chauncy's shirts on the clothes horse, and Bella started on a pillow-case.

'So he came home from the sea and sold the house, though it's little enough he'd get for it, since it was left to go to rack and ruin. He sold the furniture too – everything that was left, except the old paddle-steamer.'

'*Darroch's Folly*?' Everyone knew *Darroch's Folly*. The pathetic little paddle-steamer had become part of the town's history. The last remaining vessel of the fleet that Charlie Darroch had once owned and gambled away, the *Folly* had been left to pine alone down at the quay, grounded in shallow water.

Its decks and paddles were gashed and splintered, its single funnel caked so badly with dirt and bird-droppings that it was almost impossible to make out its original colours, its saloon windows glassless and gaping, its engines rusting, its once-sturdy little body listing pathetically to the side.

Birds roosted on *Darroch's Folly* and children brave enough or foolhardy enough to jump the gap between the pier and the deck occasionally explored her companionways and passages, but otherwise nobody ever went near the boat.

Rose had always felt sorry for the lonely, pathetic little vessel, denied its proper ending in a breaker's yard. Although she had a brother and sister, she herself had been a lonely child, and sometimes she had identified with the boat that was pining alone because nobody wanted it, while its sisters rode the waves and flaunted their brave bright colours in the sun.

'He'll not get much for the *Folly*, even for scrap.'

Bella sniffed. 'He's not out to sell her. He's got some daft notion about refloating her, and putting her back on the river.'

'What?'

Bella folded the pillow-case and began, with difficulty, to put the ironing board away. Rose hurried to help her.

'If you ask me he's a bit soft in the head. Mebbe it's all those years at sea that's done it. But he's pleasant enough, and his money's as good as anyone else's. When he's squandered it all away on that boat,' she added firmly, 'it's out of here he goes. I'm not running a charity house.'

It was clear that Bella's rheumatism was slowing her down a lot more than she would ever admit to. The kitchen linoleum wasn't gleaming as it usually did, and the furniture, the skirting boards and the wooden surround about the living room carpet lacked their customary sheen.

When Rose had eaten she rolled up her sleeves, put on one of her mother's all-enveloping aprons, and set to work, dusting and scrubbing and polishing.

Frustrated anger tingled in her when she looked into the hall cupboard and saw that Chauncy had made his bed neatly before going off to work.

It was only a narrow cot, but even so it took up most of the available space. His clothes and the few books he possessed were stacked tidily on the shelves above the bed – shelves that would surely crack painfully against his skull if he wasn't careful when he sat up in bed.

Rose's mouth was grim as she polished the cold linoleum her stepbrother had to stand on every morning. It was time, she decided, that someone stood up to Mam. Since Chauncy wouldn't dream of it, then it was up to her.

She loved Chauncy as dearly as if he was her own brother. They were much of an age, and when Leila came along she had watched Chauncy playing with the baby, caring for her, showing more patience with her than Rose herself could ever muster.

Bella had never appreciated him, but Rose well knew that it was to Chauncy, and not her mother or her sister, that Leila had always run as a small girl on those occasions when the world became too frightening to handle. He had always been there.

It wasn't right that he should have to sleep in a cupboard in the house that had belonged to his own father! But short of finding some suitable young woman and marrying him off to her, Rose couldn't think of a solution to the problem.

Piet van den Burgh came to her mind. The young Kommando and Chauncy seemed completely unlike each other, but Piet's gentleness when helping her with other patients matched Chauncy's patience towards folk like old Mr Kenway. Yes, he deserved better.

She left the immaculate cupboard and moved on to the room that had once been hers and Leila's and now belonged to the man who was, according to Bella, a bit soft in the head; the man who had laid claim to *Darroch's Folly* during Rose's absence.

The room was so neat that it was hard to believe that anyone used it at all. The bed had been made with a skill that matched Rose's own, and she had received her training in the infirmary, under the eye of a very strict matron. The only possessions on view were a pair of black-wood brushes on the dressing table. Rose gazed into the flawless mirror and wondered about the man who must have looked into it that morning. The mirror reflected back her own serious brown eyes.

She made a face at herself, then got on with her work.

By noon the place was gleaming and the housework finished to Bella's satisfaction.

'I'll just scrub the stairs before I finish.' Rose half

filled a bucket with hot water from the kettle on the hob.

'You should be going to the infirmary to see about getting your old job back. I can manage the stairs fine by myself.'

'I know you can, Mam, but I'd like to do it this time. It's been a while since I've had to take my turn.' Armed with a scrubbing brush, floor-cloth and a bar of harsh yellow soap, Rose made for the front door. 'You sit down and catch your breath. I'll go to the infirmary afterwards.'

Bella nodded reluctantly, hiding her relief well. 'I'll just heat some soup and take it in to Mr Kenway. Then we'll have some ourselves.'

Rose skipped downstairs and out to the close-mouth before starting work. The drabness that had appalled her on her journey home had been improved by sunlight. Now the buildings offered shades of slate grey, dove grey, and a soft blue grey that fell more easily on her eyes. The strongest colouring came from the sky, a clear blue touched here and there by white clouds. A seagull wheeled overhead, screaming harshly.

Rose drew in a deep breath of salt-laden air, knowing that if she walked down the side street almost immediately opposite she would come out on to the river-front and be able to look across the wide expanse of water to the layer upon layer of hills dreaming on the other side.

Home wasn't so bad, after all – though when she relaxed her guard for a moment she found herself aching for South Africa and her work at Naauwpoort Hospital.

Reminding herself tartly that the war over there wasn't going to go on for much longer, and she would have had to return home eventually, she turned back into the close and was soon on her knees on the stone staircase, scrubbing so hard at the treads that soapy water flew in all directions.

There was something pleasant about hurling all her energies and frustrations into scrubbing the stairs. It had always been one of her favourite tasks, and on many occasions she had exchanged with Leila, taking over her turn at the stairs in return for the darning, a task that Rose hated and Leila, proud of the skill in her pretty hands, enjoyed.

She worked fast, and had finished the first flight of steps when Bella crossed over to Mr Kenway's door, carefully balancing a bowl of steaming soup and a generous crusty chunk from the end of a loaf of bread on a large plate.

Rose, head down, working to a steady rhythm now, heard her mother's 'It's only me, Mr Kenway –' and the sound of the old man's door, which was always left on the latch, being opened.

It closed, then opened again within minutes. Slippered feet thumped on the newly washed stairs, regardless of the marks that would have to be washed off again, and Bella's voice, shrill and urgent, called her name.

'What is it?' Rose straightened and wiped the back of her hand over her forehead, pushing back a strand of hair that had escaped the loose knot at the nape of her neck.

Bella's face was white and flabby with shock as it peered down at her over the wrought-iron banister. 'Never mind what is it – come here when you're told!'

Then she added, with a tremble of shock in her voice and on her mouth, 'Mr Kenway's taken bad –'

The bucket was heaved into a corner of the landing, where nobody could fall over it. The brush and cloth and soap were tossed down beside it and Rose sped up the stairs, wiping her hands on her apron as she went.

There were three 'houses' on each landing – one on either side, with a single-apartment home set in the middle. There were no bathrooms; thc occupants bathed in tin baths in the privacy of their own kitchens, and shared the water-closet situated on the half-landing below their own level. The occupants of the two ground-floor flats had an outside privy beside the communal wash-house and coal shed.

Old Mr Kenway lived in a middle single-apartment 'house', a room cluttered with furniture and ornaments. The windows were tightly closed and the smell of the place hit Rose as she crossed the threshold.

It was a smell of old age and stale air, of rubbing embrocation and wet wool. The room was chilly, in spite of a pool of sunlight that illuminated the sink, a few unwashed dishes, and a thin faded carpet criss-crossed by paths beaten into its fabric by the pressure of feet over the years.

'Here –' Bella was bending over the wall-bed. 'I thought he was just having a lie-in after the party, but I can't waken him –'

The old man, looking even more crumpled and wizened than he had on the previous night, lay on his back, his buttonless pyjama jacket open on a thin chest.

His lower jaw sagged, revealing shrunken gums and a few bad teeth; his eyelids were half closed, and his skin the same grey-white colour as the pillow. His lips and the area round his nostrils were delicately shaded in blue.

The bedclothes were twisted round his skinny frame and his hands were tight claws that gripped at the thin quilt. On a little table by the bed lay an opened screw of paper containing a few peppermint sweets, a glass tumbler half filled with dusty water, and the bowl of soup, still steaming.

Rose gave her wet hands a final firm rub on her apron then took his wrist in her fingers. It was cold, but there was a thready, erratic pulse there.

'He's still alive. I think he's had a heart attack. We need a doctor – and some warm coverings.'

Her mother sat down very suddenly on a chair near the bed. 'You see to it. I'll stay with him. Go on!' she added sharply as Rose hesitated, eyeing her with concern. 'I'm not going to faint!'

Someone came bounding up the stairs, taking them two at a time, as Rose ran back on to the landing from her own home, carrying an armful of blankets hastily dragged from her bed.

She peered over the banisters and saw a young man wearing a belted Norfolk jacket over breeches and stout boots, a sporting cap pulled firmly down over his head.

'You – run and fetch a doctor!'

He stopped and tilted back his head to gape up at her as she stood above him, clutching the blankets in her arms. He had the tanned skin of a man used to being out of doors, and a square strong-jawed face dominated by eyes that, in the moment when she first encountered them, sent a strange, startled lurch of recognition and longing through her. But she had no time to dwell on it. Not now.

'What did you say?'

'Fetch a doctor – there's an old man dying here!'

He spun round without wasting any more time. As she ran back into Mr Kenway's room she heard the stranger's strong boots thudding rapidly down the last flight and echoing along the close.

Bella was crouched by the hearth, trying to light the fire. By the time Rose had tucked the extra blankets about the old man and the first flames had begun to flicker round the kindling they could hear the boots thundering back upstairs, accompanied by another, lighter, pair of feet that continued on into the room.

Rose looked up at the angular woman who came into the room. 'I told the fool to fetch a doctor!'

'Rose Gibb, mind your tongue!' Bella hissed, mortified. 'This is Doctor Anderson!'

The woman ignored them both, giving her attention solely to Mr Kenway. Rose stood back, watching until the swift, deft examination was over, then stepped forward to help when the doctor turned to the bag she had brought in with her.

The woman looked up at her in surprise, then said, low-voiced, 'Oh – you're the girl who was nursing in South Africa?'

'Yes.' Her fingers closed on the correct phial. She handed it to the doctor, who took it with a brief nod of approval and acknowledgement.

Bella sat and watched, silent for once, as they worked. They both knew that it was no use, but they were both reluctant to stand by and do nothing.

When Mr Kenway died less than ten minutes after the doctor had arrived she closed his eyes with swift but gentle fingers, drew the shabby, torn sheet over his face, and got to her feet. 'There was nothing anyone could do for him. His heart was just worn out.'

She stood looking down on him for a moment, then said, 'D'you know if he had any family, Mrs Gibb?'

To Rose's surprise, her mother's swollen fingers made the sign of the cross. She doubted very much if Bella even realized that in her need of consolation and reassurance she had turned to the religion she had long since rejected.

'Nobody. Poor old man. Poor soul,' Bella said tremulously. 'Nobody of his own here to see him go.'

'He had you,' Doctor Anderson said with abrupt kindness. 'You were good to him, I know that.'

'I did my best.' Bella, suddenly bereft of her protégé, sounded forlorn. Then she added, with an attempt to get back to her old self, 'At least he'd the sense to put money by for a decent funeral. I'll be saved the worry and cost of that. Rose, see the doctor out, then come back and help me to lay him out.'

'Lay –' Rose felt her eyebrows climb to the roots of her hair. 'Mam, we don't have to do that. The undertakers'll see to it.'

Bella's mouth set in familiar, mutinous lines. 'I looked after him when he was alive and I'll go on looking after him until he's decently under the ground. Go on now, and stop your arguing!'

8

Once out on the landing the doctor hurried off without wasting time on any further conversation.

Rose watched her go, then went on into her own house to heat water and fetch the materials needed for the laying out.

She stepped into the kitchen, then gave an involuntary startled yelp when she realized that the room wasn't empty.

The man she had sent running for the doctor had discarded his cap to reveal a thatch of tumbled gold-brown hair. As he spun round from the stove, where he was helping himself to some soup, the steaming liquid spilled over his thumb.

He muttered a stifled oath, transferred the bowl hurriedly to his other hand, and licked scalding broth from his skin. 'What the–?' he began, then checked himself just in time and tried again. 'You'll be Rose Gibb? I'm Magnus MacBride, your mother's lodger.'

He held his hand out, and as she took it Rose looked into his eyes, wide and thick-lashed, and knew again the strange sensation that had gripped her when she first saw him on the stairs.

They were more golden than hazel, those eyes, clear and far-sighted, with all the yellow-bronze smouldering heat of the South African veldt deep within them. It was hard to drag her own gaze away from them. They were saved from entirely dominating his face by being teamed with a strong, bony, slightly hooked nose and a firm mouth.

Mam's new lodger looked every inch a seaman. In fact, he had the look of a buccaneer, a man bent on going his own way, letting nobody divert him from his set purpose, be it for good or evil.

His big hand enveloped hers for a moment. When he released it he indicated the soup bowl.

'I've been working on the boat all morning, and I was more than ready for my midday meal. I didn't think your mother would mind if I helped myself,' he said briskly, without the slightest hint of apology. He opened the bread bin, foraged inside, and brought out half a loaf, which he put on the table.

'No, of course not. I'm just in to collect a few things.' She left him to his soup, and fled to the bedroom, where her mirrored reflection showed that her hair was falling in wisps about a face stained with dirty water from the stair-washing.

She hastily unpinned her hair, combed it out and repinned it more securely, then discarded her apron for a clean smock before going back into the kitchen to wash her face and hands.

Magnus MacBride was scraping the bowl when she returned.

'How's the old man?'

'He died. A heart attack.'

'I'm sorry,' he said. 'Can I do anything to help?'

'We'll manage.' Rose poured hot water from the big kettle into a bowl, rolled up her sleeves, and was about to refill the kettle when MacBride took it from her.

'I'll see to that. You'd best get yourself washed. Your face is dirty,' he said with unnecessary bluntness, softening the words at once by adding, 'And I'll make some tea. Your mother'll need some.'

With her face and hands washed, she felt much more ready for the task ahead. Over the edge of the towel she watched him as she dried herself. He moved about the kitchen confidently, with none of the clumsiness and uncertainty Chauncy would have shown.

He turned, caught her eye, and said, 'I spent years at sea, so I know how to look after myself.'

He opened a cupboard door, took out a tray, put cups, milk, sugar and spoons on it while waiting for the kettle to boil again.

By the time Rose had collected the necessary materials together he had made tea in the large pot. He poured out a cup for himself and put the pot on a tray.

'You carry this and I'll take the rest of the stuff,' he ordered, and she found herself obediently following his broad back across the landing and in through Mr Kenway's door.

He set the tray down, nodded at Bella, cast a swift glance at the covered figure on the bed, and left without a word.

'He's a decent enough lad, for all that he's got daft notions in his head,' Bella said gratefully, pouring out a cup of tea – made black and strong, just the way she liked it, Rose noticed.

'He's eaten most of your home-made soup.'

'And welcome to it.' Bella drained her cup, then squared her shoulders. 'Well, lass – let's get on with it.'

They were the only two mourners at old Mr Kenway's funeral service. Chauncy was at work, and Leila, a lady of leisure now that she had a husband to support her, twitched slim shoulders when invited to join her mother and sister and said that she was certainly not going to upset herself and her unborn baby by attending the burial of an old man she scarcely knew.

Bella, in unrelieved black from head to foot, did her dead neighbour proud, and more than made up for the lack of mourners. Although she had never been one for touching other people, even her children, more than she had to, she took Rose's arm as the two of them climbed the stairs on their way back home.

Now that they were closely linked, arm against arm,

Rose realized that her mother seemed to be smaller than before. She wondered, briefly, if it was simply a result of the fact that by going to South Africa she had broken away from Mam's domination.

Then she decided that it wasn't only that. Bella's skeleton had definitely shrunk into itself.

'What sort of treatment are you taking for your rheumatism, Mam?'

'None of your business! Don't you go talking medical talk to me, my girl,' her mother flared up at once, wrenching herself free so that she could dig in the deep recesses of her bag for the door key. 'There's nothing wrong with me that I can't cure by myself – and there never will be!'

'D'you think Mam's all right?' Rose asked Leila when she paid her promised visit to her sister's new home.

'Of course she is. What makes you say that?' Leila asked in genuine surprise, the teapot – a delicate china pot, totally unlike the big metal pot used in the Gibb household – poised in mid-air over a cup. Then she added in sudden alarm, 'She's not ill, is she?'

'Her rheumatism's worse than it was when I went away.'

Leila's face sagged with relief. 'Oh – that! For a moment you had me worried. Rheumatism's just something that happens to everyone when they get older.'

'That doesn't make it any the more pleasant to bear.'

'At least it doesn't kill folk. I don't know what I'd do if anything happened to Mam.'

'You've got Daniel now.'

Leila's lovely face flushed with momentary pleasure at the reminder. 'Yes, but – a woman needs her mother when she's carrying a child. She needs – well – the sort of advice and comfort that a husband can't begin to give. How much sugar would you like?' she added with the self-conscious pride of a newlywed unused to entertaining in her own home.

She had insisted on touring her sister all over the tiny, shining house as soon as Rose first arrived. Apart from the kitchen there was a dining room, so small that the guests would have to squeeze against the walls in order to reach their seats, the parlour where the sisters now sat, a bedroom dominated by a large double bed, which Leila busily and possessively smoothed over, although it was already flawlessly neat, and a tiny boxroom, destined to become the nursery. There was even an indoor bathroom, complete with water-closet and a small bath.

'Imagine,' Leila said, glowing as she stepped back to let her guest peer in through the door, 'I don't have to go down to a half-landing any more!'

Although Daniel himself wasn't at home signs of his ownership of the house were everywhere – a pair of brown cloth slippers perched neatly side by side in the hearth, heels on the gleaming brass fender; a folded newspaper waiting, unopened and unread, on a small table by the most comfortable armchair.

The bookcase was filled with leather-bound volumes that bore no outward resemblance, even without the titles visible, to the romantic novels Leila liked. And, of course, there was his piano, lovingly polished, the showpiece of the whole house.

'Have you heard anything more of young Mr Crawford since you came home?' Leila wanted to know, sipping at her tea, watching her sister over the rim of the cup.

Rose glanced at the handsome clock on the mantelpiece, willing the minute hand to move faster and release her from this claustrophobic little house.

'What makes you think I'd hear from him?'

A glint of green jealousy flashed in her sister's eyes, then was swiftly hidden. 'After the way he looked at you when you brought him home? I'd have thought you'd have been a guest at Crawford House by now.'

'Don't be silly!'

'I'm not. You know it's all round the town, don't you – that business of you saving him in South Africa?'

'I didn't save him. I only identified him.' Rose cursed Blair Crawford's loose tongue.

'Daniel says –'

'That must be the fourteenth time you've said "Daniel says" since I arrived. Do all married women quote their husbands non-stop?'

'As to that, I really wouldn't know,' Leila said huffily. 'No doubt they do, if they've had the fortune to marry men of intelligence and good sense, as I have. Daniel says –'

Rose took another sip and looked again at the clock. When at last the hour struck she bounced to her feet. 'I told Mam I'd do some shopping on the way home, then polish the kitchen linoleum. She's not fit to do it on her own, but that won't stop her trying if I don't get back early enough.'

'You'll do her no good at all if you fuss over her. She's not delicate, you know. It's not as if she was the one who was – in a certain condition.'

'You look well enough.'

'Oh, I am. As Daniel says, childbirth is natural to a woman, and not an illness,' Leila said primly, earnestly. Then her fingers twisted about each other, and she added with a sudden rush of words, 'Rose – does it hurt?'

'Does what hurt?' Rose looked around for her gloves.

'Having a child.'

'How should I know?'

'You're a nurse.'

'I'm not a midwife. And although the men under my care in South Africa were suffering from a great number of conditions, childbirth wasn't one of them.'

'Rose!' Colour flooded into Leila's neat little face, then receded just as quickly. 'There's no need to be vulgar!'

'I wasn't being vulgar.' Rose remembered, too late,

that Leila had no sense of humour whatsoever. 'I was just explaining that I haven't any experience of childbirth, either personally or as a nurse.' Then noting the genuine fear that glittered in her sister's eyes she added gently, 'But it can't hurt all that much, surely. If it did, nobody would ever have children, and most people have lots. Why don't you ask Mam about it?'

'Oh, I couldn't!' Leila squawked, then sank down onto the chaise longue that took up most of one wall, and burst into tears.

'Oh – Leila –!' Rose, appalled by her own heartless flippancy, dropped her gloves and gathered her sister's shaking body into her arms.

'It's just that – I feel so ill in the mornings,' Leila hiccupped wetly against her neck. 'And my waistbands won't fit any more, and – and my hair looks awful!'

'No it doesn't. You've got lovely hair.'

'Oh, Rose!' Leila twitched away and glared through her tears, seizing a handful of the offending hair. 'Just look at it! It's like straw, even though I brush it night and morning with a silk handkerchief over the bristles. It's awful!'

Rose searched her memory. One of the girls who shared her hut in South Africa had been obsessed by the damage the hot climate was doing to her hair, and had continually tried new treatments. 'Have you got castor oil and glycerine in the house?'

Leila was beginning to recover from her tears. 'Of course,' she said with damp, matronly dignity.

'Mix two tablespoonfuls of each into a small bottle with some alcohol and massage it into the roots every day. You can put in some eau de cologne to give it a pleasant scent,' she added hurriedly as her sister's thin lips parted in swift complaint.

Leila pondered over the advice for a minute, then said with a hiccup, 'Anyway, my skin will go blotchy – and I'm becoming fat and Daniel won't like me fat! He's always been very proud of my waistline.'

‘Glycerine and rosewater will take care of your skin, but as to the other – it’s not possible to carry a child without putting on weight. For goodness’ sake, Leila,’ said Rose with a sudden spurt of irritability, ‘Daniel will understand. It’s his child as well as yours.’

‘You know nothing at all about the complexities of marriage and motherhood,’ snapped Leila, quite forgetting that only a few minutes earlier she had been expecting Rose to advise her on childbearing. ‘Daniel’s a wonderful husband, of course, but being a man, he has – well –’ She faltered, then said with distaste, ‘He has certain – certain needs, and he makes demands –’

‘Leila, all husbands do. It’s part of being married.’

Leila tossed her head. ‘Well, I don’t care for that part of married life,’ she said primly, the tears threatening again. ‘I don’t care for it at all. That’s one blessing about carrying a child – Daniel can scarcely make demands on me just now. Not until long after the child’s born. But even so –’ she gulped, and dug in a pocket for the handkerchief she had only just put away ‘– it’s essential for me to look as pretty and – and desirable as I can, to ensure that he doesn’t stray.’

‘I don’t know what ladies’ magazine you got that from, but if I were you I’d stop taking it and buy a good daily newspaper instead,’ Rose said roundly, picking up her gloves and rising to her feet. ‘At least that way you’ll learn enough about current affairs to hold Daniel’s mind!’

She left the house seething with a mixture of amusement over her sister’s predicament and pity for poor Daniel, married for so short a time and already denied the pleasures of the marriage bed.

She was so busy thinking about him that she didn’t actually see him until he stood in her way and spoke her name, hat in hand.

‘Are you leaving so soon? I thought Leila would have invited you to stay for the afternoon.’

'It was only a brief visit to see the house. I've things to do at home.'

'Of course,' he said, but he didn't step aside.

'I didn't realize that you came home during the day.'

'I left some papers behind this morning, in error. I need them for an afternoon class.'

'In that case I mustn't hold you back.' She began to edge round him.

'You must come again, soon,' he said, then at last he moved out of her way and she was free to hurry away.

9

The door to Bella Gibb's flat was open, and so was the door to Mr Kenway's single-roomed home. As Rose reached the landing Bella came out of the dead man's house. Her greying hair was tucked beneath a scarf, her face streaked with dust; but her eyes were bright and lively, and her movements more free than usual.

'There you are at last. Get into your working clothes and come in here and help me.'

'What are you doing?'

'Just do as you're told and stop asking questions,' Bella snapped, and disappeared back into the single room.

When Rose joined her five minutes later she found her mother tugging at the mattress on the wall-bed. The bedclothes and pillow were heaped neatly on a table, together with a pile of books. Drawers had been pulled out from cupboards and were strewn all over the floor.

'Help me to turn this –' Bella panted. Together they heaved the mattress over and she inspected the underside.

'It's a bit stained, but it'll do.'

'It's ancient. Only fit to be thrown out.'

Bella shot a bright, contemptuous glance at her daughter. 'Listen, milady, there'll be some poor soul glad of this. It'll fetch in a copper or two.' She lost interest in the mattress and bustled over to a shabby tallboy in a corner of the crowded little room. 'Give me a hand to pull this out from the wall.'

'Mam, what are you doing?'

'I'm clearing out Mr Kenway's room for the next tenant, that's what I'm doing. And I'm taking what's due to me before that miserly old thief of a landlord gets his hands on it.'

'Mam!'

Bella, trying unsuccessfully to drag the tallboy into the middle of the room, rested for a moment, hands fisted on hips. 'Listen to me, my lassie, before you go judging your elders and betters. Who was it looked after Mr Kenway all those years ? Who was it ran back and forth across the landing with broth and tea and scones for him? Who did his shopping when he wasn't well enough to go out, and poulticed his poor old chest in the winter? Me, that's who – and never once did I look for a word of thanks or a penny in my hand. Never got it, either. I'm entitled to sell off his bits of furniture now that he's got no more need for it. Not that there's much worth selling,' she added with regret.

'He might have had relatives. Anything that's here should go to them.'

'To the devil with his relatives! Anyway, there aren't any, except a niece in England who never as much as sent the poor lonely old soul a scratch of the pen from one year's end to the other. Never bothered to come to the funeral either.'

'Even so –'

' "When I'm gone, Mrs Gibb," he says to me many a day, "what few sticks I have'll be yours," ' said Bella self-righteously. 'Well, he's gone – and so will this stuff be gone if I don't get it out of here before the landlord comes round. Now will you stop fretting and give me a hand with this tallboy!'

By the time the siren in the harbour signalled the end of the working day every piece of furniture and every item of clothing and bedding had been scrutinized and priced. Bella, buoyed up by the anticipation of making some extra money, seemed unaware of the pain from her rheumaticky joints.

Between them they packed the old man's clothes, put the shabbiest garments into a sack for the rag-man to take away, and stowed away the dishes and books and ornaments. Even the dirty, tattered curtains had been taken down from the window and pushed into the rag-bag.

'Chauncy can take the books to Hannie Simpson's pawnshop later,' Bella said. 'And he can bring Hannie back with him to give me a price for the rest. We'll mebbe get everything away tonight.'

Then she scrubbed an arm across her hot red face and stretched her back, wincing. 'Away through and make us a cup of tea, Rose – and you can put the potatoes on to boil while you're at it.'

The potatoes had already been peeled. Rose tossed a handful of salt into the heavy pot then heaved it on to the stove and made the tea.

Then she sat down at the kitchen table to study a small box she had brought with her from Mr Kenway's house.

It was thick with grime and grease, but its graceful fluted corners intrigued Rose. She emptied out the collection of buttons and pins and dust it held, then wet the corner of a wash-cloth and rubbed experimentally at the exterior of the box.

The grime had had years to accumulate, and it was solid. But within the dirt something had already been uncovered by the scratching of a fingernail; a tiny gleam that fuelled her curiosity and led her on.

Rose added soap to her armoury, and managed to clear part of one side, exposing a panel inset with a delicate floral pattern in brass.

She put the box and the cloth on to the tray and carried them back into the old man's house with her. 'Look, Mam, this is a lovely piece of work. I think it's an old tea caddy.'

Bella curled her stiff fingers gratefully round her cup and looked at the box without interest. 'If there's any tea in it you can add it to our own caddy. If there isn't, put it with the other stuff for Hannie.'

'But it might be worth more than Hannie would give you.' Rose looked at the furniture about them with new eyes. It was scratched and dulled and neglected, but the lines of the chairs and the two small tables were elegant, and the faded, torn tapestry seat of a small stool in the corner showed faint, delicate colour.

The drawers they had dragged from the tallboy were furnished with pleasing brass handles.

She put her tea down untasted and began to move about the room, studying everything more closely. 'Mam, we should clean this furniture up and have a proper look at it –'

'D'you not think we've got enough to do with our own bits and pieces? Let Hannie see to any cleaning that's necessary. I've got better use for my energy, and so have you. For a start,' said Bella, 'you can walk up to the infirmary tomorrow morning and see the matron. You've wasted quite enough time.'

The moment had come, Rose steeled herself, then said, 'I've already been to the infirmary. Mam, I'm not going back to nursing.'

'What?' Bella's cup clattered down. 'Have you lost your wits, girl?'

'You know what happened while I was away –'

'I know that you made a fool of yourself over some man – but that's all behind you now. You'll go back to see that matron first thing tom –'

'It's not behind me – not as far as she's concerned. She'd had a report in already from the lady superintendent.'

Rose smarted over the memory of the meeting, a carbon copy of the interviews she had already endured with the superintendent at Naauwpoort and the lady superintendent in Cape Town.

'She wasn't eager to welcome me back – and I found

that I wasn't eager to go back. So I told her what I'm telling you now. I'm giving up nursing, for the time being at any rate.'

There was a short silence, then: 'Nonsense!' Bella Gibb said flatly. 'It's the only thing you're trained to do.'

'It seems to me that sometimes,' Rose said bitterly, thinking of the last sight she had had of Piet, being dragged like an animal to his death, with blood on his shirt, 'there's no sense in helping folk to get better if they've got worse things to face.'

'But what else can you do?'

'I'll find something.'

'You needn't expect me to support you while you're looking for it, my lady!'

'I've got some money left from South Africa. And I'll find work. I'll pay my way.'

The older woman got to her feet, her face white with anger. 'You'd better,' she said harshly. 'Or else you're out on the pavement – daughter or no daughter!'

And she limped off to her own house, slamming the door behind her.

Rose looked down at her hands and saw that they were shaking. She had openly defied Mam and survived. But she wasn't through the woods yet. Now, somehow, she had to find a new way of earning her own living.

She began to work on the small tea caddy again, taking comfort from her task. Slowly, it emerged from its age-old coating until at last it was fully revealed, a beautifully shaped rosewood box, inlaid with brass.

She was turning it thoughtfully over in her fingers when she heard Magnus MacBride come loping up the stairs, taking them two at a time as usual. On the landing the footsteps stopped, then came towards her.

She looked up as he appeared in the doorway.

'Oh, it's you. I wondered why the door was open.' Then he came further into the room, reaching for the box. 'What's that you've got?'

'A tea caddy.' She surrendered it to him. As always, he was casually dressed in an open-necked shirt and working trousers. As always, his hair was untidy, shot through with sunshine, even in that dark, dingy room.

He studied the box, turning it round in his large capable hands, then handed it back. 'An old one, too. Might be worth something.'

'That's what I thought. All this furniture' – she waved a hand about the room – 'might be worth something if it was cleaned up and shown to its advantage.'

He lifted an eyebrow at her. 'And you're going to do it?'

'I'd like to, but Mam's going to sell it to Hannie Simpson tonight, for what she can get.' She ran a hand over the wooden arm of the chair she sat on. 'It would be a pleasure to polish this up and see what's underneath.'

'Then buy it from her before Hannie gets his hands on it.'

'What with?'

To her astonishment MacBride said, 'I could lend you twenty pounds, but no more than that. I doubt if Hannie'll offer more.'

'And where would I keep it?'

'There's an old shed on the pier where my boat's moored. Nobody uses it. It would do. I'll fetch a barrow and help you to transport the stuff there.'

He propped a broad shoulder against the wall. 'If you sell it for more than the money you owe me you'll make a profit. If not – you'll have learned a lesson.'

'You must be wealthy, to lend money on a whim,' she said dryly.

Amusement gleamed deep within those amazing tawny eyes of his. 'I'm not. That's why I can only afford twenty pounds.'

'But why lend it at all?'

'You'll have heard about my uncle?'

'I know that he lost a fortune at the gambling tables.'

'I'm a gambler too,' said Magnus MacBride. 'Only I put money on people, not horses or cards.'

'And on old paddle-steamers that nobody else wants.'

'Aye,' he agreed, unruffled.

Curiosity led her to ask, 'What's she like below decks – *Darroch's Folly*?'

'You've never been on board? I thought every child in Sandyford had been through her time and time again.'

'I never liked to pry.'

He grinned. 'Then come aboard by invitation.'

'When?'

'Now's as good a time as any,' said Magnus MacBride. 'Wash your face first, though – it seems that every time I see you you've got dust all over your nose.'

Seen from the street, her colourless, sun-bleached funnel and the top of her nearside paddle-box peeping over the harbour wall, *Darroch's Folly* looked sad and shabby. Viewed from close up, she was a disaster.

Even so, Rose sensed a thrill of excited pleasure as she followed Magnus MacBride across the uneven, weedy cobbles to where the old paddle-steamer lay at her moorings. As they got nearer she saw that he had already started to clear the rubbish that had accumulated on her decks over the years, and to scrape the thickly encrusted bird-droppings from her railings. But the vessel still seemed to be well beyond any man's help.

Once she had had another name, a more grand name. But the gilt lettering had long since faded from the gashed and splitting wood at her bows and all signs of that name had gone. Once, she had been one of a fleet of three Darroch boats – before her owner succumbed to his gambling fever and lost his little empire. But that had been many years ago.

Magnus MacBride stooped and swung a broad plank between boat and pier, then started along it. 'Come on –'

'You surely don't expect me to walk along that?' She

edged her way to the side of the harbour and peered over. The drop between boat and wall seemed deep. At the bottom dirty water washed indifferently round the wooden pilings. The space was only a matter of a few feet, but the plank looked far too narrow a bridge over that abyss.

MacBride turned, halfway along the walkway, apparently oblivious of the scummy water waiting below. 'It's the only way to go on board and see her properly. Come on –'

He came back a step or two and held out his hand. Rose stood transfixed with nervousness for a moment, then gathered up her skirts and took it. His fingers closed about hers.

'Just keep looking at me,' he commanded.

Step by step, her hand in his, her eyes locked with his golden gaze, she moved towards him, along the plank, above the water, until he put a foot firmly on the deck of *Darroch's Folly*, turned, scooped her into his arms, and deposited her on the paddle-box platform by his side. Then he released her and skipped, light-footed, to the deck.

'This way –'

She followed him down the short flight of wide steps from the paddle-box to the deck, which canted at an angle because the old steamer was lying on stones and mud instead of floating free on deep water.

She would have liked to stop there for a while, to get the feel of the boat beneath her feet. But Magnus was already leading her to a door forward of the slender raked funnel.

'This is the main saloon.'

The room was large and empty, with windows set into the walls on three sides. There was no glass left in any of the frames. It was obvious that birds had been nesting here for years.

'There's a smaller one aft –'

Again there was no glass in the windows, and the

mahogany bar that ran along the only windowless wall was white with damp.

'I've found an old man who used to be a cabinet maker. He's going to see to the woodwork for me. He'll mebbe be able to help you with your own stuff as well.'

'I've not decided to buy it yet.'

'But you will. The promenade decks are above the saloons.' Magnus took a firm hold on the railing of the nearest stairway. It crumbled, and came away in his hand.

'Mebbe we'd better leave the promenade decks until I've done some work on them,' he conceded, then added cheerfully, 'But the bridge is secure. Come up and have a look at it.'

Because a great pile of rubbish was blocking the starboard stair to the bridge they had to clamber up the sloping covered passageway to the port side.

As she picked her way carefully at Magnus's back Rose didn't know whether to laugh at the thought of this poor old hulk ever taking its place on the river again, or cry for the once-bonny boat.

Once on the bridge she had no time to think of laughing or crying. Up here, the steamer's cant to starboard was more pronounced. When she tried to walk on it she staggered, and if Magnus hadn't taken a firm grip of her hand she would have fallen and rolled from one wing to the other.

He supported her and steadied himself with a seaman's natural sense of balance. 'Here's the wheel – still in place, and still seaworthy.'

'How can you see to steer the boar?' Rose peered through the gaping holes that had once been windows, and found herself looking directly on to the funnel.

'The helmsman takes his orders from the captain – or the pilot, if it happens to be necessary to have a pilot aboard. They have a fine view from each wing. It's best for the balance of the vessel to have the bridge and wheelhouse between the boxes.'

Then he said, 'We'll go below now.'

10

As she started after Magnus down a narrow companionway into the gloomy bowels of the vessel Rose asked nervously, 'It – it can't tip right over, can it?'

'Certainly not. And she's a she, not an it.' He stopped at the foot of the companionway and turned to help her down the last few steps.

'She's as sound as a drum. Clyde-built in 1868 and sturdy enough to last for years yet,' he added proudly.

Now that they were below decks and below the harbour wall there was little light, and what there was had an unpleasantly greenish tinge.

The forward ladies' saloon below deck, with every porthole, as expected, broken and open to the elements, was a damp and dirty cave. Something crunched under her foot as she hovered in the doorway, but she didn't have the nerve to look down to see what it was.

'This is going to be a handsome apartment when I've set it to rights,' MacBride was saying with satisfaction. 'There's a smoking saloon aft, for the gentlemen.' Then his voice changed, taking on a tone that reminded her of Leila showing off her new piano. 'Come and see the engines –'

Rose had travelled aboard the smart, brightly painted Clyde paddle-steamers on more than one occasion, and she knew that the steam engines, situated at the heart of the boats and open to the public's view, were a great attraction for the men and children on board.

The ladies generally preferred to sit out on deck, or in the saloons if the weather was inclement, admiring the passing scenery.

But the engines in *Darroch's Folly* bore no resemblance

to the huge shining pistons and rods she had viewed in those earlier days. They consisted of a vast, rusted collection of metal sunk into a great pit as black and frightening as anything that a professional writer of terrifying stories could have thought up.

'Of course they need a lot of work done on them,' her guide said, reading her face despite the cave-like dimness. 'But they're sound enough. Single steeple two cylinder.'

'Clyde-built, I suppose,' she said faintly, wrinkling her nose against the terrible smell of damp and decay that hung all about the place.

'Yes indeed. I've worked in the engine rooms of ships all over the world, so I know what I'm talking about. Though I'd like to put in a diagonal compound engine instead, for greater speed. If I can raise the money, that is.'

He crossed the aisle skirting the pit and peered through the small glass porthole set into the outer wall. 'The paddles need restoration, but that's a simple enough matter.'

'Can I see them?'

His teeth showed white in a smile at the sudden enthusiasm in her voice. 'Here they are.'

He moved slightly to the side to let Rose look through the porthole. At first there was very little to be seen, other than a wash of pale green light that made her feel squeamishly as though they were deep underwater.

She pressed her face against the thick glass, peered more closely, and made out the weed-covered side of the harbour wall, viewed through the open pattern on the outside of the paddle-box. Then gradually, as her eyes became used to the light, she saw the great motionless slab of a paddle float and part of the iron spars that held it in place, within the box itself, on the other side of the glass and only inches away. A flutter of excitement constricted her throat for a moment. Every time she had been taken for a paddle-boat trip with Leila and Chauncy as a child she had spent most of her time below, watching the great paddles turn at blurred speed, beating up the water as they forced the weight and bulk of the boat through it.

'What are they made of?' She turned to Magnus MacBride and was disconcerted to find that his face, as he also turned from the porthole, was so close that she could scarcely have slipped her hand between their two noses. The greeny light showed her that his eyes weren't true gold after all, but hazel, shot through with glittering lights like gold dust.

'The floats?' A gentleman would have moved back courteously. He didn't, and she felt his breath warm on her cheek as he spoke. 'They're made of wood, bound with metal.'

'Does wood not rot in the water?'

'Not that wood. It's iron hard.' Then he added, without a change of tone, 'I like your face, Rose Gibb. It has character as well as beauty. And your hair smells of violets.'

Then to her astonishment he took her into his arms and kissed her.

During her brief courtship with Daniel his few kisses had been restrained and almost polite. At times Rose had shocked herself by wishing that he could have been more positive, more masterful with her. But he never had been.

The only other man to claim her lips had been the red-haired soldier in South Africa, and his wet, disgusting, hungry assault could scarcely be counted as a kiss.

But Magnus MacBride's embrace was something quite different from either Daniel's or the soldier's. His mouth took hers first of all in a mere touching, a tasting, then with confidence, his lips parting, the tip of his tongue demandingly separating her own lips, his arms drawing her close against his body, where she fitted like the correct piece of a jigsaw.

Pleasure and a feeling of the rightness of the situation warmed Rose. She let herself melt against him, put her hands up to shape themselves against his broad back, allowed her tongue to move and entwine with his.

Then just as she was settling into the kiss it came to its conclusion as unexpectedly and smoothly as it had begun. He drew his head back from hers, his hands slid from shoulder to elbows, where they cupped her lightly, and they were two separate people again, each breathing a little faster than usual.

'That,' said MacBride after a moment, 'was a blessing on the old lady. Can't you feel the new life in her already?'

More scandalized by her own behaviour than by his, Rose jerked back, pulling out of his grasp altogether. Her face felt hot. 'I can not!'

'It's there,' he said, unruffled. 'It's there, and you'll know it all in good time.'

As they emerged on deck a paddle-steamer whisked past the harbour on its way out of Gourock, smoke feathering from bright yellow funnels, paddles thrashing the water into creamy foam, the deck busy and colourful with passengers.

MacBride glanced admiringly at the passing vessel, then turned to survey his own sorry piece of marine flotsam.

'She's hungry to be out there again – aren't you, my lass?' he said reaching out to pat the paint-flaked funnel.

Darroch's Folly bucked a little beneath their feet as the wake from the other steamer sent in great waves that rocked her. It was as though she was stirring in agreement with her new owner's plans for her future.

Looking into Magnus's golden eyes Rose saw the dream that filled them, and was caught up in it despite herself.

'Could she truly go back on to the river?'

'Of course.'

'Are you going to sail her yourself?'

'I'll need to get a captain, for I've not got the necessary qualifications. Not yet,' he added, 'but I'm going to study for my master's ticket.'

'But the Clyde's already full of paddle-steamers.'

'There's always room for one more – then another, and another. I told you – I'm a gambler, like my uncle. Only I'm gambling this boat instead of money. I'm taking on the rest of the world instead of taking on other card-players.'

He patted the funnel again. 'But unlike my uncle, I'm going to win. Once this old lady goes back to work she'll earn the money to buy more. A whole fleet, that's what I'm aiming for. The Darroch Line.'

Rose perched gingerly on the edge of the dilapidated wooden bench, bracing herself against the slant of the deck. 'The Darroch Line.' She tasted the words in her mouth for a moment. 'It has a fine ring to it.'

'It has. I'm going to turn this ugly duckling back into a swan.' Then he asked, half-defensively, 'What are you smiling about?'

'I was just thinking that just now you sounded very like a man I knew in South Africa. A Boer. You even looked like him.'

'Tell me about him,' he said, in much the same way as Piet had ordered her to tell him something of Daniel.

Rose had never thought that she would tell anyone what had happened in South Africa. But sitting on the sloping deck of the old steamer, the wind riffling through Magnus's tawny hair and making it even more untidy, the seagulls quarrelling harshly on the mudbanks, she began to talk, and couldn't stop until it had all poured out.

He heard her out, his eyes sometimes drifting along the lines of the steamer, sometimes looking out across the Clyde to where the far shore, dappled by sun and the shadows of cloud, seemed to be rippling on the surface of the water.

When she finally finished her story they were both silent for a while. Then Magnus said, 'So – you'll take that twenty pounds I offered, and buy the old man's furniture?'

She had to wrench her mind back to Sandyford and the present. 'What's that got to do with Piet?'

'Everything. You need to test yourself, just as I do. Buy the furniture, see what you can make of it. Find out if you're going to be a failure or a success, Rose Gibb.'

'I might lose your money.'

'If you do you'll have to go back to nursing, like it or not, and repay the debt. Your mother'll have won and you'll have gained nothing by going off to South Africa.'

He leaned forward, tipped her face up to his with one finger beneath her chin, and said challengingly, 'Well?'

She looked beyond him, out over the river that stretched behind his head. Another paddle-steamer was fussing past them, coming in to the pier. Again, the old wreck she sat on shifted very slightly, like a live thing – or like something that had long been dormant and was now beginning to hope again.

'Yes,' Rose heard herself saying. 'Yes – I'll do it.'

11

After the evening meal Chauncy uncomplainingly shouldered a box of books and went off to Hannie Simpson's pawnshop. When he returned it was with Hannie himself, a big middle-aged, balding man with sly dark eyes that had a way of darting into corners and up at ceilings, looking anywhere but at the person he was addressing.

He insisted on going into Mr Kenway's house alone. After a while he came across the landing to where Bella waited in her kitchen.

She poured out a cup of tea for him. 'Well?'

Hannie packed several spoonsful of sugar into the cup, drank half the tea in one mouthful, set it down, wiped his mouth with the back of a hand and said, 'Ten pound the lot.'

'Ten pounds?' Bella was outraged. Hannie's gaze lifted to the clothes pulley suspended from the ceiling, then flickered back to where Rose sat at the table, darning one of Chauncy's socks.

As his eyes rested on her she was uncomfortably aware of their clammy weight against her skin. Then they were off again like moths in the night, fluttering to the corners of the room. But always, Rose realized with growing distaste, they were drawn back to herself, as a moth might be attracted to a flame.

The small room seemed to be full of people. Chauncy leaned against the door, waiting to help Hannie with the furniture once the bargaining was over. Magnus MacBride was polishing his boots in a corner by the stove, missing nothing of what was going on. The notes that he had given to Rose were tucked into her skirt pocket in a neat, solid bundle.

'That's all I can give you,' said Hannie. 'It's not even worth that.'

'I'd get fifteen pounds from that furniture shop in Motson Street.'

'You'd not,' Hannie said with heavy confidence. He drained the cup and put it down. 'Twelve pound – and that's my final offer.' He fisted his hands on the table and pushed himself upright, ready to leave.

'Fourteen pounds.'

A smirk touched the corners of Hannie's mouth and he began to shake his head, confident now of his bargain.

Then his jaw dropped in astonishment when Rose said, 'Mam, I'll give you fourteen pounds for the lot.'

'You?' Bella's head whipped round; her voice was a squeak of astonishment.

'Yes, me. Will you take it?'

'Wait a minute here – I'm the one that's making the offer. I didnae ken that you'd gone into the furniture business, Rose Gibb,' Hannie said with blustering belligerence.

She forced herself to meet his eyes and at once they slipped away to circle the room.

'I might be. Well, Mam?'

'Fourteen pound and ten shillings – and that's only because you and me's kenned each other for years, Bella.'

Hannie's hand went to his pocket, then halted as Rose said clearly and firmly, 'Sixteen pounds, Mam.'

Even MacBride's head was lifted now, his tawny eyes moving keenly between Rose, Bella and Hannie.

'Where would you get sixteen pounds?' Bella squawked.

'That's my business. But I'm willing to put it into your hand right now. Unless Mr Simpson wants to offer more?'

The tip of the man's tongue moistened his lips with the same nervous darting movement his eyes used. He swallowed convulsively, and Rose knew as clearly as though he had said it that, like herself, he had guessed at the value of the pathetic, neglected furniture next door.

She watched as his slow brain tried to decide whether the furniture was worth gambling his money on. She began to enjoy the game between them. She didn't like the man, didn't trust him. It would be a pleasure to best him.

Slowly, deliberately, she withdrew the roll of notes from her pocket and began to count them out on to the table. For once, Hannie's eyes stilled, fixed on the money, narrowing as he tried to estimate how much she had in all.

Then he slammed a fist on the table and said explosively, 'Be damned to the lot of you! I've got more to do with my money than throw it away on rubbish, Rose Gibb! Have it, if you want it. And much good may it do you!'

Chauncy, his face a mask of astonishment, his own gaze fixed on the notes piling up on the table, stepped aside automatically to let the man leave.

'Here!' Bella shrilled after him. 'What about the books you got?'

Hannie hesitated, spun round on his heel, and tossed a coin on to the table. 'Not a penny more,' he said viciously, and slammed out of the house.

In the silence that followed Rose smoothed out the sixteenth pound note and laid it on top of its predecessors. Then she put the remaining four pounds back into her pocket. 'There you are, Mam.'

Bella reached out a dazed hand to the money, then checked herself sharply. 'Where did you get it, Rose? The truth, now!'

In his corner, Magnus MacBride had returned to his boot-polishing, whistling softly to himself.

'That's my concern.'

'It's mine as well. You're still my daughter, you know.

You're still living under my roof!' Bella scooped up the money and checked it swiftly.

'I didn't have to sell myself for it. That's all you have to know.'

There was a sudden tremor to MacBride's whistling, then it steadied itself again. Bella's face reddened.

'Mind your tongue, lassie! At least tell me this – what are you going to do with the stuff now you've got it? It'll have to be out of there tomorrow morning, for the landlord'll be round before the day's out.'

'I know. And I'll tell you what I've done with it after I've done it.'

They matched look for look, and neither backed down. Deep within herself, Rose felt her strength growing. She had taken her first step on the road to independence, and the ground was solid beneath her.

She could almost sense Piet's approval. She could definitely sense MacBride's.

Bella's gaze dropped. She gave an angry sniff and stowed the notes away in her pocket, then stamped from the room. With her going, the tension in the air eased noticeably.

Chauncy shook his head in admiration. 'That's the first time anyone ever managed to make a fool out of Hannie. You did well, Rose.'

'I don't like the man. I don't like the way he has of looking at – at folk.'

Her voice quivered slightly on the last words, and Chauncy moved to her and put a reassuring hand on her shoulder.

On the following morning Magnus MacBride brought a man and a hand-barrow to the close-mouth. Bella watched sourly as Mr Kenway's possessions were carried out.

'I might have known he'd be in on it,' she snorted as her lodger disappeared downstairs, hefting a cupboard with ease. 'You've been letting him fill your head with his daft ideas!'

'No, he just offered to help me to take the furniture away.'

'But you're a nurse to trade, lassie! What do you know about furniture?'

'I can learn. And I can scrub and polish as well as anyone else.'

'On your own head be it,' said her mother and went back into the house, closing the door with unnecessary energy behind her as MacBride came bounding back up the stairs, his helper trailing behind him.

Because the hand-cart was small it took three journeys before everything was stored in the shed at the harbour. The man with the barrow was paid off with five shillings out of the money Rose had left, then she handed the rest to MacBride.

'That's sixteen pounds and five shillings I owe you.'

He shook his head and handed it back, folding it into the palm of her hand, closing her fingers into a fist over it. 'That's not the way to do business. You'll need a bit of money behind you to help you get started. Pay me when you've sold it, and not before.'

Then he moved a step closer and asked, devilment in his eyes and the curve of his mouth, 'Should we not bless the furniture business, the way we blessed my boat?'

She drew back sharply, reddening as he laughed. 'Certainly not!'

'Pity,' said Magnus, then: 'What are you going to do next?'

She had lain awake half the night worrying about that, but there was no sense in admitting it to him, or to anyone else.

'Now I'm going to sort out the pieces that might be worth something, and let it be known that the rest's for sale,' she said with assumed confidence. 'Once it goes I'll have room to clean up what's left. And when it's restored

I'll offer it to the man who owns that furniture shop in Motson Street. He often has some very nice old pieces of furniture in his windows, and I think he's more honest than Hannie Simpson.'

'I'll speak to the old man who's going to work on the boat for me,' MacBride offered. 'He'll mebbe be able to give you some advice.'

When she had finished cleaning the old tea caddy she took it to the store in Motson Street. The shop-owner turned it over in his hands, studying it closely.

The rosewood and brass shone, and now that the box had been relieved of its layers of grime even Rose's unpractised eye could appreciate the fine craftsmanship that had gone into its making.

'It's a handsome piece,' the man said. 'I'd be interested in buying it from you.'

Bella was a born haggler, and so was Leila, but Rose had never had the knack. She hated talking about money, though she realized that if she was to make anything from the load of furniture she now owned she would have to overcome her scruples and stand up for herself.

But to her astonishment Mr Grier named a sum that was a little more than she had been prepared to accept. Taken aback, she blinked at him.

'I think it's a fair price,' he said, and held the caddy out to her. 'I doubt if you'll get a better offer elsewhere. But you're welcome to try, for I can't increase it.'

'Oh no, I didn't – I mean, I'll take it!'

She walked down to the harbour, the money from her first sale safely in her pocket, unable to believe her good fortune. She had made an undoubted profit, and Mr Grier had expressed his interest in seeing the furniture once it was restored and ready to resell. Her feet skimmed along the pavement, wafting her in and out of the crowds on a cloud of excitement.

Blair Crawford had to call her name three times before she heard it. He dismounted from his chestnut horse and walked beside her, the reins looped over his arm.

'You look as though something very pleasant has happened to you.'

'It has. I've just sold a tea caddy.'

He blinked, and his jaw dropped. Then he said with amusement, 'I'm most relieved to hear that, for I'd quite decided that you must have found yourself a sweetheart. But a tea caddy's less threatening. How are you settling down in Sandyford, after South Africa?'

'Very well.'

'I wish I could say the same. My father didn't take well to my little escapade there. As a punishment, he's seen fit to anchor me down. I'm to take charge of the business at the harbour.' There was resentment in his voice, but it swiftly disappeared when he went on to a happier subject. 'He's looking forward to meeting you. So is my grandmother. I've told them all about your heroic rescue.'

'It was scarcely heroic.'

'Oh, I've turned it into a fine story that goes down very well at most dinner tables. Don't demean it for me, I beg of you.'

They had reached the end of the street leading to the harbour where Chauncy worked, and where the Crawford business was situated. 'When can we hope to see you at Crawford House?'

'Mr Crawford –'

'Blair, please. After all, I owe you my liberty, if not my very life. In South Africa –'

'We're not in South Africa now. Good afternoon, Mr Crawford.'

'Rose –' he called after her. She turned. His smile was infectious. It was difficult to dislike him, or to suppress him. 'Shall we say tomorrow afternoon at about three? I'll call for you.'

'No –' she said swiftly, imagining what her mother would make of another visit from the young laird. Then she added with resignation, 'I'll make my own way to Crawford House.'

Blair put one foot in a stirrup and vaulted lightly into the saddle, gathering up the reins. 'If you wish. Tomorrow, then,' he said, and went on his way, leaving her to wonder just what she had let herself in for.

12

'You look like a cat that stole the cream,' Bella said when Rose went back to the house. 'Where have you been?'

'Down at the harbour having another look at *Darroch's Folly*.' She judged it wise to keep quiet about the sale of the caddy.

Bella gave a derisive snort. 'I don't know which of you's the worst! One mooning over old furniture, the other mooning over a wreck that should have been sold for scrap long since!'

An elderly man was waiting by the shed door when Rose arrived on the following morning. He hurried forward to meet her, pulling his cap from his pepper-and-salt head.

'Mistress Gibb?' His voice was thin and gentle and in character with his appearance. His clothes were clean, but shabby and well darned and patched. 'Mr MacBride said that you might have work for me. My name's Rory Pollock.'

'You're the cabinet maker?'

'Yes, Mistress. At least, that was my trade before I was paid off.'

'You'd best come in and see the pieces for yourself.' She unlocked the door and opened it wide to let the daylight in.

He followed, his nose twitching at the smell of wood that had already begun to permeate the place. The nervousness fell away from him like a cloak shed from his thin shoulders.

She watched as he moved from one piece of furniture to another, his heavily veined hands touching, stroking, examining. He took his time, and Rose, fascinated by the obvious expertise in those hands, didn't hurry him.

When he had finished he turned to where she waited. 'You've got some bonny things here, Mistress – and some that's not worth working on.'

'But you think it would be worth restoring most of it, and reselling?'

He ducked his greying head in agreement, but said nothing. There was anxious eagerness in the eyes that studied her when he looked up again.

'Would you be willing to help me?'

A broad grin spread over his face. 'Aye, Mistress, I would that!'

'I can't pay you until the furniture's sold.'

'I'm willing to wait, if you can manage a few shillings now and then as we go along.'

'When can you start, Mr Pollock?'

Now that the thing was decided his narrow shoulders were straighter, his voice stronger. 'First thing in the morning, Mistress,' he said, 'and folk usually cry me Rory.'

Rose held her hand out, dropping easily into the local way of speaking. 'I'll see you tomorrow, Rory. And folk usually cry me Rose.'

A year earlier, Rose wouldn't have had the nerve to walk up to the pillared front entrance of Crawford House. But things had changed a lot in the past year. They had changed dramatically in the past few weeks.

Now, it was possible to cross the great expanse of well-raked gravel, to climb the flight of steps guarded by crouching stone lions, to ring the bell and say calmly to the maidservant who opened it, 'Mr Blair Crawford is expecting me.'

'Rose!' Blair almost nudged the girl aside as he came forward, hands outstretched. He drew her into the large carpeted and pillared entrance hall and the door closed behind her. 'You did come, after all.'

She smiled at him, hiding her nervousness well. 'Did you think I wouldn't?'

'I never know where I am with you,' he admitted, and slid her coat from her shoulders before leading her into a large comfortable room to one side of the hall. 'Father and Grandmother are in here.'

George Crawford was an older version of Blair. Hair that had been fair was now liberally sprinkled with grey, with two strikingly attractive wings of pure silver at the temples. He was tall and lean, with piercing blue eyes.

Rose's trained eye saw the tinge of blue round his lips and nostrils that spoke of heart trouble.

'Blair has told us a great deal about you, Miss Gibb. And, of course, I remember your stepfather.' He turned to the woman who sat in a high-backed, cushioned chair by the fire. 'This is Blair's grandmother.'

In her youth Catherine Lacey must have been a woman of striking appearance, rather than a beauty. In her eighties she was still eye-catching, with her snow-white hair dressed in a coronet, and vivid blue-green eyes dominating her wrinkled face. She held out a wizened hand that took Rose's fingers in a surprisingly firm grip – firmer than her son-in-law's had been.

'Sit here,' she commanded, and Rose had no option but to seat herself in a chair where the autumn sunlight, flooding in at the big bay windows, left the old lady in shadow but illuminated her own face clearly.

Tea was served, then the servants withdrew, closing the double doors noiselessly behind them, and Rose was left alone with the Crawford family.

George Crawford had little to say for himself. He danced attendance on his mother-in-law; it was said by the gossips in the town that there was altogether too strong a fondness between Catherine Lacey and her dead daughter's husband.

Watching the two of them, Rose wondered if the gossips had the right way of it. True, George Crawford catered for the old woman's every need and treated her with great deference. But now and then, when he thought he was unobserved, there was a different look in the eyes that rested on his mother-in-law. A look, Rose thought, of distaste, dislike.

South Africa and the war that still raged there was the main subject of conversation, and one that Rose could talk about with some authority. But she was aware of a clash of wills between father and son when Blair spoke longingly of returning to South Africa and his father, nostrils tightening, reminded him that his duty was towards his work at the harbour.

'For the moment,' Blair said. 'But there's something about that great country that pulls at the heartstrings. You know what I mean, don't you, Rose?'

'Yes, I do.'

'I fully intend to go back. Perhaps next summer –'

'By next summer the whole thing will no doubt be over,' his father told him coolly.

'In that case I must hope to go over sooner than that.'

'Blair, I cannot understand this preoccupation with war!'

'I'm sure Grandmother can.'

The old lady shook her head fondly at her grandson. Clearly he was a favourite of hers. 'Your father has every reason to hate the Boer War, you know that. After all, it took your poor sister's husband from her.'

'And I've no wish to lose a son as well as a son-in-law,' George Crawford said harshly, then added, 'But I'm sure that Miss Gibb is quite uninterested in our family arguments. Take your guest out on to the terrace, Blair, and show her the grounds.'

'I'll say goodbye now, Miss Gibb,' the old lady said, her voice hardening with bitter frustration as she added, 'People of my age revert to the nursery regime, you know. I must have my afternoon nap if I am to see the evening through. Come and visit me soon. We must have a proper talk together.'

'That's a sensible young woman.' Catherine Lacey watched her son and his guest stroll along the terrace. 'She'd make a good wife for Blair.'

George Crawford's face went blank with shock. 'A woman who lives in the town? A member of a family employed by the Crawfords? The idea's ridiculous! He only invited her here so that we could show our gratitude for the way she came to his assistance in South Africa. There's no question of any further friendship, let alone marriage!'

'What a snob you are, George,' his mother-in-law said, adding maliciously, 'No doubt if the girl's family had made a lot of money by hawking rags in the street you'd have welcomed her with open arms.'

His fair delicate skin crimsoned. Amused, she watched the flush deepen, then said, 'Perhaps it's time this family had some fresh blood running through its veins. Some good red blood to give added life to the blue.'

'That has already been tried, my dear Catherine.' Crawford's voice sounded strangled in his throat. 'It didn't succeed.'

It was her turn to flush – a patch of angry colour high on each cheekbone. She bit her lip, then said, 'I'll grant you that my daughter was a spineless creature. But this one – this new friend of Blair's –'

'There's to be no more of your nonsense, Catherine! No more encouraging Blair with his wild ideas about South Africa or anything else! D'you hear me?'

'There's no sense in playing the laird for my benefit, George. It doesn't impress me.'

The blue tinge round his mouth deepened. 'I'm the head of this household, and by God I'll be listened to!'

'And I,' said Catherine Lacey, 'pay the bills. Don't forget that.'

There was an angry silence. George Crawford, Laird of Sandyford and the man the townsfolk looked up to, struggled hard to control his temper, to slow down the ominous racing of his heart.

'Poor George.' Mrs Lacey's voice was gently mocking now. 'It really hurts you to know that pedigrees no longer pay, doesn't it? That a good business brain counts more than noble blood.'

Swallowing an angry answer he walked to the fireplace, where he was out of her line of vision. His fist convulsively clenched, his teeth bit into his lower lip.

Denied the quarrel that she sought, suddenly tired of the conversation, the old woman said pettishly, 'Ring for the servant. I want to go to my room.'

Silently, George Crawford did as he was told. As he reached for the bell-pull by the fireplace, his eyes were icy with frustrated hate.

'Grandmother likes you. I'm glad,' said Blair as he and Rose walked to the end of the terrace, where a flight of stone steps led down to spacious lawns and gravel paths.

'Why?'

'Because I want you to come back to Crawford House. I want that very much.' Blair's voice, and his eyes, were intent. 'And you will, if Grandmother approves of you.'

'And if I choose to come back.'

He laughed. 'I hope that you will.'

They stopped at the top of the steps and leaned on the stone balustrade. The lawn was edged on all sides with deep flowerbeds massed with yellow and white and pink and scarlet and orange roses.

Beyond the carefully planned tumble of colour Rose could see a shrubbery, and then the tops of trees planted further down the hill.

Over the trees, vibrantly colourful in their autumn colours, the Firth of Clyde sparkled like a young bride on her wedding morning, bordered on the far side by thick blue-grey crayon strokes roughly shading in the Isle of Bute.

A paddle-steamer churned its way busily into sight. It was one of the larger vessels that sailed down the river, trading from the Broomielaw in the heart of Glasgow. Even from a distance Rose could see that its decks were packed with passengers making the most of one of the final trips 'doon the watter' before winter closed in and the steamers were almost all put into dock to be cleaned and repainted for the following year.

Only the larger boats linking the mainland to the islands kept going during the winter months.

The steamer crossed their line of vision and disappeared behind the green and gold top of a great oak. Rose watched it go, then turned and looked at the big grey-stone house behind. Its windows, like the waters of the firth, reflected the sunlight and threw it back, glittering, into her eyes.

'What a beautiful house.'

'It does well enough,' Blair agreed with the air of one who takes good fortune for granted. His own eyes were aware of nothing but Rose herself.

Rory Pollock was waiting outside the shed the next morning, with a tattered and torn bag clutched in one hand.

As soon as Rose unlocked the door he selected a table, cleared it, and unpacked his bag, laying the contents out carefully.

'I'll use this as a work bench for the time being. It's of no value anyway,' he said briskly, arranging a complex assortment of saws, wedges, chisels and files and other items that she didn't recognize at all. Then he stood back and surveyed the jumble of furniture that had once been old Mr Kenway's home.

'I'll probably start on that old clock first.' He indicated a solid wooden piece that had lost about a quarter of its polished surface. 'If that's all right with you, Mistress.'

'You do whatever you think best.'

'But mind you, the very first thing to do,' said Rory thoughtfully, 'is to sort out the rubbish and sell it off.'

As far as furniture was concerned Rory Pollock was an expert as well as a hard worker. Within a few hours of his arrival that morning Rose knew that he was going to be a godsend.

By the end of his first week he had begun to work magic among the sorry bits and pieces from Mr Kenway's flat. Some of the furniture was put aside to be worked on. Other items were scathingly tossed aside, dismissed as being not worth the bother.

Nothing was wasted. Summoned by Rory, people began to find their way to the harbour; people from the poorer part of the town, eager to buy whatever Rose had to offer, happy to accept the items Rory had rejected.

She disliked taking money from them, but when she suggested that they should be allowed to take the unwanted items for nothing the old man looked at her with horror.

'Lassie, what are you saying? Every penny helps.'

'But most of these folk find it hard enough to buy food. It's wrong to take the few pence they can offer.'

Rory shook his head sadly. 'D'you know nothing about business, Mistress – or about folk? These people aren't looking for charity. They want to pay their own way, even if it's only a few pence.'

'I only thought that –'

'They'd not thank you for giving them the bits and pieces for nothing. Let them have their pride, will you? And remember that every penny piece you take in helps to pay for the work needed on the rest of the stuff,' he added sternly.

For most of the time Rose was his willing assistant, cleaning and polishing to his direction, watching with horror as he ruthlessly tore pieces apart, then with amazement as he put them together again and restored them to their original beauty. Under his tuition she learned a little more about her new career every day.

But she had to put her foot down when he came to her with the shabby little footstool, which looked even shabbier now that he had ripped the faded tapestry from it.

'This has belonged to some fine lady in its time,' he said. 'It's been used in her coach. It's a bonny piece of work, and someone would pay well to have it in their drawing room. But we need to have a new covering made for it.'

'I'm no use with a needle, Rory.' She wondered briefly if Leila would be willing to help, then dismissed the thought. Leila was too grand to work for anyone now, especially her sister.

'I know a lassie who's the finest wee needlewoman you'd ever hope to meet. She could do it for us.'

'I'm finding it hard enough to pay my own keep at home and give you something to be going on with. I'll not have the money to pay anyone else until this furniture's sold. And if it isn't, I don't know what I'll do.'

'She'd not look for much.'

'Rory, I can't afford to give her anything!'

'You could sell something to keep us going.'

'What did you have in mind?'

He disappeared into a corner and came back with a fluted glass vase, which he pushed into her hands.

'Not a chip on it – it's my guess it might fetch a few shillings. You could take it home with you and give it a good washing first.'

'It's ugly!' Rose turned the dirty green glass object over in her hands.

'Sometimes the uglier a thing is the more money folk'll spend on it,' Rory persisted, shuffling his feet hopefully.

'Oh well – ask the woman to let me see some of her

work tomorrow,' she said with resignation, and he gave her his rare, unexpectedly broad grin.

'If you've nothing to do in the meantime you could polish the frame of the wee stool for me,' he said, and trotted over to where his glue-pot was being maintained at the right temperature on top of an old cast-iron stove he had found on a rubbish tip.

He kept it going with an endless supply of wood that had been ejected from *Darroch's Folly*, moored a matter of ten yards away.

Rose stepped outside to study the vase in daylight. It looked no better than it had done inside the shed.

The tide was in, and *Darroch's Folly* rode high, her deck flush with the harbour wall and the arch of her paddle-box rising above Rose's head when she strolled over to take a closer look. Her funnel and decks had been scraped and scrubbed in readiness for revarnishing and repainting.

Magnus MacBride had a crew of men working on the boat now, men who, like Rory, were too old to be employable, or too unskilled to be wanted by the town's industries.

MacBride appeared on deck, backing up the companionway, dragging a great tangle of rope and wood after him. He hefted it over the narrow gangplank and on to the harbour and dusted his hands together as he came over to where Rose stood.

'That,' he said, nodding at the vase, 'is hideous.'

'Rory thinks it might earn enough to pay for some tapestry.'

He scrubbed a hand over his face, leaving a grimy stain in its wake. A shaft of sunlight teased gold lights from the thick tangle of hair about his strong face.

'If Rory says so then it probably will. I'm not happy about the engines. I think I'll have to rip them out and install new ones.'

'Can you afford to do that?'

'I've got no choice. I'm going up to Glasgow next week to see if I can't get something arranged. The next stage,' he added thoughtfully, 'is to get her out of the water entirely so that I can have a look at her keel and deal with the engines.'

'The steamer owners all take up the dry docks at this time of year. The Crawfords own the only empty dock in the town.'

'I know. And that might be a bit of a problem.' He rubbed his chin. 'But no doubt I'll overcome it.'

The evening whistle blew further along the quay, where the Crawford ships were based. Rose spun round, her eyes searching guiltily for the town hall clock, just visible over the roofs of the houses overlooking the river.

'Is it that time already? I said I'd be home in time to help Mam to make the supper. Leila and Daniel are going to eat with us. You'd best come with me right now,' she added pointedly, 'for you'll have to get yourself presentable before we sit down at the table.'

'I've work to do here. I'll get something to eat later, when I come in.'

He turned back towards *Darroch's Folly*, then swung round again and said, 'Chauncy tells me that you and Daniel Currie used to walk out together. I suppose you know that he's still in love with you?'

She felt her face flame with shock and embarrassment. 'Don't be daft! Daniel was never in love with me.'

'He is. You'd be well advised to keep away from him,' Magnus MacBride said. 'Your sister's not one to take kindly to losing her man. Anyway, you deserve better than him.'

Then he stepped across the gangplank, leaving Rose, open-mouthed, staring after him.

13

Thanks to Magnus's parting shot, she could scarcely look at Daniel as they sat opposite each other during tea. As always he was quiet, leaving the floor to Leila, who chattered away like a contented parakeet.

She was putting on weight, but she looked well. It struck Rose that the more Leila bloomed, the more tense Daniel looked.

Remembering her sister's comment that the coming baby had put a stop to the need for distasteful wifely duties, Rose came to the conclusion that Leila blossomed because she was free to enjoy matrimony without its physical implications, while poor Daniel was almost being blighted by neglect.

For some reason, she thought of the nursery rhyme about Jack Sprat, who would eat no fat, and his wife, who would eat no lean. Her lips twitched, and she had to bend her head over her plate to hide a sudden attack of inner laughter.

In the morning she sold the ugly, but spotlessly clean, glass vase for a handsome profit, bought the exquisite piece of embroidery Rory brought to the yard, and ordered more tapestry to cover the seats of four upright chairs in the shed.

Agnes Anderson, the doctor who had attended old Mr Kenway in his last moments, called at the shed a few days later, accepted a seat on a newly refurbished chair that Rory hurriedly produced for her, and offered Rose a nursing post.

'I can't pay you as much as you'd get in the hospital – I live hand to mouth myself,' she said in her deep, slightly hoarse voice. 'But I'll give you what I can. I need someone to work among the families in the poorer part of the town and help me in my surgery.'

Her eyebrows rose when Rose refused. 'I understood from your mother that you were in need of employment.'

Inwardly dratting Mam for her interference, Rose said levelly, 'She was wrong. I've no wish to go back to nursing at the moment.'

Doctor Anderson looked at the shabby table Rose was polishing, at the glue-pot sitting in an old basin on top of the stove, and said dryly, 'A trained nurse – and you'd as soon do this?'

Rose pushed a strand of hair back from her eyes and returned the older woman's gaze. 'I've not made up my mind what I want to do yet. This is as good as anything for the moment.'

The doctor stood up and Rose was surprised to see how small the woman really was. Agnes Anderson had a way of appearing to be larger than life. 'When you do make up your mind let me know. My offer remains open.'

Watching her walk away Rose nibbled at her lower lip. As the doctor had said, she was a trained nurse, and she should be using her training. But she knew deep within herself that she wasn't ready to go back to nursing.

Perhaps she never would go back to it. Perhaps she would leave Sandyford and seek her future elsewhere.

But not yet. She had a pile of furniture to renovate and sell first – and she wanted, very much, to see *Darroch's Folly* take to the water again. Besides, she owed Magnus MacBride money.

She would stay in Sandyford for a little while longer.

To Rose's astonishment and Bella's fury the restored furniture made a handsome profit.

'That's mine by rights,' her mother said flatly when Rose told her how much Mr Grier had offered.

'Yours?'

'It was my furniture you sold.'

'No it wasn't, Mam, it was mine. I gave you a fair price for it, and I paid to have it done over and made good again.'

'A fair price, is it?' Bella screeched. 'You've got the impudence to stand there and tell me that you gave me a fair price – and you making all that extra money out of it?'

'I paid you more than you would have got from Hannie Simpson. You were happy enough to take the money at the time, so that's an end of it!'

Chauncy waited, saucer-eyed and silent, for the world to end. He looked stunned when Bella turned and flounced out of the kitchen, muttering darkly to herself about snakes in the grass and greedy daughters.

Magnus MacBride, who had also been a witness to the scene, eyed Rose reprovingly when she later handed over the money she owed him.

'You should never tell anyone how much you make. That's the most important rule of business.'

'I'm not in business.'

'Oh, but you are, Rose Gibb,' he said. 'You are.'

When she gave Rory his money he pushed it into his pocket without counting it.

'I trust you, Mistress. Well –' He turned to stand by her side, and together they surveyed the empty shed, stripped of every last piece of furniture.

For a moment they gazed in silence, then Rory said slowly, thoughtfully, 'They tell me there's an old woman died in Kennart Street, and her son and his wife just want her household stuff off their hands for a few pound. If we got there before Hannie Simpson –'

*

The shed wasn't large enough to hold the new lot of furniture and allow room for working as well. In any case, as Rory pointed out, winter was almost upon them, and the furniture needed to be in a warmer, more secure place if it was to remain undamaged.

Rose searched in vain for a warehouse that she could rent cheaply.

'There's sure to be one down by the harbour,' Magnus suggested when she had scoured every possible place she could think of, and been unsuccessful.

'Everything down there belongs to the Crawfords. I don't want to go asking them for favours.'

His tawny eyes surveyed her. 'You're not asking for favours. You're prepared to pay rent, are you not? And from what I hear young Crawford would be more than willing to lend a sympathetic ear.'

She felt colour rising into her cheeks. 'What do you mean by that?' she demanded dangerously, but MacBride refused to be drawn.

'Ask your brother if there's a place for rent,' he suggested.

When he was approached Chauncy said at once that there was an empty warehouse available on the harbour, near the Crawford office.

'I know for a fact that it'll stay empty for the next six months at least. Bring old Rory to the harbour tomorrow morning. There'd be no harm in having a look at it.'

The warehouse was solid, roomy and watertight. It even had a small office at the entrance.

Rory almost skipped about the place with delight. 'It's just what we need, Mistress. We'd be snug and warm in here – I could put up a proper workbench right there, beneath the skylight.'

'But it'll cost far too much to rent!'

'It'd do no harm to ask young Mr Crawford what he wants for it,' Chauncy said.

'No harm at all,' Rory coaxed, and Rose found herself out-voted.

She dressed carefully for her business meeting with the young laird, choosing her best blue coat with the deep lapels, and sleeves that were tight-fitting below the elbow, and full above it.

The lapels and cuffs were outlined in red braid, and on her upswept hair she perched a neat little black hat decorated with a single full red silk rose and black plumes.

Chauncy winked his approval when she stepped into the wooden building that housed the offices on the harbour.

'He was right pleased to hear that you wanted to see him,' he whispered before ushering her in.

'Rose! I was beginning to think that you'd decided to shun me.' Blair Crawford came to greet her, and lead her to a chair. Then he perched on the edge of the desk, so close that she could have reached out and touched him.

Dark business clothes and a high white collar gave him an air of maturity and dignity. 'What can I do for you?'

'Well – I seem to have fallen into the furniture business –'

He grinned down at her. 'So I heard.'

'– and I'm in need of larger and more sound premises for my new delivery of goods.' She thought, as she spoke, that the words sounded impossibly pompous and over-elaborate. But she soldiered on. 'I need a warehouse, and you have just such a warehouse lying empty.'

'And you want me to give it to you. Of course I do – gladly,' he said promptly.

'Indeed I do not want you to give it to me! I want you to rent it to me, on a six-month lease with an option to renew.'

'Ah. And how much d'you expect to pay for it?'

She bit her lip, then said patiently, 'Mr Crawford, I'm

not a child to be amused and played with. I'm making you a business offer.'

He got up, went round to the other side of the desk, and sat down in his high-backed chair.

'Forgive me, Rose – I'm not used to doing business with ladies. Let me see, now –'

He drew a sheet of paper towards him and scowled over it, pencilling and re-pencilling figures. 'What about six pounds?'

She looked back at him, shocked. 'It's not enough for a big warehouse like that!'

'It's lying empty and I'm making nothing from it. If you use it, it will earn its keep.'

'Should you not consult with your father before making such an offer?'

His handsome face darkened. 'As I've been told time and time again, I'm in charge of the harbour. I've no doubt that he'll be pleased to hear that I've managed to make use of the empty warehouse. Well, what do you think? Or do you want time to consider it?'

'No need for that. When can I move in?'

'Whenever you wish. Chauncy will give you the keys. And now,' he added hastily as she began to rise, 'I have a favour to beg of you.'

'Indeed?'

'My sister Lilias is coming home in a few days' time. My father's decided to hold a small dinner party in her honour next Friday, and we both hope that you'll attend.'

She had begun to shake her head before he finished speaking. 'Oh – I don't think that –'

Blair put a hand on her arm. 'Please, Rose. I'm sure Lilias would appreciate your company as much as I will. Bring a companion, if you wish,' he added as he saw the indecision in her face. 'Ask your brother to act as your escort.'

She could think of nothing Chauncy would hate more. 'Thank you for thinking of me –'

‘That,’ said Blair Crawford, ‘is a pleasure I indulge in quite often.’

‘– but I doubt if I’ll be free to attend the dinner party,’ Rose finished firmly.

The whole thing was quite ridiculous! She found Blair attractive – disturbingly attractive, she thought as he passed close on his way to open the door for her – but any romantic thoughts he might be harbouring towards her must be nipped in the bud at once.

‘I’m sorry to hear that,’ he said formally.

She hesitated at the door. ‘Should we not sign papers to make the warehouse business binding on both sides?’

‘Ah yes, of course.’

‘Perhaps you could draw them up?’

‘With pleasure.’ Blair opened the door, then said as she was going through it, ‘I’ll have them ready to sign at the dinner party next Friday.’

‘Blair –’

‘And I’ll send the carriage to collect you and your brother at eight o’clock.’

Chauncy had stepped out of the office and was conferring with Magnus MacBride by the hulk of the old paddle-steamer.

He refused point blank to accompany her to the dinner party.

‘Oh please, Chauncy!’

‘But I work for the Crawfords – how can I socialize with them as well?’

‘It’s no easier for me than it is for you, and I’m going.’

‘Rose, you’ve got more knowledge than I have of the ways of the gentry,’ Chauncy said wretchedly. ‘I wouldn’t know what to do. I’d make a fool of myself and let you down.’

‘You wouldn’t! Chauncy, I can’t go on my own – not to a dinner party.’

‘I’m sorry, Rose, but I’ll just not do it, even for you.’

She looked up at him in dismay. 'But Blair Crawford more or less said that there'll be no contract for the warehouse if I refuse to attend!'

'The solution's quite simple,' Magnus cut in. 'I'll escort you.'

'You?' She looked with horror at his grease-smeared hands, his dirty face, his tousled hair and his faded, patched overalls.

'Me,' he said blandly. 'Don't fret yourself – I've got some decent clothes, and I know how to behave in company. I'll not let you down.'

'I don't think that would be –' she faltered, but he waved the protest aside.

'Nonsense. Consider it arranged.' As she walked back to the shed to tell Rory that she had gained the warehouse, Rose wished that she had taken the post Agnes Anderson had offered, or even returned to the infirmary to eat humble pie and let the matron and the other nurses lord it over her.

Anything would be better than the predicament she now found herself in.

14

Bella was almost beside herself with pride when she heard of the invitation to Crawford House.

Miss McKinnon, the elderly lady who had moved into the next-door flat, and had immediately become Bella's new crony, clucked and exclaimed when she heard the news. Throughout that week, if Miss McKinnon was in the house when Rose came in, the woman would blush and bridle and positively curtsey before her.

Leila was consumed with envy; even so, she graciously offered to come to the house on Friday evening to make sure that her sister was properly groomed for the dinner party.

'I can manage quite well on my own,' Rose said irritably. She was beset by nerves, and dreading the evening ahead. If it hadn't been for Blair's veiled hint that a refusal might cost her the warehouse she would have found some excuse to stay away.

'Nonsense,' Bella insisted. 'I've already told Leila to come along in good time. She's looking forward to it.'

Rose's nervousness was due as much to Magnus as to herself. Try as she might, she couldn't picture him as a suitable escort for a dinner party. The more she worried, the less perturbed he seemed to be about the engagement.

'You should be at home, with Daniel,' Rose told her sister when Leila arrived early on Friday evening.

'He's invited some choir members in for a rehearsal round the piano. He won't even know I'm gone.' Leila tossed her head and pouted. 'That dratted singing's taking up more and more of his time. Sometimes I almost wish we hadn't bought the piano.'

Then she added moodily, 'I've brought my white feather fan and pearl earrings and necklace – the Lord only knows when I'll have occasion to use them again, and at least I'll be able to say that they spent an evening in Crawford House. And they'll do very nicely with your blue gown.'

Rose had decided, against her mother's advice, that her best dress would have to do for the occasion. It was a blue silk gown with a half-train and a fine ivory lace bodice.

Bands of blue silk ran from shoulder to waist on the bodice, and the velvet hem was weighted to hold the line of the skirt when she moved. The neckline was plain, and the full lace sleeves ended just below the elbow. Leila nodded approvingly when she saw it.

'Since you'll not be able to outshine any of the ladies there,' she said with supreme disregard for her sister's self-esteem, 'it's best to be neat and unassuming.'

White gloves and Leila's pearls and white feathered fan completed the picture perfectly. Skilfully she brushed out Rose's hair and piled it on top of her head in a soft, shining dark mass, caught at the back with a small blue silk bow.

'You know, Rose, your hair's better than I thought. And your skin's not bad at all,' she said as she worked busily.

When she finally stood back and eyed Rose her gaze sharpened with envy when it reached the slender waist.

'You'll do.'

'Do? She'll make those fine ladies at Crawford House tonight look like crows sitting on a fence,' Bella said with unusual warmth. Then her eyes slid past Rose and her jaw dropped.

Rose turned, and felt her own eyes widen as she saw Magnus MacBride standing in the open doorway, with not a trace of engine oil or grime about him. He wore a black evening suit, the trousers impeccable, the cut of the satin-lapelled jacket moulding his square shoulders and lithe waist.

A snowy white stiff-collared shirt, neatly tied white bow tie, white gloves and polished black shoes completed the outfit. His hair was well brushed, and his tanned face astonishingly handsome when seen against its new setting.

'Are you ready?' His gold-flecked eyes swept over her, not missing a thing in that one brief glance. One brow rose slightly and his lips twisted in a faint smile.

The door-knocker rattled, heralding the arrival of the Crawford carriage. Leila wrenched her gaze from Magnus, shut her mouth with an audible clicking of teeth and looked around for Rose's cloak.

She was forestalled when he picked it up and put it about Rose's shoulders with practised ease.

Bella had planned to escort them down to the close-mouth and wave them away, a prospect that had been worrying Rose for days. But somehow, without any of them realizing how he did it, Magnus managed to forestall her.

As the house door closed behind them, leaving Bella and Leila inside, he took Rose's hand and threaded it through the crook of his elbow. She just had time to see that the other two doors were slightly open, with a pair of inquisitive eyes twinkling in the gloom behind each, before she and Magnus were on their way down to the carriage.

As they rattled off through the streets he leaned back comfortably in his seat and took time to study Rose again, slowly, from head to toe.

'You look quite perfect,' he said with satisfaction rather than admiration. 'Blair Crawford will be able to refuse you nothing tonight.'

She sat bolt upright, suddenly realizing what was behind the remark. 'The dry dock! That's why you insisted on accompanying me – you want me to persuade the Crawfords to let you have their dry dock for *Daroch's Folly*!'

'I hope to do the persuading myself. But if you're willing to add your voice to mine –'

'You're just making use of me!'

'You made use of me to buy your first lot of furniture.'

'You offered the money – and I've repaid every penny of it!'

'And I didn't press you for interest on the loan. You could say that I'm calling in the interest now.'

'I refuse to beg favours on your behalf!'

His eyes widened in innocent surprise. 'I'm not asking you to beg favours on my behalf.' Then he leaned forward and said, 'You're looking particularly beautiful tonight, Rose. I'm certain that Blair's going to find you as enchanting as I do.'

Rose would have ordered the coachman to turn the horses at once and take her back home if it wasn't for the fact that she needed Blair's signature on the warehouse lease.

She would have had Magnus thrown out into the gutter, but she doubted if the elderly driver was a match for the younger, stronger man.

There was little she could do but clench her hands on her fan in impotent fury and ignore him for the rest of the short journey. Never, never would she seek for, or accept, help from this man again. She had been a fool!

When the carriage stopped before the great doorway of Crawford House Magnus was first out, turning as soon as his feet touched the gravelled driveway, forestalling the coachman and reaching up to help Rose to alight.

Then he drew her hand into the bend of his elbow once again and they walked together up the flight of stone steps.

'You dare to embarrass me tonight –!' she whispered

as the big front door opened and a butler stood waiting to receive them.

'Would I do such a thing?' Magnus murmured, then they were inside and it was too late to say anything more.

The manservant took their outer wraps, opened the double doors to the left of the hall and bowed them into the large, high-ceilinged room.

There were several people already gathered in the room, which was brilliant with the light from a series of chandeliers. Rose hesitated, and felt Magnus's fingers encircle her right arm and tighten swiftly, briefly, in a reassuring squeeze. In that moment she was suddenly glad that he was there.

Four figures separated themselves from the general group and came towards them. One was Blair, another was George Crawford. The third was Catherine Lacey, tiny but erect, her claw-like hand on her son-in-law's arm.

The fourth figure was unmistakably Blair's sister Lilias, tall and very fair, immaculately gowned in gold and white, carrying herself with confident grace.

They had come only halfway across the expanse of carpeted floor when the four of them faltered then stopped.

Blair looked puzzled, while his father's face went bone white, every vestige of colour fading from beneath the skin. Catherine's remarkable eyes narrowed, then blazed at a point just behind and above Rose's right shoulder.

Lilias was the first to move, almost running across the floor, her hands outstretched, her face illuminated with naked joy.

'Magnus –' she said, by-passing Rose without a glance. 'Oh, Magnus – you've come back to us!'

The fingers that had been warm against Rose's arm fell away as Magnus MacBride said, 'Hello, Lilias' – and moved forward to take the girl's hands in his.

Standing alone, Rose felt her heart sinking as she saw the shock and anger in George Crawford's face.

15

Moonlight traced a path across the smooth waters of the Clyde, far below the terracing where Rose stood alone. Behind her Crawford House, brilliantly lit, stood out against the sky like a great liner. But she was too miserable to look up and appreciate its beauty.

Dinner had been a nightmare. The food looked delicious, but as far as she was concerned it might as well have been made from sawdust and glue. Nevertheless she had eaten it methodically, willing every second and every minute to pass by so that she could get out of the house.

Magnus, the sole cause of her rage and misery, had been seated diagonally opposite her. Most of the other guests were people who had made their wealth in the industrial shipyards and factories, and the talk, in general, was of business. George Crawford ate little and said little, but Magnus fitted into the gathering perfectly, speaking frequently and with authority.

He seemed to be quite at home in that vast, wealthy house. And so he should be, Rose thought bitterly. Hadn't he been almost one of the Crawford family as a child?

Her cloak, warm and soft, fell about her shoulders. The hands that had put it there lingered, the palms shaping themselves closely to the rounded curves of her upper arms.

'You'll take a chill if you're not careful.'

She turned, breaking free of his clasp as she did so. 'Blair –'

His face was only dimly seen in the darkness behind him. 'I know. You didn't realize that Magnus MacBride was an old acquaintance of ours.'

'I had no idea that he'd ever been in Sandyford before.'

As he moved to lean on the stone balustrade beside her, his back towards the lighted windows, his face and body became a solid, featureless outline. 'We were great friends, Magnus and Lilias and myself. She adored him.'

She still does, Rose thought, but didn't say it.

'His father and ours were partners in the mine at one time. Father had the property, Patrick MacBride had the money and the mining knowledge. But they quarrelled, and the MacBrides moved away.'

'Is that all?'

'Should there be more?'

She thought of George Crawford's face in that first moment of sighting Magnus. The skin had seemed to shrink in against the skull. The man had looked positively ill.

'The look on your father's face when he first saw Magnus led me to think that there must be.'

'You've surely realized by now that my father,' said Blair with a sudden bite to his voice, 'hates to be crossed. He dislikes people who disagree with him. He never forgives them.'

The venom in his voice disturbed her. Something in her face, which was lit by the house, must have indicated her reaction, because he added with an attempt at light amusement, 'Except, of course, my grandmother, who's a law unto herself.'

'After bringing Magnus into his house I doubt if I'll get that warehouse now.'

'Nonsense, I've already promised it to you. The harbour's not his concern,' said Blair levelly. Then as a sudden shiver rippled through her body he added, 'Come inside, it's too cold out here.'

Mrs Lacey had excused herself immediately after dinner and had gone to her room. In the drawing room Magnus MacBride, relaxed and seemingly oblivious of the effect his appearance had had on his host, was in the midst of an interested group, airing his plans for the old paddle-steamer.

Lilias, by his side, drank in every word. Her beautiful eyes, very like her grandmother's, but with more blue in them so that they were violet rather than turquoise, were fixed on his face. She and Magnus MacBride made a handsome couple. George Crawford hovered on the outskirts of the gathering, a brandy glass in his hand.

'You're talking nonsense, man. Daydreams that'll never come true.' A florid, prosperous-looking elderly man interrupted Magnus brusquely as Blair and Rose came within earshot.

'You think so, Mr Finlay?'

'You know who I am?'

'Everyone on the Clyde coast knows who you are, Sir,' said Magnus. 'You own a bonny fleet of steamers, and Captain Donlevy here' – he nodded to another member of the group – 'is captain of your flagship.'

Mr Finlay preened himself slightly, but his voice was still harsh when he said, 'Since you're so well informed, young man, you surely know enough to realize that there's no place for another owner on the Firth.'

'Competition's a fine thing. This country of ours has been built upon it.'

There was a general murmur of approval, and Robert Thomson, a man in his early middle years who had made his money in the drapery business and now owned a string of well-known shops throughout Scotland, a yacht, and a handsome mansion some four miles from Crawford House, said heartily, 'I quite agree, sir. You've got the right way of it.'

'Competition,' grated Mr Finlay, 'only works in the hands of those who understand how to use it. I'm telling you that there's no place here for you or your boat.'

'You'd need an entire fleet to compete on the Clyde now,' his captain broke in. 'Or a powerful amount of money behind you. Am I right in thinking, Mr MacBride, that you've got neither?'

'As to that, my business affairs are my own.'

'And there's your answer, Donlevy,' Mr Finlay sneered.

'Not all of it. I intend to raise the money by setting up a limited company. And I mean to challenge yourself and the other steamer barons next summer.'

'A race?' Thomson asked with keen interest, and there was a general stirring among the company. It wasn't unknown for steamer owners and captains to pit their vessels against each other, and wagering on the outcome of such races was usually heavy.

Magnus lifted one shoulder in a faint shrug. 'Why not? My flagship against yours, once I get her back into the water.'

'Flagship!' Mr Finlay's anger melted away. He permitted himself a broad grin, looking round the group, inviting them to join him in his derision. Someone dutifully sniggered. 'You'd be better putting your hopes into a toy yacht!'

'It'd sink less readily,' added the captain, and this time more than one person laughed.

Rose saw a faint flush of angry colour staining Magnus's cheekbones beneath his tan, but his voice was cool and unruffled as he said, 'I think not. She's a sturdy vessel; once I get her properly overhauled –'

'She was mebbe good enough years back, but not now. And how d'you plan to overhaul her while she's in the water, tell me that?'

'I'll be putting her into dry dock, of course.'

'There's none to be had,' Captain Donlevy said swiftly.

'You're right,' Magnus agreed, 'other than on the Crawford harbour.'

'You'll not use my property!' George Crawford pushed through his guests to confront Magnus.

'I'm willing to pay the full rate, Sir.'

'No!' Crawford spat the word into the younger man's face and turned away. Magnus, defeated but unbowed, raised an eyebrow at Finlay.

'Then it seems, sir, that our wager is null and void.'

'Tchah! You'd not have won anyway.'

'We'll never know that now,' Magnus said silkily. 'For myself, I'm convinced that I'd have done it.'

'Never.'

'You're wrong, Sir.'

The two men faced each other; Finlay's face was purpling, his big hands half curled into fists, while the faint smile still hung around MacBride's lips.

The shipping baron was the first to look away. His eyes sought and found George Crawford.

'Crawford, give him the damned dry dock, and let him prove his words!'

'I'll do nothing of the sort,' his host said abruptly.

'I think he should have his chance,' Robert Thomson chimed in. 'It's only sporting to let him have the use of the dock, Crawford.'

'I'm not in business, Sir, for sport!' George Crawford's voice was harsh.

Blair spoke for the first time. 'You're certain that you could do it, Magnus?'

'I am.'

'In that case,' said Blair, 'I'll put fifty pounds on Magnus's steamboat, Mr Finlay.'

The man, about to turn away, spun round, his jaw dropping with astonishment. Lilias gasped audibly. Her father, chewing the words savagely in his teeth, said, 'Don't be a fool! That wreck'll never see service again!'

'It might. I'm willing to put my money on Magnus.' Blair's eyes raked the group. 'Anyone prepared to take me on?'

'I'll join you!' Thomson said promptly, his eyes alight with the thought of a wager. 'I think MacBride's got a chance. Now, gentlemen – who dares to disagree with us?'

There was an instant buzz among the men. First one and then another joined the wager, most of them on Finlay's side, but a few adventurous souls putting their money on Magnus.

He nodded to his champions. 'Good of you, gentlemen – but I'm still in sore need of a dry dock.'

'You can have the use of ours,' said Blair.

George Crawford's face was suffused with instant anger. 'He'll have nothing of the sort!'

There was another buzz, this time one of protest and disappointment from those who had wagered money. Magnus glanced around their faces with detached interest. Rose, catching that glance, seeing the gleam deep in his tawny eyes, realized that he had manipulated the situation neatly.

'I'm in charge of the harbour now, Father.'

'I forbid it!'

Father and son faced each other, oblivious for the moment to their staring guests. Looking at the set of Blair's lips, Rose knew that he cared nothing for *Darroch's Folly*. In helping Magnus he had found a way to make his father pay for confining him in the dockyard office when he wanted to be off again to South Africa.

'You can't forbid it, Father,' he said now, with slow, deliberate relish. 'You told me that the harbour's my responsibility. Surely I must do all I can to make the dry dock earn its keep?'

'Blair –'

'Is anybody else using it at the moment?' Robert Thomson wanted to know.

'Nobody.'

'Well then, since it's lying idle, I can't see why you're so set against seeing it used, Crawford.'

'I decide who uses my property, sir, not a –' George Crawford, about to say '– a mere draper!' stopped, swallowing down the insult he had almost delivered to a guest, then said, '– not anybody else.'

'In that case, mebbe you'd prefer to take over the harbour affairs yourself, Father, and relieve me of my duties? If not – if you insist on my staying in Sandyford and taking charge of the harbour, then I say that Magnus has the use of the dry dock.'

For a moment it seemed that George Crawford might choke. Lilias went over to him and put a restraining hand on his arm.

'Father –'

He drew in a long shuddering breath, shook free of her as he turned from his son, and stumped from the room, slamming the door behind him.

There was a moment's silence, then someone began to talk quickly and nervously about the weather, and one by one the others joined in.

Magnus held out his hand; Blair shook it.

'We'll draw up the papers tomorrow,' he said, then turned to Rose, his face still pale with the effort of defying his father, but his eyes bright with triumph. 'Your contract's ready to be signed now.'

'It was wrong of you to defy your father like that, in front of everybody,' Rose said when the door of the small study closed behind them, shutting out the buzz of the dinner party.

'Nonsense, the old man's been inviting it ever since he ordered me to stay here and take over the harbour. I thought you'd be pleased to know that MacBride had the use of the dry dock. You're by way of being friends, aren't you?' Blair asked, eyeing her closely.

'Not particularly.'

'You brought him here as your escort.'

'That,' she said coolly, 'was at his suggestion. If I'd known that he'd been here before, and often, I wouldn't have agreed. Did you have to defeat your father in such a public fashion?'

'It was the only way. In private, he'd have had the better of me.'

'Blair, has he been suffering from bad health lately?'

'His heart, you mean? He's been told to take things more quietly – that's his excuse for making me stay here and take over part of the business. But he's well enough.' He took a document from a drawer, and dipped a pen into an inkwell. 'Don't try to make me feel guilty, Rose – it's my opinion that he'll outlive all of us.'

He signed his name with an accomplished flourish, then stepped back to allow her to sit at the desk.

'You sign there.'

She dipped the pen into the elaborate silver inkwell, then bent over the paper.

'Besides,' Blair said from above her head, 'in giving MacBride what he wants, I'll have made Lilias happy. And at the moment, Lilias's happiness is all that the old man cares about.'

'Why didn't you tell me that you already knew the Crawfords?' Rose demanded when she and Magnus were returning home in the Crawford carriage.

His eyes glinted gold lights at her in the dimness of the carriage. 'I didn't think it was important.'

'I don't care to be caught up in an old squabble that doesn't concern me.'

'An old squabble? Is that what Blair told you?'

'He told me that your father and Mr Crawford were partners in the mine, and they quarrelled.'

'Ah,' he said softly, thoughtfully, then: 'So he didn't mention the part his mother played in the business?'

'What?' The carriage juddered over a pothole in the road, and she only just managed to avoid being bounced into his arms as he sat opposite. 'What?' she repeated, recovering her balance and wedging herself into her corner.

'There was no business row. That was a tale George Crawford put out to save his own face. The mines were doing well enough – mainly thanks to the money my father had put into them, and his ability as a mining engineer. He was even planning to build a fine house up on the hill and settle in Sandyford for good. Then he and Blair's mother fell in love. That's what broke up the partnership.'

She gazed at him, astounded. They were passing a gas lamp; its yellow glow lit up one side of Magnus's face, leaving the other side in deep darkness. In that instant, with the planes and angles outlined in light and shadow, one eye glittering, he looked invincible. More than that – he looked ruthless, she realized with a quick shiver of fear.

'No wonder George Crawford hates you!'

They passed the lamp, and Magnus's voice was now disembodied, calm. 'The sins of the father are being visited upon the son. The old man's never forgiven my father – and I've no doubt that he made the rest of his wife's life a misery.'

'They didn't run away together?' Despite herself, she was intrigued.

'Oh no. There was my mother to consider, for one thing. She kept indifferent health, and as far as I know she never learned the truth. And then there was the question of the Lacey money. George Crawford married purely for that money. The Crawfords had overspent themselves, you see. George's father looked around for an heiress to keep the family solvent. As soon as he found one he made her his daughter-in-law. The Laceys – like my own father – had made their money in trade. They wanted their daughter to marry into a pedigreed and well-respected family. It was a marriage made for mutual convenience.'

The carriage jolted again, but this time Rose caught at a strap and managed to stay on her own side.

'I believe,' said Magnus grimly, 'that the poor woman

was quite starved of love. And my father possessed more than his fair share of charm.' Then he added with amusement flickering deep in his voice, 'I'm told that it runs in the family.'

She said nothing, staring out of the window at the darkened streets, lit here and there by a street lamp or a glowing window. His voice went on.

'So George fought to keep his wife – not for her own sake, but for her money. And her mother supported him all the way. She wanted no scandal to rock the very secure place her daughter's marriage had given her in local society.'

Rose shivered at the thought of such a marriage – based only on mutual exchange of wealth and power, with no loving, or even affection by the sound of it.

'So they parted – your father, and Blair's mother?'

His voice hardened. 'My own feeling is that he should have held fast to her, if she was what he wanted, and be damned to the consequences.'

'I've never thought of you as a romantic.'

'I'm not. But I believe that if something matters as much as that love affair seems to have mattered to my father, nothing should be allowed to get in its way. However, they parted, and I knew nothing of the whole business until my father was dying. By that time he had gone to South America and lost all his money in some foolhardy venture.'

The carriage halted. They were home. 'People who are dying,' said Magnus as the coachman climbed down to open the door, 'always seem to be very eager to unburden themselves of their life stories. I suppose it's their way of leaving some sort of footprint behind, to prove that they've been here.'

As they stepped into the close he added cheerfully, with a sudden change of mood, 'Now that the dry dock's secured I'm going to have to go up to Glasgow. I must fix up the old girl with a two cylinder diagonal compound engine if I want to give Finlay a run for his money.'

16

When *Darroch's Folly*, patched in readiness for the short journey to the dry dock, was eased from the muddy cradle that had been her resting place for some fifteen years there was a fair-sized crowd to see her go.

Among them Rose recognized Hannie Simpson. The big man was standing some distance away, by himself, his eyes fixed on her. When she turned her head and caught him, he made no effort to look away. Once again she felt as though his gaze was something that crawled over her face and body. She shuddered, and wrapped her arms protectively across her breasts, cradling her elbows in her palms.

She looked away from him and watched, her heart in her mouth, as a line was attached to the vessel and a tug moved into the river and took the strain. From the bridge wing Magnus gave her a cheerful wave, then his hand abruptly descended to clutch at the railing before him as the boat under his feet lurched, dragging back reluctantly on the line.

'He'll drown, you mark my words,' Bella said from beside her. 'The minute deep water gets under that wreck it'll go down to the bottom, and Magnus MacBride with it!'

'Mam, the water's not going to be that deep. Just enough to float her.'

'It'll turn over,' Bella's gloom and doom voice went on, and Miss McKinnon, her faithful shadow these days, gave a gasp of horror. 'It'll turn over and he'll be trapped.'

'Oh, Mam!' But in spite of her scoffing Rose felt a tremble of fear. She wasn't altogether certain that the makeshift work carried out on the old steamer was enough to keep her afloat.

A thin cheer went up from the men who had been working with Magnus as *Darroch's Folly*, finally giving in to the tug's urging, steadied her lurch to port and began to slip forward. Clumsily, with no grace whatsoever, she lurched over the mudbank and into deeper water, wallowing as the ground that had supported her for so long dropped away and she found herself back in her natural habitat. Magnus took his cap off and waved it jubilantly above his head. The wind carried his yell of triumph to them.

'She lying awful low in the water, is she not?' Rose asked anxiously.

'I told you – she's sinking,' Bella said with grim satisfaction. Then the steamer settled – low in the water as Rose had said, but steady now – and began to follow the tug, to the accompaniment of another cheer.

The crowd began to disperse. Bella, complaining about the cold wind, collected Miss McKinnon and turned for home.

'Are you coming, Rose?'

'In a minute. You go on.'

Alone on the pier, Rose stayed where she was, staring after the paddle-steamer until she rounded the end of the pier and disappeared from sight. By that time she had almost reached the end of her journey. Men would be waiting with ropes and chains to swing her round and drag her out of the water and on to the protective stocks.

Darroch's Folly hadn't sunk, after all. Magnus had survived his first voyage on his beloved boat.

She drew a deep breath, and only then discovered that her fingers, cupping her elbows, had dug in so deeply that her arms were aching.

January wind filled with sleet had been driving up the firth during the night, howling round the tenements, tapping at the window of Rose's small room and disturbing her sleep.

She got up earlier than usual, but even so her mother was up before her, shuffling painfully about the kitchen.

'Mam, you should have stayed in bed.'

'With every joint feeling as if a knife's being turned in it?' Bella asked peevishly, clashing pots and pans about on the range. 'As God's my witness, this winter'll be the ending of me! Me and the poor Queen both, bless her,' she added piously.

Chauncy and Magnus appeared, rubbing sleep out of their eyes. They ate silently, then made ready to go out; Magnus to Glasgow in search of yet another essential piece of machinery needed for *Darroch's Folly*, Chauncy to the harbour, where a boat was waiting to be loaded with coal from the Crawford mines.

Magnus was scarcely ever in the house now. When he did appear he was usually grimy and exhausted, impatient to eat something then settle to studying for his master's ticket in his room before snatching a few hours' sleep.

Quite often he made use of the living room, secreting himself behind its closed door with Chauncy and some prosperous-looking, keen-eyed men.

Rose knew from Chauncy that they were the men who had agreed to buy shares in the company that Magnus had set up to fund the refurbishing of *Darroch's Folly*. Try as she might, she couldn't get used to calling the boat by its new name, *Darroch's Pride*.

'Are you coming with me, Rose?' Chauncy asked as he pulled his coat on.

She indicated Bella's bent, slow-moving figure with a swift movement of her eyes while her lips said lightly, 'Och, it's too cold to go down to the harbour at this time of the morning. I'll just get some housework done first.'

He caught her meaning and joined in the play-acting. 'It's all right for you, able to stay by the fire until the day moves on towards noon,' he grumbled mildly, and left. If Bella were to guess that Rose was trying to ease her burden on a day when the rheumatism was worse she would have angrily refused assistance.

'Not bound for some fine house today – you and your old-man friend, seeking to add to your fortunes?' Bella asked maliciously as Rose rolled up her sleeves and donned a smock over her blouse and skirt.

'January's a bad month for house sales, and I've got more than enough in the warehouse to keep us going for the moment.'

'Hmm!'

Rose, scrubbing at a porridge-encrusted pot, paid no heed. Bella's resentment at her daughter's new-found career grew with each day that passed. Try as she might, she couldn't prise any more from Rose than fair payment for her lodgings. The knowledge that she was being defied by her own flesh and blood gnawed at her far more than the inflammation in her joints.

She made only a token gesture at the housework then stumped grumpily across the landing to drink tea and complain to Miss McKinnon about the ingratitude of grown children.

When Rose left the close the night's darkness was just beginning to lift. Reaching a newsboy who hugged his hands in the warmth of his armpits as he bawled out the latest headlines, she stopped to buy a paper.

Rory had arrived at the warehouse early, as always, and the fire that kept the glue-pots at the right temperature was bright and welcoming on this bitter morning.

The hum of voices reached Rose as soon as she walked in; business had done well over the winter, and she now employed two women to help with the cleaning and polishing as well as a man, another out-of-work cabinet maker, who worked alongside Rory.

She stepped inside and looked round with satisfaction and pleasure. This place had become a symbol of her independence, her little kingdom; within its doors she was contented.

There was a lot of work in hand. A man who had inherited his father's furniture was waiting to ask her if she was interested in buying it. Someone looking for a corner cupboard dropped in at the warehouse in the hope of finding something suitable. Rory wanted her opinion on a bookcase that might well be worth refurbishing, but would be costly. Now that she was employing people she had to keep her accounts and wages ledgers up to date.

A few hours passed before she found the time to read her newspaper. The main item was about the health of the old and ailing Queen, and there was a call for more army volunteers to fight in South Africa.

As Rose turned to the second page the word 'Naauwpoort' seemed to spring from the close-packed print before her. The Boers were close to taking the area, and had fired on a train only ten miles away from the hospital. The train had managed to continue, going directly to the hospital when it reached Naauwpoort so that the injured people on board, mainly Boer women and children, could be treated.

Rose read every word of the article, recalling the hospital and the land around it, and wondered what it must be like for the nursing sisters there now, nearer the fighting than ever before.

Restlessly, unable to go on with her work, she put on her warm jacket and stepped outside, drawing the salty air down into her lungs and lifting her face to the sun's frigid brightness as it broke through the clouds.

The cargo boat lying at the nearby berth was still loading coal; Chauncy, who was supervising the work, nodded to Rose as she passed.

Her feet took her, inevitably, past the small boatyard, where an elegant yacht was taking shape on the stocks, to the other side of the long harbour, where *Darroch's Pride* lay in dry dock, supported by a mountain of scaffolding.

The old steamer, clear of the water and held upright by a forest of timbers, had been stripped down completely. Huge pieces of engine lay scattered carelessly about the cobblestones. She looked for all the world like a dying queen bee with her worker attendants frantically trying to revive her.

Magnus, back from Glasgow, the neck of his shirt open and the sleeves rolled up despite the cold, was conferring with a small knot of men.

He had taken a handful of the town's unemployed, men who had been living on the poverty line for a long time, men who had lost hope and heart, and built them into a team that would have followed him to the ends of the earth.

Willing to work hard for pitifully little, they took great pride in what they were doing, and had become as determined as Magnus to see the old vessel back in business.

Rose wandered around the giant pieces of machinery trying without success to imagine how they could ever fit into the boat.

As usual there was a small group of onlookers, some sceptical, some genuinely interested. Among them Rose saw Mr Finlay, the man Magnus had been foolish enough to wager with, together with Captain Donlevy. As he studied the steamer Mr Finlay rocked complacently back and forth on his heels, a smirk on his face.

'Another five months, and she'll be making her maiden voyage.' Magnus arrived by her side, each word puffing warm clouds in the crystal air.

'D'you think so?'

'I know so. June 1901 will see the start of the MacBride fleet.' Magnus gave a cheerful salute to Mr Finlay, who returned it sourly and walked away. 'Talking of empires, how's the furniture business doing?'

'Very well indeed.'

A smart little trap swept through the open harbour

gates and came to a standstill, the horse tossing its head and sparking well-shod hooves off the cobbles. Chauncy sprang to take the reins as a woman, warmly booted and furred against the day's chill, stepped down and began to pick her way towards the dry dock.

'Well enough to supply me with chairs and settees for the for'ard saloons?'

'You're almost ready to furnish her, then?'

'I will be by the time you've got the order together. I'll have wooden benches on the promenade deck and in the smoking room – and the aft saloon deck as well. But I'd like the for'ard saloons above and below deck to be elegant, for the ladies.'

'Will the upper saloon be your first-class area?'

'Good Lord, no. I'm not going to waste time or space on first and third class. Folk can go wherever they like on my boat.'

Rose watched Blair's sister approach. 'You've got a visitor, Magnus.'

'Have I?' He swung round, then said, 'It's only Lilias.'

'She's become very fond of the harbour all at once.'

'So has Blair, I notice.'

'Blair works in the harbour office.'

'But not in your warehouse,' Magnus said smoothly, laughter dancing deep in his eyes. 'He seems to be uncommonly interested in that warehouse.' Then he said as the laird's daughter reached them, 'Good afternoon, Lilias.'

Colour glowed becomingly in Lilias Warner's pretty face. 'Hello, Magnus. Good afternoon, Miss Gibb.' The feathers on the smart little hat trembled as its wearer inclined her head. Her long-lashed violet eyes rested briefly on Rose's face, then returned to Magnus.

'Seating for about two hundred,' he went on. 'Something that the ladies would like.'

'Tapestry?'

'If that's what you'd advise. I've no notion of what would look right.'

'Where?' Lilias put a small gloved hand on his arm.

'Rose is going to furnish the main saloons of *Darroch's Pride* for me.'

'You should let me choose your colour schemes.'

'Rose can do it well enough.'

Lilias shot an angry look in Rose's direction, then said coaxingly, 'I'd like to do it, Magnus.'

'And run me into debt before the vessel as much as touches the water?' he asked in amusement. 'My dear Lilias, I could never support your extravagant tastes!'

She pouted. 'You could if you'd let me become a shareholder, as I asked. I've got as much money as you'd need.'

'Out of the question. I've already told you that I'll not take money from a woman.'

Then, as she chewed at her full lower lip he turned back to Rose, a challenging gleam in the golden depths of his gaze. 'Well, what d'you say?'

Where would she find all the furniture? How could she possibly get the work completed in the time? For about ten seconds she allowed herself the luxury of panicking, then took a deep breath and said calmly, 'I'll do it.'

'Fine,' said Magnus. 'I thought you would.'

Rory had a talent for discovering house sales. He and Rose, accompanied by Chauncy whenever he happened to be free, travelled further afield with each week that passed, visiting a motley collection of buildings around the Ayrshire coast, then striking inland.

Some of the sales they attended were held in mansions, some in more sedate family homes, one or two in castles. They all yielded treasures which Rory lovingly repaired. Then, under his supervision, Rose and her small team of women polished and finished off each item before taking it to Mr Grier in Molton Street.

To her great pleasure, Mr Grier was willing to buy almost everything that came from the warehouse.

'You've got a fine eye for good furniture, Miss Gibb,' he said appreciatively, 'and a good man there to advise you.' Then he added, a twinkle in his normally serious gaze, 'I'm thinking I'd be wise to keep buying from you. If I don't, you might take up the idea of opening a shop as well as the warehouse, and what would I do for customers then?'

'I've quite enough to do without thinking of a shop as well,' Rose told him with feeling.

With more and more furniture coming in, she was kept as busy with the cleaning and polishing as the women she employed, as well as being in sole charge of the ledgers and the cash-box. And as it was Rory's strict rule that nothing be decided without proper consultation with Rose, she was continually being summoned to this or that part of the warehouse to give her opinions.

In her spare time she studied books on furniture-making and restoration borrowed from the local library, and gradually acquired a working knowledge of the business she now found herself in.

Summoned by Rory, the poorer townspeople gathered like flocks of sparrows whenever a new shipment arrived, picking over the odds and ends that were bought specially for them; hurrying off, bright-faced, with their new possessions beneath their arms, or transported on old perambulators or barrows or even rickety sledges pulled by frayed rope.

The wooden building down on the harbour was a busy place now, warmed by the fire necessary for the glue-pots, abuzz with people most of the time, stocked with tables and chairs, sideboards and cupboards, all awaiting attention.

When a set of elegant chairs, suitable for Magnus's steamboat but sorely in need of renovation, came into the warehouse, Rose decided that the time had come to offer the unseen embroideress steady employment.

'She's given us some beautiful pieces, Rory, and I'd like her to do something with these.' She ran her hand over the seat of one of the chairs. Once, it had been covered by a handsome piece of embroidery; now the delicate stitching was shabby and faded and torn.

His eyes met hers, then slid away. 'I doubt if she'd want to come down here to work. I'll take the measurements and the materials to her, the same as usual, and you can tell me what you've got in mind.'

But her growing curiosity wouldn't accept that. 'It's time I met up with her. Ask her to come to the warehouse.'

'Best not, Mistress.'

'Rory Pollock, what secret are you keeping from me? Come on, now – out with it!'

He stared down at his feet. 'I promised the lass that nobody would know her name but myself.'

'There are other seamstresses in the town, you know. I could go to one of them instead.'

'There's none as good as she is,' Rory said swiftly.

'I'm aware of that. But at least I'd be able to speak to them face to face. Rory, I've got more embroidery work than I can handle, what with the order for the paddle-boat to do, so I'm not interested in going on in this fashion. I must be able to talk to her myself, so you might as well tell me who the lassie is.'

The old man hesitated, then said reluctantly, 'It's Meg Simpson.'

'Hannie's daughter?' Rose asked incredulously. 'The girl who ran away to be wed?'

She had heard about the Meg Simpson scandal from Bella soon after her return home. Hannie's only child, Meg had been browbeaten by her father all her life. Finally, when she had just turned twenty, she had run off with a young carter.

When they heard of it the townsfolk wished the girl well of her new life. But her father, consumed with possessive rage, had gone after the young couple and had run them to earth in a lodging house in Glasgow. Nobody knew for certain what had happened then, for Meg never spoke of it and the young man was dead, killed by a fall from the open window of the secret love-nest to the back-court below.

The subsequent court inquiry accepted Hannie's sworn statement that his daughter's seducer had stumbled and caused his own death in the act of abandoning his victim to her father's righteous parental wrath.

Meg hadn't been called upon to give her side of the story, because by that time she was close to death herself, following a miscarriage. When she was released from hospital Hannie had returned to Sandyford, grimly triumphant and totally vindicated, bringing his daughter with him.

'Aye, Hannie's lass.' Rory looked wretched. 'She's a decent soul, Mistress, for all the tattle there was about her. And Hannie leads her a terrible life. If he was to know about the work she's doing for you the dear Lord knows what he'd do to the girl –'

'Don't fret yourself, Rory. He'll not hear a word from me. But I want to talk to Meg,' said Rose firmly. 'When's the best time to catch her in, when her father's not about?'

17

Atholl Row, where Hannie Simpson lived, consisted of a single row of old tenements divided from the waterfront by the railway. The residents looked out of small ill-fitting windows on to the high railway wall, and as often as not the slice of sky above was hidden by smoke from the engines being shunted on the lines.

Atholl Row housed the poorest folk in the town. The labourers, the unemployed, the old and the helpless crowded into its dark buildings and filled its small rooms. Their children played in gutters that ran with refuse.

Hannie Simpson owned the tenement building he lived in. His flat was on the ground floor, where he could keep an eye on the comings and goings of his tenants.

The place smelled. Rose's nose wrinkled as soon as she mounted the two steps up from the pavement and entered the close's gloom.

It smelled of stale urine and food that had been cooked long ago and stagnant water. It smelled of poverty and hopelessness and misery.

The stairs at the end of the close wound up into total darkness on this gloomy winter's day. Peering aloft, Rose was thankful that she wouldn't have to venture there. The back-court, glimpsed beyond the staircase, was unkempt and littered with rubbish.

The whole place was a breeding ground for the diseases that ravaged the slum areas of towns and cities. Behind one of the two ground-floor doors a baby was howling wretchedly and a man and woman were screaming abuse. Rose knocked on the other door, waited, knocked again.

After a long time, long enough for the chill of the place to start sinking into her bones, she heard a faint rustle of sound from within.

She tapped once more, lightly, then put her mouth as close as she dared to the filthy, scabbed paintwork. 'Meg? Meg Simpson?'

The door opened just wide enough for the girl inside to put an eye to the crack. 'He's out. He'll not be back till his dinner-time,' Meg said in an anxious whisper, and would have closed the door if Rose hadn't prevented it with a firm hand.

'It's not your father I've come to see, it's you. I'm Rose Gibb –'

'I cannae speak to anyone.' Meg's voice rose in sudden panic. She pushed against the door, but Rose pushed harder. Meg fell back, the door opened, and Rose whisked in and closed it behind her.

The narrow hallway was too dark for her to see her reluctant hostess, but there was no mistaking the tremor in Meg's voice when she said, 'He'll be back – he'll not be pleased –'

'I'll be away long before he comes back, never fear. I just want to talk to you about your embroidery. Is there somewhere we can sit down?'

'In here,' Meg Simpson's voice was heavy with despair, foreboding, and a realization that she was not going to get rid of her unwelcome visitor. She opened a door.

Rose, following her, felt her mouth falling open with astonishment.

The room was a treasure cave. The heavy curtains were drawn and the place lit by a single lamp that gleamed on crystal and mahogany and silver. The Persian rugs underfoot were patterned in soft pastel shades, the velvet upholstery on sofa and chairs had the opulent sheen of ruby wine.

The surfaces were crowded with candlesticks, vases,

picture frames, china ornaments. On the walls hung massive paintings that must have come from large houses. Each painting was set off by a superb frame.

'He won't let anyone come into this house. If he should find out –'

The girl's timid voice drew Rose's stunned mind back to the reason why she had called. She turned her head and found herself looking at the most beautiful of all Hannie Simpson's possessions.

Meg, fidgeting nervously with the items on the small table where the lamp sat, was unwittingly positioned in such a way that the glow picked out the red glints in her dark hair and, as she looked up for a brief moment, the amazing beauty of her eyes. They were like sea-jewels, clear and green, fathomless and thick-lashed.

Then she stepped away from the lamp and became nothing more than a small, slight young woman, pale and thin-faced, dressed in something clumsy and dark and unbecoming.

'Please –' she said with growing anxiety, and Rose realized that she had been standing staring at both room and girl.

'I'm sorry. I was taken by surprise.' She gestured at the opulent richness all around.

'He likes fine things about him.'

'Are you not afraid of thieves?' The house was in an area notorious for petty crime.

'Nobody ever comes in and the curtains are drawn, always. Nobody knows.' Meg's small work-reddened hands twined round each other in her agitation, reminding Rose what she had come for. She seated herself carefully on the edge of a chair that she was certain was Chippendale, and began to explain her mission.

As soon as she grasped what her visitor was on about Meg's lovely green eyes opened wide. 'Oh no, I couldn't! I could never go to your warehouse. He'd not let me!'

In her agitation she walked about the room, picking

up a china shepherdess here, a framed photograph there, handling and replacing them with automatic, practised skill. 'I knew it was wrong of me to agree to do the work for Rory when he first asked me!'

'It wasn't wrong at all.' Rose got up and took the other girl by the shoulders. Not much flesh covered Meg Simpson's bones; they felt small and fragile.

'You've a great skill with the needle, Meg. There's nothing wrong in using that skill to earn some money for yourself.'

Then as the girl shook her head she asked, 'D'you not have the time to do more work for me?'

'It's not that. This all takes looking after' – she indicated the beautiful pieces around them – 'but I'm never out, so I've got plenty time to do it. I do my sewing in my own room in the afternoons, while he's out, and he knows nothing about it. But I couldn't come to the harbour. He'd not let me.'

'D'you mean you stay behind drawn curtains all the time? You never cross over the doorstep?'

'Only to go to the shops at the end of the road. He won't allow it. Not since I – I –'

Meg's small neat head drooped with shame on a long, delicate neck. Anger surged through Rose as she realized what a wretched life the girl had been living without anyone's knowledge. It was wicked, inhumanly wicked, to break someone's spirit like that. But it was just what she would expect of Hannie Simpson.

'Listen to me, Meg. It's time you earned some money of your own – and your father doesn't need to know a thing about it. Will you not come to the warehouse tomorrow morning and look at the chairs that need covering?'

'Oh no, I –'

'I can't bring them here, can I? And there's nobody else I know as good with a needle as you. You could have a quick look at them and be back here before anyone knows you've gone.'

It took another five minutes of persuasion before the girl agreed, and even then, slipping out into the dirty close, hearing the door shut behind her immediately, Rose wasn't entirely certain that Meg would do as she promised. Her fear of Hannie Simpson was so strong that it could almost be touched.

It was catching, too. Rose found herself peering out from the close-mouth, glancing to left and right before she carefully went down the two worn steps to the pavement and hurried off.

She remembered the unpleasant feeling that Hannie Simpson's sly wandering eyes had given her, thought of the hidden treasures and the intimidated girl she had just left, and decided that he was the most loathsome man she had ever known.

When a hand was laid on her arm she gasped and spun round, convinced that Hannie had seen her leaving his house.

'Magnus! You gave me a fright!'

'What are you doing here?' He threaded her hand through the crook of his elbow, scowling at a man who was loitering at a nearby close-mouth. 'A woman's not safe in this street on her own, d'you not know that?'

'I can see to myself.' The words were sharp, but at the same time she was glad that he was there, striding along by her side, his arm hard and strong beneath her gloved fingers. He was everything that Hannie was not – straightforward and reliable, honest and trustworthy.

'Mebbe you can, but all the same, if you're going to have cause to come here again let me know and I'll escort you. You were surely not looking at furniture in any of these kennels? There's nothing in this street worth having.'

She thought of the fortune that lay behind Hannie Simpson's permanently drawn curtains and said primly, 'Of course not. I was trying to get a woman to do some sewing for me.'

'Did you succeed?'

'I don't know,' said Rose as the two of them neared the end of the narrow street. 'I don't know – but I hope so, for her sake as well as mine.'

A man stepped out of a dark, damp close just ahead of them, turned his head and saw them, then stopped short. For a moment he hesitated, as though he would like to duck back, out of sight. Then he held his ground and waited for them to reach him.

'Good morning, Rose.' He nodded to Magnus.

'Daniel? I didn't expect to see you here.'

Daniel Currie's eyes darted from one face to the other. 'I was visiting the family of one of my pupils. The child's sick, and likely to sicken the rest of them if the parents don't take care. They've no understanding of the nature of illness and disease, some of them. They believe in letting Nature take its course, and as often as not Nature has little compassion –'

Then, realizing that he was letting the words hurry on endlessly, he stopped abruptly. He had lost weight, she noticed. It gave a gaunt look to his face that emphasized the bone structure under the skin and made him interestingly handsome, like a young poet stricken with some ailment.

'Are you going back home?'

'No,' said Daniel. 'I have another call to make.' He hesitated, then said in a rush of words, 'I'd as soon Leila didn't hear of you seeing me here. It angers her to think that I might be exposing myself and her to illness by coming to Atholl Row.'

Then he touched his hat, nodded again to Magnus, and slipped by them.

'He doesn't look well,' Rose fretted, then amended it to, 'He doesn't look happy.'

'Marriage may not suit him as much as he had hoped. Some men,' said Magnus, 'are misguided enough to think that marriage is the answer to all life's problems. In fact, it very often adds to them.'

'You're very cynical.'

'Just world-wise.'

'So marriage isn't for you?'

He gave her a sidelong glance, an intense look. 'Marriage has a way of creeping up behind a man when he least expects it, and getting a grip on his shoulder. But that's not to say he need be any the less world-wise about it.'

Meg arrived at the warehouse on the following day, slipping in through the open doors in the middle of the morning like a wraith from the sea-fog that was just beginning to disperse outside.

Her face was only a pale glimmer within the shawl wound round her head and the upper part of her body. Below it she wore a drab, shapeless skirt and clumsy shoes.

When she recognized Rose she smiled timidly, easing the shawl back on to her shoulders.

'I can only stay for a moment.'

'I'm glad you came. See –' Rose took her immediately to where the chairs were ranged against the wall.

Meg examined the faded tapestry seats. 'If I could take one of the pieces home with me to guide me I could make a new set for you.'

Rory had joined them. 'I'll hand it in to you tonight – when he's gone out for a drink,' he added, and she nodded. Obviously these two understood each other well, and she trusted the old man.

'Come and look over here – there's more work I'd like you to do.' Rose showed the girl a pretty little footstool in need of renovation. It wasn't part of a house sale; her name was beginning to be known, and the lady of one of the larger houses on the fringe of the town had asked her to renovate the stool.

Again Meg nodded her head. There seemed to be nothing the girl couldn't do with her needle.

'You could support yourself easily as a seamstress,' Rose told her, but Meg shrank away, her lashes fluttering as though she expected a blow.

'Oh no, I could never do that – he'd not like it at all!'

Behind her back Rory shook his head warningly at Rose. 'Meg, will you tell me what you think of this piece?' he invited, and led her over to a handsome low velvet button-back chair, a new acquisition, and one that he particularly liked.

The wooden framework had been badly treated, and Rory was looking forward to working on it.

They were studying it when the warehouse door burst open and Chauncy, who visited whenever he could, strode in. Startled, Meg whirled round and stared, wide-eyed.

A shaft of sunlight, breaking through the fog's tattered remnants, struck in through the open door, forming a halo round Chauncy's brown head and going on to pick out the flame-red highlights in Meg's hair and illuminate her white little face and the great emerald eyes that dominated it.

She stood motionless for a moment, trapped in the beam of light, then dragged the shawl over her head and stooped to snatch up the basket she had laid down for a moment.

'I must go,' she said, and brushed past Chauncy before he had a chance to speak. He turned to look after her small figure, then looked back at Rose, dazed.

'Who was that?'

'Hannie Simpson's daughter. She's the one with the great skill for embroidery. I'm trying to get her to do more work for me.'

'That's Meg Simpson? I've no mind of seeing her before,' Chauncy said, his voice slow and marvelling, as though he were waking from a deep sleep.

'That's little wonder. Her father never lets her out of the house, it seems. So if you see her around here again keep your mouth shut about it or you'll get the girl into bother.'

Rory, running his fingers along the back of the chair, said longingly, 'If I was only a younger man I'd like fine to thrash that Hannie Simpson, so I would!'

Rose went to him, and gave his arm an affectionate squeeze. 'And I'd be there to cheer you on, so I would!' she said.

18

At the end of January Queen Victoria died, and Sandyford, together with every city, town and hamlet in the land, went into mourning, and prepared to sample the novelty, after all those years, of being ruled by a king instead of a queen.

But neither life nor death can halt the passing of time, and by the time winter's grip eased and spring began to make itself felt the town was back to normal, and Rose was busier than ever.

The lady who had asked her to renovate the footstool was only the first to approach her. Word went round swiftly, and scarcely a week went by without Rose being summoned to take afternoon tea with the mistress of some big house or another, and to give advice on the restoration of old furniture.

The moneyed folk felt safe in the presence of the neatly dressed, well-spoken young businesswoman who advanced into their drawing rooms with unselfconscious poise and charged reasonable rates for work that was very well done.

The women who came from working stock themselves, and whose husbands or fathers had been astute enough or talented enough to make their fortunes in industry, trusted her because she was like themselves, with none of the 'airs and graces' that those with inherited wealth tended to put on.

The women who had been used to riches all their lives knew that she was friendly with Blair Crawford, and had visited Crawford House on more than one occasion. As far as they were concerned Rose was eminently respectable, almost one of their own kind.

A few of them even took her into their confidence, confessing shameful financial problems that they dared tell nobody else. Rose listened, and bought from them discreetly.

Their neighbours never noticed that the furniture taken for renovation didn't come back, and Rose made certain that once any necessary work was carried out the items were resold in other areas, where they were unlikely to be recognized.

She felt pity for these distressed gentlefolk. In their own way they were suffering almost as much as some of the poor souls who gathered eagerly at the warehouse for the bits and pieces that she and Rory now bought in specially for them.

'You realize that you're encouraging these people for no good reason?' Blair Crawford said disapprovingly when he called in at the warehouse on a day when a cluster of shawled women and ragged children, barefoot despite the cold weather, were triumphantly carting off their latest bargains. 'There's no money to be had in selling to them.'

'And there's no harm in helping them,' Rose returned sharply.

'As you wish. My grandmother would like to see you.'

'Why?' The question was ungracious, but Rose had had a busy day, and she was in no mood for idle conversation. She was anxious to attend a house sale where she hoped to buy some more chairs for the paddle-steamer.

'Because she's been confined to her bed for the past few days. She'd like you to come to tea.'

'I'm very busy just now,' Rose said reluctantly.

He leaned back against the wall and beamed down at her. 'I can understand why she's taken to you. You're alike, in a lot of ways. I'll tell Grandmother that you look forward to seeing her soon,' he added, and went back to the office where, Rose well knew, he dallied around and left all the decisions to Chauncy, a willing workhorse.

Leila, suffering permanently from backache, mourning for her lost figure, behaved as though pregnancy was a fatal illness instead of a natural function.

On the one occasion when Rose, tired out after a day's work and irritated by her sister's constant carping, had dared to say that, Leila had almost attacked her.

'What do you know about it, Miss? Flouncing about the town, in and out of all the fine houses, having the time of your life – wait till it's your turn!'

'I doubt if it ever will be my turn,' Rose retorted, and Leila, freed from restraint because the menfolk weren't there and the only bystander was her mother, snapped back, 'You wish it was you in this condition and not me. You wish it was you married to Daniel, don't you? You always wanted him –'

'For the love of God, girl, calm yourself down!' Bella pushed her younger daughter into a chair and held her there. Leila bounced and seethed under the restraining hands.

'She's jealous!'

'I'd not envy you if Daniel was the last man in the world.'

Leila burst into loud sobs and leaned against her mother's shoulder. 'Not content with m-maligning me, now she's maligning D-Daniel,' she bawled like a spoiled child.

Rose, suddenly contrite, patted her sister's hand. 'I'm sorry,' she said, then walked out of the kitchen, ignoring the muffled, squashy 'No you're not!' spoken into Bella's comforting shoulder.

Leila became increasingly difficult to please, and Daniel looked increasingly unhappy. His eyes were shadowed and he was withdrawn, with very little to say for himself.

'Times I worry about these two,' Bella unexpectedly confided to Rose one day. It was noon, and they were sitting companionably at the kitchen table, drinking tea.

'What's there to worry about? I thought you were delighted with the marriage.'

'I am, but –' Bella hesitated, then said, 'They're just not happy together.'

'Once the baby comes everything'll be find.'

'I hope so,' Bella said without conviction, then Miss McKinnon came tapping at the door and the conversation went no further.

As far as Rose was concerned Leila and Daniel would have to look out for themselves. She had more than enough to do, particularly when her mother was confined to her bed.

Doctor Anderson was called in, and left some new embrocation for the aching joints. She looked even more tired than usual.

'Ah, Doctor,' Bella said from her pillow, her voice richly Irish with sympathy, 'you look as though you could do with climbing into this bed yourself.'

'March is a bad month for illness. I've got a lot of sick people to see to,' the doctor said harshly, with a sidelong glance at Rose who stood by the door. 'There's no time for rest. I'll be back next week. I'll see myself out.'

'That woman's a saint,' said Bella when they were alone again. 'How you could have refused to help her when she came to you in her hour of need, I'll never know.'

Rose ignored the jibe. She had other things on her mind. 'Mam, would you not think of getting someone in to do the heavy work for you now you're not able?'

'Certainly not!' Bella reared up in bed despite her aching bones. 'Where d'you think I'd find the money to pay for a servant?'

'Not a servant, just someone to help you with the floors and the stairs. I'd pay for her.'

'I've no doubt you would – you and your secret fortune that's been built on my good nature! Just you mark this, my lady – Bella Gibb will have no servant, nor no cleaning woman neither, in her house as long as she's got breath in her body. And as long,' she added, 'as she's got a daughter who can do what she's not able to do for herself. Cleaning woman, indeed!'

'Mam –'

'I'd not be able to hold my head up in the street if word got about that I'd taken a cleaning woman!' said Bella, and would hear no more on the subject.

Rose hoped, as she plied the polished door-knocker, that Leila wouldn't insist on her staying for the entire evening.

It was a miserable March night. The islands and the far side of the river had been hidden from sight all day; the grey water had blended into the sky, and it was impossible to see where one met the other.

In mid-afternoon the rain had come sweeping in across the water in a solid curtain. It still pattered on Rose's umbrella, and she had had to step carefully along the pavements to avoid the puddles.

At home, Magnus and Chauncy and the man who had become overseer of Magnus's workmen were gathered round the kitchen table discussing boilers and condensers. Bella was spending a cosy evening with Miss McKinnon.

Under Rose's arm was a book on antique furniture that she had just taken from the public library. She hoped to make her way back through the downpour once she had delivered her message, and spend the rest of the evening reading in her own room.

To her great surprise it was Daniel, relaxed in shirt sleeves and waistcoat, who opened the door. For a moment he gaped at her, then hurriedly stepped back, holding the door wide.

'Rose! This is a pleasant surprise – come on in.'

The hallway was small and square; as she stepped inside, close to him, her nose tingled with the agreeable smell of soap and masculinity. 'Mam asked me to hand these things in for Leila.'

He made no attempt to take the small parcel, but opened the door to the parlour.

'It's a miserable night; we've set a good fire in here.'

The room was warm and comfortable, the picture of cosy domesticity with the curtains drawn against the night. An open book lay on a small table on one side of the hearth. On the other, an identical table held a bundle of half-completed knitting.

'Is Leila at home?'

'Take your coat off. It's not often we can enjoy your company.' Daniel slipped the coat from her shoulders and urged her to sit on the small sofa opposite the fireplace. 'She's just gone along to a neighbour's for a minute,' he said over his shoulder as he went back into the hall with her coat. 'She'll be glad to see you here when she gets back.'

'I can't stay long, I've things to see to at home –'

He came back into the room and closed the door behind him. 'You'll surely wait for a moment or so, just until she gets back. She'd never forgive me if I let you go away without seeing her.'

He sat down in his own chair and studied her intently, as though he hadn't seen her for a long time. 'You're looking well, Rose.'

'I'm fine.' She tried not to fidget beneath that steady scrutiny. 'How's the school-teaching getting along?'

A shadow settled on his face. 'No easier than it's ever been.'

He launched into a diatribe about his pupils. Much to Bella's delight, Daniel had recently been appointed headmaster of the small school where he had worked for several years.

The school catered for children from the poorer part of the town.

'It's heart-breaking, Rose, to see the poverty among my pupils, when there's so much wealth not a mile away up the hill. Some of these folk that have built their fine summer houses,' said Daniel hotly, 'came from the slums themselves, and yet their only thought is to keep every penny they earn with no regard for those less fortunate than themselves. It's no wonder that the townsfolk resent them coming to settle here, among us!'

'They spend money in the town, and some of the girls in your school will find work with them.'

'Aye, there's always that to be grateful for, I suppose,' he said with irony. 'They've got little chance of getting much more from life – from the moment they're born. Most of their fathers are unemployed, or working in the Crawford mine. D'you have any knowledge of the sort of diseases that can cripple a miner?'

'I saw a fair bit of it while I worked in the infirmary.'

'Aye, of course you did.' The bitterness faded from Daniel's eyes. They were suddenly intent on Rose's face again. 'How could I forget that? That's how we met, you and me.'

Without her mother's knowledge, for Bella would certainly not have approved, Rose had taken to attending the local Church of Scotland with some of the other nurses while working at the nearby infirmary. Daniel had been the choirmaster and organist at that church.

'And that's how you and Leila met, in a way,' Rose pointed out. Daniel had called at the house one day when she was on duty. A day when Leila, so much prettier and more feminine than Rose, was at home. A day when Mam was quick to see the instant attraction between her younger daughter and the schoolmaster, and to fan the spark into a flame. Daniel and Rose had never walked out together again.

He ignored the reminder. 'What future can there be

for these children, Rose? Some of them are bright enough, but that stands for nothing these days. Money's the key that opens doors – and only money. Intelligence has little to do with it. There's no fairness in such a system!'

'I'd no idea that you cared so much about them, Daniel.'

He flushed slightly, then admitted, 'It's only since I began to think of my own child and the sort of future I can give him that I've realized how little some of those children have to look forward to. It's when you're about to become a parent,' said Daniel, his eyes seeking and holding hers again, 'that you think over things that are to come – and think back on things that might have been.'

The little clock on the mantelpiece chimed out the half hour.

'Mercy – is it as late as that? I must go –'

She began to rise, but he was on his feet first, catching her hands in his. 'Stay for a wee while longer!'

'I thought Leila would have been back by now.'

'Och, she loses all track of the time when she starts gossiping,' Leila's husband said impatiently. 'She'll not be back for hours yet.'

She dragged her hands free and took a step back. 'You said –'

'You'd not have stayed if I'd told you the truth.' The words tumbled over each other. His eyes glittered down at her and colour suddenly rushed to his pale face. 'And I wanted to be with you for a while, to look at you – talk with you. We've not had a moment alone since you came home.'

'There was no reason for us to be alone.'

'After all that we meant to each other before you went away?'

'You chose to marry my sister.'

'Because you'd gone away!'

'I left because I could see that you only had eyes for

Leila, once you met her. You never looked the road I walked on after that!'

He brushed the words aside with an impatient movement of one hand. 'I was a fool, Rose, a blind infatuated fool.' The words spilled out, tumbling over each other. 'I should never have let you go. I know that now.'

Although her passion for him was long past she could still feel pain for the girl she had once been, the girl who had wept over his sudden coldness.

Anger at the memory of that pain and at being tricked into entering the house sharpened her voice when she said, 'It's too late, Daniel. You wed with Leila and now she's carrying your child.'

'You've no need to remind me of that, for she's not let me forget, not once in the past eight months!' His face twisted with misery. 'If ever a woman could make a man feel – unclean and unnatural, it's Leila. Not a kiss I've got from her since she found out that I'd burdened her with a child. Not a loving touch, not a caress –'

'Daniel, it's wrong of you to be talking to me about my own sister in this way.'

'You loved me once – mebbe you still care for me the way I care for you. Who else can I talk to but you?'

Then, to her horror, he reached out and caught her shoulders, dragging her against him, his mouth sealing hers as she tried to speak.

For all his protestations about caring, there was no love or tenderness in the kiss. All she knew was his great hunger, the trembling urgency in the limbs pressed tightly against hers, the realization of what might happen if she didn't put a stop to it now.

Her arms found the strength to push him away. 'No!'

'Yes!' Daniel said huskily, imperiously. 'You know that you want me as much as I want you!' He reached for her again.

She struggled against him, but his wanting, after months of denial from Leila, carried him beyond reason.

He caught her shoulders in determined hands and pushed her on to the sofa, following her down, claiming her mouth again, his body pinning her against the seat so that the fingers of one hand were free to claw at the buttons on her dress.

'Daniel, for God's sake!' Fear began to invade Rose as she realized how determined he was.

With a great effort she managed to wrench herself away, and as he reached for her again she cracked her open hand against his jaw. His head jerked round with the force of the blow and his hands fell away from her.

She jumped up, her palm stinging as though she had just been caned.

Daniel, his hand clapped to his face, glared at her. 'You little – !' he said thickly, then he was on his feet in one movement, his free hand reaching out for her.

She jumped back and snatched up the only weapon she could find – Leila's knitting needles, shrouded in soft white wool.

'You keep back from me, Daniel Currie!'

He hesitated. His eyes ranged between the sharp points of the needles and the smooth white skin of her throat, exposed by the buttons he had managed to unfasten.

The angry heat went out of his face. 'Rose' – his voice was a low groan. 'Rose, I need you!'

She backed away from him. 'And I mean what I say, Daniel. If you come near me I'll have to hurt you.'

He stopped, assessing the situation. His tongue flickered over his lips.

Then into the sudden silence between them came the frantic rattling of the door-knocker. Fists pounded on the door, the knocker sounded again, a child's voice shouted hoarsely, 'Mister Currie! Mister Currie!'

The wildness faded immediately from Daniel's eyes. He shook his head, as though trying to clear his clouded brain, then wheeled away from her and went into the hall without another word or glance.

Left alone, Rose dropped her sister's knitting and drew the back of her hand across her mouth, which felt bruised and swollen. Then with clumsy, trembling fingers she fastened her buttons, thankful that he hadn't managed to tear any of them loose.

She pushed the last one into its buttonhole and started to tuck a loose lock of hair back into the soft knot at the back of her head.

Then her hands stopped their busy work as Daniel burst into the room, his face ashen.

'It's Leila. She fell on some steps. She needs help – quickly!'

19

Leila, huddled on the sofa in her neighbour's front room, insisted shrilly and persistently on going home at once.

'If you can carry her, Daniel, she'd be as well home.'

Daniel, kneeling by his wife's side, her hand in both of his, stared at his sister-in-law. 'Are you out of your mind? It could harm the child.'

'The child's less likely to be harmed if Leila's content,' Rose snapped at him, then turned to the woman of the house. 'Get me some blankets to wrap her in. We're taking her home.'

Once she was settled in her own bed Leila calmed slightly, though she took a death-like grip on Daniel's hand the moment he set her down.

'Don't leave me!'

His face, already pale, turned grey. His eyes were glassy with terror. 'Rose!'

Her nursing training came back to her as though she had never been away from the infirmary. Deftly, unfeelingly, she peeled her sister's gripping fingers back one by one.

'Go away, Daniel, and let us get on with the birthing.'

As soon as he was free he scuttled backwards to the door, mouthing assurances that he would be nearby; then he gained the door, and fled.

'Daniel!'

'Let him go,' Rose said crisply. 'We'll manage better on our own.'

Leila opened her mouth to argue, but was prevented by a deep spasm that convulsed her body. Rose took firm hold of her hands, and bore the pain of her sister's grip stoically until Leila relaxed.

'I w-want Ma-am!' Tears coursed down her face.

'Daniel'll send someone to fetch her.' Rose ferreted through the chest of drawers and found what she was looking for – a length of clothes line in the bottom drawer, placed there in readiness for the birth.

Working swiftly, she knotted it to the head of the brass bedstead and put the ends into Leila's hands. 'Pull on that when you feel the pain coming on,' she said, and began to strip off her sister's underclothes.

'Rose, I'm f-frightened!' It was a wail that threw Rose back in time to the days when they had both been little girls. Leila, always a coward, had been easily frightened.

She went to the head of the bed and cupped her sister's tear-stained face in both hands for a moment. 'Don't be, Leila,' she said gently. 'There's nothing to be frightened of. I'll not let anything happen to you. Now lie quiet for a moment and get all the rest you can while I put a sheet under you and fetch some water to wash your face.'

But Leila's baby wasn't in the mood to wait. Rose encountered Daniel at the top of the stairs, and just had time to reassure him and ask him to bring a basin of hot water and a flannel when Leila's desperate scream of 'Rose! O God – Rose!' summoned her back to the bedroom at a run.

Leila, poppy-faced, eyes staring, was dragging at the ropes with all her might. 'Dear God –' she gasped. 'Oh Rose – what's happening?'

One glance was enough. 'You're having a baby, that's what's happening. Push, Leila – make as much noise as you need to, but push now – and push hard!'

Leila screamed, a throat-wrenching sound that rang in Rose's eardrums. She sucked in her breath and screamed again, and again.

On the crest of the third cry a small blood-spattered head burst from between her thighs and slid into Rose's hands. A moment later a neatly tucked and folded little body followed, and as Leila collapsed back on to the bed, gasping for breath, a mouth opened in the tiny screwed-up face and the baby, not waiting to be held upside down and smacked, gave out her first mewl of displeasure at being forced from her comfortable resting place.

Gently, working more by instinct now than by training, Rose turned the slippery little thing over and hooked a finger into its mouth to clear it of mucus. The baby choked and spluttered, then the mewl became a louder, stronger cry.

'Rose?'

'You've got a daughter, Leila. A little girl.' Rose's voice shook.

'Daniel wanted a boy.'

'Be damned to what Daniel wanted! It's not Daniel who had to give birth to her.'

Leila gave a ghost-like giggle then asked, 'Is she all right?'

'She's beautiful,' said Rose thickly. 'Give me a minute, then you can hold her and see her for yourself. Oh, Leila – she's so beautiful!'

To Bella's disgust she didn't reach the house until after Charlotte Isobelle Currie's arrival. When she did appear on the scene, some ten minutes after the baby's birth, it was in a cab hired by Magnus.

'He's a good soul when all's said and done,' she said, sailing into the house, ready to take over, her rheumatism forgotten in the excitement of the moment. '"I'll not have you walking the streets on a wet night, Mistress Gibb," says he, "not with your rheumatics." And that Chauncy standing there wringing his hands, not knowing what to do for the best. Where's my daughter and the new little lamb?'

Leila, pale and limp, sweat-drenched but immensely proud of herself, lay in her marriage bed, her baby in the crook of her arm. Daniel, by her side, watched the two of them with loving possessiveness.

'Out you go, now, and let her get her rest,' Bella commanded, sweeping both Rose and Daniel out of the room then closeting herself with her daughter so that they could talk about the birth uninterrupted.

The little maid arrived back from her evening off just then, wide-eyed and half-relieved, half-disappointed at missing all the fun.

Rose sent her to make tea for Leila and Bella and Daniel, who had sunk into his usual chair in the parlour, white-faced and shaking with reaction.

'You'll stay and have some tea?' he asked automatically, but she shook her head.

'You've got Mam now, and your little daughter. You don't need me.'

He caught her hand as she brushed past his chair. His eyes were diamond-brilliant against his pallor as he looked up at her. 'You think not, Rose?'

'I know not, Daniel,' she said, disentangled her hand gently, and left him.

As she reached the pavement Magnus MacBride, his coat collar turned up against the cold damp night air, stepped forward from the shelter of a doorway.

'I thought you might be coming out soon. I sent the cab away, but I can fetch another if you want.'

'I'd as soon walk.'

He fell into step beside her. 'How's your sister?'

'She's well enough. And the baby's strong and bonny for all that she's two weeks early. A wee girl.'

Tired, she stumbled slightly on a broken piece of paving, and he steadied her with a firm hand beneath her elbow. It stayed there as they walked homewards, and she was glad of it. The rain had stopped falling at last, but the pavements were still wet.

'Do you know,' she said wonderingly, 'that's the first time I've acted as midwife on my own.'

'I've no doubt you made a good job of it. You'd make a good job of anything you set your mind to.'

'You think so?'

'I'm sure of it, Rose Gibb. "When I was young, I had not given a penny for a song,"' he said surprisingly, '"Did not the poet sing it with such airs That one believed he had a sword upstairs."'

'What did you say?'

He laughed. 'It's from a poem. It's always stuck in my mind, but I never knew the sense of it until I met you. I'd not hesitate to give a penny for your song, Rose. You sing it with passion and such strength.'

They were passing the harbour. On an impulse, Rose said, 'Can we go in for a minute? I want to take a look at *Darroch's Folly*.'

'*Darroch's Pride*,' he said patiently, as he had been saying for the past few months.

He pushed open the small door set in the great gates and helped her over the sill. She waited in the dark night as he had a word with the watchman installed in the office.

When he returned she was doubly glad of his supporting, guiding hand, for there were few lights on the harbour. Magnus, sure-footed, led her over the cobbles, into and out of the deep shadow of a cargo boat that had been loaded that day and was due to leave on the early morning tide. To her left the Clyde was invisible, but she could hear it lapping against the stone walls.

A fishing boat from further along the coast passed on its way to the open sea, its lamps reflecting in the water, the voices of its crew loud in the still night. Then it was gone, and the waves made by its wake broke loudly against the wooden pilings that supported the harbour.

The paddle-steamer was a huge bulky shape against the moonless sky. A faint dusting of stars clung to her funnel and outlined her bridge and deck saloons. In the dark, where the patches and shabby paintwork couldn't be seen, she looked noble.

'You think you'll manage it?' Rose said after a long

silence. Magnus's hand beneath her arm urged her forward, and she moved with him into the shadow cast by the boat.

'The Darroch Line? Of course I will. This' – his arm indicated the great star-dusted bulk cradled in the stocks – 'is my flagship.'

'You sing a fine song yourself.'

'Will you give me a penny for it?'

'You told Lilias Crawford that you'd not take money from a woman.'

'Then will you offer payment in another way –?'

'Perhaps –' she said, her voice suddenly trembling.

As his hands touched her face the damp night air fell away and a great warmth suddenly mounted in her heart, in her bones and veins, in her breasts and her loins.

It mounted like a wave until she felt that it was long past breaking point – then as Magnus MacBride's hands moved to her shoulders and his mouth took hers the wave crumbled and fell, bathing her in its flaring warmth. With a sense of shock that would have been numbing if every part of her hadn't become so deliciously, painfully alive, she realized that all she had wanted for a long time was to be with Magnus MacBride, to be held in his arms.

Hungrily, she returned the kiss, a shudder running through her body, from fingers to toes.

When he finally raised his head one of his arms tightened, drawing her closely against him. Gently, the fingers of his free hand cupped the nape of her neck, his thumb spreading wide to follow the angle of her cheekbone and caress her earlobe, a caress so shockingly, startlingly intimate that it sent another tremor through her.

The hand moved again, unhurriedly, to her throat, unbuttoning her coat and then the top buttons of her blouse with a slow deliberation quite unlike Daniel's earlier frenzy. He bent his head again and his mouth claimed hers, only breaking now and then to stray over her nose and eyelids and forehead, then returning to her eager lips.

His fingers slipped inside the opened neck of her blouse, caressing the warm smooth skin of her throat, dipping lower until they were resting on the upper slopes of her breasts, trailing across the valley between them.

She felt her whole body grow taut and eager under that intimate touch.

She had no idea how long they stayed in the dark beside the dry dock, locked in each other's embrace, exchanging kiss for kiss, caress for caress, silently and totally wrapped in each other.

It was Magnus who finally drew back, his breathing swift and erratic.

'Rose Gibb, you're the one that could take a man's mind off everything that should matter to him,' he said huskily. 'I could swear that you once lived on a rock and sang poor sailors like myself to their doom.' Then he added, his arms releasing her reluctantly, 'I think I'd best take you home.'

'Magnus –'

He stopped the words with a soft kiss on the end of her nose, folding her hands closely in his. 'Rose, I've got my boat to see to, and you have your warehouse. But one day, when we've both made our fortunes and gained our dreams, perhaps then I'll be free to come to you and –'

He broke off, and drew her arm through his. 'Until then, it's time you were home, Rose Gibb.'

They walked in silence, his upper arm warm and firm against her shoulder, to Bella's house where Chauncy was waiting for them in the kitchen, too worried about Leila to go to bed.

'You're certain that she's well?'

'Very well, and no doubt eager to show the baby off to you as soon as you can visit her.'

'Are you sure Mam's fit to look after her? She's not going to make herself ill over it?' Even though Bella cared little for Chauncy, he cared for her, Rose thought, and was angry with her mother for not realizing what a fine stepson she had.

'This baby's done her more good than any medication. Daniel's there, and the maidservant. All Mam needs to do is rule the roost and cosset Leila and nurse the baby. She'll be as happy as a queen bee,' Rose assured him, every nerve-end aware of Magnus's presence at the table, his capable hands, the hands that had only recently caressed her, curled round a mug of tea.

Later, in bed, she listened to the muted sounds he made as he moved about his room, and remembered his kisses and his caresses, and the great hunger they had wakened in her. Then she thought of what he had said to her.

'One day –' she thought, and stretched luxuriously, smiling into the dark. One day.

She held the words close as she drifted into sleep.

20

Catherine Lacey, swathed in a powder-blue bed-jacket of soft wool, leaned back against a pile of pillows and studied her visitor as the housekeeper left the room, noiselessly closing the door behind her.

'I've been hoping for the chance to have a talk with you for some time.' Although she looked very frail the old woman's voice was surprisingly deep and strong. 'But my grandson tells me that you've been too busy to visit me up until now.'

'I have a business to run. And my mother's health has been poor.'

'It was never poor before, as I remember. Your mother worked in the meat market, didn't she? As strong as any man.'

'In her time,' said Rose. 'Now she's paying the price of having to work hard in all sorts of weathers.'

'I believe you must be very like her in nature. Blair,' said Mrs Lacey, 'thinks very highly of you. He admires you, and so do I.'

She leaned forward slightly. 'What do they say about me in the town?'

'I've no time to listen to gossip, Mrs Lacey. And even if I had I wouldn't think of repeating it.'

Blair's grandmother laughed, a tinkle of tiny faint bells. 'Then I'll tell you. They say I'm the power behind the Crawford family. That I hold the purse strings.'

She eyed her guest slyly, then said, 'My grandson wants to go back to South Africa. I want him to remain here, where he belongs. There's an estate to run, and business to see to. His father's not a strong man, and Lilias is a flibbertigibbet.'

Rose sipped at her tea and refused to comment.

'A sweet girl, but good for nothing but marriage. Since she lost her first husband' – the dry tone implied that Lilias had been widowed through her own carelessness – 'there's nothing to do with her but marry her off again.'

Then her voice sharpened. 'But not to Magnus MacBride! Lilias must marry money.'

'Mrs Lacey, your family concerns are none of my business.'

The old woman ignored the interruption. A frown knotted her delicate eyebrows. 'Lilias is easily led – like her mother. Magnus MacBride is living under your mother's roof, is he not?'

'Yes.'

'What d'you think of him?'

The question took Rose aback. The memory of that night weeks ago, when Magnus had held her in his arms and kissed her in the shadow of the old paddle-steamer, came into her mind. She had the uncomfortable feeling that Catherine Lacey's blue-green eyes could bore into her innermost soul and read it like a book.

After a moment, choosing her words carefully, she said, 'He's an honest man.'

'He's handsome, and full of charm, like his father. It was difficult to dislike that man, but I managed it.' The woman's voice hardened. 'Oh, I managed it all right, when I saw the danger in him! But my daughter didn't. She fell for him, and all but ruined her marriage. I don't want his son back here, causing trouble!'

'The days when the folk at Crawford House were able to decide who should live in Sandyford are over, Mrs Lacey.'

'More's the pity. I don't want my granddaughter falling in love with the likes of Magnus MacBride, or him with her.'

'There's little danger of that. He's got nothing on his mind but that paddle-steamer of his.'

The old woman's hand fluttered against the silken quilt that covered her. 'Enough of Lilias and Magnus MacBride. I wanted to talk to you about my grandson.'

Rose wished with all her heart that she had never come to Crawford House. 'I can't see that Blair has anything to do with me.'

'Can't you? I've no time for beating about the bush, my dear, not at my age. Blair needs a strong wife, not one of those namby-pamby rich girls. I've got more than enough money, so he has no need to marry for it as his father did. What he needs is someone like you.'

'I'm not a piece of property to be bought and sold.'

'If you were, I'd not think of you as a fitting wife for Blair. You've started your own business, they tell me. How is it going?'

'Well enough.'

'It takes money to make a business prosper. How are you managing?'

'That's my concern.'

'Money – and goodwill,' Catherine Lacey said slowly. 'I hear that you're getting custom from neighbours of ours. I hope you realize' – the meaning in her voice was unmistakable now – 'that they came to you because you're known to be a friend of my grandson's. That's what I mean by goodwill. If someone in a position of importance was to say a word against you – think what it would mean, Miss Gibb.'

Rose stood up. 'Thank you for the tea, Mrs Lacey. I must go now.' Then she said deliberately as she took the proffered hand in hers, 'Threats don't frighten me; nor do they bring me to heel. I think I could manage to run my business very well without the help of your neighbours. And without your help too.' The hand she held was as icy cold as the diamonds that garnished it.

'Visit me again, Miss Gibb.' Mrs Lacey's voice followed her as she walked to the door. There was an undertone of amusement in it. 'I think we understand each other very well.'

Leila was a besotted, devoted mother. Her every waking moment was spent with Charlotte, and the Currie household revolved round the baby.

Leila was often at her mother's house now; too often, in Rose's opinion. When she got back from her unsettling visit to Catherine Lacey her sister was sitting on one side of the kitchen range, with Bella on the other, bouncing a be-ribboned Charlotte on her knee.

'Well?' Bella asked eagerly. 'How did you get on with Mrs Lacey?'

'You're getting to be a right friend of the family at the big house,' Leila put in, her voice and eyes sharp with envy.

'We had a cup of tea and a wee chat, that was all.'

'A wee chat about what?' her mother wanted to know.

Rose looked at the two faces upturned to hers and wondered what they would say if she told them that Catherine Lacey had more or less tried to blackmail her into marrying Blair Crawford. Then she said mildly, 'She was asking me about the warehouse. Is Daniel not at home today, Leila?'

'He's off on one of his missions of mercy to some family or another.' Leila's mouth had started to take on a thin look whenever Daniel was mentioned. 'He thinks more of these folk than of his own daughter. You'd think he'd want to be with Charlotte.'

'I don't see why, when you'll not even let the man hold her for more than a few seconds.'

'Him! He juggles her up and down until she's sick.'

'Ach, men know nothing about how to handle bairns,' said Bella placidly, continuing to bounce the baby.

'I'm sure he'd be willing to learn.' Rose had seen the yearning in Daniel's eyes as he watched Leila with his daughter.

Leila hated to be crossed. 'And what makes you think you understand my husband better than I do?'

'Times, Leila, I think that everyone understands Daniel better than you do. You should talk to the man now and again.'

'How can I when he's never in the house?'

'Pay no heed,' Bella said to her younger daughter, who had been initiated into the mysteries of motherhood and was now her companion and equal. 'She grows more thrawn by the day, our Rose. It's making all that money that's gone to her head.'

Rose turned away. She could talk until she was blue in the face, and she still wouldn't be speaking their language.

As she went out of the door Charlotte hiccuped, and Bella gave a yell of anguish as a stream of half-digested milk, dislodged from its rightful place by the joggling the baby had been enduring, landed on her good black weekend dress.

The heavens smiled on Magnus MacBride on the May day when *Darroch's Pride* was due to take to the water again.

The sky was a pure translucent blue, its surface scarcely disturbed by the occasional snowy wisp of cloud, and the Clyde sparkled brightly enough to dazzle the eye. There was a cheerful holiday atmosphere about the small knot of shareholders and the much larger crowd of interested onlookers gathered at the harbour.

The centre of attraction, the once-shabby, neglected paddle-steamer glittered in the May sunshine. Her single funnel was newly painted in scarlet, with one glossy black band midway along it; her hull was black with scarlet trimming along her length just under the main rails, and her open-work paddle-boxes were painted scarlet, decorated with an intricate design in white and gold around the letter 'D'.

The teak forecastle and saloons had been varnished to a high smooth gloss, and the name *Darroch's Pride* was laid out in gold letters surrounded by the scroll design echoed on the paddle-boxes. The house flag, the letter D in black on a scarlet background, fluttered from the high mast forward of the main saloon.

There was a lump in Rose's throat as she gazed at the boat that had once been the laughing stock of the town, and had proved, with Magnus's help, to be the ugly duckling that turned into a swan.

'She's a fine vessel,' Blair said from behind her. 'MacBride has to be congratulated. Nobody ever thought he could do it.'

'I did.'

'You – and Lilias,' Blair said wryly.

His sister, beautiful in a red silk dress with gold lace at throat, wrists and hem, stood with Magnus, who looked extraordinarily smart in an immaculate white shirt and well-tailored jacket and trousers. Lilias, twirling an elegant little black and scarlet parasol, was sulky. Magnus had astounded her, and the rest of the town, by asking Bella Gibb, his landlady, to perform the launching ceremony.

Dressed in her best dark green silk gown, tightly corseted and wearing a new feathered hat bought specially for the occasion, Bella clambered, with the combined help of Magnus, Chauncy and Rory, to the platform that had been built for the launching. She looked smugly out over the heads of the people below her, bellowed in a voice that startled young Charlotte awake 'I name this ship *Darroch's Fol- Pride*!' and hurled the champagne bottle with such force that it smashed into a hundred pieces against the trim hull.

The supporting chocks had already been removed and the launch-way was well smeared with tallow. Champagne sprayed over the black paintwork just below the vessel's name, the shards of glass fell glittering to the ground like a handful of diamonds, the checking chains were eased, and *Darroch's Pride* hesitated shyly for a moment before yielding to gravity and beginning the move backwards and downwards. Once started, she picked up speed, eager to reach the water again.

'She's away!' Magnus led the time-honoured shout, waving his hat in the air, his voice rising above everyone else's. Meg clutched at Chauncy's arm without thinking. He covered her fingers with his own hand and they stood together, Meg's small slim figure erect in the shelter of Chauncy's burly shape, both of them entranced by the sight of the steamer sliding smoothly down the ramp towards her new life.

Then the boat's stern met the water and amid a great lacy fountain of spray she entered the Clyde, dipping in a deep, gracious curtsey to the onlookers as the length of her bounced then steadied and rode in deep water.

The crowd, rich and poor alike, shareholders and onlookers, raised a cheer as the drag chains rattled into action, stopping the boat before she travelled any further.

The tugs moved in to swing her about and take her off to her new berth – not the place where she had mouldered alone for so many years, but a good deep-water mooring near the dry dock. There, she would be completed and furnished and made ready for her trials and her maiden trip.

Bella, flushed and delighted with her part in the proceedings, was assisted down from the platform. Magnus gallantly offered her his arm and led her to where rows of trestle tables had been set up on the harbour so that everyone – not just the invited guests, but all those present – could sit down to a meal.

At first the folk who had just come to stare hung back shyly, but Magnus, having seated Bella and reserved a chair for himself by her side, urged them forward to the tables. Soon cloth caps and top hats, patched cotton dresses and silks were jostling together and the chirruping of a hundred voices soaked into the warm air.

'It's more like a Sunday school picnic than a launch,' Blair murmured as he and Rose found seats for themselves.

'It's what Magnus wanted.'

'And Magnus,' said her escort, with a jealous edge to his voice, 'always did get whatever he wanted.'

There was a growing demand for Meg Simpson's exquisite embroidery. Mistresses of the big houses in and around Sandyford sent chairs and footstools and even curtains to Rose, asking if her seamstress could renovate them.

As the weeks passed and her father remained unaware of her activities Meg's confidence grew. She was amazed to find that her sewing was sought after, and that she could earn money from it. She began to visit the warehouse regularly, and as often as not Chauncy found some reason to be there on those occasions. As the old paddle-steamer had bloomed under Magnus's loving care, so Meg bloomed in the warmth of Chauncy's friendship.

It took time and patience to overcome Meg's shyness. Chauncy Gibb had both, but he worried about Hannie.

'Rose, if he finds out about the lassie coming to the harbour there's no knowing what he'll do.'

'Are you frightened that you'll get the same as the last man who looked at his daughter?'

Chauncy glared at his stepsister. 'I am not! I can see Hannie off if I have to.' Then his open, honest face darkened. 'But I'm afraid for Meg. I'd speak to her father, but she'll not let me go near him.'

'She'll be all right, Chauncy,' Rose comforted. 'There's no reason why Hannie should find out.'

Rory was worried about Meg too. 'Times I wish I'd never asked her to let you see that first piece of embroidery, Mistress,' he said, watching Chauncy escort Meg to the harbour gate. 'I've mebbe brought more trouble down on the lassie's head. You can see with half an eye that she's taken a right liking to your brother. And what'll her father have to say to it when he finds out?'

Rose sprang to her stepbrother's defence. 'Chauncy would make a fine husband for any girl.'

'He's the marrying kind, is your Chauncy,' Magnus agreed, then turned to gaze at *Darroch's Pride* with the same sort of expression in his eyes that Chauncy had whenever he glanced at Meg.

As he and Rose went back into the warehouse Rory said with a sly sidelong look, 'Now there's a man who doesn't recognize the right woman when he sees her.'

'You mean Lilias Warner?' Lilias still came regularly to the harbour, although now that the new engine was being fitted Magnus had little enough time for her, or for anyone else.

'No,' said Rory, unabashed. 'I didnae mean her, and you know it. She's not woman enough for the likes of Magnus MacBride.'

Rose tried to quell him with a glance, but Rory, as she well knew, wasn't a man to be easily quelled.

21

By dint of a lot of hard work from every member of the small workforce in the warehouse the sofas and chairs for *Darroch's Folly* were finished two weeks before the boat was due to undergo her trials.

Magnus was delighted with them. 'She's going to have one of the most elegant saloons afloat on the Clyde. You've done a grand job, Rose!'

She flushed with pleasure under his praise. 'It's all thanks to Rory – and Meg. She designed the seat covers and found the women to make them.'

'But you're the one who made it all possible. Did I not tell you that you'd do well in the furniture business? You're like me, Rose Gibb – you're not afraid of a challenge.'

Then he looked down at the carefully detailed account she handed to him, and said thoughtfully, 'Ah.'

'It's not excessive. You'd not get furnishings like that for almost double the price anywhere else.'

'I'm not disputing that for a moment. It's very reasonable – very reasonable indeed. But unfortunately,' said Magnus with his most disarming grin, 'I've no spare capital at the moment.'

'You must have!'

'Well – scarcely any. And the little I do have must be held against an emergency.'

'Magnus –'

'The reboilering cost more than we'd bargained for. And I've found a good captain, so that's another expense –'

'Are you telling me that I'm not going to get my money?'

'Not at all!' said Magnus, shocked. 'I'm going to give you shares in the company instead.'

'I don't want shares!'

'In a year's time they're going to be worth more than this' – he held out the bill.

'I want my money, Magnus!'

He sighed. 'Oh, very well. But I can't give it to you for a wee while.'

'How long?'

'A year and a half, say.'

'A year and a half?' Her voice rose to a squeak of disbelief.

'Mebbe. I'll try for a year.'

'Magnus MacBride! D'you mean to say that I –'

'Come outside. The fresh air'll do you good.' Hurriedly, aware of the interest her raised voice was causing, he took her arm, and led her outside and along the harbour to where *Darroch's Pride* was moored.

'Look at her, Rose.'

'Never mind her – I'm looking at you. And all I'm seeing's a man who told me that the order he gave me would be well worth my while!'

'You're beginning to sound like a harpy,' Magnus said reprovingly.

'I'm sounding like the businesswoman you said I should be! What would you do if folk expected trips in your steamboat for nothing?'

He shuffled his feet like a schoolboy, and grinned placatingly down at her. 'I'd think they showed great good taste wanting to take a trip on my boat and not someone else's. But with the fine saloons I'll have, thanks to you, what other boat would anyone choose?'

'Oh – Magnus!' She could have struck him. He must have seen it in her face, for he stepped back hurriedly and stumbled over a capstan. The sight of him trying to recover his balance would have been funny if she hadn't been so angry.

'I've a good mind to sell off the chairs and sofas and leave you without them!'

Magnus steadied himself and planted his feet securely on the cobbles again. 'Now what sense would there be in that? My passengers would have to stand in the fore deck saloons – and how long is it going to take you to sell off all these chairs?'

He was right. She struggled with her anger for a long moment, then said, 'Very well. Where are the shares?'

He grinned widely, and had taken her in his arms and planted a kiss on her cheek before she realized what he intended. A cheer went up from the men swarming over the steamer as Rose, blushing furiously, pulled away from him.

'I'll have them made over to you and delivered tomorrow. Think of it, Rose – you're part of the Darroch Line now! *Darroch's Pride* is partly yours!'

'Humphh!' But as she looked up at the great ornamented paddle-box, the letter D at its base, Rose felt the anger drop away from her. Magnus might be the most exasperating man she had ever known, but he was right. It was good to know that now she was part of the company that had given new life to *Darroch's Folly*, and turned her into *Darroch's Pride*.

He delivered the shares first thing in the morning then announced, while she was carefully stowing them away, 'I'm going to need Rory now that the boat's completed.'

'But I can't spare him just now!'

'Confound it, woman, I only loaned him to you.'

'You did no such thing. I'm his employer, and I need him.'

'So,' said Magnus, 'do I.' They glared at each other. Rory, delighted to be the bone of contention between them, came bustling from the interior of the warehouse. 'Wheesht, the pair of you – squabbling over a poor old man like two cats that found the same mouse!'

'You're not a poor old man,' Magnus told him crisply. 'You're a valuable asset. And I found you first.'

'But I was the one who gave him work.'

'Now Rose, I said at the time that –'

'Will you wheesht when I tell you! Now,' Rory went on when they lapsed into silence, glaring at each other, 'this is what we'll do. I'll start the days off here in the warehouse, and leave young Malcolm to follow out my instructions while I spend the afternoons with the boat. Will that please you?'

'And what if there's a sale on?'

'I'll go to the sale with you, Mistress. And,' said Rory, forestalling the swift protest forming on Magnus's lips, 'when there's a sale on I'll give the evening to the steamer. Are you agreed?'

Reluctantly, they nodded.

'That's better. I've never in my life,' said Rory as he went back to his glue-pot and the task in hand, 'met two folk more like each other, and less aware of it.'

Darroch's Pride's trials were held one drizzly May morning with Magnus and his new captain, George Urquhart, on her bridge together with the Board of Trade officials.

Rose was on the harbour to witness the moment when the gleaming, oil-slick engines began to thump in their bay and the hard wooden floats started to flicker past the slits in the paddle-box, slowly at first, so that she could count each one, then faster and faster until they became a blur.

A bell tinkled in the engine room and *Darroch's Pride*, under her own power at last, began to back out of her moorings, the water creaming at her stern and beneath the paddle-boxes.

From the bridge wing Magnus watched anxiously as the last thick mooring line splashed into the water and was hauled on to the aft deck and coiled neatly. His dreams and hopes, his future and his good name rested on this day.

Watching him, Rose knew what was going through his mind. The same excitement, the same worries, gripped her. The old paddle-steamer had come to mean more to both of them than anyone else realized.

As though her thoughts had reached out and touched him Magnus suddenly turned and looked down, straight into her eyes. They held each other's gaze for a moment then he nodded slightly and smiled before turning back to watch the stretch of dark water between boat and harbour broadening and lengthening.

Skittishly, getting the feel of her new freedom, the vessel continued to back off until she was well clear of the pilings, then the bell tinkled again and the paddles slowed and stilled.

For a few moments *Darroch's Pride* continued to swing back under her own momentum before the paddles started to revolve the other way, stopping her skid and coaxing her forward.

The wheel was swung over and her bow began to turn to the open water. And at last she was away, turning her stern on the harbour that had been her home for so long, thrusting eagerly through the rain-pocked water, leaving behind a broken, foaming green-silk and white-lace wake.

A steamer coming in on the first run of the day from the Broomielaw in Glasgow gave a skirl of welcome and encouragement on her whistle. *Darroch's Pride* returned the salute and continued on her way upriver to the clear stretch of water off the village of Skelmorlie, where she would do her trial run over a measured distance known as the Skelmorlie Mile.

When she returned in triumph in the early afternoon her siren sounded as she came in to her mooring. From all over the harbour people came flocking to welcome her back and to hear the result. One look at the beaming faces on the bridge told Rose that it was good news.

'Sixteen and a half knots we did!' Magnus came straight to her when he disembarked. Despite the thin, insiduously soaking rain that darkened his tawny hair and plastered it in damp curls to his forehead, his face was alight, the gold flecks in his eyes sparkling. She had never seen him so happy.

'Sixteen and a half,' he exulted, taking her hands in his and gripping them so tightly that the bones protested. But not for all the world would she have let him know that. 'And I'm certain she could have done more, but Urquhart wasn't for it in case her boilers burst. The old lady's never gone so fast in her life!'

Then he composed himself with an effort, and turned to talk to the Board of Trade official who had followed him down the gangplank at a more sedate pace.

The damp weather that had attended the trials cleared away for *Darroch's Pride*'s first official trip two days later. The sun shone down benevolently on the great crowd of people thronging the harbour and trooping up the gangplank.

Breaking with tradition, Magnus declined to fill his vessel with dignitaries for the first trip, and instead invited all those who had supported the new line financially, or worked on the boat, together with their families.

They were all dressed in their best – workers and shareholders alike, a moving, chattering rainbow-coloured mass of people swarming over the decks and overflowing into the saloons.

At first, as had happened at the launch, they tended to divide automatically into two classes on this classless boat, but the great crowd of children present soon made that an impossibility.

Mothers screaming 'Ye wee rascal ye – come here tae me at yince!' and mothers calling 'Don't go too far, dear, and stay away from the rails' were soon united in the common task of looking after all the children collectively. Fathers couldn't help but mix at the observation points by the engines, those who had helped to put them in with their own hands explaining the intricacies of pistons and cylinders to those who had contributed the necessary money.

Bella Gibb ushered aboard a hand-picked group of neighbours and settled them in the forward deck saloon, by the windows where they could get a good view.

Rose, who had invested in a red-and-white-striped full-sleeved blouse, a red skirt, and a straw hat with red ribbons round it for the occasion, left them clucking like a coop full of excited hens and went back on to the deck.

Vans and carts lined the harbour, and hampers were transferred to the steamboat and carried down below to be stowed away. As *Darroch's Pride* didn't have a dining saloon Magnus had hired a field just outside Rothesay on the Isle of Bute, so that he could hold an open-air picnic for his guests.

'I hope the merchants realize that they'll have to wait for their money,' Rose commented when he joined her by the rails. He nodded, unperturbed.

'I told them that. I also told them that when I purchase my next steamer they'll be asked to supply food for the dining saloon. They seemed to be quite agreeable.'

'Your next steamer? Magnus, it's going to take years to get back the money you spent on this one!'

'No it won't. You wait and see.' He was immaculate in a dark blue uniform with a white peaked yachting cap, white shirt and black tie, with not a trace of oil or grime to be seen.

His bearded captain, on the bridge wing above keeping a watchful eye on the comings and goings at the gangplank, was wearing a similar uniform, decorated in his case with gold braid.

Blair Crawford arrived, nodding cheerfully to left and right as he progressed along the harbour. Seeing the two of them at the rails, he waved and came hurrying across the gangplank.

'Is Lilias not coming?' Rose asked.

'Lilias has never been any good on the water,' Magnus said casually. 'She'll not set foot on a boat. Come down below and see how she looks now.'

Blair joined them as they headed for the nearest companionway. Magnus led the way, and Blair insisted on going next. When Rose reached the last few treads both men were waiting with outstretched hands to help her.

'I'm not in my dotage yet, thank you,' she said, and took neither hand.

Under the awed eyes of a group of men and lads who hung over the alleyway rails the engineer and his two-man crew were darting in and out of the great sections of machinery below, industriously and self-consciously polishing metal that was already gleaming.

The filthy lumps of machinery Rose had seen on her first venture below decks had been replaced by an intricate pattern of metal so well oiled that it had a golden sheen to it.

A bell tinkled on the engineer's platform, and the men working on the engines scrambled up a narrow metal stairway to take their places.

'We're about to cast off. Come up to the bridge,' Magnus invited.

Rose shook her head. 'I want to stay down here for a while.'

'Surely you want to see us leaving the pier,' Blair protested.

'I can do that at Rothesay on our way home.'

'I don't understand you, Rose,' he said, torn between staying with her and snatching at the chance to go on to the bridge.

'I do.' Magnus smiled at her; the smile he had tossed to her from the bridge just before he took *Darroch's Pride* out on her trials. 'Are you coming, Blair?'

Blair hesitated. 'I'll stay with you.'

'Go on!' She flapped at him as though he were a hen. 'I'd as soon be on my own.'

He went at last, reluctantly, just as the great engines groaned into life. The piston nearest where Rose stood slowly heaved its powerful bulk up and forward; its head completed a tight anti-clockwise circle then pulled back as its partner moved forward.

Steam hissed briefly, then the second piston completed its circle and the first moved into action again, a little faster. It was like watching a gigantic cyclist pumping the pedals of his cycle round backwards.

Rose flew to the other side of the alleyway and pressed her face to the thick glass of the viewing porthole.

A huge paddle passed by inches from her nose, then another and another. Faster and faster they skimmed by as *Darroch's Pride* backed away from the pier, until they were going too fast to be counted. The underwater-green light in the interior of the paddle-box faded to daylight as the steamer cleared the pier.

The bell rang and the paddles slowed, allowing the steamboat to move back under her own momentum. They stopped completely, as did the pistons behind Rose. Then, at another command from the bridge, the pistons moved into action again, this time in the opposite direction.

Forced round by the engines, the paddles began to move again, at increasing speed. Water first spattered from them, glittering in the sunshine that slanted through the petal-like apertures in the outer covering of the paddle-box, then it was hurled away as they moved faster, flying until the other side of the porthole was streaming, and nothing could be seen except the blur of paddles whirling round, biting into the water, driving *Darroch's Pride* across the Clyde to the Isle of Bute.

22

On deck, almost everyone was crowded at the rails, watching the water breaking at the bows then creaming along the boat's elegant flanks, turning up a swathe of deep green just below the surface, flecked with white foam. Behind them their wake was a ribbon still linking them with Sandyford, which was rapidly falling back into the distance.

Seagulls dipped and soared alongside, screaming for tit-bits. On the upper promenade deck, where every seat was occupied, there was music from an accordion player who had been hired for the summer.

A large paddle-steamer passed by going the opposite way, and *Darroch's Pride*'s passengers crowded to the rails to wave and cheer. The two-funnelled steamer in the black, red, blue and yellow livery was easily recognizable as the *Ivanhoe*, the pride of the Caledonian Steam Packet Company. Her siren boomed out a greeting to the newcomer, and her captain flourished his cap from the bridge.

Magnus, beaming, returned the salute, and soon the *Ivanhoe* was churning her way into the distance astern and *Darroch's Pride* was skirting a flock of white-sailed racing yachts, many of them owned and crewed by the wealthy Glasgow manufacturers who had built magnificent houses for themselves on the shores of the Clyde. These houses could be glimpsed as chimneys and turrets sheltering among shrouding trees on the hillsides.

Rose gave a sigh of contentment. Below her feet *Darroch's Pride*'s new engines throbbed confidently, and around her people jostled and laughed and chattered. Rory and her mother were nowhere to be seen. Bella had announced that she and Miss McKinnon would stay in the forward saloon, where the wind couldn't ruffle their hair.

Rory was probably in the aft saloon with his own cronies, each of them with a glass in his hand. In the midst of the noisy, happy band of seafarers there was only one person who stood alone, leaning on the rail, staring down into the tumbling water. She went to him and touched his arm. 'You're wishing that Meg could have been here.'

Chauncy flushed, then shrugged and admitted, 'I was just thinking – it's not right that she had to miss this. Of all the folk, she's the one that should have been here.'

'I know. But Hannie would have found out if she'd come on the boat.'

'I'll have to talk to the man,' he said fiercely. 'I can't bear to go on like this, not able to walk the town with Meg on my arm in case that old rascal of a father of hers should hear about it. I'll have to go to him!'

Then he sighed, and shook his head. 'But she says that if I do, she'll have no more to do with me. You'd think she'd want to be free of him!'

Rose thought of the secret treasure cave that was Hannie's home, and of the greatest treasure of all, guarding it for him, sharing his secret.

'He's her father. It's hard to break a lifetime's habit.'

'You did it. You've broken away from everything, and I admire you for it.'

'I went away, to South Africa. It's easier to look at things from a distance. And being away changes folk a lot.'

'I love her, Rose,' said Chauncy wretchedly, his eyes on the surging green-white water below. 'It's breaking me in two. I never thought that loving someone could hurt so much.'

Her heart ached for him. Chauncy deserved happiness, but could find it only with the one girl in town who was denied to him, and to every other man.

'Escort me up to the bridge,' she said firmly, linking

her arm in his, and he dragged himself away from the railing, and from his own private misery, and did as he was told.

From the water, Rothesay pier was as busy as a piece of honeycomb seething with bees. As *Darroch's Pride* drew near the bees resolved themselves into people, disembarking from or crowding on to the three steamers already berthed.

The Isle of Bute was one of the most popular areas with the Glasgow people, who rated trips doon the watter from the Broomielaw in the heart of the city to the mouth of the Clyde and its islands as their favourite leisure-time activity in the summer.

Darroch's Pride had to hold off for ten minutes before one of the steamers came churning out, made shapelessly squat and clumsy by the bulge of her paddle-boxes as she came towards them, then suddenly, miraculously, streamlined and graceful as she passed by and they saw her from the side. Her decks were thronged and as she went by music from a small band on her after deck mingled with the strains of the accordion still playing on the deck below the bridge of *Darroch's Pride*.

Rose was on the bridge to see the steamer brought in to the pier. From her vantage point on one wing, just behind the slender funnel, she looked down on the forward promenade deck, awash with parasols and pretty hats.

Captain Urquhart brought the steamer in to her berth as sweetly as a loving hand might brush a baby's cheek. There was a scattered burst of applause from the crowd who had gathered on the pier to watch the new line's flagship make her first arrival at the island.

'Magnus, look!' Rose caught at his arm. 'There's Mr Finlay.'

The man who had scoffed at Magnus when he first spoke of his plans in the drawing room of Crawford

House was standing at the back of the crowd, eyes locked on the boat that had just come in.

At sight of him Magnus doffed his cap and bowed low, winning another round of amused applause. His face, as he straightened, glowed with pride in his vessel, and in his captain.

Mr Finlay acknowledged the salute with a slight, stiff nod of the head, and marched off along to the other end of the pier, where one of his own boats, *Island Princess*, was loading passengers.

A row of carts and traps waited on the pier for the Sandyford party. The hampers and crates were transferred to some of the carts by a willing chain of shirtsleeved and waistcoated men while their womenfolk and children settled themselves into the other vehicles.

Then with a farewell toot on the siren *Darroch's Pride* left the busy pier and went off to circle the island and give her crew the opportunity to become more used to handling her, while Magnus and his guests enjoyed their picnic.

When they returned to the pier three hours later the steamer was waiting for them. Children who had sped down the gangway like young colts were carried back up, half asleep and worn out by food, fresh air and exercise. Rory, his face sunburned until it glowed like a lamp, approached it with the help of two friends, both of them as inebriated as he was himself.

Rose watched, her heart in her mouth, as the three of them missed the narrow wooden ramp and began to head perilously close to the water's edge.

Chauncy jumped forward and led them away from the danger, but it took several tries before the three men managed to thread themselves on to the railed passageway and staggered up it, with Rory clutching tightly at the rails and complaining loudly, 'The bugger'll no' stay still!'

Bella, already on board and on her way back to the saloon, her little group of followers in tow, tutted loudly and glared. Miss McKinnon, who had been persuaded to take a glass of port after her meal, and had then sampled at least another two without persuasion, hiccuped, clapped a gloved hand to her mouth in haste, and peeped, round-eyed, over the tips of her crocheted fingers to see if anyone had noticed.

They left Rothesay in style, with the accordion blaring, the folk on the pier cheering, the passengers flourishing caps, parasols and babies in an ecstasy of delight.

On the bridge, Rose and Blair and Magnus beamed at each other. There was no denying it – *Darroch's Pride*'s maiden voyage had been an outstanding success.

From Rothesay Bay the steamer skirted Toward Point, a finger of mainland that stretched out from the opposite shore to Sandyford.

They had just cleared the point and were entering the open stretch of water that would take them back home when George Urquhart touched Magnus's arm. 'Look yonder, Mr MacBride.'

All heads turned to see a steamer following them from Toward Point, curving round to come parallel with them.

'By God, it's Finlay's boat – *Island Princess*.' Blair studied the oncoming boat, his brows knotted. 'I thought she'd be well out of the area by now.'

'She should have been at Gourock thirty minutes since,' Magnus told him. 'She's been hiding behind the point, waiting for us.'

'Why?'

'Because,' Magnus explained to Rose as though she were a child, 'Finlay wants to force us to race. Urquhart, ring down for more speed.'

'You can't race him just now – this is only your maiden trip.'

'It's unsporting of him to take you unawares like this, before you've got the measure of your vessel,' Blair agreed, but there was a sparkle in his eyes as he watched the other steamer come on.

'Blair's right. You've got every right to ignore him, Magnus.'

'Ignore him be damned!' said Magnus as *Darroch's Pride* began to surge faster through the water. Below the bridge people were beginning to throng the rails, looking back at the boat that was gaining on them. 'If he wants a race, he'll have it!'

'Are you insane?'

'I wagered the man. You were there at the time, Rose.'

'But you can't win against the *Island Princess*!'

'She can get up to eighteen knots,' George Urquhart chipped in, gnawing on the ends of his moustache. But Rose was alarmed to see that he, too, had a gleam in his eye.

'If we can't better him, at least we'll give him a race he'll remember,' said Magnus. 'We're in for a fast trip home.'

If Finlay and his captain had expected to reach and pass *Darroch's Pride* within a few minutes they were disappointed. As they began to get close enough to snap at her heels the steady thump of the smaller and older steamer's engines increased to a faster, and then a frenzied, beat.

Egged on by the promise of an additional bonus, the sweating stokers in their tiny space by the engines hurled coal into the furnaces. Every pound of steam that could be summoned was forced into action. The ladies on deck found their parasols bucking in the wind and the sea hissed as the steamer raced through it, paddles beating it to a froth.

Rory and his friends spilled out of the saloon bar, demanding to know what was going on. When they spotted the *Island Princess* clinging tenaciously to *Darroch's Pride*'s wake they started to scrabble through their pockets for the price of a wager.

'Take the children into the saloons!' Magnus ordered

through a megaphone, and there was a great rush for cover. Passengers who had set out on a pleasant excursion lurched and staggered as the steamer began to quiver like a dog held back when it ached to spring.

Bella Gibb came storming out of the forward saloon, and was almost bowled over by a crowd of mothers trying to get their small children in through the same door. Miss McKinnon followed her, spinning out of the door as the racing boat bucked and into the arms of a brawny man who, fortunately for her, was at the rails.

One glance to starboard, where the *Island Princess* was now drawing level, told Bella what was happening.

'Magnus MacBride, you mad fool,' she screamed up at the bridge. 'What d'you think you're up to now?'

Magnus leaned precariously over the bridge rail. 'Racing, Mrs Gibb!'

'Then you can just stop it right here and now and not humiliate me in front of all those folk!' she screeched in return, head tilted so far back to look up at him that the wind caught her hat and had half dislodged it before she grabbed at it. By her side Miss McKinnon, clutching at her friend's arm, was gaping up at the bridge in terror.

'It's a matter of honour, Mrs Gibb!' Magnus bellowed, and she shook her fist at him. Miss McKinnon, shaken off, reeled away, and Bella snatched at her and caught her just in time.

The steamers were running in tandem now, lashing up the water and leaving tumbling wakes behind. As *Darroch's Pride* began to tremble in earnest Rose held on for dear life and wondered if the passengers on the other boat were in as much disarray as the people below her.

'They're gaining on us – they're getting the better of us,' George Urquhart yelled.

Magnus shook his head. He was hatless now, and his dark gold hair was whipping about his square face. 'No quarter given, man – keep after them!'

'Fifty pounds says this old lady can do it!' Blair

bellowed. Magnus turned and grinned at him, a white-toothed, almost savage grin.

'Be damned to what your fifty pounds has to say – *I* say she can do it!'

'Come on, *Darroch's Pride*!' Rory's voice rose from the tumult of sound below. Looking down, Rose saw him dancing about with excitement, raising both fists to shake them above his head. His mouth was a great cavern in his red, sun-baked face.

As she watched, the boat lurched and he tumbled backwards, into the arms of two of his friends. Befuddled by drink, they collapsed under him, and the tangle of legs and arms rolled against the bulkhead, mercifully away from the railing that guarded the drop to the sea.

Her own hat blew off. She made a grab for it, but it had gone, skipping down to the alleyway at the side of the forward saloon, then through the rail. Her last sight of it showed it floating to the water, the red ribbons fluttering bravely.

Then to her great relief she saw the shoreline coming towards them swiftly, and realized that the race was almost over.

As the *Island Princess* began to draw in front a great blast of noise from the funnel sent Rose flying for shelter into Magnus's arms.

'What was that?' Her voice was underlined by a shrill chorus of female squeals from below.

He set her on her feet again. 'We're only blowing off the excess steam.'

Then she was forgotten as he leaned over the rail again, straining his eyes towards Finlay's vessel, by now drawing ahead and fast closing with the pier.

'We've lost!' Blair's voice was sharp with bitter disappointment.

'Not,' said Magnus grimly, 'until the last moment. Keep her on course, Urquhart.'

The captain snapped an order to the helmsman, spoke

into the tube connecting bridge and engine room, and eyed his employer uneasily as the *Island Princess* gained a clear lead and began to take the turn that would bring her in west of the pier.

Then, and only then, as his rival's wake showed a clear change of direction, did Magnus MacBride concede defeat.

'Slow engines,' he said crisply. 'Bring her round and set her in neatly, Urquhart. At least we'll arrive in style.'

Shoulders slumped, he walked to the end of the wing and slammed an angry fist on the rail. After a moment he turned back to face his guests, the familiar grin breaking out again.

'There's always another day. And if Finlay –' Then he broke off, the grin disappearing as, despite the frantic ringing of the telegraph, *Darroch's Pride* continued to plough through the water.

'Urquhart – slow engines, man. Are you deaf?'

George Urquhart, his ear jammed against the speaking tube, looked up. 'The engines are jammed at dead centre.' He spun round and bellowed a series of instructions at the man who gripped the wheel.

Darroch's Pride continued to head towards the pier at a frightening rate. To Rose, gripping the bridge rail so tightly that her hands were numbed, it looked as though Sandyford harbour and the warehouse were rushing out to meet the boat.

Then as the helmsman dragged on the wheel the steamer began to turn her flank to the shore, a move that checked the headlong dash and turned it into a sideways skid.

They were so close to the pier that Rose could make out the sheer panic on the faces of the people standing there, saw some of them begin to edge backwards, away from the boat bearing down on them.

The sideways skid began to lose momentum. The telegraph rang from the engine room.

'She's freed herself!' Magnus yelled, and his captain shouted back, 'But too late!' as the vibration under their feet slowed and stopped.

'Astern, man – astern!' Urquhart screamed into the tube. The pistons began to beat again, using their great might to rein in the vessel's headlong dash, shuddering her to a reluctant stop.

It happened almost in time to save them, but not quite. They were too near the pier. The slow exodus of onlookers from the edge of the harbour turned into a rush for safety, with people scattering like flies.

A string of oaths that Rose had never heard before, even from wounded and delirious soldiers in South Africa, ripped their way out of Magnus's throat. He spun round, plucked her from the railing, and tossed her into Blair's arms.

'Look after her,' he said. Then, as Blair wedged her into a corner and placed himself in front of her as a barrier, Magnus snatched up the megaphone and roared at the rest of his mesmerized passengers, 'Hold on! We're going to collide!'

Then he himself was pitched across the bridge, flying past Rose and Blair in a whirl of arms and legs, as *Darroch's Pride*, already beginning to back out of danger, collided with the wooden pilings of the pier.

There was a crunching, screeching noise, and a great clamour of screams and yells from the decks. A fountain of wood chips fanned through the air as the boat lurched from the shock then began to pull back, grinding along the edge of the pier.

At another swift order from George Urquhart the engines stopped and *Darroch's Pride* came to a standstill just as Magnus picked himself up.

'Well,' he said. 'We almost made it.'

Then he peered over the edge of the bridge on to the promenade deck and found himself looking down on a collection of kicking black-stockinged legs, and a wide range of bloomers and petticoats.

23

'I've never been so embarrassed in all my life, Magnus MacBride,' Bella raged when Magnus and Chauncy came home that evening. 'Shown up in front of all my friends like that!'

He let the words rain down on his broad shoulders, then shrugged them off. 'Now Mrs Gibb, you must admit that it was an exciting ending to her first trip.'

'Exciting, is it?' Her voice soared up the scale. 'The whole lot of us arse over tip with our legs up in the air like a lot of strumpety music-hall dancers, and everyone on the pier having a good look? I'll never be able to hold my head up again!'

Chauncy hurriedly busied himself with the kettle, filling a bowl with warm water so that he could wash himself. Magnus's lips twitched, and Rose, who had heard it all over and over again while she and her mother waited for the culprits to come home, bent her head over the sock she was darning.

'I don't think the folk on the pier did have a good look, Mrs Gibb,' said Magnus, keeping his voice level with an effort. 'They were all too busy taking shelter in case we took the whole place into the river with us.'

'It's a wonder you didn't!'

'We might have, if the engines hadn't released in time. But there's no great harm done. I'll have a starting engine installed to make sure they don't jam again, and the pier's had worse bumps in the winter storms. All the old lady needs is a lick of paint where she rubbed against the pilings, and –'

'And what about Miss McKinnon?' Bella wanted to know. 'Frightened half to death – and when she opened her mouth to scream, didn't her teeth fall out of her mouth and go over the side?'

Chauncy, drying his face, gave a muffled cough into the towel and hunched his shoulders, keeping his back turned to his irate mother. Peering up from her darning, Rose saw Magnus's features shimmering and disintegrating for a moment before, with a great effort, he controlled them.

'Tell Miss McKinnon I'd be happy to pay for – for whatever medical attention she may need.'

'I should think you would, my lad! Now – you'd best sit down and have your supper. Rose, give me a hand here.' She began to set the table for the evening meal, adding as she worked, 'I doubt if anyone's going to go near your boat again after this. I know Miss McKinnon won't, for one.'

Magnus took off his jacket, unfastened his shirt cuffs, and poured water into the bowl that Chauncy had just emptied. 'I doubt that,' he said easily. 'Folk like a boat with a bit of spirit to it. And nobody can deny after today that *Darroch's Pride* has spirit.'

He was right. By the morning the whole town and most of the coastline knew about the race and its outcome. Mr Finlay woke to find himself adversely cricitized for having forced the agreed race on Magnus without due warning and arrangement, and for having used his largest and fastest vessel in an attempt to discredit the newcomer.

Magnus, on the other hand, was commended for his courage and determination. When the boat went into service several days later, on a regular short run between Sandyford and Rothesay, the passengers flocked on board. In the week after the race no less than three associations came forward to charter her for special outings, to Magnus's delight. Charters brought in more money than regular trips.

Rory was treated to free drinks in every public house in the town in return for his story of what it had been like to be on board *Darroch's Pride* during the race, and even Miss McKinnon, when she eventually became the proud owner of a new set of dentures, just as large as the previous set, but slightly better-fitting, began to look on the trip as a privileged adventure.

'It was well worth losing fifty pounds,' Blair said enthusiastically. 'What a race! We gave Finlay a run for his money.'

'Next time it'll be a different story,' Magnus assured him. 'Next time I'll decide when and where, and I'll have a faster boat by then, so he'll have to look to his laurels.'

'Magnus, by the time you can afford a faster boat,' Rose pointed out, 'Mr Finlay'll be retired.'

They were all sitting round Bella's kitchen table. Blair had taken to dropping in now and again, much to Bella's delight.

'Have you no faith? I'll have a second boat by the beginning of next summer – I must have it by then if I'm to develop the Darroch Line.'

'How can you afford it?'

'By being careful with the money *Darroch's Pride* is bringing in now. It'll be a while before I can commission a boat, like Finlay – but there are always folk willing to sell for the right price. All I have to do is keep my eyes open for the boat I need.'

Bella shook her head. 'If you ask me, Magnus MacBride, you're getting above yourself.'

'Not me.'

'Oh aye? Mark my words' – she stabbed at the table with a finger for emphasis – 'you'll be the talk of the town before this summer's out, the way you're going. The talk of the town!'

But her forecast was wrong. It was to be her own son-in-law, not her lodger, who was to be the talk of the town.

*

Although the gardens of Crawford House flourished above the town, summer brought its problems to the people huddled in the slum area down below.

A predominantly wet winter had led to an increase in the lung conditions that plagued the poorer townsfolk, and the beginning of July brought in an epidemic of measles that set Leila into a panic in case her precious little Charlotte should take ill.

'She's a healthy baby, and well cared for – there's no reason why she should fall ill. Who would she catch it from?' Rose asked reasonably.

Leila clutched the baby to her. 'There's Daniel – visiting the sick children in their houses. He could bring the disease back and infect Charlotte. But does he care about his own daughter? All he can think about is other folk's children!'

'Is the outbreak bad, then?'

'So he and Doctor Anderson think. But you know Daniel,' said his wife resentfully, 'always more concerned about other families than his own.'

The next day Meg confirmed what Leila had said. 'Atholl Row's over-run with the sickness. Those poor wee souls – Atholl Row's where all the diseases start. Doctor Anderson's working day and night there to try to help them. And so's Mr Currie.'

'He's a decent-hearted soul – for a schoolmaster,' put in Rory, who was listening with interest.

Rose remembered the day the doctor had come looking for her to offer her work. 'Rory, could you manage on your own for a day or two?'

'Aye, nae bother.' He eyed her with mild curiosity. 'Is there somewhere else you have to go?'

'There is,' said Rose. 'I think it's time I went back to nursing. At least – until the measles epidemic's over.'

As she came out from under the railway bridge and

crossed Atholl Row a flat-bed cart clattered by her, carrying a small, roughly made coffin. Two men stood at a close-mouth watching the cart move away from them.

One of them started running after it. When he reached it he put out a hand and laid it protectively on the coffin, then slowed to a walk and kept pace with the vehicle, his face bitter and hard and withdrawn.

He wore shabby dirty clothes; the man who stayed at the close-mouth was well dressed, but the expression on his face was no less bitter. It changed as his eyes landed on Rose.

'What are you doing here?' he wanted to know as soon as she reached him. It was the close-mouth, she remembered, that he had been coming out of the day she visited Meg Simpson.

'I've just heard about the epidemic. I didn't know it was so bad –'

Daniel's mouth twisted. 'Nobody ever knows what's going on in this part of the town. Nobody cares; but they'll have to, this time, for the disease is out of control. The school's had to be closed. There was scarce a child in my classroom, and those that came were already sickening.'

'Where's Doctor Anderson?'

He jerked his head to indicate the building behind him. His eyes were shadowed; he looked exhausted. 'In there. The child that was taken away just now died last night, but nobody would come and remove her. The parents put her on top of the chest of drawers because two of the others are sick and they could scarcely share the bed with a corpse. I'd to see to it myself today.'

He added with disgust, 'It's wonderful how a bit of authority can make folk aware of their bounden duty. Agnes is with the other children now.'

'You should go home and rest, Daniel.'

He summoned up a faint smile. 'Home? I can't go home – Leila's out of her wits with fear in case I infect

Charlotte. There's a widow-woman called Jinty in one of the houses – she's given me a bed to use when I've the time to sleep.'

Then he added in a burst of angry helplessness, 'Nobody cares about them, Rose! These folk are just left to live or die as Fate pleases.'

'What about the infirmary?'

'It could only take the first dozen cases. The rest must be nursed at home – where's there's no room, and others to sicken after them.'

She brushed past him and went into the building. The foetid smell and the chill of the place hit her before she had gone three steps into the narrow passageway.

The steps to the upper floors were so worn that they almost merged into each other in the middle. Rose prudently went up one side, holding on to the slimy wall to guide herself. Daniel, more sure-footed in this place than she was, guided her with a hand under her elbow.

'It's the first door.'

The single-roomed apartment, no larger than the flat Mr Kenway had inhabited, was cold and sparsely furnished. A woman who looked middle-aged, but was probably still in her twenties, huddled by the unlit fire, rocking a small baby in her arms. Another woman, plump and red-haired, was talking to her soothingly.

Agnes Anderson, as weary as ever, as indomitable as ever, was bent over the wall-bed where two small tousled heads tossed on a ragged pillow. She looked up as Rose and Daniel came in.

'What brings you here?'

'I've come to help.'

'You know what to do?'

'Yes.'

'Number ten, two closes down from here – a family called Kennedy on the second floor. All the children have sickened,' Agnes said. 'Take what you need from my bag. I'll be at your back as soon as I can be spared from here.'

'I'll show her where it is,' Daniel offered.

As she foraged in the huge shabby bag Rose heard the red-haired woman say soothingly, 'Give him to me, Mary. I'll take him into my house for a while and let you tend to the others. He'll be fine with his Auntie Jinty, won't you, my wee mannie?'

'She's distracted with grief, poor soul,' the woman said, low-voiced, to Rose as they left the house with Daniel. 'The bairn that died was her first-born, and her favourite if the truth be told. Best to get the littlest out of the way before he takes the sickness himself.'

She bent her head protectively over the mewling baby in her arms. Her round face, out of place in this area where most of the folk looked gaunt and drawn, was soft with maternal love.

'Is your own family free of the measles?'

'Jinty has no family,' Daniel said, and the woman cast him a fleeting smile.

'I'm on my own, pet. My man was killed in the mines before we were wed a month, and left me childless.'

She disappeared through another door on the landing.

'She's a good neighbour.'

'I don't know what we'd all have done without her,' said Daniel. 'Come on.'

She followed him, groping her way down the treacherous stairs to the close and out into the street, where she drew in several deep breaths before plunging into the Kennedys' close.

During the following two weeks day blended into night and minutes and hours lost all meaning. In almost every house in Atholl Row Rose found the same story – bleak-eyed parents old before their time, men with lungs tortured by coal dust, undernourished children, most of them barking and sneezing with the onset of measles, or with their normally pale little faces already aflame with the rash.

Scarcely a child in the street escaped from the pestilence. In most houses there were three or four or five youngsters in the one bed, each at a different stage of the illness.

Doctor Budge, the town's senior doctor, came to see the situation for himself. A meeting was held in red-headed Jinty's house, almost the only flat that was free of the disease.

'How can anyone fight an epidemic properly in this street?' Agnes Anderson wanted to know, her voice hard with frustration. 'How can we disinfect rooms with sick children still in them? The town should be ashamed of these buildings!'

Budge, a gentle-faced grandfatherly man, nodded his agreement. 'I'll have carbolic given out to every household immediately, to be sprinkled on the floors. But full-scale disinfection's impossible, given the situation.'

'If the town had the sanitary officer it's been promised for the past year things might improve.'

'I'll put the matter before the Council at their next meeting, Agnes.'

'Again,' said Daniel.

'Again,' the doctor agreed. 'Councillors can take a long time to make up their minds.'

'Tell them,' Agnes suggested, 'that if they don't make their minds up this time, there'll be a revolution on their hands. And I'll be leading it!'

Leila, blind to the fate of any child other than Charlotte, fumed over what she saw as Daniel's desertion. Bella, unable to be of much practical use because of her rheumatism, sent Chauncy with baskets of food that she herself could ill afford.

When Rose went home to have a longed-for bath and a rest between clean sheets, Bella said tartly, 'Isn't it enough that Daniel's staying away from his home, without you doing it as well? You've done your share, surely! If you've any sense you'll keep out of it from now on.'

'Not until the epidemic's over,' Rose said grimly, dragging the tin bath out of the kitchen cupboard and emptying pot after pot of boiling water from the range into it. Then she added a bucket or two of cold water, tested the temperature, and began to strip off her clothes.

'Rose, see sense!'

'You're the one that wanted me to work with Doctor Anderson, Mam. Now I'm doing it; and I'll stay with her until she's no more need of me.'

In answer Bella gave a sudden shriek of horror. 'My God, lassie – what's that on your arm?'

Rose twisted her head to look at the red mark marring the creamy smoothness of her shoulder.

'A flea bite!' Bella said, appalled. 'Watch where you put those clothes!' She hurried to fetch brown paper to spread over the floor.

'Drop everything on there,' she instructed, then flew into the hall as fast as her stiff joints could take her and reappeared with the bucket she kept for washing the stairs and the wooden tongs that were used to push clothes into the big wash-tub in the back-yard wash-house.

'Fleas – in my house!' she moaned as she picked up each garment with the tongs and crammed it into the bucket. 'There's never been fleas in my house – never!'

'That's because they all live in Atholl Row.' Rose, naked, stepped into the tub and let herself slide down into the deliciously hot water. Her mother handed her a cake of yellow soap and a rough cloth.

'You scrub yourself good and well – I'm away to put this lot into the wash-tub, then I'm coming back to give your head a proper going over. I've no doubt that it's alive with lice!'

'No doubt,' Rose agreed, and Bella gave a scandalized gasp, then stumped out of the kitchen.

*

It was bliss to scrub every inch of her skin until it tingled and glowed, then to sit near the range, combing her long silky hair until it was almost dry. It was bliss to crawl thankfully into her own bed and fall into a sound sleep.

She woke to daylight, and to the sight of Magnus MacBride standing by the bed, a mug of steaming tea in his hand.

'Your mother's gone in to see Miss McKinnon,' he said as Rose blinked up at him in sleepy wonder. 'She says you're not to be wakened, but I thought you'd like to know that it's nine o'clock.'

'What?' She sat up in horror. 'I should be in Atholl Row by now! Mam should have wakened me!'

'That's what I thought.' He sat on the edge of the bed and offered her the mug, then grinned as the hands reaching for it suddenly retreated and snatched at the sheet. 'I've seen women in bed before.'

'No doubt you have, but not this woman.'

His eyes rested on the high neck and long sleeves of her nightgown. 'You're very well covered. Drink your tea while it's hot.'

He smelled of outdoors, of fresh air and sea-salty air. He looked healthy and strong, free of the sickly misery she had become used to. Over the rim of the cup she let her eyes feast on him, drawing strength from his strength to fortify her for the day ahead.

'Is it bad?'

She nodded. 'You've never seen such poor souls, Magnus.'

'I expect I have. Every country has its poverty, some worse than others. Britain's mebbe better at hiding hers from sight – tidying it away.'

'Two babies died yesterday. If it wasn't for Doctor Anderson –'

'You've been doing your share.'

'So has Daniel. I never knew he'd so much caring in

him.' Her fingers tightened on the mug. 'But what's the point of just fighting the diseases in a place like Atholl Row? These slums are breeding grounds. They should be torn down.'

'And then where would the people live?'

'New housing should be built for them.'

'And who's to do that?' Magnus asked with maddening reasonableness.

'The landlords, of course! They're the ones taking the rent for those hovels in the first place. They should put the money to good use instead of lining their own pockets with it.'

'D'you know who the Atholl Row landlords are?' Magnus asked mildly.

'I can find out.'

'It's not worth it, Rose. As I said, every country has its poor and its oppressed. It's the way of the world.'

'Easy enough to say when you've got a roof over your head and warm clothing and food in your belly!'

To her astonishment he grinned. 'The singer with the sword in the attic again. You know, Rose, you look your best when you're in a rage –'

He reached out and took a handful of the long dark hair that hung loose about her shoulders, the backs of his fingers brushing against her skin as he did so. 'And when your hair's down and your eyes are huge and soft with sleep –' he added, allowing his body to sway slightly towards her.

She clutched the empty mug in both hands, holding it before her breasts like a shield. 'Go away, Magnus, and let me get dressed,' she commanded, her voice trembling slightly.

For a moment she thought that he was going to defy her. His breath skimmed her lips, his eyes moved from feature to feature, intently studying her brows, her hairline, her nose and mouth and chin. Then he laughed, shrugged, and got up.

'Aye, you'd best be off before your mother comes back,' he advised, and went out.

The outer door opened and closed and his footsteps clattered their way down the first flight of stairs. She felt relieved at his going – and at the same time, offended he hadn't stayed.

24

The measles epidemic ended as suddenly as it had arrived.

Thirty-three children had taken measles, twenty-two of them in Atholl Row, the rest within a half-mile radius. Five children under school age had died, as well as two in their first year at school. All the dead children came from Atholl Row.

'I'm grateful to you, Rose. You did a fine job.' Agnes Anderson's handshake was like the woman herself – firm, sincere and brief.

'If I can help you again, I will.'

'You can – if you really mean it,' Agnes said promptly. 'I know you've got other fish to fry now, but if I could have your assistance two days a week I'd be grateful.'

Having witnessed the woman's tireless devotion to her work it was difficult to deny her anything.

'What would you want me to do?'

'Just visit the folk here and in the streets round about. Visit as a friend, and advise them when they need it. Let me know if there's anything I should be seeing to. I'd as soon prevent trouble before it happens than have to clean up the mess when it's too late.'

'Two days a week, bringing back fleas and God knows what!' Bella fretted when she heard the news.

'It was only the one flea. If it bothers you as much as all that I'll find lodgings in the town.'

'You will not! I'll not have the neighbours thinking I put you out. Anyway,' Bella added self-righteously, 'if I don't keep an eye on you the dear Lord only knows what you'll be up to next.'

Daniel and Agnes drew up a petition and took it along

to the Town Council. They came to the Gibb house from the meeting in a dejected mood.

'We're going to get a sanitary officer, so that's one step in the right direction,' Daniel admitted. 'But the Council doesn't own the buildings in that part of the town, so they can do nothing.'

'They don't want to do anything, you mean,' Agnes corrected him.

'Can they not force the landlords to do something?'

'That would be too much trouble altogether,' Agnes said crisply. 'Besides, they've no wish to step on anyone's toes. Half of the Council are High Kirk elders, and we all know that the High Kirk wants land gifted for its new hall. No sense in making an enemy out of the goose that lays the golden egg.'

Rose tried to make sense of that statement, and failed. 'What has the land for the High Kirk hall to do with Atholl Row?'

'D'you not know? The Crawfords have promised to give land for the kirk hall, and it's the Crawfords who're the landlords in Atholl Row. Every building but Hannie Simpson's.'

'What?' Rose looked up, shocked.

Magnus, watching her, raised an eyebrow, then shrugged.

The shrug said: I told you it was no use.

Blair was alone in his office when Rose arrived. As always, his face lit up at the sight of her.

'Rose! I've missed you.'

She shook her head as he indicated the seat opposite him. 'D'you have an hour to spare? I want to show you something.'

Intrigued, he reached for his hat and stick. 'Do we need the carriage?'

'No,' said Rose. 'I don't think we do.'

*

A group of children playing in the gutter looked up inquisitively as they heard the tap of Blair's walking stick on the cobbles. Two women gossiping at a close-mouth fell silent and watched them go by, their faces closed and suspicious, as Rose led her companion across the cobbles and into the next close.

'Good God!' said Blair Crawford as the stench hit him. 'Rose –'

She ignored him, and he had no option but to follow her past the worn shabby stairs leading to the upper floor and out into the back court, a small area piled with rubble and refuse.

A child's perambulator, ragged and with one wheel buckled, had been abandoned in a corner. The wash-house door hung askew on its hinges; a glimpse inside showed that the ceiling had collapsed and the place was unusable. A mangle stood in another corner, beside an old mattress. The ground was uneven, and littered with bricks with a puddle of stagnant water here and there.

Blair hurriedly groped for a handkerchief and held it to his nose. 'What are we doing here?'

'I thought you might like to see it, since you own it.'

Understanding dawned in his eyes. 'You mean – my father owns it.'

'You'll inherit it one day. This is where I've been for the past two weeks, Blair. This is where I've been helping to fight the measles epidemic. Your factor collects rent from the poor souls who live here. The Council can't do anything – or won't, because they're afraid of annoying the Crawfords.'

'And you think that I can put everything right? Obviously you don't know what my father's really like – or my grandmother, for that matter. They pay little heed to me.'

'You can surely try!'

'There's another way of going about it,' Blair said slowly. 'You could marry me.'

'Blair, be serious!'

'I am being serious. You could do a lot to help these people if you were my wife.'

'That's impossible!'

'Why?' asked Blair.

'For one thing, your father wouldn't want you marrying someone from the town – a woman whose brother works for the Crawfords.'

'My father likes you. I don't think he'd stand in our way. Anyway, be damned to what he thinks. I love you, Rose,' said Blair earnestly, standing before her in the small, dirty back court. 'I love you, and I need you. Marry me!'

'No.'

His eyes darkened. 'Is it MacBride? If so, you might as well put him out of your mind. He's not the marrying kind – if he was, Lilias would have led him to the altar by now.'

She felt herself flushing angrily. 'It's nothing to do with Magnus. Can you not see that there's no future for you and me and leave it at that?'

There was a pause before he said, 'No, I'll not leave it at that. I'll keep on asking until you give me the answer I want.' Then as she began to speak he held up a hand. 'And in the meantime I'll talk to my father about this place. Will that please you?'

'Yes.'

'Consider it done,' he said. 'And now – for God's sake can we get out of here?'

Daniel Currie left his wife and child one beautiful late August evening when the waters of the Clyde were calm as a millpond beneath the placid grey-blue sky, and the Isle of Bute and the Cumbraes to the west were outlined in orange flames as the sun sank behind them.

After finishing for the day in the warehouse Rose had

lingered on the harbour to watch the sunset, and to see *Darroch's Pride* return from her last trip of the day.

The boat came towards her from the fiery glow of the sky, a squat dark shape at first, dim against the flaring vivid colour. Then Rose picked out the smoke pluming from the single funnel, and the funnel itself, a slim pencil line against the sky.

As she drew nearer the water could be seen breaking on her bow and curling back in two wings to form a widening V-shaped train to the sides.

The cry of her attendant seagulls and the regular, steady beat of her engines came to Rose, carried across the water on the still air. There was a skirl of music from the accordionist, and the shrill cheep of the siren as *Dannoch's Pride* neared her home.

The boat was close enough now for her to hear the telegraph ringing, and the swish of water along her sides as *Darroch's Pride* swept by the pier, then began to move back towards her mooring as the engines went into reverse.

Magnus, in his usual place at the edge of the starboard wing, took off his cap and flourished it as he recognized Rose standing there. The sinking sun haloed his bared head, picking up the russet lights in it until it looked as though he, like the sky, was afire.

The steamer edged delicately against the pilings, Captain Urquhart's sharp eyes noting the exact moment when the engines should stop, allowing the boat to drift into her berth with the gentlest of bumps against the pier.

Then the gangway was run into place and the passengers filed ashore; sun-kissed, contented, tired, children lolling against adult shoulders or being trailed like puppies at the end of long paternal arms. Lovers squeezed their way down the gangplank with arms wrapped round each other, wives slipped their hands into the crooks of husbands' elbows.

Above them all, looking down on them like a benevolent god, Magnus unbuttoned his jacket and loosened his tie, duty done for another day.

Rose wondered, as she made her way home, if Magnus ever gave a thought to Lilias Warner, who had been in the Borders for the past month, visiting her late husband's family. Probably not, she decided as she went into the familiar close. At the moment he was so absorbed in his work that nothing else mattered to him.

Unlike Lilias, Rose was content to wait on the sidelines, and let time settle things. She had no doubt that it would.

She opened the door to the sound of Leila sobbing, and Charlotte yelling in sympathy.

Bella was pacing the kitchen, the weeping baby tucked into the crook of her arm. Leila was huddled in the armchair by the range, her pretty face swollen and distorted by grief. In one hand she clutched a sodden handkerchief.

'Rose, thank heavens you've come home at last. Hold her, for any favour.' Bella pushed the baby into her elder daughter's arms and sank down on a chair at the table.

'What's wrong?'

'Don't you come the innocent miss with me,' Leila stormed, struggling to get out of the chair. 'You knew. You knew about Daniel all the time!'

'Knew what? Is he ill?'

'Ill?' Leila gave a bark of mirthless laughter. A large tear trembled on the edge of her chin and she scrubbed it away.

Bella prised the damp wad from her daughter's hand and offered a clean handkerchief in its place.

'My God, I wish he was ill! He's left me, that's what he's done. Run away with some slut from Atholl Row!'

A series of pictures flooded Rose's memory. Daniel's face when he stepped from a close-mouth in Atholl Row and turned to see his sister-in-law and Magnus

MacBride walking towards him. Jinty, the buxom young widow who had let Daniel sleep in her house when his wife refused to let him come home, smiling faintly at Daniel over the head of the baby in her arms.

Jinty, pretty and red-haired and warm and affectionate.

Jinty, who certainly knew, unlike Leila, how to make a man feel like a man.

'How could he do it to me?' Leila's voice wailed on. 'How could he make me the laughing stock of the town?' A fresh paroxysm of tears took hold of her and she said wretchedly, 'Oh – Mam!'

Bella put her arms round her, rocking her to and fro. 'There, there, Mam's with you, it's all right.'

'It's not all right!' Leila hiccupped. 'What are they all going to say when they hear about it? Mam, what am I going to do?'

Charlotte's little fingers gripped in panic at the bow at Rose's throat, and her wail rose above her mother's.

'For a start you can stop frightening the life out of Charlotte,' Rose said crisply, and the two women glared at her.

'You're heartless, you are!' Bella said.

'I'm practical, that's what I am. Look, I'm going to settle Charlotte in my bedroom, and when I come back we'll talk about what's happened.' Rose threw the last words over her shoulder on her way out of the kitchen.

Ten minutes later she went back to find Leila hiccupping and sniffling, but considerably drier than she had been.

'Ch-Charlotte –'

'She's sleeping on my bed, well boxed in with cushions. She's quite safe. Now' – she sat down at the kitchen table – 'what's this about Daniel?'

Mutely, Leila held out a crumpled piece of paper. Rose smoothed it out on the table and recognized

Daniel's careful flowing script, somewhat blotted by his wife's tears.

My dear Leila,
By the time you read this, I will be far away from Sandyford. You must know as well as I do, Leila, that our Marriage has not been a happy one for some time. After a great deal of thought, I have decided that we both deserve our Freedom and our Happiness, you with Charlotte, I with a woman I have grown to Respect and to Love in the past few months. I have made arrangements with the Bank Manager to have everything signed over to you. He will advise you.

Forgive me for not having the courage to tell you this face to face. I know now that my future lies with Jinty.

Your husband,
Daniel

Leila was studying her face. 'You know who it is,' she accused.

There was no sense in denying it. 'I know Jinty. A widow who lives in Atholl Row.'

'Atholl Row!' Leila's tears began to flow again. 'I told you, Mam – he's deserted me for the sake of some whore in Atholl Row!'

'Leila! Mind your tongue!'

'Whore!' Leila screamed. 'Whore, whore, whore!' She snatched up the note and tore it into fragments, throwing them willy-nilly over the kitchen floor. 'That precious piano of his is going to be sold first thing tomorrow morning – that's for sure!'

Then the momentary defiance faded, and she said again, on a rising note of despair, 'What am I going to do?'

'Never you mind, pet, I'll look after you. Now dry your eyes. He's not worth crying over.'

'That's not what you said when I got married! You were as proud as a peacock at having a schoolmaster for a son-in-law!'

'Aye, well – I didn't know how he was going to turn out,' Bella defended herself.

'And as for you –' Leila turned on her half-sister. 'You'll be glad now, won't you? You always wanted him – you were always jealous!'

'Don't be silly, Leila.' Rose's pity began to wear thin. When her sister wailed, for the umpteenth time, 'What am I going to do?' she answered, 'For a start, you could wash your face and brush your hair before Chauncy and Magnus come in and find you looking a mess.'

'That's not what I meant!' But all the same Leila got up and looked into the mirror. 'I meant, what am I going to do without Daniel?' she asked, her hands automatically lifting to tidy her hair. 'How am I going to support m-myself, and Ch-Charlotte?'

The tears threatened to well up again.

Bella opened her mouth to reassure her daughter, but Rose spoke first.

'You could work for me.'

'What?' They gaped at her. Bella was the first to pull herself together.

'Don't be ridiculous, Rose. Leila – wash your face.'

'I'm not being ridiculous. I'm working for Doctor Anderson for two days a week. I could do with someone in the warehouse when I'm not there.'

Leila stared at her out of drowned eyes. 'But what about Charlotte?'

'Take her with you. The sea air'll do her good. You're a seamstress, Leila, and I've plenty of work for you to do at home on the other five days of the week. No doubt some of the ladies in the town would be glad to know of a good seamstress as well.'

'You mean – support myself?'

'Why should you always look to a man to do that for

you when you're capable of doing it yourself – and with only yourself to please into the bargain?'

Leila's eyes rounded. She gnawed on her lower lip.

'If you ask me,' said Rose, 'you'll be a lot better off on your own.'

'I'd not go so far as to say that –' her mother began, and was stopped by an imperious gesture.

'I might,' said Leila.

25

As the pleasure steamers were making their last trips for the summer and coming in to be refurbished and repainted, it came as a shock to Rose to realize that she had been back home for a year.

In the past twelve months she had built up a thriving business, become involved in the doings of Atholl Row, met Blair and Magnus.

She had had her first proposal of marriage – one that Blair repeated regularly with dogged persistence. And she had fallen in love with a man who exasperated and enchanted her beyond measure, a man who, at the moment, gave all his time and energy to his precious steamboat. But with the quiet confidence that she had developed over the year Rose was certain that everything would work out as she hoped, in time.

In the past year Leila had become a mother, and lost a husband to another woman. And Chauncy, too, had fallen in love.

The Boer War was almost over, by all reports. Piet's people had lost, as was inevitable, since they had taken on the might of the British Empire. But they had given a good account of themselves, and Britain had paid dearly in lives lost.

Over the year Bella had undeniably grown more frail. Only her determination not to give in to the rheumatism that plagued her, and a fixed belief that her grown children could never cope without her, kept her going.

As there wasn't room in the flat for Leila and the baby, it was decided that Chauncy should move into his half-sister's house as a lodger, to enable Leila to keep the house on.

'That means that we'll have to tighten our belts,' Bella said grimly to Rose. 'But I'll manage somehow – I always have.'

'I'll pay more into the house, Mam.'

'Are you sure you can afford it?' Bella asked with heavy sarcasm.

Rose hid a smile. 'I think I can.'

'I know we could all live in comfort if you'd only do as Blair Crawford asks, and marry him,' Bella said, then, as her daughter stared at her she added, 'You're a fool, Rose! Keeping a fine upstanding young man like Blair waiting as if he was just anybody!'

'How did you find out?'

'Blair came to me, as any decent young man would, to let me know his intentions,' said Bella self-righteously. 'Then the poor soul begged me to put in a good word for him. My God, girl, it was all I could do not to say yes for you there and then!'

'He'd no right to tell you!'

'And who would have, if not him? Would you? Oh, no, not you! You were sleekit and tight-mouthed even as a bairn, Rose Gibb. The things you've kept from me in the past – and me your own mother, too.'

'I always told you as much as you needed to know.'

'You didn't tell me when you were walking out with Daniel Currie.'

'What good would it have done me if I had? The minute you set eyes on him you decided that he'd be better for Leila instead of me.'

'It made sense! You were in employment where you could mebbe meet up with a rich patient, or a doctor. Leila had little chance of meeting the right man working as a seamstress. And then off you went to Africa, and never told me about that until it was all arranged.'

'Because you'd have stopped me.'

'Of course I would! I'm your mother, though there's some would doubt it if they knew the way you treat me.'

A self-pitying whine crept into Bella's voice. 'And what good did going off to the war do you? You were sent back home in disgrace.'

'I did nothing to be ashamed of, Mam, and you know it!'

They faced each other across the kitchen. Rose's hand was white-knuckled on the handle of the soup ladle, while Bella's swollen fingers twisted round each other in angry frustration.

'Well, now you're doing something to be ashamed of, all right! Turning down Blair Crawford – Blair Crawford of all people!'

Then she added, 'If it's Magnus you've got your sights set on you might as well forget him. He'll never be able to afford a wife.'

'Magnus has nothing to do with it!'

'No? I might be old and I might be daft, but I'm not blind. I've seen the way you look at him – and the way he looks at you sometimes, when he thinks nobody's watching. But he's not the right one for you, Rose.'

Then her voice softened, became almost pleading. 'Lassie, you could be the laird's wife, and your old mother could live in comfort for the rest of her years.'

'There's more to life than being rich.'

Bella glared, all pleading forgotten. 'Aye – there's being selfish too. My God, Rose, I'll never understand you!'

'You never did, Mam,' said Rose.

She rounded on Blair when he next came to the warehouse, drawing him into the little office area so that nobody else could hear her.

'What do you mean by telling my mother that you'd asked me to marry you?'

He had the grace to look slightly embarrassed, but stood his ground. 'I thought she might talk you round, since I can't.'

'It's nobody's business but our own. Now that she's got the thought in her head, there'll be no getting it out again.'

'In that case,' said Blair with a grin, 'you might as well give in, and say yes.'

'I'll say yes if and when it suits me to say it, and not before.'

'You're a hard woman, Rose,' he said. 'But I think we'll wear you down in the end – me and your mam.'

In January Magnus MacBride called a meeting of the Darroch Line shareholders and announced that he had found the second paddle-steamer he had been searching for. It was a larger vessel than *Darroch's Pride*, a two-funnelled boat able to do the longer trips round Arran and up into the Kyles of Bute, a favourite trip with the holiday-makers because of the unparalleled beauty of the scenery.

He met with stiff opposition. *Darroch's Pride* had had a very good opening season, largely due to the popularity of her young owner, and she was now coping valiantly with a reduced winter run, taking passengers and cargo to and from Bute in all but the worst of seas.

But some of the businessmen who had put their money into the company when it was first floated were reluctant, now that profits were being seen, to sink all of these profits into the purchase of another vessel.

'It's too soon,' one of them said, and there was a murmur of agreement.

The meeting was being held in a room in the little Town Hall built by Blair Crawford's grandfather and gifted to the town by the family. Blair himself was the only shareholder absent, for his father was ill and Blair had had to go to London on business in his stead.

From her vantage point in the front row Rose, the only woman shareholder, saw Magnus's jaw tighten and his eyes harden.

'Too soon? This is the best time to add to the fleet. Gentlemen,' he appealed, forgetting about Rose, 'have you never heard of striking while the iron's hot?'

'Have you never heard that a fool and his money are soon parted?' a dry voice asked from the middle of the room. There was a rumble of laughter, and Magnus flushed beneath his tan.

'The fool, sir, is the one who hesitates, and loses everything. Follow my judgement and by this time next year you'll be getting finer dividends than *Darroch's Pride* alone can bring you. I promise you that!'

'By this time next year you'll bc on at us to add to the fleet again,' someone else pointed out.

'And why not? The more vessels we have the more power we have. More power brings in more money. Gentlemen, the age of the individual steamboat owner and the small company is almost over. We all know that. The railways are competing at a rate we can't hope to match. We must enlarge, or go under!'

Magnus's fist crashed on to the table to emphasize the point. Then he added, 'Since the matter's arisen, I might as well say here that I've been talking to the representatives of one of the railway companies. They're impressed by the success *Darroch's Pride* has enjoyed in her first season. They're pleased to see that we're not afraid to use her in the winter, and that she's up to coping with heavy seas. They'd be willing to give the Darroch Line a contract for next year – if, gentlemen, we have a vessel that can undertake longer trips.'

There was an interested buzz. 'Name the company,' someone called, but Magnus shook his head.

'Not at this stage in the negotiations.'

Chauncy, seated beside him in his role as secretary and treasurer, raised a hand to gain attention.

'I can vouch for the truth of what Mr MacBride's telling you.'

'And as to the steamboat I have in mind,' Magnus

pressed home his advantage while he had it, 'I'm talking about a Gourock boat we all know – the *Anna Forrest*. She's being replaced in May by a paddle-steamer that's being built for her owners, but there's years of good work in her yet. And very little refurbishing, apart from a clean and an overhaul, and a coat of the Darroch colours.'

'How much?' someone wanted to know.

'Nine hundred and fifty pounds.'

There was a murmur throughout the room. 'How much are you thinking of bidding for her?'

'The price asked.'

'Man, man.' The last speaker got to his feet, shaking his head sadly. 'You don't know what you're about. Offer less – you'll mebbe get her, and save us all some money. If,' he added hurriedly, 'we agree to the purchase in the first place.'

It was Magnus's turn to shake his head. 'The asking price is fair, and I want that steamer. I've approached the bank, and they'll stand guarantee for half the money, but no more than that. We must raise the other half ourselves. I'm putting all I have into buying the boat, but I need another three hundred and fifty pounds. As you all know, I hold a majority of the shares. I'm willing to sell some of them off to raise the money.'

There was a long pause. He eyed them challengingly, and crashed his fist down on the table again.

'Come on, gentlemen! Are none of you prepared to back me? Are you so unsure of the outcome when you've seen how well *Darroch's Pride* has done? D'you not want to see the Darroch Line pennant fluttering at the mast of a second fine boat?'

There was another uneasy pause, then Rose got to her feet, crossed to the table where Magnus and Chauncy sat, and turned to face the body of the hall.

'I'll buy another fifty pounds' worth of shares,' she said, her voice ringing out clearly. 'Come now, gentlemen – are you going to let me stand alone, or are you going to follow me, and show your faith in the Darroch Line?'

'God bless you, Rose,' said Magnus as they left the hall after the meeting. 'If it hadn't been for you leading the way, they might not have followed at all.'

A cold blast of January wind met them as they rounded the side of the building, and he took her arm and drew her closer for warmth. There was sleety rain in the wind, promising icy pavements in the morning.

Because of the sea-salt in the air Sandyford and the other communities on the coastline rarely had snow, but freezing rain was commonplace in the winter.

With her free hand Rose drew her scarf closer about her head. 'You'd have brought them round. You've got a silver tongue, Magnus.'

'I'd as soon have the silver in my pocket as in my mouth,' he said wryly, then asked, 'What do you think about the new steamer?'

'I can see the sense of it – but to tell the truth, I'm wondering myself if you're going about it too fast.'

'Yet you were willing to put fifty pounds of your own money towards it?'

'I've got faith in you.'

He stopped, drew her into the shelter of a close, and folded the scarf back from her hair. His eyes glittered down at her in the dim light from a gas standard outside. 'Rose, what would I do without you?'

'What would I do without you?' she asked honestly.

His hands were warm on her neck. 'You'd manage very well.'

'I don't think so,' she said, and lifted her face to his, her lips parting as he kissed her.

Leila's self-centred ruthlessness proved to be an asset to the business. She dealt crisply with difficult employees and customers, but at the same time she was able to charm anyone she needed to impress.

Before long she was accompanying Rose and Rory to sales, where she proved to have a good eye for a bargain. As the winter slid by then gave way to spring, and Charlotte celebrated her first birthday, Leila gained confidence and maturity and began to enjoy her new-found freedom from marriage.

'I've still got the ring on my finger and I've still got the title,' she told Rose. 'And I've the bed to myself at night, thank the Lord!'

Charlotte, too, blossomed under the new regime, accompanying her mother to the warehouse for two days each week, accepting the attention given by one and all with an air of queenly condescension that reminded Rose strongly of Leila herself as a child.

Shortly after her first birthday she found her feet, and had to be curtailed by a rope with one end about her plump little waist and the other tied to the office desk. Otherwise she would have been all through the warehouse, poking her snub little nose inquisitively into every nook and cranny.

She was a bonny child, with her mother's neat features and dark eyes and her father's thick brown wavy hair. Meg Simpson was one of her favourite people, and one of her most devoted servants.

'That lassie should be wed, with a family of her own,' Leila said, watching Meg play with the baby one day.

'Chauncy would agree with you.'

'Rose, why doesn't the man go and face Hannie Simpson? He's sick with love for Meg. You should just see the look on his face every time Charlotte says her name when he's in the house.'

'Meg says –'

'I know what Meg says, for I've heard it often enough. I think it's time Chauncy took matters into his own hands, for there's altogether too many people in on the secret now. Hannie must be even more daft than I thought, or he'd have realized something was afoot.'

'I don't think,' said Rose, 'that Hannie Simpson could ever believe that Meg would disobey him. So he never gives it a thought.'

26

Although Leila was becoming popular with the customers it was Rose that old Mrs Lacey sent for when a set of chairs at Crawford House needed attention.

'The six chairs in the small drawing room,' she said, leading the way to the room in question.

As her son-in-law's health had deteriorated, hers had improved. She walked slowly, with the aid of a sturdy stick, but there was still vigour in her movements. 'And the matching love seat and sofa. You know the pieces I mean.'

'Yes, I do.' Rose had been to Crawford House often enough now to know her way around. Occasionally she took tea with the old lady, sometimes she dined with the family. Now and then she was Blair's partner at a social occasion, but these events were few and far between now that George Crawford's heart complaint was troubling him and Lilias was away from home.

Puffing slightly, Mrs Lacey gained the small drawing room and seated herself on an upright chair conveniently near the door, watching closely as Rose studied the furniture.

'There's a bad scratch on the leg of this chair, did you know that?'

'Happened several years ago. Blair was a very clumsy youth. Can you fix it?'

'I think so.'

'And you might have a look at those curtains while you're here – been in the Crawford family for over seventy years, I'm told. Specially made for George's grandmother, but the embroidery's needing attention. I hear that you've got some very good seamstresses.'

'Yes, I have.' Rose crossed to the tall windows. She had often admired the heavy curtains that hung there, and the exquisitely stitched flowers and birds which decorated the borders.

'I'll have them taken down tonight and packed with the other things, ready for tomorrow. Pull that bell-rope and we'll have tea.'

Rose had plenty to keep her occupied at the warehouse, but she knew better than to argue. She pulled on the bell-rope as commanded, and sat down near the old lady.

'I hear that your sister's working with you now. She's the one who lost her husband to another woman, isn't she?'

'Yes.'

'How's she managing without him?'

'Very well.'

'Hmmphh.'

The door opened and the housekeeper ushered in a maid carrying a laden tea-tray. She smiled at Rose with frosty amiability and watched while the maid arranged everything on the table between Rose and the old lady. Then she moved forward to pick up the teapot.

Catherine Lacey held up a frail hand to stop her. Early spring sunshine sparkled off the rings on her fingers. 'Miss Gibb will pour the tea.'

'Very well, Ma'am.' The housekeeper followed the maid out, closing the door silently.

'I had a communication from Lilias yesterday,' Mrs Lacey said as she took her cup. 'It looks as though she may soon marry again.'

'Indeed?'

'An eminently suitable marriage. Someone she met in the Borders; the son of a lord, no less.'

'How pleasant for you.'

Catherine Lacey's eyes twinkled quick appreciation of the slight irony in her guest's voice, but she merely said,

'It will please her father to know that she'll become the Honourable Mrs whatever. And in time, one hopes, her ladyship. The first title in the Crawford family.'

She put her cup down. 'Her first husband was heir to a peerage, you know. Pity she didn't manage to hold on to him. He was a pleasant enough young man in his own way, and entirely suitable for Lilias. Blair tells me that Magnus MacBride has bought another steamboat.'

'Yes. She's being repainted now.'

'And you're a shareholder in his company. You must have faith in him.'

'I think he's a good businessman.'

'Unlike his father, or his uncle. Yes, it's a relief to know that Lilias is all but settled again,' the old lady mused, then added, her eyes flickering up towards Rose, 'That leaves Blair free.'

'Free?'

'He won't have to support his sister. He's free to make the right sort of marriage too – in his own way.'

Although Rose hadn't finished her tea, she put her cup down. 'I take it that Blair's told you.'

'He tells me everything.' Catherine Lacey leaned forward, her voice suddenly brisk and businesslike. 'Why did you turn him down.'

'A marriage between the young laird and someone of my – station – would be absurd.'

'Blair doesn't think so, and neither do I.'

'And what about Mr Crawford?'

'George,' said his mother-in-law decisively, 'will do as I wish. Besides, he approves of you.'

'As a daughter-in-law?'

'As a businesswoman. Blair's never been good at business; George has the sense to know that a level-headed wife would be an asset to the boy. Well?'

'I don't love him.'

'Tchah! Love fogs the senses and gets in the way.

Fondness makes for a better marriage,' the old lady said crisply.

Rose thought of Magnus, of the way she felt when she was near him, and kept quiet.

'Blair's also told me that you'd like us to do something about some houses in Atholl Row.'

'I doubt if there's much anyone can do about them. If I had my way of it they'd be razed to the ground and the folk rehoused.'

'Mebbe you should concentrate on getting the tenants to keep themselves and their homes clean. It's dirt that spreads disease.'

'How can anyone keep a hovel clean? Have you seen those tenements, Mrs Lacey?'

'Certainly not – and I don't intend to see them either. These tenants are asked to pay very little rent. You get what you pay for. If they want something better they must find it themselves. The Crawfords do a great deal for Sandyford, but we're not a charity.'

'Mrs Lacey –'

'Miss Gibb,' the old woman said slowly and clearly, her eyes fixed on Rose's face, 'the houses belong to the Crawfords. Only a member of this family has the right to do anything about them.' Then she added silkily, 'I think you follow my meaning.'

'Marry Blair, and you can have your way where Atholl Row's concerned,' Leila said thoughtfully. Then she laughed. 'I wish the old woman would put that sort of offer my way!'

'It's – it's unspeakable!' Rose raged, stamping up and down her sister's small front parlour. 'How dare she think I can be bought!'

Leila put a comforting hand on her arm. The two of them had grown closer now that she was working in the warehouse.

When Rose had left Crawford House, seething

inwardly over Catherine Lacey veiled offer, it had seemed natural to go straight to Leila.

'Don't let the old so-and-so bother you, Rose. She just thinks that money can buy anything.'

'It can't buy me!'

'But you like Blair, don't you?'

'Yes, but –'

'But – there's Magnus MacBride. If I was you, I'd choose Blair. You know where you are with him.'

'That's not what I want from life.'

'Be honest with yourself, Rose. When will Magnus ever be in a position to marry? It's going to take years to get the Darroch Line together. And when it happens – when he's got the time and the money, will he want to marry anyway? Has he ever definitely asked you to be his wife?'

'Not in the exact words, but –'

'There you are, then,' Leila said reasonably, getting to her feet as an angry wail from the hallway proclaimed that Charlotte had managed to entangle herself in the umbrella stand again. 'There are far worse things in life than being the mistress of Crawford House.'

The Boer War, that long and bitter struggle which the British had mistakenly looked on, at first, as a matter of minor importance, came to an end in May of 1902, just before the Darroch Line's new paddle-steamer, resplendent in her new colours and renamed *Tansy*, undertook her maiden voyage in May, round the Kyles of Bute.

Maroons exploding on the railway line early in the morning woke most of the townsfolk to the news of the war's end. Most of the factories closed for the day, and the people streamed out into the streets to cheer on a procession of the town's Volunteers and the local brass band. The shops and public buildings broke out in a rash of Union Jacks, church bells pealed out, and the schoolchildren, too, were given a holiday.

Rose sent her employees home and sat alone in the

warehouse, studying the newspaper she had bought on her way to the harbour. 'The long, arduous and costly war has been brought to an end,' the newspaper article proclaimed. 'With honour and security for the future.'

For the British, perhaps, but not for the Boers, Rose thought.

'Coming to watch the procession?' Magnus asked from the doorway.

When she shook her head he came further into the warehouse, glancing at the newspaper spread on the desk.

'You're thinking about Piet,' he said, and came round to lean on the desk by her side. His hand took hers, turned it over so that he could wind his fingers through hers.

She let her head droop against his shoulder, grateful to have him near.

George Urquhart became the *Tansy*'s captain, and Magnus, who had not yet sat his master's examination, took on another captain for *Darroch's Pride*.

As before, he invited the people who had been instrumental in assisting in the formation of the Darroch Line on the new boat's maiden trip. Because *Tansy* had a dining saloon, there was no picnic, but a special lunch served on board.

The route, one of the most beautiful of all the Clyde passenger trips, took them past Toward Point, where Mr Finlay's steamboat had once waylaid *Darroch's Pride* and forced her into the race that had almost ended in tragedy, then past Rothesay Bay, across the mouth of Loch Striven, a long finger of water reaching into the broken mainland, and into the Kyles, a narrow neck of water, barely negotiable.

Colintraive slid by on the starboard side, the hills behind it rising smoothly and placidly from the waterline, then the land reached inquisitive fingers from either side, fingers that almost met, with scarcely more than a ship's breadth of navigable water between them.

The engines slowed and the passengers crowded the rails, marvelling as *Tansy* eased her way along the narrow channel until the bottleneck fell away behind them. The engines began to speed up again and the water at their bows broadened into a great stretch as they passed a fleet of yachts that, from a distance, resembled a flock of large gulls nesting on the water.

The land on either side presented every shade of green, from the soft mossy darkness of the trees, through mid-green bushes to the rich emerald sheen of grass. The hills in the far background, glimpsed between the rolling folds of the nearer land, were a misty grey blue.

Once round the northern tip of the Isle of Bute, *Tansy* continued down the Kyles on the other side, to anchor at last in Ettrick Bay, where they had lunch in the neat little forward dining saloon below the main deck.

Then the paddle-steamer left the Kyles behind and moved into the Sound of Bute, with Arran's mountains, known as the Sleeping Warrior because of the outline they showed from a distance, to starboard.

'What I really want now,' Magnus said as he and Rose stood alone on the bridge wing watching the southern end of Bute disappear behind them and the large and small islands of the Cumbraes come up to starboard, 'is one of those new turbine steamers.'

'Surely not!'

'It makes sense. They can go at speeds the paddle-steamers can't match. They look better, their movement is smoother –'

'But paddle-steamers have more – more character.'

'You're being sentimental.'

'Nobody could be more sentimental than you are over *Darroch's Pride*.'

'That's different,' said Magnus. '*Darroch's Pride* was the first of the Darroch Line. But as soon as I can afford it, I want a turbine. And I want an office too. Chauncy was pointing out that it's time we had proper rooms. I'm going to ask Blair if I can rent a building on the harbour.'

She looked up at the set of his chin, the glint in his golden eyes, and felt a moment's unease, remembering Leila's words.

'Magnus, when will you decide that you've got everything you want?'

'Never, I hope,' said Magnus.

Hannie Simpson came thrusting his way into the warehouse on the following afternoon, when only Meg and Rose were in the place.

Meg had come to deliver some work and had stayed longer than usual, sketching a design on a chair that had just been bought in. Rose was working on the accounts, for the following day was Saturday, and she had to pay her employees.

Rory and some of the others were at the other end of the harbour, putting the finishing touches to some work on the *Tansy*.

The door was open to the early summer warmth, and the harbour outside was quiet, for once. Then the peace was broken as heavy feet came pounding over the cobbles and a fist slammed on the open door. Rose looked up from her work to see Hannie standing in front of her, breathing deeply, his small eyes red and menacing.

At first sight of him she almost dropped her pen. She managed to put it down carefully, managed not to look at the far corner where, she knew, Meg was working as she said, her voice pitched to reach the girl and warn her, 'Good afternoon, Mr Simpson. Can I be of assistance to you?'

'I've come for my daughter!'

'What makes you think she'd be here?' Rose kept her gaze on the man, wondering if he had heard the faint rustle from the shadows.

'I was told she was here,' said Hannie belligerently. 'Told that she's been coming here, behind my back, ever since you set up this place. Working for you without my knowledge and my permission! Where is she?'

He spun round and glared about the place. Rose took advantage of the respite to glance quickly at the corner. Nothing stirred, and the shadows were still. Evidently Meg had had the sense to melt into the background.

'She's not in the warehouse. And even if she was, it would surely be her concern, not yours.'

He swung back, as she had intended him to. As long as his attention was on her, Meg would be safe.

'I'm her father!'

'Meg's old enough to live her own life.'

He slammed a huge fist on the desk before her, and the inkwell jumped nervously. 'So you *have* seen her!'

'I see nothing wrong in her doing some work for me now and again.'

He thrust his face close to hers and she couldn't help recoiling, even though the tall desk was between them.

'Nothing wrong? Nothing wrong in enticing my daughter away from me? So you're not content with underpricing me, selling off furniture to folk that could only come to me before – bankrupting a man who's been plying his trade in this town since you were only a babe in arms –'

Then he added viciously, 'As for that brother of yours – he's no better!' His voice rose, and saliva flecked his lips.

Fear began to touch Rose with its icy fingers. All she could see outside – beyond his burly shoulders – was the empty harbour. Her only ally was his terrified daughter, crouched in hiding. Where, she wondered desperately, were the men who were usually passing and by-passing the open door, going about their work?

'Mr Simpson, I'd be glad if you'd leave at once.'

'I'm quite sure you would, Missy. But I'm not in any

hurry to leave.' He sketched a mocking bow, then straightened. 'Don't let me keep you back from your work, My Lady. I'll just have a look around to make certain you're not lying to me –'

'Not without my permission!' She came round the desk and blocked his path, a move that placed him squarely between her and the door.

'That's no way to talk to me, Missy.' He looked around, then reached out and picked up a handsome little clock that Rory was working on. 'No sense in getting me angered, is there? Just tell me where Meg is, and I'll –'

'Get out of here.'

He opened his hand and the clock fell against a chest of drawers, then to the ground. As it landed, something inside it gave a smothered chime.

With a cry of distress and anger Rose bent to pick up the small broken object. Hannie's fingers tangled in her hair and pulled, bringing her upright with a gasp of pain.

'Leave it,' he said, his small eyes inches away from her own. He released her hair and caught at her shoulders instead. The tip of his tongue ran over his lower lip. 'And leave Meg too, for the moment. We've got other fish to fry, you and me!'

She managed to bring both her arms up to act as a barrier, and he transferred his grip to her wrists, but only succeeded in capturing one. Her free hand flailed up and dug into his cheek, her nails leaving bloody trails behind them as they tore their way down to his chin.

He yelped, and shook her as though she were a rag doll. She felt her teeth rattle together.

'Spirited, are you?' Hannie panted into her ear. 'All the better, lassie!'

'Let me go!'

'When I'm good and ready,' he said, capturing her

freed wrist and forcing her back step by step before him, into the dimness of the warehouse.

27

She opened her mouth to scream, but Hannie was ready for her. Skilfully he whirled her around so that she was pressed against him. Both her wrists were taken into one big hand while the other was clamped across her mouth.

He laughed breathlessly into her ear, Meg apparently forgotten. 'That's got you trussed like a chicken. That's shown you who's your master! Now –'

She could feel his big body pressing tightly against her, hard with excited anticipation. She was as helpless as a child in his grip, forced deeper into the store, to where a pile of discarded cushions made a convenient nest, hidden from the door by a stack of furniture.

'Since Chauncy Gibb's pleasuring himself with my lassie, by all accounts, I'll pleasure myself with his sister,' he panted. 'I'll teach you to look down on the likes of me, then I'll see to it that that brother of yours never looks at another man's daughter again –'

One foot hooked round Rose's ankles. She fell, with Hannie's solid weight on top of her. The air was driven agonizingly from her lungs and she was only dimly aware of his hands on her body, his mouth slithering over her face, as she struggled to breathe.

There was a flurry of movement from the corner of the warehouse, a voice shrill with fear screaming, 'Leave her be!' and Hannie grunted with astonishment under a hail of blows from Meg's small, determined fists.

They can't have hurt him, those blows, but they had the effect of taking him by surprise. His head whipped round, away from Rose, and his daughter clawed at his face.

'Leave her be, Father!'

He gave a yelp of pain as she swiped at him again, then his crushing weight left Rose and she sucked air greedily into her starving lungs.

Realizing that the man was after Meg now, she reached up and caught hold of his jacket, pulling as hard as she could.

'Run, Meg,' she wheezed, then as the girl hesitated she urged, 'Run! Go and get someone!'

She managed to lock her hands round one of Hannie's wrists. When he lurched to his feet Rose went with him, clinging for dear life. As his daughter turned towards the door Hannie's free hand caught her arm and pulled her back with a jerk that almost dislocated her shoulder and brought a scream of pain to her lips.

'Whore! Jezebel! Sneak away behind my back, would you?'

He wrenched free of Rose, swung his hand back at shoulder level, then swung it forward again, the palm catching Meg's uplifted face with a crack that set Rose's teeth on edge. The girl's head danced on her delicate neck, and if her father hadn't been holding her she would have been tossed against a pile of furniture by the force of the blow.

Hannie drew his arm back again, but this time Rose was ready for him. She hurled herself against his broad back and managed to throw him off balance just enough to make the second blow miss its target and fan harmlessly past Meg's head.

With a roar of fury he released Meg, who folded up silently, and turned on Rose.

Backing away from him, trying to circle round to the door, she collided with the work bench that held Rory's tools. Without taking her eyes from the pawnbroker's blazing, crimson face she reached one hand behind her, fumbling for some sort of weapon. Her fingers closed on a hammer, and she brought it round so that he could see it.

'Get out, Hannie. Get out now!'

He laughed jeeringly and began to move towards her, one hand outstretched. 'Give it to me, lassie. Or d'you want me to take it from you?'

She moved back, only to stumble against the arm of a sturdy chair. Hannie pounced, and the hammer went spinning harmlessly off into a corner as his hand closed on Rose's shoulder, then moved swiftly to her mouth to muffle the scream that had begun to rip its way into the air.

'If it's a fight you're wanting, Simpson,' said Magnus levelly from behind him, 'why not take on a man, instead of a lassie?'

Hannie let go and spun round, his great fists doubled.

Round his great muscular arm Rose saw Magnus standing in the doorway, feet sturdily apart to balance his weight, hands hanging by his sides. His face looked as though carved from granite, his eyes were coldly murderous.

'Are you all right?' he asked tersely, his eyes locked on the older man's face.

'Y- yes.' Her voice shook. She would have run to him if that cold face and expressionless voice hadn't intimidated her.

'Come on!' Hannie invited, his voice shrill with excitement. 'I'll take you all on, the whole lot of you. Come on, MacBride –'

'Not in here,' Magnus said. 'Not where we might harm the furniture.'

With a catlike movement so fast that neither Rose nor Hannie saw it coming he sprang forward, took the older man by the shoulders, spun him round, and threw him out of the door. Hannie grunted his surprise as his shoulder crashed against the door-frame, then he measured his length on the cobbles outside.

Rose clutched at Magnus's arm. It was rock hard beneath her fingers. 'Magnus, let him be. Just get him out of here!'

He shook her off, spared her one glance from eyes as hard as flint.

'See to the lassie,' he said, and sprang through the doorway as Hannie climbed to his feet.

Meg whimpered and began to pull herself upright, her green eyes blank and dazed. A huge angry swelling was already marring one side of the girl's face.

'You're all right, Meg?'

She tried to pull free of Rose. 'Father – he'll kill Chauncy –'

'No he won't. Not now.'

As though in response to the sound of his name, steps came rattling hurriedly over the cobbles and Chauncy himself, his eyes wild in an ashen face, appeared in the doorway.

'Meg –' he said in an agony of fear. 'Meg – !'

Then he saw her, and came to her, arms outspread. She left Rose and went into his embrace like a wounded bird blindly seeking the only safe shelter it knew.

Chauncy's arms enfolded her closely, fiercely, as though they would never again let her go, and his brown head sank to pillow itself on the red curls that nestled against his shoulder.

Rose, no longer needed, no longer wanted, left them together and went to the doorway.

Word of the fight had already spread like wildfire, and the men she had so sorely needed moments before were swarming from all over the harbour – dockers who had been unloading a ship with equipment for the mines, the ship's crew, bystanders who had simply been at the harbour to watch the unloading and were now promised unexpected and better entertainment.

They were already forming a circle round Hannie and Magnus. As Rose reached the doorway Hannie reeled back from a blow to his mouth.

He cursed, spat redly on the ground, and rushed forward. Magnus, standing fast, met him with another blow – one that was checked before it managed to land on its target. Then it was his turn to stagger under a solid fist.

'What's going on?' Rory asked, tugging at Rose's arm.

'Hannie came looking for Meg.'

'And me not there to look after the pair of you! Are you all right?' he asked anxiously, his eyes on the torn sleeve of her dress, the hair loosed from its knot by Hannie's grasping, groping fingers.

'I'm fine, and so will Meg be – now.' Rose clutched his arm as Hannie and Magnus closed again. 'But I'm feared that Hannie might kill Magnus. Do something, Rory! Stop them!'

'It's more than my life's worth to put an end to another man's fight, Mistress,' Rory said self-righteously, then gave a yell of triumph as Magnus laid Hannie flat on the stones. Judging from the cheer that went up, not many of the men in the circle were for Hannie.

'That's it, Magnus lad,' Rory crowed, 'teach him a lesson he'll not forget. Come on, Magnus –!'

Hannie bounced to his feet, bellowing, put his head down and charged at the younger man. Magnus sidestepped the rush and managed to get in a blow that must have made Hannie's ear ring. Rory's encouragement rose to an unintelligible shriek of excitement.

Magnus landed another telling blow and Hannie reeled away, then came back with fists flying. His nose was bloody now, and there was a scarlet splotch on Magnus's cheekbone that would soon become a bruise.

He was fighting with cold control, judging the older man's mindlessly furious rushes and flailing punches, avoiding them with comparative ease, and skilfully landing blows just where he wanted them.

'Hit the man again, Magnus!' Rory screamed raucously, his own bony fists windmilling.

Rose watched helplessly as the pawnbroker was sent

reeling by a well-placed punch that split the skin above his right eye and sent a spray of blood into the air when he shook his head to clear it.

He dashed an arm across his face to mop the crimson stream that threatened to blind him, then threw himself at the younger man.

He was tiring visibly already, stumbling a little, feeling in the air for his adversary with wheeling arms when blood from his cut forehead ran into his eyes again.

Soon his mouth was puffed and bleeding and there was a great bruise on one cheekbone.

Magnus's fist coolly slammed into Hannie's mouth once again, and the man stumbled backwards, men scattering before him. For a moment it looked as though he would trip and go over the edge of the harbour into the water, but instead he keeled over and fell, landing with a crash that knocked the wind from him.

Magnus stood waiting, fists at the ready, his chest heaving as he sucked in air. 'Get up, Hannie,' he said, his voice grating.

'Magnus, leave him!'

If he heard Rose, he gave no indication. 'Get up!' he repeated.

Then, when Hannie stayed where he was, body limp and eyes closed, Magnus said contemptuously, 'Give me a hand with him, somebody. Get him out of my sight and back to wherever he belongs!'

As he bent over Hannie's prone form, hands out to grasp the man by the front of his waistcoat, the pawnbroker's arm suddenly moved, arcing through the air, the piece of chain in his fist hissing as it sought out his adversary's downbent face.

There was a great roar from the onlookers as Magnus managed to whip his head back out of reach. The chain links caught one ear, and Rose saw blood shower down onto Hannie's face.

The man's shoulders heaved up from the stone as he

tried to get to his feet, toppling his opponent. But Magnus managed to pin him down, forcing the hand that held the chain back over Hannie's head, back and back until it was pinned to the ground a matter of inches from the edge of the harbour.

He lifted it before slamming it down on to the cobbles again, then again and again until the pain-paralysed fingers uncurled and the chain that was meant to cut Magnus's face open fell free to slither like a vicious serpent over the edge and splash into the water some twelve feet below.

That, Rose thought with sick relief, was the end of the matter. But before her horrified gaze Magnus MacBride wrenched Hannie to his feet and hit him – a blow that had all his bone and muscle and power behind it; a blow that she heard clearly above the excited baying of the crowd. A blow that snapped Hannie's head back just as his own open-handed slap had done to Meg.

The hand that had been supporting Hannie opened and the man collapsed, only to be picked up again as though he were a bag of rubbish, and hit once more.

After the fourth such blow Hannie rolled away as he crashed again to the ground, gathering his knees beneath him, trying to get away. His head hung almost to the cobbles and his battered face dripped blood onto them.

He was caught and hauled to his feet again. Once more Magnus's fist slammed into the red mass that had been a recognizable face a short while before.

This time Hannie went down on his back, one hand held out in feeble supplication. The plea was ignored. Magnus plunged after him, swept him upright, supporting him solely with one hand, for Hannie was incapable of standing, and knocked him to the red-stained cobbles again.

Rose broke free of Rory's restraining hand and ran into the circle, dragging back on Magnus's arm. He swung round on her, pulling himself free, his face tight with rage.

'Magnus, for God's sake! The man's half dead – can you not see that for yourself?'

The sight of him frightened her. His face was bruised and one side of his head was drenched in blood from the wound Hannie had dealt him with the chain. The shoulder of his shirt was torn, dark and sticky. But it was his expression, rather than his injuries, that struck cold fear to Rose's heart. It was set hard, a marble mask dominated by eyes that burned with cold hell-fire.

'I'm seeing to it that he'll never lay a finger on you again,' said Magnus with ice in his voice, and turned back to his victim, now grovelling on the cobbles before him, whimpering through split and swollen lips.

'Do something!' she screamed at the onlookers. 'D'you want to see murder done here?'

To her great relief one or two of them moved forward, though some of the others roared their protest. It was like a cock-fight, or bear-baiting, Rose thought, struggling against nausea as Magnus, resisting the grip of the men who took hold of him, was pulled away from Hannie.

She dropped to her knees beside the pawnbroker. His eyes had rolled into his head so that only the whites showed, and he was gurgling, choking on his own blood. Rose dragged him on to his side and wiped his face with a fold of her skirt.

'Somebody get an ambulance wagon,' she said. 'Quickly!'

As one of the men ran to do as she ordered she glanced briefly at Magnus. He had pulled his jacket off at the beginning of the fight, and now his shirt and waistcoat were bloodied and tattered, the buttons ripped from both garments in the struggle so that they gaped open from the strong pillar of his throat to his flat belly. Sweat ran down his chest.

Their eyes met, but only for a few moments. Cold, devoid of every emotion but revenge, he faced her down.

28

'How could you do it? How could you keep on hitting the man when he was half dead?'

'He deserved all he got – and more,' Magnus said icily. His face, brilliantly colourful here and there from the blows Hannie had managed to get in early in the fight, was still closed to her, the face of a stranger.

'He didn't deserve to be beaten like that!'

'I've seen worse done in my time. And done worse, too. A seaman's life means survival – winning and not losing.'

'But you could have killed him. Mebbe you have.' Rose tied the bandage around his head and went to the sink to empty the bowl of blood-stained water, thanking the Fates that her mother was with Leila and still unaware of what her lodger had been up to.

'You should go to the infirmary and ask after him,' she said over her shoulder.

Magnus picked up his jacket. 'I'll do nothing of the sort.'

'Then I will.'

'You won't!' He dropped the jacket, rounded the table in two strides and caught her arm, wrenching her round to face him. 'I'll not have you going near that man, not after what he tried to do to you.'

'Don't order me about, Magnus. I don't belong to you, or to the Darroch Line.'

'You think not?' he asked, his voice rough. 'We've belonged together since first we set eyes on each other, Rose Gibb. You know it, and so do I.'

'Let me go!' Half angry, half afraid, she wrenched herself free of his hooked fingers.

'Don't touch me! You're – you're frightening me!'

The door-knocker thumped as though the hand that held it was determined to force it through the door.

'You'd best answer it,' said Magnus bleakly, and turned to retrieve his jacket from the floor.

Two burly police officers were standing outside.

'We're looking for a man named Magnus MacBride, Miss. Is he inside?'

'Aye, I'm here.' Magnus called from inside the house, and they pushed their way past Rose, hands moving swiftly to the truncheons at their belts.

Magnus was standing by the kitchen range, the jacket on over the blood-stained rags that were all that was left of his shirt. He was quite relaxed, even smiling – a smile that didn't reach his eyes.

'Gentlemen, at your service.'

They glanced at each other, then the man who had asked for Magnus took a step forward. 'Magnus MacBride, I must ask you to accompany us to the police station, where you will be questioned in connection with a breach of the peace and an assault on one Henry Simpson.'

Magnus nodded, and moved forward. When one of the men put a hand on his arm he shook it off. 'No need to worry, lads. I'll not give you any trouble. It was Simpson I'd the quarrel with, not you.'

As the three men, Magnus in the middle, reached the half-landing and began to descend the second flight of stairs he looked up at Rose, standing at the banisters. For a moment his eyes blazed into hers with an impact that surged through her, weakening her so that she had to tighten her grip on the railing in order to remain upright. Then he had gone, and she was alone.

As soon as she got back into the house and shut the door her knees gave way, and she sank to the hall floor, shaking so hard that she couldn't summon up the energy to get to her feet again.

While she still huddled there someone came running up the stairs, taking them two at a time. The knocker flew into action, beating an urgent tattoo on the door.

'Rose? Rose, are you in there?'

'Blair?' She pulled herself upright and opened the door. He stepped inside and took her into his arms.

'I went to the warehouse to see you, and Rory told me that you'd been attacked.' He held her back at arm's length. 'Are you all right?'

She nodded, and began to say, 'I'm fine.' But the tears that had been held back for so long began to pour down her face, and instead she heard herself saying, 'Oh Blair – I'm so glad you're here!'

She clutched at him tightly. Blair was safe, Blair was reliable. Blair would never terrify her the way Magnus had that day.

'Let me be with you always,' she heard him whisper, his mouth warm on her neck. 'Marry me, Rose! You can't refuse me this time!'

There was a gasp from the open door, and Rose lifted her head to see Bella standing there, the shopping bag dropping from nerveless fingers.

'You've come at the right time, Mrs Gibb,' Blair said, his voice ringing with triumph. 'Just in time to agree to let me marry your daughter.'

'Oh – Rose!' said Bella, and swept the two of them into her embrace.

Hannie Simpson recovered from the beating he had received, although he faced a considerable stay in hospital while his injuries mended.

As soon as the man was well enough Chauncy went to the infirmary and informed him quietly and firmly that he was going to marry Meg.

'Meg's going to stay with my sister Leila until we get wed,' he told the pawnbroker. 'If you try to stop us I'll finish the job that Magnus MacBride started, I promise you that.'

The man glared at him through swollen eyes and said nothing.

'And I believe the police'll be coming in to have a word with you,' Chauncy added as he rose to leave the ward. 'It seems that you've had the burglars in, Hannie. Good day to you.'

Magnus appeared before the police court the day after the fight. He was fined three guineas, and was later put out by his landlady.

'He's in his room now, packing his things,' Bella said when Rose got home from the warehouse.

'Oh, Mam!'

'I'll not have a convicted criminal staying under my roof,' said Bella. Then, sharply: 'Where are you going?'

'To talk to Magnus.'

'If you take my advice, you'll have nothing to do with him,' Bella called after her, and was ignored.

Magnus, stowing the last of his possessions into his seaman's bag, looked up as she went into the bedroom. Someone had renewed the bandage about his head. His bruised face was as hard and expressionless as stone, his eyes hooded.

'I'm sorry – about Mam.'

He shrugged. 'She's got the right to decide who stays under her roof.'

'Where will you go?'

'There are plenty of rooms to let.' He pulled the mouth of the bag shut, then straightened up and looked fully at her for the first time. 'Your mother tells me you're going to marry Blair Crawford.'

'Magnus –'

'You're a fool, Rose,' he said coolly, almost contemptuously. 'What happened to your dream of independence? Was the thought of being the lady of the manor too tempting for you?'

'How dare you!'

'I hope you'll be very happy together' – he came towards her, and she had no option but to step aside and let him pass – 'but I doubt it.'

Bella appeared in the hallway as the landing door closed.

'Good riddance,' she said, her face and voice as implacable as Magnus's had been.

29

Rose Crawford returned from her wedding trip to find herself the mistress of a house where she felt like a guest, and the wife of a man who worshipped her, but in the way that he might worship a lovely painting or a piece of exquisite jewellery, not a flesh and blood woman.

Rose would have preferred to delay the wedding until she had grown used to the idea of being Blair's wife. But he and his grandmother, abetted by Bella, had urged an early marriage on her, and had had their way.

Leila designed the wedding gown, in white satin with a tight-fitting bodice that was skilfully folded and tucked and cut low in a way that made the most of Rose's full breasts. The plain skirt was slightly trained and embroidered round the hem only with white silk flowers, which were echoed on the bodice. The sleeves were puffed at the shoulder, then tight to the wrists, where they frothed with white lace.

The lace veil was also embroidered round the edges, and hung from a diadem of orange blossom.

It had been decided that Rose should prepare for her wedding at Crawford House, which was just as well, for Bella's small house would never have held the hairdressers and dressmakers and maids who had been required to prepare the bride.

When they had finished with her Rose looked at the stranger reflected in the glass. The dress made the most of her tall, ripe figure. Her face was becomingly flushed with excitement, and her dark hair was piled high to show off her long slim neck,

'You're a real lady, Rose,' Bella said tearfully.

'Mam, don't start crying!'

'Let her cry,' Leila advised as Bella retreated to a sofa, her face buried in an ample handkerchief. 'She's been looking forward to crying at this wedding for the past two months.'

As the veil was being put into place the door opened and Catherine Lacey came in, elegant in lilac silk, leaning on the housekeeper's arm.

'Let me have a look at you, girl.' She lowered herself into a chair, and nodded. 'You'll do. You'll do very well. Effie –'

The housekeeper came forward, holding out an opened flat box.

'My wedding gift,' the old woman said. 'I want you to wear them today.'

Leila gave a gasp of delight. Bella came hurrying over to peer into the box.

'Would you look at these!' She stared in awe at the flawless string of creamy pearls, the matching bracelet and earrings. Then she turned to her daughter and said, 'What do you say to Mrs Lacey, then?'

'Mam!' said Leila, scandalized and embarrassed.

Catherine Lacey smiled. 'Oh, I think Rose and I understand each other. And now I must go, or I'll be late at the church.'

The pearls, glowing softly against Rose's throat and wrist and on the lobes of her ears, provided the perfect finishing touch to her wedding outfit. Chauncy, waiting uncomfortably in the big entrance hall, looking like a stranger in his smart wedding clothes, stared openly as his stepsister came slowly down the stairs with Leila and Bella in attendance.

'You look grand,' he said as he came forward and took her hand. Then he added with a grin, 'Almost as good as my Meg looked on our marriage day.'

Paris was everything that Rose had imagined it would

be; everything that Blair, who knew it well, had said it would be.

Each day brought its own wonders and its own magic, but at night, when they were alone in their beautiful hotel suite, the story was different.

From their wedding night Blair was diffident about touching his wife and making love to her. At first he passed it off by confessing, with an endearingly awkward reluctance, that he was a novice to lovemaking.

Rose, herself a novice, had thought that they might explore and experience the pleasures of married love together, but as time passed without the matter becoming resolved she began to fret.

Her own appetite sharpened to the point where it became a keen hunger. Blair had a good body, slender but well-muscled and long-legged. At night, in the darkness, when he lay close to her, she began to want him more and more.

But when she made the mistake of trying to rouse him he drew away, shocked and angry.

'For God's sake, Rose, you're not a street wanton – don't act like one!'

'I'm your wife!'

'I'm well aware of that,' Blair said into the darkness. 'And I expect my wife to behave like a lady, not a – a trollop.'

'Blair –'

'It's late, Rose,' he said. 'Get some sleep.'

The bedroom windows were open and a pleasant breeze fluttered at the curtains. It touched her face but it could do nothing to cool the burning need deep within her body.

Magnus came unbidden to her mind. Since he had walked out of her mother's house she had seen him often on the harbour. But each time they merely nodded to each other like acquaintances, never stopping to speak.

Rose, recalling the animal ferocity of his attack on

Hannie Simpson, told herself that a man with such deep dark passions could never be the man for her.

Even so, lying unfulfilled and unsatisfied beside Blair, she couldn't keep Magnus from her mind. That same dark passion must have another side to it, she thought, tossing restlessly, trying to settle her twitching limbs and ease the wrenching need deep in her belly.

She remembered the warmth of his fingers on her breast on the night he had kissed her in the shadow of *Darroch's Pride*, the night she had delivered Leila's daughter, and a groan burst from her lips.

Blair, disturbed, moved restlessly then settled again. She pushed her head deep into her pillow so that he couldn't hear, and wept.

Blair woke her in the dawn light. 'Rose?' he asked tentatively.

She turned to face him. His hand cupped her face, tangled itself in the mass of dark hair that spilled over her shoulders.

'I love you,' whispered Blair. 'I do love you!'

He kissed her, then slowly, carefully, began to unfasten the small bows that held the bodice of her nightgown closed over her breasts. She lay still, afraid to respond in case he drew back from her.

While Paris began to waken to a new day below their window he made love to her gently, tenderly, but without passion.

She lay in his arms, her eyes closed, and tried not to think about Magnus.

The telegram arrived that afternoon.

Rose stared at the words 'Mrs Blair Crawford' on the envelope, wondering for a bemused moment why the receptionist had handed it to her. The name seemed to be alien to her.

'Open it,' Blair said impatiently. She did as she was

told, read the few words inside, and passed the slip of paper to him with a shaking hand.

'Mother has pneumonia. Can you come home. Chauncy.' It was only when Blair read the words aloud that they became real.

'She must be bad or he wouldn't have asked me to go home.' She looked up at her husband in sudden panic.

'It'll be all right,' Blair said gently, taking her hands in his. The telegram, crumpled in his palm, scratched at her fingers.

'We'll leave right away,' he said.

'Yes, we must.'

She thought that there was a note of relief in his voice at the prospect of ending the honeymoon. She knew that there had been a note of relief, scarcely hidden, in hers.

Bella Gibb was delighted to receive a visit from her daughter, Mrs Blair Crawford, but annoyed about the honeymoon being cut short on her account.

To Rose's irritation the same matron who had refused to reinstate her on her return from South Africa met her in the hospital foyer, her face wreathed in a smile that sat ill on her normally frigid features.

'Good afternoon, Mrs Crawford. Your mother's in Livingstone Ward.'

'Thank you.' Rose, who had once nursed in Livingstone Ward, turned to the stairs, only to find that the matron remained firmly by her side.

'She's much better now,' the woman chattered on as they mounted the stairs. 'Mrs Lacey sent instructions that she should have a private room, but Mrs Gibb insisted on going into one of the main wards, so we – ah, here we are. A visitor for you, Mrs Gibb.'

Bella, in one of the beds nearest the door, lay back on a pile of pillows.

'Rose!' Her voice was a shadow of its usual self. 'What are you doing here?' Then her eyes moved to the matron, and she added dryly, 'A visitation, is it? In that case, it must be my turn to die.'

The woman tutted briskly. 'Come along now, Mrs Gibb, we know we're getting stronger every day, don't we? Well – I'll leave you two together, shall I?'

'That woman,' said Bella weakly when the matron had gone, 'is a fuss. She tried to put me into a cupboard of a room with nobody to talk to. I soon told her a thing or two! What sort of way's that to treat a sick woman?'

Her eyes fastened on Rose's blue silk dress and matching cape, the froth of ivory lace at her throat and wrists, the pearl earrings, the wide-brimmed hat decorated with ivory and pink silk roses. 'You look every inch a lady,' she said contentedly, then, her voice sharpening: 'But you should have been away for another two weeks at least.'

'Chauncy sent me a telegram.'

'Chauncy,' said his stepmother witheringly, 'hasn't the sense he was born with! What did he want to go and do a thing like that for?'

'Hush, Mam. I'd have been angry with him if he hadn't let me know that you were ill.'

'All the way from France, just to find that I'm fine,' Bella said peevishly, then added, 'Since you're here you might give me a drink of water.'

It was strange to be in Livingstone Ward again, bending over a bed, supporting a patient's head, holding a tumbler to parched lips.

But instead of a starched white uniform Rose wore silk and jewellery, and as Bella gestured with her hand and Rose took the tumbler away Blair's gold wedding ring flashed on her finger.

Bella allowed her to pat her mouth dry with a soft, lacy handkerchief, then said, 'Well? Are you happy?'

'Yes, Mam, I'm happy.'

Bella nodded, content to accept her word. 'My daughter, the lady of the big house.' She chuckled. 'You should just see the way I'm treated in the shops now. It's yes, Mrs Gibb this and yes, Mrs Gibb that –' She stopped, and began to cough.

'Hush, Mam, you're talking to much. Lie quiet and I'll tell you about Paris.'

'What would I want to know about a place like that for?' Bella said, but she had tired herself out, and for the next ten minutes or so she was content to listen.

When her eyelids began to droop Rose said, 'I'd better go and let you get some rest.'

'Aye, that man of yours'll be pining for you.'

'When you're well enough to leave the infirmary, Mam, you'll come to Crawford House.'

Bella's eyes flew open. 'I'll do nothing of the sort!'

'There's a room all ready for you. Mrs Lacey herself said –'

'Mrs Lacey says altogether too much. It was her that nearly had me shut away in a room all on my own. No, no, Crawford House isn't the place for me.'

'If I can live there, so can you.'

Bella shook her head. 'It's different for you, lass. I think it must be because your father, whoever he was, belonged in a big house. But not me. I'll go to Leila's for a few days, then I'm going home to my own place.'

'But you'll be on your own now.'

'Miss McKinnon'll keep an eye on me and do my shopping until I'm able.'

'Mam, you can't go on living in a tenement when your daughter's in the big house on the hill.'

'I belong in a tenement. I'm happy where I am.'

'Would you not like a wee place near Leila?'

'I would not!' said Bella decisively. 'I'll stay where I am, thank you, and you can just tell that to Blair. And to Milady Lacey. Besides,' she added with a twinkle in her eye, 'I'm an important woman in my own street now, and I'd not miss that for anything in the world!'

30

George Crawford had become an invalid,and spent most of his time in his suite of rooms on the first floor of the house. Blair found more and more responsibilities piling onto his shoulders.

'I hate this damned estate,' he said peevishly to Rose.

'Would you like me to take over the accounts for you? I know what I'm about,' she said confidently. 'I've done well enough with my own books at the warehouse.'

He brightened. 'Would you, Rose?' Then he added diffidently, 'Wouldn't it take up too much time?'

'I've nothing else to do,' she said dryly.

She had returned from Paris to find that the running of Crawford House was not to be her concern.

'No sense in burdening yourself with it until you have to, my dear,' Catherine Lacey had told her. 'Mrs Hamilton is very capable, and the servants work well for her. And I'm very happy to go on instructing her.'

'What's left for me to do?'

The old lady smiled. 'Why, there's a great deal for you to do, Rose. You will be the hostess when we entertain. You will have social duties. And you will no doubt have a family to think of, in the near future.'

Not, Rose thought but didn't say, until Blair becomes a proper husband to me.

Their private life had deteriorated even further since their return home. Blair was as affectionate as ever, but once his family home enfolded them he became even more reluctant to make love to Rose.

The frustration this caused, and her enforced idleness as a member of the upper class, began to gnaw at her, until finally, a month after her return home, she walked down to the harbour, scorning the use of a carriage.

At first sight of *Darroch's Pride*, taking on a consignment of passengers, she stopped short, memories flooding.

Then she walked on, past the Crawford office, past the small wooden hut that had once been a store and now bore the words Darroch Steamship Line in bold red letters, and went into the warehouse, sniffing at the familiar, beloved smell of wood and cloth, varnish and glue.

Leila's face lit up. 'Rose! What are you doing on the harbour?'

'I'm coming back to work.'

Then as the pen dropped from her sister's fingers she went on hurriedly, 'I know that we'd decided that you should take over the business, Leila, but I shall go out of my mind if I don't occupy my time more fully. I'm tired of arranging flowers and pouring afternoon tea. So I want to come back to the warehouse – if you agree.'

'Of course I agree! But what does Blair have to say about it?'

'Blair's in London, and I'll tell him about it when he comes back. Anyway, Mam's coming out of hospital in a few days, and you'll need to be free to see to her.'

Rory came in at the door and stopped short, his thin old face flushing with pleasure. 'Mistress Crawford! It's good to see you, lassie. But what brings you here?'

'I'm coming back to work, Rory. For a few days each week, anyway.' She took the hand he offered, and shook it warmly.

'Welcome back, Mistress Crawford!'

'Rory,' she said, 'my friends cry me Rose.'

When Blair returned from London he kissed the tip of his wife's nose and said indulgently, 'If it makes you happy, my darling, go and work at the warehouse.'

'Your grandmother's worried about what the neighbours might say.' She wound her arms around his neck, glad to see him home again, wondering if his loving greeting might be the sign of an improvement in the situation between them.

He laughed. 'Who cares about the neighbours? You're a Crawford now, and in this part of the world the Crawfords are answerable to nobody.'

Later, in bed, she dared to reach out for him once the light was out. To her surprise he responded immediately, turning towards her and catching her in his arms so roughly that she had to bite back a cry of surprise.

Silently, swiftly, he stripped her and moved to lie on top of her as her body quickened to the urgency in his. She looked up, and the moonlight filling the room showed his face clearly, eyes closed, features set and intent, as though he was completely absorbed in something that he could see within his own head.

His knee pushed impatiently between her thighs, then he was entering her, taking her as she had wanted him to since the night of their wedding.

'Oh – Blair!' she whispered.

His eyes flew open at the sound of her voice and locked on to her face, silvery in the moonlight.

'Rose?' he said, as though astonished. And she watched the desire drain out of his face, felt it go from his body, felt his manhood slacken within her.

He rolled away from her, and she reached out to touch him.

'Blair, what's wrong?'

He flinched at her touch, a tremor rippling his skin. Bewildered, she drew back hastily.

'Blair –'

He said nothing, and they lay side by side, not touching, not speaking. It was as though a wall had suddenly been placed between them.

When she tried to talk to Blair about the gulf that was

slowly opening at their feet, leaving her on one side and him on the other, he denied that there was anything wrong at all.

'You know how much I love you, Rose. Don't I tell you often enough? Don't I bring you gifts? Can't you see it in my eyes every time I look at you? Don't you know how happy it makes me, being able to introduce you to people as my wife, my own dearest wife?'

'But when we're alone together you –'

'I what?' he asked, a sudden chill in his blue gaze.

She hesitated, searching for the right words, then said, 'You make me feel as though I'm being kept at arm's length.'

'That's nonsense! I can only suppose,' he said coolly, 'that you came to marriage with some strange expectations of what it's all about.' Then he added quickly, 'I was thinking about Atholl Row. Do you still want something done about it?'

'Of course I do.' She knew that he had brought up the subject purely as a red herring. But she couldn't afford to ignore it.

'The factor tells me that two of the houses have fallen vacant. They're in the same building, an end tenement. If we could rehouse the other two families in that building we could pull it down and rebuild. It would be a start.'

'Can you do that?'

He smiled down at her, his eyes alight with love. 'If you want it done.'

'Oh, Blair!' She put her arms about him, and he hugged her willingly.

But from then on he avoided any attempt on her part to talk about their personal problems.

Her work at the warehouse and her work on the Crawford accounts helped to keep Rose's growing misery and bewilderment at bay most of the time.

She started going to sales with Rory again, and although at first her new neighbours stared and whispered and raised elegant eyebrows over the fact that the new Mrs Crawford was actually working, the scandal of it soon tired them and they grew to accept the situation.

Leila had done a magnificent job in her sister's absence. The business was thriving, and an additional employee had been brought in. Leila and Rory, after conspiring together, had approached Mr Grier, owner and manager of the furniture shop in Motson Street, and suggested to him that they should start making new furniture which could be sold in his shop.

'You mean he agreed?' Rose asked in astonishment. Mr Grier was very proud of his furniture emporium, and most particular about every item sold there.

'Certainly he agreed. He's a charming man, if you just know how to deal with him. He needs to be flattered just a little – like any man.' Leila, beaming, showed her a handsome tapestry footstool. 'He wants four of these stools. And if they sell, we'll try him with a small table. That is,' she added, eyeing her sister apprehensively, 'if you agree.'

'What does Rory think?'

'It was his idea.'

'In that case,' said Rose resignedly, 'I'll have to go along with it.'

Now that she was visiting the harbour again a meeting between herself and Magnus was inevitable. She had no way of knowing when or how it would come about, and what they would say to each other when they finally came face to face.

It happened when she least expected it. A new collection of furniture had come in, and as usual Rory had set the pieces not worth renovating aside to be sold to the poorer folk in the town.

An old woman had come with a cart trundled along by

her small grandson, barefoot despite the autumn chill. The woman's faded eyes lit up at the sight of a mattress, stained but still whole and sturdy enough.

'How much, Missus?'

Without hesitation Rose named a sum that was low even for a 'poor sale'. The woman beamed her relief and dug into a tattered old purse for the necessary coins.

'Come on, then, Calum,' she said to the child, and they started tugging it through the door and out to the cart.

'Wait a minute, it'll drag on the cobbles if you don't get help.' Rose came round the office desk, looking into the depths of the warehouse for someone to take an end of the clumsy mattress.

There was nobody in sight, so she took a grip on it herself. It was heavier and more difficult to manage than she had realized.

Slowly the three of them managed to get it through the door and across to the cart. But it balked like a nervous animal when they tried to lift it up on to the vehicle.

'Hold on,' a familiar voice ordered, and the mattress was taken from the three of them and flipped dexterously on to the cart.

'There you –' Magnus stopped short as he turned and saw Rose, who had been hidden from him by the mattress's bulk. His eyes, suddenly flat and expressionless, skimmed by hers and went on to the woman. 'D'you have something to tie it on with?'

'Aye'. She dug into the bag she carried and brought out a tangle of string.

'That'll do.'

As he worked on it Rose watched his broad, capable hands, his bent head, the set of his shoulders. He wore his navy-blue jacket and trousers, and the white peaked cap was at a jaunty angle on his head.

He must have come off the *Tansy*, which hadn't been at

her moorings when Rose had arrived thirty minutes earlier.

He finished unravelling the string and lashed the mattress securely in place, securing the seamanlike knots with deft speed.

'There you are, Ma'am.'

When the old woman and the lad had gone he turned to Rose and touched the peak of his cap. 'Good afternoon, Mrs Crawford.'

'Good afternoon, Mr MacBride.'

'You're looking well,' said Magnus.

'And you. Where are you staying?'

'I found a set of rooms to rent in Lomond Place. It suits me well enough.'

For a moment longer they stood gazing at each other, neither saying anything. His face was carefully blank, his eyes guarded. She had no way of knowing what he read, if anything, in her own features.

Then he saluted again and strode away, leaving her alone.

31

As the year dragged to its close Rose settled into a steady routine of work and social obligations.

As Blair's new wife she was required to hold a series of At Homes and dinner parties; a frightening prospect at first, but with Catherine Lacey's assistance she coped, and even began to enjoy these events.

She became involved, too, in various charitable projects, and enlisted Leila's aid in planning a big Christmas party in the Town Hall for the town's poorer children.

'You've taken to your new life like a duck to water,' her sister told her, then laughed. 'Mam must have the right way of it – being conceived in a big house has given you the background you needed.'

Bella had long since moved back into her own flat, despite protests from Chauncy, Leila and Rose.

'Meg and me would have taken her in gladly,' Chauncy said, a worried frown drawing his brows together.

Leila shook a finger at him. 'Don't you be daft! You've got enough to think of, with Meg's baby on the way. I was near driven out of my mind while she was staying with me. It was like being a child again – do this and don't do that, where are you going, mind you're not late back. And me with a daughter of my own, too! I tell you, I was glad to get the place to myself again when she decided she was well enough to go home.'

'All the same –' her half-brother fretted.

'Miss McKinnon's there to keep an eye on her,' Rose pointed out. 'And you're in the next street, Chauncy, if you're needed. Best let her go her own way. She'll do that anyway, whatever we say.'

Blair was spending more and more time away from home, leaving the work of the harbour and the mines and the estate to Chauncy, his mine manager and his factor. Rose found herself being consulted by these men when problems arose during his absence, and blessed the commercial experience she had accumulated while building up her own business.

'Everyone manages fine without me,' Blair said when she tried to point out that he should spend more time in Sandyford. 'I'm not needed here. I never was,' he added almost sulkily. 'The old man could easily have let me go back to Africa. He keeps me here out of damned stubbornness!'

'He cares about you, Blair. It would make him happier if you were home more often.'

George Crawford's heart condition had become much worse. He was now an invalid, and a private nurse was in daily attendance.

Blair shrugged. 'Someone has to visit the suppliers and the buyers. Now that he's not able, I must do it. He can't have it every way.'

Christmas brought a flurry of extra social engagements that kept her too busy to fret over matters between herself and Blair. A few days before the Christmas celebrations Magnus called a meeting of the Darroch Line shareholders.

Sitting at the back of the hall, her husband by her side, Rose studied Magnus as he explained to the shareholders why it was essential to buy a third steamer for the 1903 summer season.

A new maturity had begun to overlay the youthful enthusiasm she had first encountered when he showed her round *Darroch's Folly*. He had gained his master's ticket, Chauncy had told her, and was now qualified to captain one of his own steamboats.

He had done all that he had set out to achieve, and more. His business was doing well, and he was popular and well known, not just in Sandyford but up and down the coast.

Confidence added new dimensions to his rugged face and his tall, broad-shouldered figure. Confidence and perhaps, thought Rose with a shiver of remembered fear, a ruthlessness that she hadn't seen or even suspected until the day of the fight with Hannie Simpson.

Hannie had come out of hospital to find his daughter on the brink of marriage to Chauncy Gibb, his house stripped of everything, even the wallpaper, and his once-feared name a subject of amusement and derision. He had left the town; rumour had it that he had gone to stay with a brother in Glasgow, but nobody knew and nobody cared.

Magnus may have stopped short of killing him that day on the harbour, but he had destroyed the man utterly in every other way, as far as Sandyford was concerned.

She brought her straying thoughts back to the matter in hand in time to find that Magnus had won his argument, as she knew he would.

'And now, gentlemen – ladies and gentlemen,' he corrected himself, his eyes finding Rose without hesitation, 'since this is the festive season I'd be pleased if you would all join me in some refreshments in the next room before we venture into the night air.'

There was a general murmur of approval, and a general move towards the inner door.

'We should go home. I promised your grandmother that I would play a game of cards with her –'

'Nonsense.' Blair put a hand beneath his wife's arm and steered her away from the main exit. 'Grandmother can wait for a little longer.'

As the Crawfords came into the room Magnus

excused himself from the group he stood with and came to meet them, beckoning a waiter with a loaded tray.

'Good evening, Rose. Blair.' He took two glasses from the waiter, handed them over, took a third for himself and raised it to them in a brief toast. 'Marriage suits you, Blair. I've never seen you look so well.'

'You should try it yourself,' Blair said cheerfully.

Magnus smiled – a smile that didn't quite reach his eyes. 'Some men were born to marry, and others, like myself, were not.'

'Then you're the loser, I can assure you. On the other hand, I should be grateful that you're not the marrying kind. Otherwise,' Blair explained when Magnus looked puzzled, 'you and I might have been at loggerheads over which of us was to win Rose. I'll admit that at one point I thought it might have been you.'

'Blair!'

'No need to be modest, my love.'

'Let's just say that the best man won,' Magnus suggested.

'You must come to a soirée we're having on Christmas Eve.'

'Thank you, I would be delighted.'

Rose swallowed down some wine, welcoming the fiery bite of it in her throat, and said lightly, 'So – there's to be a new steamer.'

'My aim is to add one vessel to the fleet every year.'

'Indeed? And when will you be satisfied?'

His eyes shot gold lights at her. 'When I have the finest fleet on the Firth of Clyde. I hope, next year, to commission a brand-new vessel, instead of buying from other companies.'

He grinned, then drawled in a fair imitation of some of the more well-to-do folk in the area, 'Pity your little yard only stretches to building yachts for jumped-up tradesmen, old boy. I might have been able to put a spot of business your way.'

Blair laughed, and Rose asked, 'Are you still set on a turbine engine?'

'Oh yes. Something sleek and fast.'

'For myself, I prefer the paddle-steamers.'

'So do I,' said Blair.

'And I,' said Magnus, 'but paddle-boats are already slipping into the past. It makes sense' – a harsh note crept into his voice, and his eyes rested on Rose – 'to put the past behind us, and only think of the future.'

'I agree.' Blair accepted another glass from the waiter. 'I'll drink to your future, Magnus, for I've got all I want in the world now.'

'Yes,' said Magnus. 'I know that.'

Bella Gibb died very suddenly early in March. Chauncy, who called in on her every morning on his way to the harbour, found her lying in her bed.

'Her heart gave out,' Agnes Anderson told Bella's shocked family when she was summoned. 'It was weakened when she had that bout of pneumonia.'

She looked down on the dead woman. 'It's as good a way to go as any. No suffering, no knowing.'

'It's the only way God could have taken her,' Leila said tearfully when the three of them gathered in Bella's parlour to arrange the funeral. 'Not knowing. She'd never have agreed to go if He'd asked.'

'Oh – Leila!' Rose hugged her sister, half-laughing and half-crying. 'Only you could put it like that.'

Leila blinked back a fresh onslaught of tears. 'I miss her already. The times she's near driven me to my wits' end, too. I never thought I'd miss her like this.'

They all felt bereft. No matter what had happened in the past, Bella had always been there; even when Rose was in South Africa the knowledge that Bella was at home in Sandyford had given her world a centre to revolve round.

They clung together for comfort during the first few

days of their bereavement, gaining a comfort from each other that they couldn't get from anyone else.

A great crowd of folk attended the funeral. Bella, during all her years in Sandyford, had made her mark on the town, and there were many present who could have testified to the compassion that she had always tried to keep hidden from public view.

Miss McKinnon, red-eyed and pink-nosed, wept into a large black-bordered handkerchief throughout the funeral service and became volubly maudlin at the reception for the mourners in the Co-operative Halls, when someone mistakenly decided that what she needed to cheer her up was a glass of port.

Magnus was there, sternly handsome in black, shaking Rose's hand formally as she stood with Leila and Chauncy at the door, welcoming the guests.

Catherine Lacey insisted on attending. 'It's the least I can do for your mother,' she said briskly to Chauncy at the reception. 'She was a good woman, and we mustn't forget that her husband saved George's life.' She sighed and added, 'Though it's little enough enjoyment the poor man's getting out of his life now. Is that your wife over there? Pretty little thing – she has beautiful eyes. I see you're about to become parents.'

'Next month,' Chauncy said, crimson with pleasure at the old woman's praise of his beloved Meg, and with embarrassment at her outspokenness.

'Mmm. You're fortunate – very fortunate,' the old woman said dryly, her eyes moving beyond Chauncy to where Rose stood, slender and flat-bellied.

Once Bella Gibb had been laid to rest in the cemetery beside her husband her house had to be cleared. None of them wanted anything from the place.

'It seems like stealing,' Leila said, voicing all their thoughts.

Chauncy nodded. 'I think the gypsies have the right way of it, burning a person's belongings.'

'We're not burning anything of Mam's,' Rose told him sturdily. 'There are plenty of folk who'd be glad of some warm clothes and bedding, and some good furniture. They can have it all.'

'I can't take to do with the clearing out,' Leila said swiftly, 'I just can't!'

'I'll do it,' Chauncy offered.

'And I'll help you.'

'It wouldn't be seemly for the mistress of Crawford House to be doing that sort of work.'

'I'm helping,' Rose insisted, and he gave in with some relief.

They packed up Bella's clothes and put her few pieces of jewellery aside to be given to Charlotte in the future.

'And to Meg's baby, should it be a girl,' Rose insisted.

'And your own children, when they come,' Chauncy said, stowing the small box carefully in his pocket so that he could take it home for safe-keeping.

Rory and another man from the warehouse brought a horse and cart to take the furniture to the harbour, where it was to be sold off.

It was like the time she had taken old Mr Kenway's bits and pieces away, Rose thought, watching the men carry the pieces down the stairs. A wave of nostalgia, of wanting to turn the clock back to that day when she was standing on the brink of a new career with the rest of her life before her, swept over her.

All at once Chauncy's broad back, going away from her down the first flight of stairs, was Magnus's. As her brother reached the half-landing and turned to go down the next flight he glanced up, and instead of Chauncy she saw Magnus's rugged face, coldly alien under a snowy white bandage.

It wasn't the day Mr Kenway's belongings had left that she was remembering now, but the day of the fight, the day Magnus had gone down those stairs between two policemen.

She swayed and had to clutch at the banisters for support. The face below hers frowned in concern, and became Chauncy's again.

'Are you ill, Rose?'

She dug her fingers into the banister rail so tightly that they hurt.

'I'm fine. I just got dizzy, leaning over the stairwell.'

'And now,' said Rose as she and Chauncy stood in the empty house, their voices echoing against bare floorboards and uncurtained expanses of window, 'there's the scrubbing out to do.'

'Och, the place is clean enough.'

She gave him a mock scowl of horror. 'Chauncy Gibb! Mam would be shocked if she could hear you. She'd not dream of moving out of a house without cleaning it thoroughly. And since she's not here to see to it for herself –'

'You're surely not thinking of doing it?'

'Who else is there? Meg's not fit, and Leila won't set foot in the place.'

'We'll pay a woman to do it.'

Rose briefly recalled Mam's screech of horror long ago, when Rose had suggested getting in a cleaning woman to help with the heavy work.

'She'd hate that. It's my place to do it, Chauncy. Besides,' she added as he opened his mouth to make a further protest, 'I want to do it. It's been a long time since I rolled up my sleeves and did some good hard scrubbing.'

It was fortunate for her that Blair was away from home once again. She put on a plain skirt and blouse and arranged to borrow a bucket of hot water, cloths, a scrubbing brush and soap from Miss McKinnon, firmly turning down the woman's offer of help.

This was something that she wanted to do alone, the last duty she could perform for Bella.

And it was a duty that would be performed well, she promised herself, even to Mam's exacting standards.

She kindled the kitchen fire, filled the big kettle, and put it on. Then she carried the bucket of hot water into the living room, unbuttoned the neck of her blouse and rolled her sleeves up to beyond the elbows, and set to work.

As she scrubbed industriously, soapy water flying from her brush, the wooden floor taking on a pale brown cleanliness beneath her rinsing cloth, all the frustrations and sorrows of the past months fell away. She began to sing, and the suds flew even faster.

By early afternoon the living room and the two bedrooms were finished. The hall linoleum was polished, and the brasses on the front door shone.

There was only the kitchen to do. She emptied the bucket of dirty water into the stone sink and was just refilling it from the kettle when she heard someone running up the stairs, taking them two at a time. The sound echoed through the empty rooms, and set Rose's heart leaping into her throat.

She knew that tread well, though it had been a long time since she had heard it last.

32

Her hands stilled at their work. The flow of water from kettle to bucket dwindled then stopped as she stood motionless.

Knuckles rapped on the door. She straightened, laid the kettle down gently, noiselessly. She wouldn't answer. He couldn't know that she was here – that anyone was here. He had no key. If she didn't open the door he couldn't come in. She wouldn't open the door –

The knuckles rapped again; the noise of their onslaught boomed down the hall and rolled around the empty rooms. She stepped out of her shoes and crept to the kitchen door on stockinged feet, her hands pressed tightly against her mouth as though she were trying to keep herself from calling out to him.

The newly polished letter box flew open. 'Rose?' said Magnus into the open slot. 'Open the door, Rose. I know you're in there.' Then he knocked again.

Suddenly realizing that if he wasn't stopped he would have the whole building roused, and the womenfolk at their doors, peering inquisitively up and down the stairs, Rose flew to open the door.

'What kept you so long?' Magnus wanted to know, thrusting his way past her into the hall.

'What are you doing here?'

'I'll tell you that when you've closed the door,' he said crisply, and forged ahead into the kitchen. When she followed him she found him warming his hands by the range. 'It's got cold enough for snow out there,' he said conversationally, removing his smart bowler hat, stripping off his heavy coat. Beneath it he wore a dark suit and white shirt. At the neck of the shirt a pale grey silk stock was fastened with a pearl pin. He looked successful and assured.

'What brings you here?'

'I came to talk to you. I've just come back from Glasgow, and I happened to meet Leila, who mentioned that you were here. I came,' he said again, by way of explanation, 'to talk to you.' Then he added with a sudden heart-stopping grin, indicating her outfit, 'If I'd known that dress was to be so informal I'd have made time to change. As it is, you'll have to excuse my appearance.'

Her blouse and skirt were, she knew, spattered with dirty soapy water. Her hair, loosened by her exertions, hung in ringlets about her neck. She was quite sure that her face, too, was spotted and splashed by water flying up from the scrubbing brush.

She pushed the mental picture of her own appearance away and tried, for the sake of serenity, to pretend that she was immaculately dressed, and in the drawing room of Crawford House.

'If it's about the Darroch Line, surely you could –'

'It's not about the Darroch Line.'

'Then I can't see –'

'Dammit, Rose,' he interrupted her impatiently, 'I just wanted to talk to you, to be alone with you for a few minutes! How long is it since we were last alone?'

'The day you almost killed Hannie Simpson.'

He glowered at her from beneath his brows. 'You'll never forgive me for that, will you? For giving the man the thrashing he deserved.'

'Deserved? He was half dead, pleading for mercy, and you –'

'All that time in South Africa, those months among soldiers, and you still think that Britons should always be gentlemen, don't you?'

'In South Africa the soldiers were under the command of their officers. And the officers didn't –'

She stopped suddenly.

'Didn't what, Rose?' He was watching her, eyes narrowed. 'Didn't ever hit a man when he was down? Didn't drag your Kommando friend away to be shot when he was recovering from his wounds? Accept the truth, Rose! Men aren't angels – or beasts. We're just human. We all have our base side, as well as our better side.'

She was angry with him, furious with him for bursting in on her, taking away the brief contentment she had been experiencing.

'Go away, Magnus. I've work to do.'

'When I'm ready.' He leaned back against the wall, arms folded, and studied her with tawny eyes that bored through her own gaze, tunnelling into the thoughts beyond, seeking them out and forcing them to give up their secrets to him.

'Are you happy with Blair?'

'Very happy.'

'You said that too quickly. No regrets?'

'None.'

'I have,' said Magnus, and suddenly his voice was so gentle, so intimate, so raggedly exposed that it hurt her to listen to it. 'Oh, my darling, I have.'

'Don't! You've no right to speak to me like that!'

'Right doesn't come into it.' He unhitched his shoulder from the wall and came towards her. 'We've grown apart, you and I. In another year we'll be so far apart that we won't know how to talk to each other at all, except about the weather and what's happening in Parliament. Before that happens, I want to –'

The knocker rattled, and they whirled, like startled intruders.

'Mrs Crawford?' Miss McKinnon's voice came skirling through the letter box. 'Are you still there, Mrs Crawford? I brought you some tea.'

In one movement Magnus was behind her, his hands on her arms, his voice low.

'Don't answer.'

'I must!'

He dipped his head, put his lips to her ear. 'D'you want her to find us alone together?'

'Mrs Crawford?'

'She'll think you've gone out to – to buy something,' Magnus urged in a whisper. She turned to look up at him, a movement that was to be the undoing of both of them. Now their faces were almost touching, their eyes locked.

'Oh – Rose –' said Magnus, a groan in his voice.

He lowered his head and let his mouth fasten on the curve of her neck, tracing a fiery line of kisses from her ear to her shoulder, nuzzling deep into the open collar of her blouse. His touch sent a deep shudder through her body, and in answer he pulled her into his arms, seeking and taking and holding her mouth with his, his tongue greedily probing and twisting round hers.

'– tea, Mrs Crawford –' Miss McKinnon's voice receded and died as Rose pressed tightly against Magnus, all the frustration of her nights with Blair flaring up into a hunger that couldn't, wouldn't be denied. She twined her arms closer about him, wanting to draw him into the depths of herself, to make him one with her for ever.

He pushed the material of her blouse aside, and kissed her shoulder. She felt the buttons fastening the blouse give as he pulled impatiently at it so that his lips could reach the swell of her breast.

Everything was swept away by her great need for his loving, the need that Blair had fuelled, but had not satisfied. The need that, Rose now knew, only Magnus could truly satisfy. Her marriage, her husband – everything was forgotten, consumed by the urgency of the moment.

Magnus undressed her, his breath quick and harsh in his throat. When she stood naked before him he said, low-voiced, 'Let your hair down.'

His eyes, hot with his wanting, followed the movements of her raised arms and tautened breasts as she loosed the knot on top of her head and allowed her hair to fall about her shoulders like a dark silken curtain. He reached out, took two fistfuls of it, and drew her to him. Then he bent his head to fasten his mouth onto a rosy, erect nipple pushing its way through the tresses.

She wove her fingers into the thick tawny hair against her shoulder, and he returned to claim her mouth again, briefly, before lifting her into his arms.

'Rose –?'

'Yes – oh, yes!'

They spoke in whispers, though Miss McKinnon had long since gone back into her own house, the unwanted cup of tea in her hand, and there was silence from the landing. They spoke in whispers not so much because they were afraid of being heard, but because they suddenly inhabited a world so exquisitely beautiful, so precious and fragile, that the sound of one voice might easily shatter it and cast them back into cold reality.

He sank to his knees and laid her tenderly, like a mother putting a child into its crib, on the linoleum-covered floor before the range. Then he picked up his jacket, thrown impatiently aside earlier, and folded it, putting it beneath her head. After that, slowly and deliberately, he explored her body with his mouth, warming and covering her with sweet, soft kisses until she was moaning and twisting beneath his lips, devoured in the fire that flared through every part of her.

'Magnus, for God's sake!'

He laughed, a low, exultant laugh, and pulled off his clothing. Then, mother-naked, he came to her and into her without further hesitation.

All the yearning that had kept her awake night after night while Blair slept by her side rushed to meet him. She gripped at him with arms and legs and mouth, drawing him deep into her body, holding him to ransom, determined not to let him go until she had drained him of everything he had to give.

She had never dreamed, never imagined that loving could be so fierce, so intense, so pleasurable. They rolled over the floor together, Rose above Magnus, then Magnus above Rose, unaware of the hard cold surface beneath them, intent only on each other.

Rose heard her own voice gasping endearments, commands, pleas. She heard Magnus answer, but she didn't know what words either of them used. This, she thought, drunk with love, dazed with her ecstasy in him, was the other side of the dark passion that had caused him to thrash Hannie Simpson. This was Magnus MacBride – a man with all of a man's emotions. And at that moment she was glad, so glad, that he was such a man.

At the peak of their loving her body arched strongly beneath his, she cried out and heard his answering cry mingling with hers – then at last they were still, clasped in each other's arms, breathless, cast ashore on a great final triumphant wave of pleasure that left them exhausted and deliriously happy.

Magnus moved first, raising himself on one elbow to look down on her. She felt the perspiration on her naked breasts and belly cooling as the protective warmth of his body was removed. His russet hair hung in soft curls over his forehead, his eyes were wide and clear, the golden lights in them sparkling down at her. His mouth curved into a smile.

'Rose –'

'Hush.' She stopped him with a finger on his lips. They parted, and his teeth fastened on the ball of her finger, nibbling and teasing. Then his head dropped to her breasts.

Mistily, she thought of Blair, and wondered why she felt so free, so innocent. Then, as Magnus's kisses began to rouse her once more she gave herself up to pleasure, resolving to deal with guilt whenever it arrived.

This time, the razor edge of his hunger dulled, he took her tenderly, slowly, and with love. They joined, parted, joined, rose together, as though swimming languidly through a warm foreign azure sea, to a climax that was far sweeter but no less passionate than before, then collapsed again into a tangle of smooth naked warm limbs, touching, stroking, kissing each other with delicious laziness.

'I knew from the first moment I saw you –' he whispered into her hair. 'The day that old man died, do you remember? I knew that you were my only future. But I was arrogant enough to think that there was all the time in the world, time to put the Darroch Line on its feet, time to build up something to offer you, something worthy of you. I should have told you, but I thought –'

Pain began to flower dully within Rose: the pain of remembering that it was all too late.

'And now,' she whispered desolately, tasting her own salt tears on his smooth shoulder as she spoke, 'it's too late.'

'Is it?'

She stirred in his embrace. 'You know it is.' Now the guilt came, burning into her, tarnishing the joy she had known only moments before. She closed her eyes against his look, and felt moisture squeeze beneath the lashes. Magnus's mouth gently touched first one closed lid, then the other.

She opened her eyes, and saw his lips shining wet with her tears. He released her and began to get up. She wanted to reach for him, to pull him back, but she fought against the impulse, and against further tears that threatened to cloud her vision. She wanted to be able to look at him clearly, to imprint him in her mind, to have that, at least, to comfort her through the rest of her life.

His body was slim-hipped, long-legged. The hair at his groin and on his chest was reddish, his shoulders pleasingly broad, his skin satin smooth. The muscles moved easily beneath it as he bent to pick up his clothes.

She sat up, pushing her long hair back. 'An artist should paint you in the nude.'

He paused, startled for a moment, then grinned down at her with a wry, almost bitter twist of the mouth. 'An artist should paint us both in the nude, and call it the Garden of Eden.'

Then the trace of amusement faded from his eyes. He swallowed hard, took a step towards her. Hurriedly, knowing full well that if he touched her again she would be unable to resist him, she got to her feet and picked up her petticoat.

'And we know what happened in the Garden of Eden – afterwards,' she heard him say, low-voiced.

She dressed hurriedly, listening to the small sounds he made as he moved about the room, but she didn't look at him until she was fully clothed again, her hair pinned up.

Then they faced each other across the width of the kitchen for a long silent moment before Magnus said abruptly, 'I came here today in the hope that you'd tell me you'd never loved me. Perhaps then I could have wished you well. But now –'

'I'm Blair's wife, Magnus.'

'Yes,' he said. 'Yes.'

He put his coat on then combed his fingers through his hair and settled his bowler hat carefully in place.

Watching him, she knew that she could never again pretend that what had been between them before her marriage was dead and gone.

'Rose, it's not too late,' he said abruptly, almost angrily.

'It is!'

'Who gives a damn what other people say?' He reached towards her. 'All you have to do is walk out of here by my side, and face them – Blair as well. We could be together, always.'

She put her own hands behind her back, locking the

fingers firmly together to keep them from straying towards him. 'I can't. I can't do that to Blair.'

His eyes flashed red-gold flame at her. 'But you can do it to me!'

'You're stronger than he is. You can exist on your own.'

'Can you?'

'If I have to.'

'I wish to God,' said Magnus, 'that I'd paid that penny for your fine brave song. Then you would have been mine, and not his.'

He turned and went out, leaving her alone, completely and totally alone, in the empty house that had once belonged to Bella Gibb.

33

The Darroch Line's new paddle-steamer's trials were held on a glowering April day when a grey curtain of rain hid the islands and the far mainland shore, and a keen cold wind came scudding in from the west, over the open sea, driving the water before it.

Now and again, when the curtain thinned, it showed that the islands which on sunny days seemed to be stretching languid green limbs into the water had turned into surly crouched beasts, threatening the mainland.

The foam-capped waves came in high and hard, marching in row upon row on the shore, slapping against the rocks, clutching at mudbanks and grasses and pebbles with greedy fingers, sliding reluctantly back, then gathering their energy and making a fresh assault.

Blair had arranged to go on board *Bracken* for the trials; Rose, who had work to do at the warehouse, accompanied him to the harbour.

It had always seemed unlikely to Rose that Blair's infrequent, almost frigid attentions could bear fruit, but in the days following her stolen moments with Magnus she had wondered more and more if she was carrying Magnus's child. Surely the depths and intensity of the loving they had shared in the tenement kitchen must bear a result?

Surely, a voice whispered deep within her mind, such infidelity must bring its own punishment?

Whatever the risk, she found herself desperately wanting Magnus's child. She had no idea what she would do if she found that she was indeed pregnant. Pass if off as the Crawford heir? Face Blair with the truth, and let him use the pregnancy to free her from a marriage that had become an empty shell? She had no idea. She only knew that she wanted the comfort of knowing that Magnus's child was within her.

When the usual cramps and the usual bleeding occurred after two weeks, she wept.

Magnus was becoming a popular guest in the larger houses above the town, particularly among those households with unmarried daughters; each time Rose encountered him she marvelled at the way they were able to talk to each other as mere acquaintances.

But now and again, when she turned her head and caught Magnus's eyes on her and felt a flutter of longing deep in her belly, she remembered their fierce, illicit coupling, and knew that he too was thinking of it.

The steamer was handsome in her new colours, rain sluicing over her decks. Her stokers had got up a good head of steam, and the smoke from the double funnels was being wrenched away by the wind to stream into the air and fragment.

Magnus, burly in his sou'wester and oilskins, stood by the gangway, talking to Chauncy. He nodded as the Crawfords arrived.

'Rose. Blair. We'll be casting off in a few minutes.'

Blair ran an appreciative eye over the steamer. 'I thought you might have decided to put the trials off until a better day.'

'No need. She'll be doing bad-weather runs anyway, to Arran. I'd like to see how she handles the Skelmorlie Mile in this weather. I'm hoping that she'll make better time than *Tansy*.'

'Are you taking her out yourself?' Rose asked.

'I'll captain her once she starts work, but for the moment Urquhart has the bridge. I want to spend time down in the engine room during this trip. Are you coming, Blair?'

The tide was in, and the gangway tilted at a sharp angle; Magnus scaled it with ease, Blair gripped the rails and pulled himself uphill to the deck. Rose lifted her face to the rain and watched them both taking their places on the bridge as the mooring ropes were cast off.

Blair waved, his fair, handsome face beaming with youthful delight at the thought of the trip ahead. Magnus turned his head, looked for her, found her, and lifted one hand in a brief salute. She brushed the rain from her face and stood watching the steamboat edge neatly away from the harbour and disappear into the grey drizzle.

Leila arrived at the warehouse an hour later, shaking rain from her umbrella, stamping her booted feet, happy to get into shelter.

'Where's Charlotte?'

'With Meg. I brought the chair-back Meg's been working on. I told her that it was far too wet for her to come out.' Leila opened her parcel and spread the cloth out for her sister's inspection. 'Isn't it beautiful?' Her fingers touched the delicate, flawless stitching reverently. 'You should just see the gown she's making for the baby!'

'I must visit her soon. How is she?'

Leila screwed up her pretty nose. 'Fat as a butterball, poor lassie.' Then she added, lowering her voice and looking round to make certain that nobody else overheard her, 'But I've never seen her look so happy. It's almost as if she's pleased!'

'Of course she's pleased. So were you, when Charlotte was born.'

'Well – yes, but that was after she was born, when she looked so pretty in her perambulator, with her little lacy caps and her nice gowns. But before that, when you feel all fat – I don't understand Meg. It's almost as though she doesn't mind any of it.'

'What do you mean?'

'Och, Rose, you know very well what I mean?' Leila's face bloomed like a poppy. 'Surely she couldn't care for that part of it!'

'Leila, just because you disliked the more – private side of marriage, it doesn't mean that every woman does.'

'But I mean – you can't – you can't say that you like it, Rose? No matter how much money Blair has!'

Rose thought of her marriage bed, then she thought of Magnus, and a great wave of physical longing surged up in her.

'You can't!' her sister said again in disbelief.

Someone came slipping and sliding over the cobbles, splashing through the puddles. The warehouse door, closed against the inclement weather, was thrown back against its hinges, and Chauncy burst in, bareheaded and without his coat.

'There's something amiss. *Bracken*'s coming back, and she's under tow!'

Rose was out on the harbour, the icy rain sluicing down on her unprotected head, before she realized that she had begun to move.

A small sturdy paddle-steamer was emerging slowly from the mist. Behind her, wallowing helplessly in the heavy seas, came *Bracken*.

Magnus – Rose thought, her heart gripped by fear. Blair – Her eyes strained through the rain, but none of the figures on the bridge seemed familiar.

'D'you want to catch your death of cold?' Leila drew her under the shelter of her umbrella.

Chauncy, too tall to share their shelter, waited tensely beside them, the rain darkening his hair and plastering it to his skull.

'Can you see them, Leila? Can you see Blair, or Magnus?'

'Not yet. But there's no need to think that anything's happened to them. The engines have broken down, that's all.'

Rose shook her head impatiently. She knew that one of them was hurt.

The steamer that towed *Bracken* came in close, dipping towards the harbour then by-passing it to bring the crippled Darroch boat in alongside.

'Take her lines,' the captain on the towing vessel boomed through a loud-hailer. 'I'll cast her off as soon as you've got her.'

Then he added, 'And fetch the ambulance wagon, there's an injured man aboard. Steam-pipe fractured –'

'Leila, send somebody for the ambulance wagon, quickly,' Rose ordered, swinging round on her sister. 'And fetch some baking powder from Harvey's Bakery, it's only a step away.'

As *Bracken* slid silently along parallel to the harbour, only the faintest ripple of a wake at her bows and flanks when there should have been a great foaming of water, Chauncy said, 'There's Blair.'

'Then it's Magnus,' Rose said, and felt the blood drain from her heart.

The stern mooring rope thwacked on to the harbour. Someone snatched at it before it could slip back into the water, then looped it securely round a bollard and began to pull as Chauncy ran to help.

Blair stood by the rail near the paddle-box, his face white and strained. More men were running from all over the harbour now. A team of them were pulling on the rope that linked *Bracken* to the shore, dragging the vessel in hand over hand.

Slowly her stern began to swing towards them. The forward line was thrown ashore, falling short on the first try. The deckhand deftly coiled the line back in with controlled urgency, threw it again, and made the harbour wall this time.

It was hauled in as fast as the men could work, first the thin line, then finally the thick looped rope appearing, slippery and dripping with water. Over a bollard it went, and another half dozen men lined up to pull on it as the steamer that had brought *Bracken* home cast off the towing line.

Now that the steamboat could be hauled in fore and aft the men made short work of the task, although to Rose, waiting on the cobbles, it seemed to take a long time.

'I got some!' Leila appeared by her side, a large drum clutched in her arms. 'And I sent a lad running for the ambulance wagon.'

Bracken was alongside now. As soon as the gangway was run into place, before it was roped securely, Rose sped across it, swaying dizzily over the dark water as the gangway jerked beneath her weight, then stepping safely on to the paddle-box.

Blair met her on the deck. 'Thank God you're here! It's Magnus –'

'Where is he?'

'In the engine room.' He was shaking with reaction. She ran for the companionway, throwing herself down it with reckless disregard for life and limb.

A small group of men were huddled on the engineer's deck. They parted, and she fell to her knees beside Magnus, who was lying on his back on a pile of sacking. His head was turned to one side, arms thrown out either side of his body as though he had been tossed down carelessly. His waistcoat and shirt had been cut from the upper part of his body, and lay shredded around him.

The right side of his face and his torso were lobster red, the skin blistering. The tender inner part of his right arm and the palm of his hand were equally blistered, showing how he had thrown his arm up to protect his eyes when the steam-pipe fractured.

His legs and the fingers of his uninjured hand moved slowly, ceaselessly, in protest against the searing agony that was eating him alive. His teeth were locked tightly together in a futile attempt to hold back the whimpers of pain.

'He was alone down there, trying to clear a valve that had jammed,' someone was saying above her head. 'The pipe fractured, and the steam –'

'Open that.' She thrust the tin into the nearest hands, then folded her skirt back and unfastened her petticoat, regardless of any masculine eyes that might be fixed on her.

'Did you splash him with cold water?'

'Aye, as best as we could.'

'Good.' She stepped out of the petticoat and tossed it to someone. 'Rip that up. Go on, man!' she added as he hesitated, eyeing the delicate garment.

She scattered the baking powder liberally over the angry, scarlet skin then laid the clean strips of torn petticoat gently on top. There was a stir among the watching men and Rose looked up to see Agnes Anderson.

'I heard that there had been an accident,' the woman said briefly. She knelt, and said almost at once, 'It looks bad.'

'Steam scalds. I put baking powder over them, and clean cloths.'

'The best thing, for the moment.'

Magnus groaned, and his left hand fisted itself, then opened out again, the fingers reaching into empty air. Rose touched them and they immediately curled about her hand, holding so tightly that she felt as though the bones were going to break.

'He needs morphine.' Agnes opened her bag.

Someone shouted from the top of the companionway, 'The ambulance wagon's here!'

'In that case, he might have a chance,' said Agnes grimly.

They had to wait until the morphine took effect before they could move Magnus, prising his fingers loose, one by one, from Rose's hand.

Agnes travelled in the ambulance wagon with him. As she gathered her skirts briskly about her skinny shanks and climbed aboard she glanced over at Rose and raised her brows in silent invitation. Rose shook her head, and stood in the rain with Blair and Chauncy and Leila, watching the ambulance wagon disappear through the harbour gates, wanting to go with it, with him, but unable to, because she was another man's wife.

'Poor MacBride,' Blair said. 'What a stroke of bad luck, just when he was building the business up so well. I suppose,' he added thoughtfully, 'that whether he survives or not, that's the Darroch Line finished.'

34

Blair was by no means the only person to assume that the Darroch Line had collapsed. Magnus MacBride had been the force behind the entire venture, and with Magnus MacBride lying in the infirmary, drifting in and out of consciousness and as close to death as any man would want to be without stepping across the divide, it naturally followed that there could be no Darroch Line.

'That's not necessarily right,' Rose argued with Blair, with Chauncy, with Captain George Urquhart.

'Oh, we'll go on with the summer programme that Mr MacBride had already agreed for *Darroch's Pride* and *Tansy*,' George Urquhart assured her. 'But it's going to cost a fair bit to put *Bracken* right. She'll have to go into one of the big yards at Greenock or Port Glasgow. Even if we went ahead with the repairs and got her through her trials she'd miss the first half of the summer trade. Mr MacBride was counting on the money she was going to bring in.'

He shook his head doubtfully. 'My own feeling is that it might not be worth putting out the extra cost on her.'

'But we should surely use her!'

The two men eyed each other, then: 'I don't know, Rose,' Chauncy said slowly. 'Do we have the right to go ahead and mebbe bankrupt the man while he's so ill? You told me yourself that there's all sorts of conditions can come from severe burning. Pneumonia and the like. He may well need every penny that's left to him. Not that there's much,' he finished gloomily.

'Magnus would fight, and so should we.'

'Can we, without him?' George Urquhart wanted to know. 'Several of the shareholders have already lost heart. They want their money back. And there'll be more.'

'Give me a list of shareholders. I'll go and see them.'

'With all due respect, Mrs Crawford –'

'I'm a shareholder myself, Captain Urquhart. And if you're not prepared to try to save the Darroch Line, then I'll do it.'

'But you don't have the authority to speak to folk on Mr MacBride's behalf.'

'I'll get it,' said Rose tightly, and two hours later she was among the people flocking into the infirmary for the afternoon visiting hour.

She had wanted, every minute of every day since Magnus's accident, to see him. But it was scarcely seemly for Blair Crawford's wife to go rushing to another man's bedside, and even if she had been free to do as she wished Magnus was too ill to have any visitors for the first few days. But now he was out of immediate danger, and now she had good cause to visit him.

She arrived on foot, and unannounced, so that there was no time for the matron to arrange a welcoming committee.

'You won't stay long, will you? He can't really talk at the moment,' the ward sister said as she led the way to a screened bed.

'Can he hear me?' Then she added as the girl nodded her neatly capped head, 'Could he sign a paper?'

His right hand's bandaged.'

'With his left hand, then. And perhaps you could witness it. It's very important.'

'The matron should –'

'Never mind the matron,' said Mrs Crawford of Crawford House. 'You'll do. I'll let you know when I need you.'

The right side of Magnus's body and face were swathed in bandages. The healthy tanned skin on the left side of his face stood out against the mass of bandages. His only visible eye was closed.

But when Rose said his name his eyelid lifted at once to expose an eye unharmed by the steam jet, but drugged and sleepy.

She sat down, and took his hand in hers. His fingers closed over hers at once, just as they had done in *Bracken*'s engine room.

'Magnus, we've got to keep the Darroch Line going while you're in here. Isn't that what you want?'

His left eyebrow tucked down as though asking her what sort of daft question that was.

'Chauncy and George Urquhart'll do all they can, but they're not happy about making decisions. And decisions must be made. Will you trust me to make them?'

The visible corner of his mouth twitched into the faintest semblance of a smile. His hand squeezed hers, then relaxed.

'I'll try to do what you'd do yourself, I swear it. I'll keep the Darroch Line going.' She drew a paper out of her bag.

'I must have a signed paper giving me the authority I need. You'll have to sign your name as best you can with your left hand. Can you do it?'

His eyelid dropped, then lifted again.

'I'll fetch the sister,' said Rose.

The effort that it took Magnus to scrawl his name left him exhausted. After the sister had deftly added her own signature as witness, she said, 'I think it's time he got some rest.'

'I'm just going.' As the sister vanished round the screens Rose stooped over the bed, took his hand in hers. 'I'll be back soon to let you know how things are coming along.'

His eyelid drooped, then fell. His fingers relaxed their

hold on hers. Rose bent and kissed Magnus on the forehead before leaving him.

She went straight back down to the Darroch Line office. 'Get *Bracken* back into dry dock as soon as you can, and do whatever's necessary to repair her and make her ready for her trials,' she instructed Captain Urquhart.

'I doubt if the line can afford it.'

'I'll see to the cost – you just see to the steamboat, Captain.'

His brows knotted in a puzzled frown. 'Did Mr MacBride authorize you to repair *Bracken*?'

She produced the paper with Magnus's drunken left-handed scrawl across the bottom. He eyed the document, stroking his beard nervously. 'But did he –'

'Captain Urquhart' – she was a Crawford of Crawford House again – 'get *Bracken* back on the water. I'll worry about the money.'

'Yes, Ma'am,' he said meekly.

'You're not serious!' Blair stood before the drawing room hearth, filled with flowers now that the warm weather had arrived, and gazed down at his wife.

Rose returned his look. 'Perfectly serious.'

'My wife, trailing round a tribe of hard-headed businessmen, begging them to –'

'Not begging them, Blair. Convincing them that it makes sense to keep their money in the Darroch Line. And they're not a tribe, they're individuals. I shall treat them as individuals.'

'You're my wife, Rose. Not Magnus MacBride's guardian angel.'

'It's being your wife that'll get me in to see these men in the first place. They'd have little time for me if I was just Rose Gibb. As for being a guardian angel – I'd do the same for you if it was your business that was on the brink of destruction.'

'Why can't you stay at home and play the lady of the manor?' he grumbled affectionately.

'Because that's still your grandmother's place, and I'm used to having something to do.' She linked her hands round his arm. 'Come and see the tribe with me, Blair. Add your voice to mine.'

'I can't. I have to go to Newcastle for a few days.'

'All the more reason for me to have something to do while you're away.'

'Oh, very well. But I don't think it's going to work. If you ask me, the Darroch Line's finished. Another investment that went wrong.'

'If that's what you really think, sell your shares to me.'

'What?'

'I mean it. The more shares I have the more power I'll have. And I need the power in order to make the decisions.'

He laughed, and shook his head. 'One day, Rose, I must try to persuade you to take over the Crawford interests. You'd no doubt make me a very wealthy man.'

Then he dropped a kiss on her nose and added, 'I'll not sell you my shares in the Darroch Line. But if you're as set as all that on having them I'll give them to you, as a gift.'

'I'd as soon pay you.'

'I'll not take your money.'

'In that case,' she said, 'I accept.'

During the following week Rose visited Magnus's shareholders, one by one.

They received her because she was Blair Crawford's wife. Some of them gave her a fair hearing because they knew about the success she had made of the furniture business.

Others, she knew with inward fury, could not see past the swell of her breasts against her jacket bodice, the sheen of her black hair beneath the neat feathered hat perched atop her head. To them, she was a woman, and a woman could know nothing of business.

Many of them wanted to be relieved of their shares, and would have clamoured for a return of their investments even if Magnus's envoy had been a man.

'There was something about the fellow,' one of them said to her, jingling the gold watch-chain that stretched across his ample belly, 'that instilled confidence. A gambler, like his uncle, but a gambler with his head screwed on the right way. But now –' He drew in his breath sharply, wagging his balding head. 'Now I'd not give tuppence for the future of the line, and that's a fact.'

'I myself own a number of shares, and I have every faith in the Darroch Line.'

The man smiled indulgently down on her. 'But you've got your husband's money behind you, Mrs Crawford. You'll not be all that concerned as to whether or not your shares bring you a good dividend.'

She got to her feet with an angry flounce of skirts. 'Since you're so set on retrieving your investment, sir, I'll buy your shares from you.'

'Eh?'

'At the price you first paid. It's as fair an offer as you'll get anywhere.'

'Does your husband know –'

'I'm reimbursing you from the proceeds of my own business, Mr Fielding,' said Rose icily, longing to hear the crack of her palm against the man's witless face.

She bought more shares before the week was out, and was forced to call on the bank and borrow heavily against the furniture business.

'Are you quite certain that this is what you wish, Mrs Crawford?' the bank manager asked discreetly, pausing before putting his signature to the document.

There was no time to think things through, no time to allow herself to doubt, or panic. She was working purely by instinct, and she herself didn't know whether the instinct was that of a woman with a good head for business, or a woman hopelessly in love with the wrong man and hellbent on doing everything she could for him.

'Quite certain,' she said coolly, firmly, and the deed was done.

He accompanied her out on to the pavement when their business was completed and handed her up into the Crawford carriage.

As the coachman clucked to the horses and they set off, Rose bowed to the manager, then sat back and lifted her gloved hands before her face, studying them intently. As she had expected, they were trembling.

She twisted them together in her lap and tried not to doubt what she had done. It was too late for doubts.

She now owned a good third of the Darroch Line shares. She was the largest single shareholder apart from Magnus MacBride. She had put herself into debt to buy the shares. She had put her own company's future into jeopardy.

Come what may, if she were to continue to hold her head high in Sandyford the Darroch Line must succeed!

35

It took longer to repair *Bracken* than anyone had first thought, for the damage done by the burst steam-pipe was considerable.

With every day the vessel lay in dry dock the cost of her repair mounted. Magnus, certain of her successful trials, had chartered her out for several sailings, and rather than lose the charters altogether Rose and George Urquhart and Chauncy decided that they must themselves charter a steamer from another line to fulfil the engagements.

Then *Tansy* suffered a mild engine fault that confined her to the harbour for a week and involved a costly part replacement. The Darroch Line was reduced to one steamer – sturdy little *Darroch's Pride*, still paddling several times a day between Sandyford and Rothesay Bay.

Rose watched the small reserves of money she had managed to put together dwindle daily. News of Magnus's accident had spread, and the people who had enjoyed their trips on *Darroch's Pride* flocked back to express their own form of sympathy. Many of them even travelled by train from Glasgow to board the boats at Sandyford instead of sailing all the way down the Clyde on the paddle-steamers that plied out of the Broomielaw.

But even when *Tansy* went back to work the money was going out faster than it came in. The repairs to *Bracken* and the hiring of charter steamers were gobbling up the money that *Darroch's Pride* and *Tansy* made. Rose lay awake at night and worried while Blair slept by her side; she went about her charity work in the town, visited Meg and admired her lusty new baby boy, and secretly fretted about costs all the time.

Magnus was making a good recovery from his injuries, but it was slow, as the doctors had predicted. For a long time he was too ill to think about the paddle-steamers. But gradually, as he fought his way back to health, he began to ask questions.

Rose told him only about the crowded decks at each sailing, and kept silent over the problems. She longed to spill out everything, to ask him what she should do to recoup the losses, but she couldn't. And she let Blair, involved in his own concerns and in the responsibilities piled on his shoulders because of his father's steadily decreasing health, assume that everything was going well.

The work on *Bracken* was finally finished, but the vessel still lay in the dry dock, waiting for a date for her trials.

'Every week – every single day – that we've to wait means more money lost!' Rose fumed, pacing the floor of the Darroch Line office. Her stepbrother and George Urquhart watched her sympathetically.

'If it's any consolation to you, Mrs Crawford, we're not the only people to be suffering misfortune. Have you not heard that Mr Finlay's lost the *Island Princess*?'

'What?'

Chauncy nodded. 'It's true. They've discovered that she needs to be reboilered, and she's had to be taken off the Arran run.'

'That's the run Magnus planned for *Bracken*, in competition with Finlay,' the captain said ruefully. 'Now neither of them are on it. I hear that he's thinking of selling his boat and commissioning another vessel instead, to be built for next summer.'

'Is he, indeed?' said Rose thoughtfully.

'I can't think what you'd want to see me about, Mrs

Crawford.' Mr Finlay peered across his desk at his visitor.

'You'll have heard about Magnus MacBride's accident?'

'The whole coast's heard. A sad misfortune, and not one I'd wish on anyone. Not even a young upstart like MacBride,' he added.

'Upstart or not, he's built a fine steamboat line. You can't deny that, Mr Finlay.'

'I can't. But if you're here to ask me to put my hand in my pocket just because a competitor meets up with a bit of ill fortune, you might as well walk out of that door now, Madam.'

'I hear you've met up with a bit of ill fortune yourself.'

'*Island Princess*? What of it?'

'And not a steamboat free to take over her run, they say. The new Darroch boat, *Bracken*, was meant for that run,' said Rose.

'That,' the old man said tartly, 'is typical of his impudence!' Then his dry, barely sustained courtesy suddenly flaked away and he barked, 'Get to the point, lassie! If you're after chartering MacBride's boat to me to take *Island Princess*'s place, I'm not interested. There are plenty of –'

'I'd not dream of leasing her to you.'

'What?' He sat back and eyed her for a long moment. 'I'd heard that you were taking to do with the boats while MacBride was in the infirmary. Though why you should trouble yourself's beyond me.'

'I'm a shareholder. I own thirty-one shares in the line. Magnus MacBride holds fifty-one. The other eighteen are shared among four investors.'

'Aye? Well, if you're out to sell the steamboat to me –'

'I'm out to give her to you.'

There was a pause, broken only by the voice of a street vendor calling her wares outside. Then Finlay said cautiously, 'You're what?'

Satisfied that she had gained his full attention, Rose leaned forward in her chair.

'I'm out to give her to you. And *Tansy*, and *Darroch's Pride*. Mr Finlay, am I not right when I say that you've got no family to inherit your shipping line?'

'Aye, you are.'

'So what's going to happen to it?'

'What business is that of yours, Ma'am?'

'You're not a young man, Mr Finlay. How many more years do you intend to stay in business?' she challenged him crisply. 'You must have thought of the future.'

'I'll sell – when I'm ready!'

'Sell to one of the railway companies, and have the Finlay Line absorbed into a large fleet as though you'd never existed? Or sell the boats off one by one? Why not hand it over to a younger man when you're ready? A man who could either buy you out or run the business for you and let you retain your financial interest?'

'A man like Magnus MacBride?'

'Exactly.'

'By God,' said the old man, 'you've got plenty of impudence – I'll say that for you!'

'I'm making you a sound business proposition. The Darroch Line needs money if it's to keep going –'

'Let it founder!'

'Mr Finlay, you started up your own line when you were a young man yourself. I can't believe that you've grown so old and crabbit you've forgotten what a struggle it was then. Hear me out,' said Rose coolly when he opened his mouth to speak. He paused, shrugged, and shut his mouth again.

'I'm suggesting an exchange of shares. I sign over my Darroch Line shares to you, making you the largest shareholder apart from Magnus himself, and you sign over a number of shares of equal value in the Finlay Line to me. We just heard today that *Bracken*'s trials are set for next Wednesday. She comes out of dry dock on the

Tuesday. She could be on the Arran run within ten days, Mr Finlay.'

'Go on,' he said cautiously.

'A merger between the two lines, but each line to keep its own name and its own colours. The two lines to share *Bracken*, and the profit she makes, for this year at least. If you want to commission another steamer for next year, a guarantee from the Darroch Line that they'll take *Bracken* off the run when your new vessel's ready, and their word that they'll not compete against you on that run.'

She paused, marshalling the plans she had so carefully worked out, going over them one by one.

'A mutual agreement that each line will respect the other's identity. And you'll underwrite the full cost of repairing *Bracken*, for one year only. At the end of that year the Darroch Line should be in a position to reimburse you.'

'And if it isn't?'

Rose swallowed hard, and said, '*Bracken*'ll be forfeit. She'll be yours.'

'You must have great faith in MacBride's ability to get his business back on its feet within the year.'

'I have.'

'Does he know about this?'

'He's given me the power, as a major shareholder, to make whatever arrangements I deem necessary to keep the business going while he's ill. And there's one more thing.'

'Aye?' His voice was cautious, but grudgingly interested.

'When you retire Magnus MacBride will be your natural heir. That means that he'll either have first refusal to buy the Finlay Line for a fair price, should you decide to sell, or he'll become the manager of a combined Darroch Finlay Line, and you'll be a major shareholder. But that's in the future.'

'I'm glad to hear it. You're not for turning me out to pasture right this minute, then?'

She was relieved to hear crusty amusement in the words. 'Not until you're good and ready, Mr Finlay, I can assure you of that. For the moment, it means that you'll get your Arran run back, and the Darroch Line will be free of its financial problems for the next year. What do you say?'

'I'd have to consider it.'

'Of course. I hope you'll be on board *Bracken* next Wednesday for the trials.' Rose stood up and gathered her things together. 'You can give me your decision after that. Good day, Mr Finlay.'

'I don't know what to tell Mr MacBride when I visit him,' George Urquhart said gloomily. 'What am I going to say, Mrs Crawford?'

'You'll merely tell him the truth. That *Bracken* did very well at her trials, and that she starts on the Arran run next week.'

'He's got to know the whole truth of it some time, Rose,' Chauncy pointed out.

'I know that!' She surveyed them both with exasperation. 'You two look as though there's been a funeral, when all that's happened is that the Darroch Line's solvent again.'

'And in old Finlay's hands.'

'It is not! I told you what Mr Finlay and I agreed on together. The papers are being drawn up now, making every point clear. And once they're signed,' said Rose, uncomfortably aware of two pairs of accusing masculine eyes fixed on her face, 'I shall go to the infirmary and I shall tell everything to Magnus. He'll realize that I had to do it, even if you don't.'

All the same, she was far from certain of Magnus's approval as she walked up the infirmary steps a week later. She had deliberately stayed away from him after her talk to Mr Finlay, because she wanted the agreement to be made final before Magnus got as much as an idea of it. It was the only way, she kept telling herself as she went into the main ward.

The only way to save the Darroch Line and keep the business intact for Magnus when he was well enough to take up the reins again.

The bandages had been removed. At first sight of Magnus's uncovered face Rose wanted to cradle him in her arms. With an effort she held back, drawing a chair to the bedside while he looked at her with a mixture of pleasure and apprehension.

The right side of his face was a map of lobster-red and white, where new skin was growing over the burned areas. One side of his mouth was still puffy and stiff, and his right eyelid drooped.

'Well?'

'I've never seen you look so interesting, Magnus MacBride.'

His apprehension fled. He grinned, the left side of his mouth curling up, the right remaining solemn. 'I made them give me a mirror. I look like a monster.'

'You'll improve. The main thing is that you're getting better.'

'There's no doubt of that.' He leaned back on his pillows, easing his bandaged arm with a slight grimace. 'I'll soon be out of here, and back on the bridge of *Darroch's Pride*.'

'It'll be a while before you can get back to work.'

He brushed the warning aside. 'So they all say. But what I need is to get back to the water. That'll do me more good than anything. That,' he added, low-voiced, 'and seeing you again. I've missed you, Rose.'

'Blair's father's not been at all well,' she said evasively. 'I've scarcely been able to get away from the house.'

His eyes were fixed on her, devouring her features. 'You look more beautiful every time I see you, Rose.'

'Did George Urquhart tell you how well *Bracken* did on her trials?'

'Aye, he did.' He gave a sigh of pleasure. 'I knew she would.'

'She almost killed you.'

'She's got spirit.' He grinned again. 'I like my women to have spirit.'

'She's on the Arran run, with Captain Urquhart on the bridge.'

'That's what I'd planned for her. How much did the repair work cost? I asked him, but he never got around to telling me.'

She took a deep breath, then said, 'It cost more than the Darroch Line could afford.'

He sighed, his left brow tucking down. 'I was afraid of that. But once I'm on my feet again I'll find a way of clearing the debts. How much time did they give me to pay?'

'The yard wanted their money at once, since you were in here and they'd no way of knowing how long they might have to wait.'

Worry clouded the tawny eyes that were more hazel than gold since his accident.

'Confound them! What did you do?'

'What I had to do to keep the line going.'

'But what –' He stopped suddenly, then said, 'Rose, what's been going on while I've been lying here? George Urquhart looked decidedly uncomfortable when I tried to –'

'Just keep quiet and listen, will you, and don't say a word until I've finished?'

Nervousness made her voice sharper than she had intended. He looked at her with sudden apprehension, but said quietly, 'Go on.'

At first, when she began to speak, his gaze was locked

on her face. By the time she had finished his uninjured arm had been lifted to cover his eyes. All she could see, in the shadow between his elbow and shoulder, was his unsmiling mouth.

When she finally stopped he lay still and silent.

'Magnus?'

Slowly, he drew his arm down from his face and turned to look at her. His eyes were brilliant topaz with anger.

'What have you done to me?'

'I've saved the Darroch Line for you.'

'And sold me to Finlay!'

'No! I told you, you'll each run your own line. He's given his word on that, and it's in the agreement. I brought a copy – read it for yourself.'

With a sweep of his arm he knocked the document to the floor. 'To hell with the agreement!'

'You're bound to it as much as he is.'

'I didn't make it!'

'I did, and I had your permission – your signed and witnessed permission – to do what I thought fit to keep the business running.'

'What you thought fit?' he asked with stinging contempt. 'From what I hear you're not even a shareholder now. You handed your shares over to old Finlay – all the shares you could gather into your possession – so that he could get a foot well and truly in the door.'

'Without Mr Finlay's money the Darroch Line would have foundered while you were lying here.'

'Go away, Rose,' Magnus said quietly.

'Magnus, it's for the best. You'll see that when you –'

He turned his head away from her.

'Magnus, please listen –'

Then as he lay still, ignoring her, she got up and walked away from him, out of the ward.

36

Rose returned to Crawford House, tired and dispirited, to find the doctor's landau on the gravel sweep outside the front door. With a sudden sense of foreboding she looked up at the windows of her father-in-law's room on the first floor. The curtains were drawn.

As she hurried up the steps and in at the open front door Doctor Lang and Blair came down the staircase.

'Blair –?'

'I regret to say, Mrs Crawford,' said the doctor pompously, 'that Mr George Crawford passed away peacefully ten minutes ago.'

'Oh, Blair, I'm so sorry!'

Her husband was dry-eyed, very pale and preoccupied looking, as though completely immersed in his own thoughts. 'Grandmother's in the drawing room. I'll join you both shortly, my dear.'

Catherine Lacey was enthroned in her favourite high-backed chair by the flower-filled hearth, her walking stick planted firmly on the carpet before her, her two ancient ringed hands clasped on its handle.

She looked at her grandson's wife with huge bright, dry eyes. It seemed that nobody was going to weep for George Crawford.

'So – he's dead at last,' she said, a grotesque triumph in her voice. 'All those years of waiting for me to die so that he could get his hands on the purse strings. And it was all for naught. I outlived him, as I intended.'

Then she added, almost under her breath, 'But it will be strange without him. I didn't realize until now how much I shall miss him.'

*

Rose was appalled, and repelled, when she realized how little George Crawford's family cared about his death.

After those few telling words in the drawing room Catherine Lacey had said nothing more about her son-in-law. Blair seemed to go about in a dream.

Lilias, who arrived with her young husband and a mountain of luggage, wept for her father on her first evening home, but her tears were very quickly over. Lilias had her own life now, and nothing else was real to her.

The funeral, as befitted George Crawford's station in life and his importance to the town, was a very impressive affair.

A funeral supper was held in Crawford House, and there was also a supper in the church hall for the Crawford workers. The whole town had an air of gloom about it. It was just like the days after Queen Victoria's death. The Town Hall flags were lowered to half mast, the shop windows were shrouded with black crepe, and the boats on the river flew their flags at half mast on the day of the funeral.

Lilias, beautiful in unrelieved black, left on the day after her father's funeral, using as her excuse vague domestic matters that clamoured for her attention.

'If I was you,' she said to Rose as she settled her hat in place and drew on her gloves, 'I would persuade Blair to do over the whole house. It sadly needs it.'

She cast a look about the house that had been home to her for most of her life, and wrinkled her nose. 'It looks so – so Victorian. Blair must bring you to visit us some time soon. Our new house is very modern indeed – very fashionable.'

Then she departed, and Rose and Blair and Catherine Lacey were alone, facing the future together.

Rose didn't go back to the infirmary. There seemed little sense in it. She heard, through Chauncy, that Magnus was badgering the doctors to let him get out of the infirmary. Now that all three boats owned by the Darroch Line were at work, and everything going smoothly., there was no longer any need for her to be involved in the business.

As Magnus had so coldly reminded her, she was no longer a shareholder. And while she was in mourning for Blair's father it didn't seem right that she should be immersing herself in business affairs.

She tolerated the mourning period for a long month, then put on a neat grey suit with a black hat and a dark blue blouse, and went to the harbour.

'You'll have heard that Magnus is out of hospital at last?' Leila asked.

Rose felt her heart stop, then throw itself painfully against her ribs. 'No, I hadn't heard. Have you seen him?'

'Not yet, though he's been down at the harbour. He's expecting to get back to work any day now.'

Then she asked with concern, 'Are you sure you should be here? There's folk that'll say it's not right, you being the laird's wife now, and old Mr Crawford scarcely in his grave.'

'I don't give a fig for what folks say, Leila. That house is stifling me. If I don't get out of it now and then, I'll die!'

'Well, if you're certain –' her sister said, then beamed, and hugged her. 'Oh, Rose, it's so good to see you back again, where you belong!'

Blair was scarcely at home in the winter following his father's funeral. When he was in Sandyford, he was quiet and preoccupied.

Even so, it came as a complete shock to Rose when he announced one evening in February that he had decided to sell Crawford House.

His grandmother's face turned grey. Her eyes were as

hard and as cold as diamonds as she said, 'Don't talk arrant nonsense!'

'My mind's made up, Grandmother. The matter's already in the hands of the solicitors.'

'You're mad!'

'On the contrary,' said Blair. 'I've come to my senses.'

'You can't sell your heritage – your children's heritage!' Her stick pounded on the soft thick carpet. 'There have been Crawfords here for generations! If your father knew –'

'My father,' said Blair coldly, 'is dead. I own the house now, and the land. It's mine to do with as I wish.'

'It's a sacred trust for those who follow on!'

'I don't see it in that way.' He took up his favourite stance before the fireplace. 'I watched my father kill himself trying to keep this place going on what money you allowed him, and I don't intend to do the same.'

'My money will go to you when I die. To you and Lilias. You know that! There will be more than enough to keep the estate going.'

'My father may have been prepared to wait, but I'm not. The estate's mine to sell if I so wish.'

'Lilias will never agree to it!'

'Lilias,' said her brother, 'has no say in the matter. The estate is going to be sold, and then I'll be free to do as I wish.'

The old woman looked at him with real hatred in her eyes for the first time in his life. 'I forbid you to sell!'

'Grandmother,' he said ruthlessly, 'for the first time in my life you have no authority over me. I won't need your money when the estate's gone. I'll have my own money then. I'm not content to be your lapdog, as my father was.'

'And where, pray, am I to go when you sell my home out from under me?'

'To Lilias, I suppose – if you wish. On the other hand,

you can afford to buy your own house, and hire a companion.'

'You will not sell Crawford House! Listen to me, Blair –'

'Why should I listen to you?' Blair asked, cool amusement in his voice. 'You're not a Crawford, and never were. You bought your way into this family, Grandmother – you're still wealthy enough to buy your way into some other social set. People with my background only know how to spend money – people with your background know how to trade with it.'

The cane that was never far from the old woman's hand swept up, and Blair stepped back just in time to avoid a vicious slash at his legs.

The stick swung in a wide arc and knocked his recently emptied tea cup from the low table before the fire.

The fragile china flew into the hearth and shattered into a hundred pieces. Rose gave a cry, and ran to pick up the pieces.

'Leave it, my dear. The servants can see to it. Well done, Grandmother. I've always admired your spirit,' said Blair, and walked out of the room.

'You knew!' The old woman rounded on Rose, her eyes blazing. 'You knew about this and you did nothing to prevent him, or to warn me.'

'I knew nothing. He didn't say a word to me.'

'You must stop him!'

'It seems to me that Blair's made up his mind. Neither of us can stop him.'

'You're his wife, girl! You've got more control over him than anyone else. It's your fault,' she added viciously, her mouth square and ugly as it spat the words out. 'Your fault! If you'd given him an heir he'd never have thought of selling Crawford House.'

Anger simmered in Rose. She had received as much of a shock as Mrs Lacey. Her future, too, was suddenly a closed door to her. 'Has it ever occurred to you, Mrs Lacey, that the fact that Blair and I have no children may be as much his fault as mine?'

'Nonsense, girl! My daughter faced the same problem with his father, but she managed to produce a son and a daughter, and there's no reason why you shouldn't, for you're a sight more strong-minded than she ever was.'

Rose felt as though someone had thrown cold water in her face. 'You know about Blair?'

'Of course I do. He's his father's son, in every sense of the word. Raised by George to think of wives as pure and delicate. Taught to satisfy his appetites and find his pleasures elsewhere.'

She thumped her cane on the floor again. 'If you're wise, you'll see that your own son's told otherwise, when you have one.'

Rose remembered Blair's almost panic-stricken reaction to her need for him in the early days of their marriage. She remembered the way he had said 'You're not a street wanton – don't act like one!' and 'I expect my wife to behave like a lady, not a trollop.' She thought of his increasingly frequent periods away from home, the way he returned from those business trips refreshed and relaxed.

She knew now why her marriage had turned out to be a hollow mockery instead of a proper communion between a man and a woman.

'You must have realized' – Catherine Lacey's voice was saying. It sounded far away.

'No – no, I never did.'

'Too busy with your own concerns, I suppose. Well, now that you do know you'd best put all your wiles to work and get that heir.'

'You think I could have his child now? Knowing what I know?'

'Why not? My daughter managed it. And she was a spineless creature compared to you. If you're as proud as all that,' the old woman said contemptuously, 'Blair doesn't even need to be the father. Not as long as he thinks he is. But however you go about it, remember that you're Blair's wife, and it's your duty to give him an heir!'

Catherine Lacey left Crawford House a week later, sitting straight-backed in the carriage that took her to the station, not once turning her head to bid farewell to the house she had come to look on as her own.

'Blair –' Rose said as they stood together at the top of the steps and watched her go.

'Hush, Rose.' There was steel in his voice. 'She's had the running of this place for long enough, and I'm damned if I'll change my mind for her – or for you. I've waited for a long time to be free of the whole Crawford kingdom.'

'What about all the folk who work on the estate, and in the mines and at the yard and the harbour? What's to become of them?'

He shrugged impatiently. 'They'll not be out of work. The businesses'll be bought over by men who want to keep them going.'

'But this town has always looked to the Crawfords for guidance and protection.'

'Then it's about time,' said Blair, 'that it learned to stand on its own feet. We're in the twentieth century now, my dear. We're Edwardians. The days of the feudal system are long over.'

He was so steeped in his own interests that she wanted to take him by the lapels and shake him. 'But it's frightening for a man not to know who his new employer might be, or how safe his position is. And how long he might be able to continue to feed and clothe his family.'

'Rose, we can't take responsibility for the whole town. Even if I could, I refuse. From now on I'm thinking of myself. And you,' he added.

'Where are we to go?'

'Where else but back to South Africa?'

She gaped up at him, then said faintly, 'South Africa? For how long?'

'For ever. Now that the Boers have been put in their place,' Blair said exultantly, 'it's the perfect place for folk like us to settle. I'm going to buy some land, start farming. We'll make a new life for ourselves, you and me. A new Crawford kingdom, Rose – far away from here.'

37

Once the news of Blair's decision spread through the town there was, as Rose had predicted, wide-scale alarm on the part of all the families who relied on the Crawford estate for their livelihood, and a great sense of shock throughout the town at the thought of losing their laird.

A deputation of businessmen and councillors called at Crawford House in their stiff white collars and best suits. They spent an entire evening with Blair, and returned to the town without having managed to make him change his mind.

'You'll be all right, Chauncy,' Rose assured her stepbrother. 'Leila's keeping on the furniture store, and there'll be room for you there.'

'No need to worry about me. Magnus has already offered me a place with the Darroch Line, and I've agreed to it. It's the rest of the men I feel sorry for, them not knowing what's going to happen next. Rose, before you go away – would you stand godmother to the baby?'

Rose felt herself blushing with pleasure. 'Me?'

'Who else would we have wanted?' her stepbrother wanted to know. 'It was you who brought Meg out of that house where she was held prisoner.' He took his wife's hand in his own and held it tightly. 'It was thanks to you that we found each other.'

'We hoped that you'd say yes,' Meg chimed in, 'but we weren't certain, with old Mr Crawford dying so recently, if you'd be able to attend the christening.'

'I'd not miss it for anything in the world!'

The happy parents beamed, then eyed each other uneasily. Chauncy shuffled his feet, and it fell to Meg to say hesitantly, 'We – we've asked Magnus to stand as godfather to young Edward.'

'He's been a good friend to us,' Chauncy hurried to intercede.

'He'd never agree to it, surely.'

'He has. The thing is,' said Meg, 'Chauncy says that there's been a quarrel between the two of you, and we wondered if – if it might –'

Rose's mouth had suddenly gone dry. She moistened her lips, then said, 'It'll not make any difference as far as I'm concerned. I'd not let anything stand in the way of being Edward's godmother – or anyone.'

'Those were almost Magnus's exact words,' Chauncy said with relief, and his little wife shot him a swift, reproving glance.

He went crimson, but insisted doggedly, 'Well, it's true. Rose – Magnus knows now that old Finlay isn't out to take the Darroch Line away from him, or even interfere with the way Magnus chooses to run it. I think he'd like it fine if you made your peace with each other.'

Rose bent over the crib and put her finger into the baby's loosely curled fist. The tiny hand closed on it at once, even in sleep. 'He's not made a move towards me.'

'It's his pride,' Chauncy said awkwardly. 'If you ask me, he's ashamed of the way he turned on you when he first heard of it. But I'm sure he'd welcome the chance to clear the air.'

'You two were always such friends,' Meg's soft voice chimed in. 'It would be good to see you making up your differences before you go away, especially now that you're to be Edward's godparents.'

Rose drew her finger gently from the baby's grasp, careful not to waken him. She straightened and faced the man and woman who stood close together, eyeing her hopefully.

'No,' she said. 'There's no sense in it, for Magnus and

I are bound to our own ways now. Best to leave things as they are.'

Still mindful of the period of mourning for her father-in-law, she dressed for young Edward Magnus Gibb's christening in a lilac silk gown with pale grey ribbons knotted down the bodice, and at the cuffs and on the skirt. Her hat was wide-brimmed, lilac with grey feathers. She attended the christening alone, because Blair was in London.

Magnus wore a new russet-coloured suit that matched his hair. The new skin that had grown over the scalded area of his face was still somewhat tender looking, but now it was a healthy golden colour, sketched over here and there by faint scars. The eyelid on the injured side still drooped a little more than its partner, giving him a rakish air.

With a faint smile that was still lopsided, still dragged back by the right side of his mouth, he came forward to greet her as she went into Chauncy's small house.

Why was it, she wondered, that scarring on the face ruined a woman for life, yet added to a man's attraction?

The smile faded when he said, 'I hear that you're leaving us soon.'

'Blair wants to settle in South Africa.' The words had a strangely hollow ring to them. She couldn't believe in them. Ever since Blair's announcement, she had felt as though she were living in a dream.

'It'll not be the same without Crawfords at the big house,' Chauncy said unhappily, then his eyes lit up as Meg appeared in the doorway with her baby, in a foam of snowy white ribbon and lace, in her arms.

Young Edward, a placid baby at any time, was on his best behaviour during his christening.

When he was placed in Rose's arms, his forehead wet with water from the font and his round face, so like his father's, screwed up in hurt puzzlement, she held him close and looked over his head to see Magnus watching her.

Their eyes met, and the shock of that meeting was so great that she automatically tightened her hold on the baby, fearing that she would drop him. For a time that was only seconds, yet seemed to last for an eternity, she and Magnus looked into each other's hearts and souls, then with an effort Rose lowered her face to her nephew's warm, silky little dome.

From there, head bent, she could see Magnus's hands, folded over each other, strong against the rough material of his suit, the scarred right hand hidden in the clasp of the left.

All at once the thought of leaving him, of leaving Sandyford, was unbearable.

The mines and the small shipping interest were sold to a consortium from Lanarkshire. The boatyard, timber yard and a fair slice of Crawford land went to another consortium. And in June, when the pleasure steamers were out on the Clyde again, the house was bought by a Glasgow whisky merchant seeking a pleasant summer home for his large family.

'How my father would have hated that,' Blair said, almost with relish, when he told Rose the news. 'Grandmother will be furious when she hears.'

Then, reading the expression on his wife's face, he added, 'No need to look at me like that, Rose. I merely sold to the highest bidder. And these days, whether we like it or not, the tradesmen are the folk with the money.'

He worked with feverish haste, anxious to get away from Sandyford as quickly as he could. All the pieces that Lilias and her grandmother wanted were packed and dispatched.

The rest was sold off as swiftly as he could manage it. Room after room was emptied, servants dismissed.

The house began to echo to the voices and footsteps of those who were left.

'In a few weeks' time we'll be in South Africa,' Blair exulted. 'Just think of it, Rose! Remember how wonderful it was before?'

She remembered. She remembered the magnificent golden-red soil, the low hills stretching into the distance under a sky of infinite blue. She remembered the liquid-eyed, shy Kaffir children. She remembered how much she had missed Africa when she came home, and how she had yearned to go back.

But everything had changed. She and Blair would be going to an Africa where Piet's people had fought for their freedom, and lost. A land that didn't belong to its people any more, be they black or Boer.

She thought of her husband's arbitrary attitude towards the Crawford employees who had worked all their lives for the family and had been cast aside, no longer needed. She thought of Blair taking that same self-centred arrogance to Africa, imposing it on the people there.

On the night before they were due to depart, Leila entertained them to supper in her house. Blair was first out of the door when they were leaving. As Rose was about to follow him, Leila drew her back into the hall and pushed a small package into her hand.

'Magnus asked me to give you this,' she said, low-voiced. 'You've not to open it until you reach South Africa, he says.'

In the morning, dressed for the journey, Rose opened the package during a last walk along the terrace. There was no message in it, no word at all. Just a small plain cardboard box, and inside it, on a bed of cotton wool, a single penny with a hole bored through it so that it could be hung on a fine-link chain.

She lifted it out and the sunlight caught it as it revolved on its chain. It had been burnished until, in the light, it was as tawny as Magnus MacBride's head, as golden as the flecks of light in his eyes.

With fingers that shook slightly she opened the catch and put the chain about her neck. A paddle-steamer was churning its way along the Clyde far below her. She tasted the salt air on her lips.

'Rose!' Blair arrived at her side, hat in hand. He didn't bother taking one last glance over the garden. 'The bags are loaded. It's time to leave for the station.'

The coin was cool against her throat. She drew in a deep breath, then said, 'Blair, I'm not going to South Africa with you.'

He looked down on her, astonished. 'Of course you are! It's all arranged.'

'By you. I was never consulted.'

'Rose, for God's sake! You're my wife!'

'But not your possession.'

'You can't stay here on your own.'

'Yes I can. I've got Leila, and Chauncy –'

Panic flared in his eyes. 'Rose –' He put his arms about her, holding her tightly, trying to draw her towards the house. 'I need you! We'll talk about it in London.'

She drew away from him. 'I'm not going to London.'

'Dammit, Rose –' He put a hand on her arm; then as she shook her head he let her go and stepped back, his handsome face twisted with anger.

'You're my wife!' he said again. 'D'you want to make a laughing stock of me?'

'I didn't think it mattered what the people here thought of you.'

His expression hardened. 'I'm going to London now, as planned,' he said coolly. 'I'm taking your luggage with me, and I'll expect you to join me there. If you don't – be damned to you!'

She watched him walk away from her, striding down the terrace, slamming the French windows behind him.

*

When she was quite certain that Blair was on his way to the station, Rose left Crawford House for the last time, empty-handed, taking only the clothes she wore.

The pleasure-boat season was in full swing and the harbour seethed with adults and children, perambulators and bicycles, parasols and straw boaters and sailor hats and floral bonnets.

There were four steamers in, each with its own group of passengers surging on board. One of them was *Darroch's Pride*. Rose's mouth went dry as she saw that Magnus was on the bridge. For a moment she almost turned away, then, unnoticeable in her plain travelling dress and wide-brimmed hat, she forged ahead and joined on at the tail end of the chattering mass of people boarding the little paddle-steamer for the trip to Rothesay.

As she went up the gangway the lad at the top held out his hand for her ticket, then drew it back hastily, gaping at her.

'Mistress Crawford!'

'Wheesht!' she instructed him as he half-turned towards the bridge to signal to Magnus. 'No need to say a word to anybody. D'you mind allowing a stowaway on board just this once, Lachie? I've no money for my ticket.'

He grinned, taking the truth for a joke. 'On you go, Ma'am. We're just about to leave.'

She stood by the railings immediately below the bridge, so that if Magnus were to look down all he would see would be an anonymous straw hat with a streamer of blue ribbon round it, and watched the harbour and the warehouse recede as the stretch of water between *Darroch's Pride* and the land widened.

Then she walked to the bows, where she leaned on the rail and looked down at the green and white water foaming and hissing as it was sliced by the paddle-steamer's bows.

It was a perfect day; hot and still on shore, and with a cooling breeze on the water. The accordionist on the upper promenade deck struck up something slow and pleasant to the ear. The music flowed on to the warm air, trailing behind them with a wake of its own. The gulls nagged alongside in the hope of coaxing breadcrusts from the passengers.

Rose filled her lungs with the salty air, and knew that this was where she belonged. As the boat surged on, paddles churning the water into lacy foam that glittered silver in the sunlight, all the frustrations and tensions of the past months fell away.

She was still young, still able to make a new life for herself. She thought of Blair, and realized that he was already part of her past, and she was part of his.

'Rose? Rose, I thought it was you!'

She turned, her eyes dazzled by the sparkling water. 'Hello, Magnus.'

He had left his peaked cap on the bridge and his tawny hair was ruffled and tumbled by the wind.

'I thought,' he said slowly, 'that you were leaving for London today.'

'Blair left. But I'm staying.'

'Oh?'

As she moved, the sunlight caught the burnished penny on its chain, nestled against the creamy skin of her throat. The coin flashed like gold.

'I didn't mean you,' said Magnus, 'to open the box until you were in South Africa.'

'Are you certain of that?'

A grin spread slowly over his face. 'Well – mebbe I took a gamble. And mebbe I won.'

'I'm glad you did.'

'So am I.'

They stood smiling at each other, then he said huskily, 'God, Rose, I want to kiss you!'

'It wouldn't be seemly, Mr MacBride. Not in front of all those folk.'

'No. But as soon as we can get away from them –'

'I'm a fallen woman, Magnus. A wife who's deserted her husband. Can you take the scandal?'

A shaft of sunlight illuminating his face picked out the gold lights in his eyes. His teeth were white against his tanned face as he laughed.

'Let them say what they want, and be damned to the lot of them.'

Happiness flared up in Rose, spreading from her heart until it tingled in the tips of her fingers and her toes, bringing with it all the passion that she had thought lost for ever.

'Oh – Magnus!' she said, with her heart in her voice, then turned and leaned on the rail, looking over at Rothesay Bay, blinking back the tears that threatened to overflow.

Magnus's shoulder came to rest against hers, firm and warm. His hand landed beside hers on the rail.

She turned her hand over and their fingers interlaced, clinging tightly in a promise of for ever, as the paddles spun and *Darroch's Pride* sped as straight and as true as an arrow towards the far shore.

Bibliography

The Golden Years of the Clyde Steamers (1889–1914)
by Alan J. S. Paterson

The Clyde Passenger Steamers by Kenneth Davies

One Hundred Years of Army Nursing by Ian Hay

More Compelling Fiction from Headline:

KAY STEPHENS

WEST RIDING

An absorbing saga of love and ambition in the Yorkshire hills

Rhona Hebden is the daughter of a mill owner in the West Riding of Yorkshire, a girl whose pretty heart-shaped face and tumble of auburn hair disguise a strength of will and character that surprises even herself. When she inherits shares in Bridge House Mill from her late father, she leaves her home in the familiar row of back-to-back houses in Halfield town and determines to break through the Depression years of the 1930s to make the knitting pattern and yarn business a going concern.

When civil engineer Wolf Richardson announces a plan to flood the beautiful Halfield valley in order to create a reservoir, Rhona's Yorkshire pride comes to the fore and she sets out to thwart his scheme. But Wolf is a hard man to win over and Rhona finds that she has more than met her match. Moreover, she realises that she is disturbingly attracted by his dark, brooding looks and fiery ambition. Then the war intervenes, bringing unpredictable tragedies, and Rhona is swept up by the effort to fight and survive. During a weekend leave, she hastily marries an old childhood friend, only to find herself longing once more for Wolf. Whilst battling against the heartbreaks of war, Rhona discovers that her greatest struggle is that of her own conflicting emotions and the desire to give up all for love.

Full of passion and ambition, WEST RIDING is an absorbing novel rich in emotion and infused with the spirit of the rugged Yorkshire countryside.

'A nicely crafted love story' *Yorkshire Evening Post*

More Compulsive Fiction from Headline:

THE LAND IS BRIGHT

A Liverpool saga in the great tradition of Catherine Cookson

ELIZABETH MURPHY

'Better is a dinner of herbs where love is than a stalled ox and hatred therewith.' Proverbs 17

When her Mam dies in childbirth, little Sally Palin becomes a second mother to her two brothers and baby Emily, the apple of her eye. Sally is determined that her sister shall leave the mean streets of their Liverpool home and enjoy a better life, but the success of her dream is bittersweet.

To escape a fever epidemic that ravages the city, Emily is sent away to her rich, childless Aunt Hester, to grow up in the healthy country air with luxuries the Palins could never provide.

But despite these material advantages, Emily fails to find happiness, and settles for a loveless marriage to an elderly widower, while Sally enjoys love and fulfilment with her husband and children, even though they must struggle against unemployment, illness and tragic loss . . .

'. . . an evocative novel of life behind the scrubbed doorsteps at the turn of the century. Gently paced, it nonetheless conveys the grinding miseries of poverty and making ends meet in the pre-welfare days . . .' *Books*

'Elizabeth Murphy draws on her knowledge of her home town Liverpool to conjure up a cast of colourful characters . . . in a family saga that you just won't be able to put down.' *Prima*

FICTION/SAGA 0 7472 3192 3 £3.99

More compulsive fiction from Headline:

MALCOLM ROSS

A rich West Country saga in the bestselling tradition of POLDARK

On a Far Wild Shore

Young, beautiful and newly widowed, Elizabeth Troy travels to her late husband's Cornish home hoping to find comfort in its fertile hills and valleys. But she is shocked to discover the vast, decaying acreage of Pallas is now solely her responsibility – a legacy as unexpected as it is unwelcome.

Elizabeth's plans for her inheritance provoke the bitter hostility of her sister-in-law, Morwenna, whose word has been law at Pallas for thirty years. To bring the troubled estate back to prosperity Elizabeth must look for help elsewhere. And there are many very willing to be more than a friend to the widow – David Troy, a poor relation whose sober exterior hides some disturbing secrets; Courtenay Rodda, the sensual newspaper proprietor; and James Troy, the rich and worldly wise American cousin who begins a thrilling but dangerous liaison with Elizabeth . . .

'The book is beautifully written, the characters depicted with a passionate realism that held me entranced. I simply loved it!' Patricia Wendorf, bestselling author of *Larksleve*.

FICTION 0-7472-3001-3 £2.95